WARMASTER 8: CHARNEL KEEP

MELISSA MCSHANE

Cover design by Etheric Tales www.etherictales.com

Map by Matt Pivots

CHAPTER ONE

"No coffee?" Aderyn said.

She'd woken early, just after sunrise, and decided to let Owen sleep a bit longer. If her instincts were right, she and her friends would be going to the front soon, to defend the city of Shantos, and they would need all the rest they could get. Just her bad luck that this was one of those times when she knew instantly she wasn't going to fall back asleep no matter how long she lay in bed.

But when she entered the Jeweled Cuckoo Inn's dining room, she'd discovered one person had risen even earlier than she. Livia sat at the table they'd all come to think of as theirs, picking at a plate of eggs scrambled with sweet peppers that turned them bright orange. No coffee pot was visible. No small coffee cup sat at Livia's right hand.

Livia glanced up when Aderyn spoke. Her eyes were puffy and closed nearly to slits, and she slumped in her seat as if she was still mostly asleep. "No coffee," she confirmed in a hollow voice that might as well have pronounced Aderyn's doom.

"Did Neeva... she couldn't have run out of coffee, that's unlikely. Do you need me to go down the street to the coffee seller and bring you a pot?"

Livia shook her head with dramatic exaggeration. "I'm not drinking coffee today. Or for the foreseeable future."

That shocked Aderyn as deeply as if Livia had said she was leaving the team. "What? Why not?"

Livia poked at her mound of eggs with her finger, testing their heat. "I told you I was going to see about replacing *acid ray* with a different seventh level spell. In addition to focused meditation for an hour every day and the complete abjuration of the spell I want to get rid of, I have to show my dedication through sacrifice. Specifically, sacrifice of a beloved habit. So... no coffee."

Aderyn sat opposite Livia, still staring. "That's a really big thing for you to sacrifice."

"Only in the sense that I'm addicted to the stuff. Giving up coffee isn't as hard as controlling my temper or abstaining from sex." Livia smiled, but it was a ghastly expression. "I knew it would be difficult, but it's been a while since I didn't start my day with coffee, and I didn't realize just how much I depended on it to energize me. I feel like I'm thinking through cotton wool. And my appetite is gone, though that could just be that I don't love eggs." She pushed her plate away.

"Is there anything we can do to help?"

"If you can remember not to offer me coffee in the morning, that would be great. I was taught from childhood never to turn down hospitality, so that would be hard to resist." Livia rose from the table. "I'm going back to bed. I thought getting up early would help me get past the need, but I just feel weary."

Aderyn watched Livia walk away, then pulled Livia's abandoned plate toward herself. It didn't look like Livia had taken even one bite, and Aderyn loved eggs, particularly in the southern style. No sense letting food go to waste.

As she ate, she idly reviewed the Codex, reading over the [**Fated One's Destiny: Crush the Horde**] quest.

An army of monstrous orcs has emerged from the Blighted Range, intent on conquering the southern human lands. Destroy their leaders and push the army back into the mountains.

Victory conditions:
Death of Glasha, orc commander general
ACHIEVED Death of Ornok, second in command
Death of ?
Death of ?
Death of ?
Destruction of Charnel Keep
Orc army retreats

Reward: [75,000 XP] plus any XP gained through actions taken to complete the quest.

She never liked not understanding the details of what was required to complete a quest. But running around the Southlands, searching for orcs who might be the leaders not yet named in the quest description, was impractical, not to mention counter to her duties as second in command of the human armies. So what she was *going* to do, once the day was sufficiently advanced, was talk to Commander General Varoun to discuss plans. And share with him the knowledge of the orc stronghold, Charnel Keep.

The system hadn't told her much about the place when it had appeared as one of the quest completion requirements, just that it counted as a dungeon and was where the orcs' headquarters were, if orcs had anything so organized as a headquarters. It had claimed saying more when Aderyn hadn't seen the dungeon was against the rules. That got Aderyn thinking about what rules the system had to abide by. It was the system! It made rules for other people!

And yet, there had been the Sorrowvale dungeon. The system had been grateful when Aderyn and her friends destroyed it, which implied the system didn't like Sorrowvale—so why hadn't the system destroyed it first? It couldn't be because it lacked the power. But if there were rules the system had set for itself—

Aderyn shook her head and scooped up more eggs. If the system was limited by rules, that might mean it didn't have as much power as everyone thought, and that idea scared Aderyn. She didn't want to learn the system's power could be hindered. That could mean anything.

She dismissed the Codex and finished eating. Varoun was a South-lander, so he might still be asleep, but on the other hand, the orcs were attacking a major city, Shantos, so it was possible he had sacrificed sleep in favor of military strategy. She would go back upstairs to the privacy of her room and contact him with the <**Farspeaker**>.

She met Owen entering the dining room as she exited. "You didn't wake me," he said, kissing her soundly.

"I thought you should get as much sleep as possible. You didn't see Livia, did you?"

"No, just you. You ate already?"

"I did, but the important thing is Livia has given up coffee as part of replacing her acid spell—"

Owen whistled. "That's intense."

"Yes. Anyway, she asked that we remember not to suggest she have coffee or offer to bring it to her. She says that helps."

"Makes sense. Will you sit with me while I eat?"

Aderyn smiled. "I'd love to, but I need to speak to Varoun. I don't know what the situation around Shantos is, and we may be needed there."

"Fair enough." Owen kissed her again.

In their bedroom, Aderyn dug Varoun's coin and her <**Farspeaker**> out of the little pouch at her hip and pressed the coin into the slot at the top of the palm-sized oval mirror. The mirror's surface fogged over with a thick mist that roiled like boiling water. Aderyn waited. After several minutes, the surface cleared, and Varoun's face looked out at her. "Aderyn. You have news?"

"No, sir, I was hoping *you* did. We're recovered from our exertions at the Ivory Palace and we're ready to return to the fighting. I hope I didn't wake you."

The elderly general grimaced. "I don't get more than a few hours' sleep these days. Fortunately, old age means I need less of it. What do you know about the fighting near Shantos?"

"*Near* Shantos? I thought the city was besieged."

"Not yet, but soon. Janesh ordered the evacuation two days ago, as a precaution. The orc forces are numerous, and the regiments in the area are only barely holding them back. Kingfisher and Monkey Regiments are hurrying to reinforce that position, and Hawk and Ox are a few days behind them, but at the moment Colonel Hasanth only has the three Shantos regiments for the defense."

Aderyn almost asked why a colonel was in charge of the Shantos defense, but then she remembered that army's general, Chandar, had been sent to find the orcs that continued to strike human settlements and disappear into the wilderness. Chandar, a talented Pathseer, hadn't been insulted by what looked like a demotion. "But Colonel Hasanth is holding them off away from the city, yes?"

"For now. He's had to give ground twice." Varoun looked very weary for a moment. Then the moment passed, and in a sharp, alert voice, he said, "I'm sending you to take command at Shantos. Hasanth is smart and a good military man, but he's a linear thinker who tends to see war as a series of problems to be solved one after the other. I need you to develop several contingency plans for the defense of Shantos—and for abandoning it if it comes to that."

"I understand." The idea of planning battles didn't intimidate Aderyn, but the lack of information did. "What information do we have about the disposition of forces?"

"I'll give you everything I have when I send you there. How soon can your team be ready?"

"I'm not sure. Let's say... one hour? We'll meet you in the command tent?"

"Agreed. I'll see you then." Varoun's image vanished.

Aderyn returned the coin to the pouch and sat on the bed for a moment. Discussing the orc stronghold would have to wait, if things were as dire as Varoun said. She was already coming up with possibilities. If they could hold off the orcs until the other regiments arrived... though if they couldn't, someone would have to secure the evacuation of any people left in Shantos... and falling back to Shantos itself, turning this into a siege, might make sense—unless the orcs didn't take the bait and swept past the city on their way to Lake Dannis and Ikharatia beyond. She needed more information before she could plan further than this.

She rose and hooked the <**Farspeaker**> pouch to her belt in its usual place. Time to get everyone moving. And hope Livia was awake again. Aderyn didn't know how much her friend depended on her morning coffee and hoped Livia hadn't chosen the worst possible time to give it up.

THE EBONY OVAL of *world door* snapped shut behind Aderyn. She took a few stumbling steps before catching her balance. Between the blazing sun and the choking humidity, the day was shaping up to be uncomfortably hot. Sweat prickled Aderyn's armpits and hairline, not that sweating did any good in this climate.

Varoun's <**Wand of World Door**> had deposited her in the middle of a typical army encampment. To Aderyn's untrained eye, they all looked alike: same drab brown or gray canvas, same churned-up mud paths that were hardened or mucky depending on how recently it had rained.

The few soldiers in the area glanced once at her as they hurried past and then pretended they hadn't wanted to stare. Since Aderyn wore the gray coat of an officer and the insignia of a general, they all knew who she was, and as a female general was a novelty, Aderyn didn't mind their staring. But one thing she'd learned about Southlanders was their love of showing hospitality to strangers, and staring was counter to proper hospitality.

World door opened again, and Owen stepped through. Aderyn didn't know why he never stumbled as she did upon exiting. Owen approached her, but scanned the tents instead of looking at her. "Doesn't look like an attack is imminent."

"The orcs have to sleep, too," Aderyn said, "and our scouts report they don't rise until several hours after dawn. They think it's because they stay active until nearly midnight."

"Midnight? Doing what?"

"None of the scouts who got close enough to learn that ever returned." Aderyn tried not to imagine what might have happened to them. "And it's not important enough to risk more soldiers. At least, I hope it isn't. Everyone who tried *scrying* reported an occlusion, something like the skill [Obscure], which implies the orcs do things they don't want us knowing about. But with the main body of the orc army pressing our troops hard, that's been the priority."

Owen wrapped his arms around her, hugging her close and pressing the links of her mail shirt, what Isold had identified as <Gossamer Mail>, against her body. "You sound like a real general. Oops. That was patronizing. Sorry. I meant, I know you weren't sure about being able to do this, but the way you talk, it's like you never had any doubts."

She hugged him back. "I understand. Thank you for having faith in me. It helped."

Weston came up beside them. "Should it be this quiet?"

"I'm guessing most of the soldiers are forming up into companies in preparation for battle." Aderyn stepped away from Owen and took another couple of steps to where she could stop a soldier hurrying past. "Where's Colonel Hasanth's tent?"

The woman saluted properly, but her eyes were wide. "General, sir, ma'am, I mean, the colonel is just that way. Should I escort you?"

Aderyn looked around. Isold had just emerged from *world door* and only Livia remained to make the transit. The stray thought struck Aderyn that there was no transportation spell that would move a large group across great distances. "No, I don't want to keep you—is it that tent?" She pointed at a tent, bigger than those surrounding it, a short distance away behind her.

"That's the command tent, ma'am, and Colonel Hasanth's personal tent is beside it."

Aderyn took pity on the soldier, who was clearly torn between doing her duty in providing an escort and not spending any more time in the company of high-ranking officers than she had to. "Thank you, private, that's all."

The private saluted again and ran.

"They're intimidated by you," Isold murmured.

"I know. Nothing I can do about it except go back in time and be born a Southlander man." Aderyn shrugged. "Everyone's here? Let's go meet this colonel."

The command tent was empty. Aderyn thought about going

through the papers and maps on the makeshift table at the tent's center. The later it got, the more she fretted over her lack of information. But she'd gain information faster if someone could organize it for her. Instead, she went to the other tent and clapped loudly the way she'd been taught. It wasn't as if you could knock on a tent flap.

She heard murmuring, too low to be distinct, and then a private in soldier's garb but without armor pushed the flap back. "Yes?" he said. He took her appearance in, then widened his gaze to include her companions. "That is—yes, general?"

"I'd like to speak to Colonel Hasanth, private." Aderyn closed her lips on *if he's available*. She wasn't going to be overbearing, but she outranked the colonel, and if he turned out to be one of those who didn't think women could lead troops, she wasn't going to give him an opening to disdain her.

The private ducked back inside the tent. Aderyn, waiting for an invitation to enter, backed up a step when the tent flap opened again and a large man stepped out. Colonel Hasanth was built along the same lines as Weston, big through the shoulders and chest, but with the beginnings of a paunch spoiling the line of his uniform coat. He had thick, graying black hair cut very short around the sides and back, but longer on top, and the way it curled made Aderyn think of a badly-shorn sheep.

Hasanth looked down at Aderyn. His expression was cranky, and his voice, when he spoke, sounded like gravel bathed in acid. "The northern girl. I told General Varoun we have this under control. We don't need your help."

He sounded so certain Aderyn doubted herself for about half a second. Then she came to her senses. "This is not about help, colonel. I am here to take command by order of the commander general. He judges my skills are needed here. So unless you want me to inform General Varoun that you think your understanding is superior to his, I suggest you give me your full cooperation."

"So the commander general doesn't have faith in my abilities?"

Aderyn's heart sank. Hasanth not only didn't think women could command, he was taking Varoun's orders personally. "That's not what General Varoun said. We anticipate the arrival of four other regiments within a few days, and my orders are to take command of the unified forces. Which means directing the overall strategy. General Chandar trusted you, or you wouldn't be in command now."

"Spoken like a woman, conciliatory and weak," Hasanth scoffed. "You think you can lead troops talking like that?"

Owen shifted, and Hasanth's eyes shifted to him. "Who's the boy who wants to defend you?"

"Enough," Aderyn said, keeping a tight rein on her anger. "Hasanth, you have three choices. One. You hand over command to me amicably, give me your support, and keep your rank. Two. You defy me, I strip you of your rank, and you can explain to Varoun why you made things complicated."

Hasanth continued to gaze at her contemptuously. "And the third?"

Aderyn swiftly Assessed him. "My husband kicks your ass from here to the orc army and back. We'll see how long you maintain your reputation when your soldiers see you whipped by someone half your size."

"Hah," Hasanth barked. "As if—"

"You're a level twelve Staffsworn with fifteen ranks in [**Advanced Weapon Proficiency**]. He's level seventeen and his weapon skill ranks are nearly double yours." Aderyn advanced on Hasanth without flinching, and Hasanth backed up into the tent wall. "Take your chances, if you want, but if you continue to defy me, he'll make you look so ridiculous you'll never lead again."

"You let him fight your battles for you?" The sneer in Hasanth's voice was weak, but it was there.

"Commanders don't do everyone's jobs for them. They use their resources wisely. If you don't understand that, then maybe you really aren't deserving of your rank." Aderyn leaned closer and lowered her voice to make Hasanth bow to hear her. "Three choices, Colonel. It's up to you. Are you going to make that the last time anyone addresses you by that rank?"

Hasanth licked his lips. Then he laughed uproariously. "Now I know you've got the balls to lead this army," he exclaimed. "Come, let me show you the disposition of troops." He strode toward the command tent, not waiting for Aderyn.

Aderyn exchanged glances with Owen, who shook his head slightly.

Aderyn agreed with him. [Sense Truth] told her Hasanth had been intimidated into that response and had backed down rather than be humiliated. Well, Aderyn could let him have his pride. But she was going to keep a close eye on him, in case his pride became more of a problem than it already was.

CHAPTER TWO

At the planning table, Hasanth swept the papers into three untidy piles and moved them to the edges so he could lay out a larger sheet of thick, brownish paper that nearly covered all of the tabletop. "Shantos," he said, pointing one meaty finger at a crudely-drawn picture of a building with towers. "It's in a hilly area, lots of terrace farming, but the hills don't come this far north. That means fighting on the open plains, and we're at a disadvantage against their goretusks."

"Goretusks?" Adelyn asked.

"Monstrous giant boars. Some of the orc archers ride them into battle. They're fast, though not maneuverable, but that doesn't matter when you're being trampled." Hasanth's bitter smile spoke volumes. "Their riders can deliver a dozen volleys and be gone before we reach their position."

He dug around in a box filled with green and yellow figures and laid them out across the map. "This is what things looked like last night. For once, nobody gained ground. The orcs always disengage at sunset, taking a defensive action to return to their camp. We've tried making night sorties with our highest-level soldiers, but the orcs always see them coming and we're lucky our men escape with their lives."

"That sounds like something we should look into," Livia said. "Tonight."

Aderyn nodded. "I agree." Livia had spells that would either tell them what they needed to know or reveal how the orcs were keeping their movements secret. "For now, though—" She tapped one of the yellow figures, the one in the center of the arc formed by three of them. "These are your three regiments. Have you had word of reinforcements?"

"Not a blasted thing," Hasanth growled. "Have we been deserted?"

"Of course not. There are four regiments on their way, two from Ikharatia and two from Tielana—south and east. I don't have a way to contact the Ikharatia regiments, but General Rajman reports that Ox and Hawk Regiments are no more than three days' march from this position."

"It may not matter," Hasanth said. "The orcs are constantly reinforced by more orcs coming from who knows where. We've already been reduced by a sixth of our original numbers."

"Let's not defeat ourselves before the orcs can," Aderyn said. "How far are we from Shantos?"

"Couple of miles. Too close."

Hasanth's pessimism was starting to annoy Aderyn. "Far enough for our purposes. You've set up a good defensive position here, so let's stick with that. If we're outnumbered—"

"Which we are."

"Fine. *Since* we're outnumbered, our goal is to hold our position and do as much damage to the enemy as we can. We don't want this to turn into a siege, though if it did, at least those goretusks would become useless."

Hasanth frowned. "What do you mean?"

"The orcs who are mounted can move quickly, surround marching soldiers and kill and be gone. But that strategy can't work against a city, because it can't be intimidated by a flight of arrows. The most the goretusk riders could do is circle the city, shouting insults."

To her surprise, Hasanth's lips twitched in a near-smile. "I see. But we still don't want Shantos to fall."

"No." Aderyn examined the tactical map. No strategy survived the first five seconds of a battle, but she could picture in her mind's eye the most likely attacks the orcs might make, the great sweeping rush of gore-tusks stampeding through the eastern flank, the sky dark with arrows in flight. "Get everyone together by platoon. I want to have a word with the soldiers."

Hasanth looked skeptical, but he said "Yes, general" without hesitation.

When Hasanth was gone, Aderyn said, "This is not a great position. If those reinforcements don't reach us soon, the Shantos division might be all but wiped out."

"What, no optimistic cheer?" Weston said.

"I'm saving it up for addressing the troops," Aderyn said. "Until then, I'm going to indulge in pessimism."

"You've stood firm all this time," Aderyn shouted with [Amplify Voice]. "Remember what we're fighting for. Shantos will not fall!"

The massed shouts of more than a thousand voices filled the air. It didn't cheer Aderyn, because she knew how big the regiments should have been and couldn't help comparing that number to the much lower one she saw before her. [Improved Assess 3] couldn't give her a total of soldiers the way it could identify how many orc grunts there were in a given fighting force, but she could estimate.

"Platoons, your captains have their orders. Be prepared to move out in ten minutes," she went on. She saluted the army, waited for the return salutes to taper off, then jumped down off the tall stool Hasanth had provided. It didn't look very military, but Aderyn wasn't tall and it was either the stool or have everyone salute the top of her head.

"We'll join Leopard Regiment, Colonel Hasanth. I want to get a good look at these goretusks, see about developing a countering strategy," she told the colonel.

"If you say so. You'll want shields," Hasanth said. "Arrow volleys are deadly."

Aderyn chose not to reply with sarcasm about knowing that already. "We'll do that, thank you."

She pressed her forefinger to the round socket on the back of the
<Farspeaker> and held it there until sparks of white lightning like a
bright web shot through it and a silver coin appeared. Aderyn handed
the coin to Hasanth. "Let me know if anything changes."

"Good luck, general." Again, Hasanth managed not to sound like
he was sneering at the idea of Aderyn being a general and his superior
officer, but Aderyn hadn't stopped watching him.

As they trudged eastward to where Leopard Regiment was positioned, Owen said, "Shouldn't he lead from the front?"

"He will. He's taking direct command of Eagle Regiment. I don't
think he's a coward, but I have reservations about his reticence to
commit fully to an attack."

"How do you know that?" Isold asked.

"It was what Varoun said about him, that Hasanth is a linear
thinker. Hasanth comes up with a plan of attack, maybe even a good
one, but if any part of it goes wrong, he's likely to retreat and regroup
rather than change tactics on the fly. I should keep an eye on him, but
the goretusk riders are a more serious problem. I need to be able to
Assess them if we're going to defeat them."

They followed the flood of soldiers to the eastern side of the
encampment, where a level three Spiritsmith dressed in uniform and
armor, though he wasn't likely to fight, handed out round shields
painted dull yellow with a gray diagonal stripe. Aderyn guessed it represented the Southlander kingdom's colors of gray and gold. The wooden
shields weren't heavy, but they were awkward for someone who, like
Aderyn, had no skills in armor use. She hefted hers a couple of times and
practiced moving it swiftly to cover her head and torso.

Beside her, Owen moved his shield rapidly and more elegantly than
she had. "I get it," he murmured to himself. "Individual protection, not
a testudo."

Aderyn didn't bother asking him to explain what was clearly a refer-
ence to his own world. "Comfortable?"

"Enough." He lowered the shield. "Historically speaking, cavalry
does best when it has a lot of open, flat terrain to maneuver through."

"Cavalry? Is that goretusks?"

"Anything that carries a warrior into battle. Horses, goretusks, elephants... the point is that this is ideal for their purposes." He gestured at the open plain beyond.

Aderyn gazed out into the distance and saw movement. "The orcs are moving. We need to find a better position."

"There's nothing here but plains."

"Let's see what we can do about that," Aderyn replied.

She and her friends and her regiment's bannerman ran, surrounded by the platoons of Leopard Regiment, for just a few minutes. The cloud of dust that was the orc army didn't seem to grow, but Aderyn knew that was an illusion. Soon enough, it would look like the orcs were about to overrun them.

"Archers, be prepared to loose arrows," she shouted with [**Amplify Voice**]. "Everyone else, stand ready to attack." From earlier battles, she knew orc archers used shorter bows than the human Deadeyes did. She wasn't going to count on it for a huge advantage, but everything helped at this point.

Several platoons of archers split apart and lined up facing the oncoming horde. Without a spoken signal, they loosed their bows simultaneously, dimming the sky with deadly rain. The orcs weren't close enough to be distinguishable as individuals, but the arrow onslaught left a couple of gaps in the front line—not enough gaps for Aderyn's comfort. Again, the archers shot, the deep twang of their bowstrings no longer coming in unison, and shot again. Still the horde advanced.

Then, with a tremendous shout, the right side of the orc army broke away and sped toward Aderyn's position, moving like a river in full flood. The sky turned dark with arrows that hissed down upon them. Aderyn lifted her shield to protect herself and staggered slightly at the thump of arrows fletched with bright red embedding themselves in the wood. She peeked over the shield's edge to see another volley headed their way. Once it hit, she screamed, "Livia, *now!*"

The ground rumbled, and Aderyn caught sight of the earth shifting between them and the goretusks, rearing up to make a great frozen wave as Livia cast *move earth major*. She lowered her shield. Distantly, she heard the cries of battle being joined elsewhere. Then huge, hideous boars with tusks banded with rusty iron poured around either side of the earth mound, their riders shrieking defiantly as they bore down on the soldiers.

"Go! Go!" Aderyn shouted, but even **[Amplify Voice]** couldn't carry her words over the noise of fighting. Owen was already in motion. She followed him, letting **[Keep Pace]** maintain her speed while she frantically looked around to assess the situation. All around her was chaos as soldiers sped toward the goretusks, trying to narrow the distance before their riders could shoot again. She had just enough time to actually Assess the oncoming enemy before they clashed.

Name: Orc Rider [532]
Type: Monstrosity
Power level range: 11-13
Attack(s): short bow or javelin
Immune to: none
Resistant to: none
Vulnerable to: bright light, *daylight, sunburst*

Orc riders make a bond with their goretusk mounts—you'll notice they paint their goretusks with colors and symbols representing their position in the horde. Killing a goretusk demoralizes its rider and makes the orc easier to kill. Plus, goretusks are even more deadly than an orc under most circumstances, so you might want to do that anyway.

More agile and flexible than an orc grunt or masher, orc riders are masters of the bow and javelin. And they do it while riding bareback on animals not meant to carry humanoids. It's too bad they're vicious monsters who hate humans and delight in killing them, because that's impressive by any standards.

NAME: Goretusk [532]
Type: Magical beast
Power level: 15
Attack(s): gore, special
Immune to: none
Resistant to: bladed weapon damage, elemental fire damage
Vulnerable to: bludgeoning damage, mind control effects

Special: trample

Goretusks are more dangerous than the orcs that ride them. Their thick hide makes them resistant to swords and daggers, as well as providing them with limited immunity to fire. Beating them to death works just fine, as does a mental attack; they're stupid and easily distracted by [Charm] or [Coercion]. But you'll need to be quick on your feet, because goretusks are *fast*. If you wait for them to close with you, they've already trampled you and are on their way back for another attack.

That's right, their special attack. Goretusks know their sharp tusks are most effective against a fallen enemy, so they use a type of [Overrun] to knock an opponent down and trample them. A goretusk weighs over six hundred pounds—I'll leave it to your imagination how much trampling hurts. Then they come back and gore their fallen foe with those tusks. Don't get knocked down.

While orc riders feel a bond with their goretusks, that bond is not reciprocated. Goretusks pressed into service as orc mounts are deeply resentful of captivity and look for opportunities to escape so they can hurt or kill their riders. The orcs see this as a fun challenge. It's up to you what use you can make of it.

Aderyn paid little attention to the number of enemies. She was sure there were more of them on the far side of Livia's mound of earth, blocked from the range of [Improved Assess 3]. The goretusks were bearing down on them, gobbets of thick spittle dripping from their jaws, and the riders had all switched from bows to javelins. Aderyn braced herself for the impact, but the javelins didn't fly. Instead, the riders held them ready to stab down at the humans when they were in range.

The goretusks were big, but not enormous; they weren't as tall at the shoulder as Owen, which still made them tower over Aderyn. Their black, warty hides were streaked all over with paint in weird shapes and symbols, and the rusty iron rings banding their tusks looked like they were dripping with rust-colored blood in the humid air. Aderyn was too focused on searching for weaknesses to fear them. The blue crisscrossing lines of [Discern Weakness] shrank to blue dots, not very many of them—one at the base of the throat, two more over the unnaturally large eyes. Then the two groups clashed, and Aderyn had no time for more.

Owen dodged the rider's javelin and tried to reach its far side for [Outflank], but the goretusk was too heavy for [Overrun]. "Aderyn!"

Aderyn concentrated on the rider. Thin white lines stretched out from him in three directions. She imagined pulling the rider forward over the head of the goretusk along one of those lines, and the rider abruptly slid forward and tumbled to the ground. Aderyn struck, but not fast enough—the goretusk made an eerie, high-pitched howl like a whistle blown inside a tin can and reared up on its hind legs to stomp the rider into the ground. Aderyn, at a loss, followed Owen's lead as he impaled the distracted goretusk. With the help of [Discern Weakness], she stabbed the goretusk through the eye, and it slumped over the dead body of its rider.

**Congratulations! You have defeated [Goretusk].
You have earned [15,000 XP]**

Another rider bore down on them before the system message faded. "Come on!" Owen shouted.

They fought for what seemed like hours, sometimes tumbling the riders out of their seats to be trampled by their mounts, other times killing riders where they sat and sending the goretusks rampaging across the battlefield. It wasn't until Aderyn paused to wipe charcoal-bitter orc blood off her face that she realized the goretusks were retreating. Caution won out over a desire to celebrate. She wished desperately for a *fly* spell to reconnoiter the battlefield, even if it made her a target.

Then she realized she had another option.

In all their fighting, she and Owen hadn't moved far from their initial position, and Livia's mound of earth was a few hundred feet to the north. "Stay here!" she told the bannerman. She ran, dodging fallen bodies without stopping to see if any were alive, and clambered up the curve of the mound. Its roughly wavelike shape meant the slope was difficult for the first dozen steps and gradually flattened into something easier to climb. Keeping low to the ground, Aderyn climbed to the top.

She estimated she was about fifteen feet off the ground, not very high, but high enough to give her a sense of where the battle was.

Her heart sank. Off to the left, Eagle and Owl Regiments were still fighting hard, clashing with orc grunts and mashers and elites, but what frightened her was that the remaining cavalry—strange word, but she liked it—had broken off their assault on Leopard Regiment's position and gone to support the other orcs. A glance around showed why. The ground near Aderyn was torn and ravaged, pocked with deep, wide pits and muddy in some places. Livia and any Earthbreakers in the platoons had made the orc cavalry's work impossible, so they'd turned to easier prey.

Now that she was standing still, the battle lust had worn off and she was tired. But it was too soon to give up. "Everybody listen!" she shouted, letting [**Amplify Voice**] carry her words across the battlefield. "We have to pursue! Attack the cavalry from behind!"

Her bannerman blew a series of notes reinforcing her command. Sluggishly, the remaining soldiers lurched into motion, moving more freely with every step. Aderyn scrambled and slid down the mound to rejoin her bannerman and found her friends gathering beneath the pile of earth. "How are we doing?" She checked the team roster, but nobody was seriously injured.

"Fine," Livia answered, flexing her stone arm. "I made sure the Earthbreakers knew what kinds of attacks to use. None of them are higher level than eleven, but that's still enough for [**Excavate**], and they all have either *create pit* or *hungry pit*."

"It was effective," Weston said. "And Isold using [**Fascinate**] to hold the goretusks' attention meant a lot of riders got distracted trying to make their mounts obey. Easy kills."

"Then let's join the others," Aderyn said.

"We should run," Livia said. "I want to conserve my resources for fighting rather than cast *transport*."

They ran, even Livia, chasing the soldiers who were chasing the orc riders. Owen held Aderyn's arm to keep her from stumbling as she Assessed the horde while she moved. Then, surprise rooted her to the ground, and she pulled free of Owen's arm. "Look!"

Ahead, a pure white goretusk whose hide looked crazed like cracked glass with thin, irregular black lines mowed down an incautious soldier. Its rider stabbed down with his javelin, a powerful movement that embedded the tip deeply enough the rider had to yank on it twice to free it from the soldier's body. The rider took a moment to survey the battle-field, and his eye fell on Aderyn, watching her so intently she felt he'd impaled her in place as well. He was ugly even for an orc, his head shaved except for three long stripes of black hair, and a mass of scar tissue centered on a blind white eye disfigured his face.

Then the rider threw his head back and laughed. It was a choked, horrible sound, the sound of something gurgling a death cry. He turned his back on Aderyn and rode away.

CHAPTER THREE

Aderyn Assessed the figure. The casual way he rode angered her, like he'd dismissed her as useless.

Name: Drorg
Type: Monstrosity (orc rider)
Power level: 14
Attack(s): short bow, javelin, short sword, special
Immune to: none
Resistant to: bladed weapons, bludgeoning weapons
Vulnerable to: *daylight, sunburst*
Special attacks: ferocious might, fear aura

Drorg is the captain of the orc riders and as vicious and cunning a creature as you will ever meet. He delights in torture and, if possible, causes as much pain as he can before he kills. Drorg has fought many duels among his people and won all of them—naturally, since orcs duel to the death.

Drorg has many abilities in common with the orc elites: he has enhanced toughness, and he can inspire fear in his victims. Never turn your back on Drorg, because he is good at striking weakness.

Drorg loves only one creature, and that's his goretusk, who he

named Kirda. Unlike all other orc riders, Drorg refused to accept that Kirda might ever turn on him, and he beat and tortured the creature into submission. Don't feel sorry for Kirda—just because she's too afraid of Drorg to betray him doesn't mean she isn't brutal in her attacks on others. That white hide of hers is paint, by the way.

When Drorg is at the head of his riders, they become even fiercer than usual. You would, too, if being flayed alive was a possible result of failure.

"That's their leader," Aderyn said, breathless from running. "Drorg. I think he's on our list, but there's no time—we have to stop the orc cavalry from stampeding the regiments!"

"Hold on," Livia said, coming to a halt. She clenched both fists at waist level and muttered a long string of nonsense words. As her voice grew in volume, she lifted her fists slowly to shoulder height and then punched the air in emphasis of her last words.

The earth in a thirty foot circle centered on Drorg cracked like a sheet of ice, and everything inside that circle, crust of earth, orcs, and goretusks, lifted off the ground and flew in a mad tangle of flailing limbs into the sky, stopping about twenty feet above the ground. No, not flying—it looked as if they'd fallen into the sky, and they slammed into an invisible barrier above like it was solid ground. Aderyn didn't waste time asking Livia for an explanation. With a cry of defiance, she was off again, with her friends surrounding her.

"Stay out of the circle!" Livia shouted. Aderyn didn't need a reminder. If it was an ongoing effect, it was one she didn't want to find out about the hard way. The other orc riders didn't stop or flee; they slammed into the human soldiers like the wave Aderyn had pictured before. Humans fell or darted out of the way. Aderyn feared there were a lot more who fell than evaded.

Owen reached the nearest orc rider and attacked its goretusk, skewering it from behind. It squealed, sounding just like an angry boar, and struggled to turn around even as its rider fought to remain in control. Aderyn used [Reposition] to drag the goretusk to one side, giving Owen the chance to [Outflank] it. The rider continued to beat desperately at the goretusk, which was maddened with pain and ignored him.

Aderyn struck at the goretusk's tiny eyes and miraculously scored a fatal hit. The goretusk reared up in agony, tossing its rider to the ground, and collapsed in death. Owen was there instantly to skewer the rider with a two-handed thrust to the chest, impaling him.

Congratulations! You have defeated [Goretusk].
You have earned [15,000 XP]

Congratulations! You have defeated [Orc Rider].
You have earned [6250 XP]

Owen pulled his blade free and shouted, "They outnumber us, and they kill faster than we do!"

"I know!" Aderyn glanced around. Everything was chaos. She couldn't see what was happening more than a few feet in front of her. Then she darted to one side, warned by **[See It Coming]**, and raised her sword to block a javelin blow from another orc rider bearing down on her. It took longer to kill this rider, who had better control over his mount. When the orc and the goretusk were dead, Aderyn said, "Where's Livia? I need to get up high."

Owen grabbed her free hand and towed her after him so they wouldn't get separated. They ducked and dodged blows, never engaging with the enemy, until they found Livia standing on the edge of disturbed earth that marked where *hungry pit* had claimed more victims. "Get me up high!" Aderyn shouted.

She expected Livia to lift her alone, but instead Livia slung an arm around her waist and carried them both aloft on a rising pillar of earth and stone. Aderyn took a look around, Assessing in every direction. The humans were definitely taking a beating. Flags indicated where the commanders of Eagle and Owl Regiments were. Both regiments were positioned so their troops made lines reinforcing each other. Her Warmaster's vision showed her where the defenders' line was weakest, and where they needed to move to shore it up. But communicating that information was going to be difficult.

She pulled out the <**Farspeaker**> and Hasanth's coin, but before she could contact the colonel, the banner of Eagle Regiment dipped in a circle and began to retreat. "No, don't!" Aderyn screamed, as if Hasanth could hear her. She fumbled the coin into the slot and waited for the mirror's fog to clear. Its surface continued to roil with thick gray clouds. Aderyn watched helplessly as orcs poured into the space where Eagle Regiment had been and closed with Owl Regiment. Between the orc army and the orc riders, Owl Regiment was caught in a pincer.

The mirror still didn't clear. Cursing loudly, Aderyn shoved the <Farspeaker> into its pouch and gestured to Livia to carry them back to earth. "Signal the soldiers to press the orc riders westward," she told her bannerman. There hadn't been time for her to learn the many signals the flags sent or all the bugle calls, but like she'd told Hasanth, generals didn't try to do everyone else's jobs for them. The bannerman, Emri, was a level two Pathseer with an incredible memory not only for signals but for names, historical events, and army regulations. Aderyn had reservations about anyone that low a level coming anywhere near a battlefield and had gotten the whole team's agreement on protecting him.

Another eternity of fighting passed. Aderyn stopped being aware of anything beyond the next orc to kill and the next system defeat notice. Finally, she took a javelin blow to her side that tore her coat and dragged the fine mesh of the <Gossamer Mail> across her side, painfully abrading her flesh. She distracted the orc long enough for Owen to kill it, but instead of pressing the attack, she took a defensive stance and caught her breath, pressing one hand hard against the wound. When Isold reached her with the <Healing Stone>, she was Assessing the crowds, comparing the orc numbers to what they'd been that morning. "We've barely made a dent," she told him.

"And we have moved southward," Isold said. "My map shows that we have given up at least a quarter mile of territory."

"Crap." She glanced around for Owen, but he'd moved out of sight. When she took a step in Emri and the banner's direction, [Keep Pace] tugged her to her right. "Emri, signal for the soldiers to regroup and withdraw to the south and west. We need to gain a better position, even if it means giving ground. I wish I knew where Eagle Regiment went." In the dust and furor of the melee, she couldn't see either of the other regiments' flags.

"It's a pity Livia is so against the *fly* spell," Isold said with a tight smile.

"'There's no thundering way I'm learning a spell that tears people off the ground where we all naturally belong,'" Aderyn said in a fair approximation of Livia's sardonic voice. "I'm rejoining Owen. Stay with Emri, all right? I'll be right back."

Isold nodded.

With [**Keep Pace**] tugging her along, Aderyn raced to find Owen. The <**Healing Stone**> had revitalized her somewhat, though it was just an illusion and not a real regeneration of reserves, and she determined to make use of the illusion for as long as possible. She saw a system defeat notice just as she found Owen, who was standing over a dead orc elite and breathing heavily. "Come with me," she said. "We're regrouping."

"I don't know how much difference it will make," Owen said.

"We no longer have the numbers to do anything but hold a position." Aderyn headed in the direction of her banner. "And we can only do that if we regroup."

"What happened to Eagle Regiment?" Owen asked. He jogged easily beside her.

"I don't know, but I'm guessing it's what I feared—Hasanth saw they weren't making progress and withdrew to find a better position. Which would be fine if he was on his own, but he nearly got Owl Regiment destroyed with that maneuver."

The Leopard Regiment banner had moved as Aderyn instructed, and the soldiers fought a perfect defensive withdrawal, which raised Aderyn's spirits. At least something had gone right today. When she reached the banner, she found not only Isold, but Livia and Weston gathered there. Isold was busy healing a deep wound in Weston's upper chest while Livia paced around them, watching for an attack.

"How are your resources?" Aderyn asked Livia.

"Low," Livia said. "Not critically low."

"Can you *move earth* again?"

"That's pushing it, but yes."

This time, Livia sent Aderyn aloft on her own. Guided by the ghostly images of [**See It Coming**], Aderyn dodged the few enemy arrows that came her way and scanned the horizon. To her surprise, the sun was near setting. The orcs didn't look like they'd lost any fighters, though the numerical count revealed by **[Improved Assess 3]** told her that was just her imagination. She still couldn't Assess the human regiments for a total count, but all three definitely looked smaller than before. However, her maneuver had worked; Leopard had shored up the weak flank of Owl, and Eagle had returned from wherever Hasanth had directed them and was fighting fiercely on Owl's other side.

Aderyn waved at Livia, who brought her back to earth. "We just have to hold out another half hour. The orcs will withdraw at sunset."

"The riders have already retreated," Owen said. "I think they were rattled."

"Disrupting the terrain really screwed with their plans," Livia said, grinning.

Aderyn agreed. Without the Earthbreakers' tactics, the battle would not have gone their way. The orc riders were far more efficient than she'd guessed.

"What happened to Drorg and the others you—what *was* that spell?" she asked.

"*Reverse gravity*," Livia said. "Creates a small field in which, well, you get it. It takes enemies out of the fight and then they get injured when the effect ends and they fall. But it means we didn't fight Drorg."

"Shouldn't we go back to the battle?" Weston said, rotating his shoulder.

"I don't know about you all, but I'm exhausted," Aderyn said. "If I head back into the fight, I'll be at a disadvantage. But let's move closer so the banner is more easily seen."

It seemed everyone was at the end of their endurance, humans and orcs alike, because it wasn't more than five minutes before the orcs disengaged and ran northward. Aderyn had Emri signal "do not pursue," and she and her friends walked back to camp. Aderyn wished she could sleep, but there was still so much to do: send out parties to search for the wounded, send other parties to retrieve their fallen dead, find spellslingers of high level who hadn't exhausted their resources to try to penetrate the obfuscation the orcs laid on their camp. Eat. Now that the rush of battle was over, she was starving.

It wasn't until she'd spoken with the bannermen of Eagle and Owl and arranged for retrieval parties that she realized she hadn't seen Hasanth. The thought made her even wearier than before. Hasanth needed disciplining for that stunt he'd pulled, and Aderyn had a terrible premonition that disciplining meant relieving him of command. Her subordinate officers were supposed to use their initiative, true, but that initiative shouldn't put other soldiers at risk.

She decided to put it off until after she'd eaten. At least then she wouldn't be on edge and in a mood for disproportionate punishment. As it was, the food tasted bland, like her stomach knew what was coming. Aderyn missed Private Nandi of Raven Regiment. Her current personal servant, Isman, was dutiful and hardworking, but lacked Nandi's quick responsiveness and anticipation of Aderyn's needs.

She finished her meal without having any idea what she'd eaten and told her friends, "I have to deal with Hasanth. Livia, can you find any spellslingers who can cast *scry* or similar observation spells?"

"I assume you mean the ones who aren't exhausted," Livia replied. "I'll take care of it."

"Do you want me to come along?" Owen said.

"I do, but that's self-indulgent. If this conversation goes wrong, there's nothing you can do about it. And I need to let Hasanth keep face, which can't happen if anyone else witnesses his humiliation. Or what he thinks is humiliation." She kissed her husband wearily. "I'll be back soon. If I'm not—"

"I'll ride to the rescue, and humiliation be damned," Owen said.

She found Hasanth in his command tent, speaking to a couple of officers wearing Eagle Regiment insignia. Hasanth glanced her way when she entered without clapping, then returned to speaking with the officers as if she wasn't there. Aderyn assumed a casual pose and waited. As she'd hoped, the officers started looking at her every time they finished a sentence, pausing to give her room to speak. Aderyn remained silent. Finally, one of the officers said, "Sir, shouldn't we—"

"You'll finish your report," Hasanth said.

"Yes," Aderyn chimed in cheerfully. "Finish your report. I'll wait."

This unnerved the officers even more. Finally, they saluted and hurried out of the tent. Hasanth busied himself at the table, moving papers around at random. [**Read Body Language**] didn't work on anyone but her partner, but Aderyn didn't need the skill to know Hasanth felt guilty. No one with a clear conscience could fail to meet his superior's gaze.

Aderyn let his restless movements continue for a few seconds more. Then she said, "You know why I'm here."

"I won't justify myself to you," Hasanth said, still without looking her way. "I take responsibility for my command, and it's impractical for me to go running to you for direction every time a crisis occurs."

"Funny, and here was me thinking the <Farspeaker> was meant for just that," Aderyn said. "Your retreat nearly caused Owl Regiment's destruction. Will you take responsibility for that, too?"

"You dare challenge me?" Hasanth roared. "You upstart girl, with your flashy Warmaster skills—you've never led troops in battle, and you *dare* tell me I don't understand tactics?"

"That is exactly right, colonel," Aderyn said in a low, forceful voice. "You're a conservative thinker who reacts too slowly to changing conditions. Anyone would have seen the results of your maneuver, but apparently all you saw was a threat to your own forces. You didn't consider the bigger picture."

"What I did was sound military strategy—"

"Sound strategy," Aderyn said, cutting him off, "if yours is the only regiment in the field. Are you going to claim sound military strategy when you explain the unnecessary deaths of men and women to their loved ones?"

Hasanth raised his fist. Astonished, Aderyn dodged the blow he leveled at her face. "What in *thunder* has gotten into you?" she breathed. "Attacking your commanding officer is a punishable offense." With **[Bonded Mind]**, she told Owen, *Better get over here now.*

"You're not my superior," Hasanth roared, "you're a jumped up northern nobody who has no idea what it means to lead troops in battle. I'm ten times the soldier you are!"

He aimed another blow at Aderyn. This time, she used **[Reposition]** to move him swiftly away from her until he struck the tent wall. It wasn't a heavy impact, but Hasanth shook his head as if disoriented. "What did you do to me?"

"That's enough," Aderyn said. "I officially strip you of rank,

Hasanth, and I'm sending you to Ikharatia for Varoun to deal with. Strike at me a third time, and you'll see what else a Warmaster is capable of." She stared him down, hoping her [Bluff] skill was high enough to keep Hasanth from pummeling her before Owen could arrive.

Hasanth lowered his fist. Confusion distorted his features. "Strip me of rank?"

"Did you think attacking me could result in anything else? You're the only one who doesn't believe I'm your commanding officer."

Loud, rapid footsteps sounded outside, and Owen pushed aside the tent flap. He hesitated, taking in the scene, then walked with measured steps to stand beside Aderyn. He put a hand on the <Sunsword's> basket hilt, but didn't draw and activate the weapon.

"You can't do that," Hasanth said weakly.

Aderyn said nothing. She removed the <Farspeaker> and slotted Varoun's coin into it. Varoun's face appeared immediately. "Yes?"

"I need someone to take Hasanth into custody pending military trial. I'm afraid our spellslingers don't have the resources for *world door* after today's battle."

Varoun's expression of confused dismay was comical, but Aderyn didn't want to laugh and maybe break the spell she'd put on Hasanth. "Very well, general," he said. "I'll join you shortly." His image vanished.

"General Varoun is coming here?" Hasanth now sounded like a vassal informed of the king's imminent visit to a disorderly house.

"You should have your servant pack your things." Aderyn almost said *Don't try to run*, but decided not to give the man ideas. Besides, if Varoun himself was coming, Hasanth wasn't the only one who needed to prepare.

CHAPTER FOUR

Aderyn and Owen escorted Hasanth to his personal tent and stood outside. "Are we making sure he doesn't flee?" Owen whispered. "What happened in there that you needed me to come quickly?"

"He took a swing at me—Owen, don't get upset!"

"Aderyn, people trying to hit you is something I take very seriously. You're a good fighter, but your primary skills aren't in attacking people. You have to let me defend you in situations like this—or am I wrong, and you could have killed him with impunity?"

He looked so angry Aderyn was glad she could tell his anger wasn't directed at her. It warmed her heart that he wanted to protect her. "I know. And I called to you as soon as I knew Hasanth was a problem. I told you you couldn't come with me, and I stand by that—but I think, now, it would have been better if you'd waited outside the tent. You're right. My sword skills are high enough, but it would have been a fatal fight."

Owen put an arm around her shoulders. "You're right, and that's a good compromise. I just—Aderyn, I need you to be as safe as this profession of ours allows."

"I understand. I feel the same." She tapped the **\<Ring of the Cat\>**

he wore on his left hand, with its single remaining gem. "You've already cheated death twice."

"Someday, we won't face danger every day." He squeezed her lightly and released her. "Did you see the quest update?"

"I haven't had time." She called up the Codex and focused on the golden dot that enlarged into [**Fated One's Destiny: Crush the Horde**].

An army of monstrous orcs has emerged from the Blighted Range, intent on conquering the southern human lands. Destroy their leaders and push the army back into the mountains.

Victory conditions:
Death of Glasha, orc commander general
ACHIEVED Death of Ornok, second in command
Death of ?
Death of Drorg, orc cavalry commander
Death of ?
Destruction of Charnel Keep
Orc army retreats

Reward: [75,000 XP] plus any XP gained through actions taken to complete the quest.

"I suppose it was too much to hope for that he broke his neck falling when *reverse gravity* expired," she sighed.

"I choose to see it as having expanded our knowledge," Owen said.

"That's much better."

With a snap, the black oval frame of *world door* flashed into being, and Varoun's image, flattened into a portrait of himself, appeared within it. Aderyn and Owen waited the thirty seconds it took for Varoun to emerge, not speaking. Aderyn listened for movement inside Hasanth's tent, or the sound of canvas tearing that might mean he'd cut through the tent side in a break for freedom, but there was no noise, not even the quiet rustling and occasional knock of wood on wood that meant someone was packing up. Aderyn hadn't really expected otherwise. No doubt Hasanth was going to appeal to Varoun. It wouldn't do any good, but she found, to her surprise, she respected him for not giving up.

Abruptly, Varoun broke free of *world door* and strode to meet Aderyn. "What in thunder is going on?"

"Hasanth made a terrible error during the battle that nearly got Owl Regiment destroyed," Aderyn said. "Then, when I told him there would be consequences, he took a swing at me. Twice."

Varoun's vexed expression didn't change. "That's unacceptable. Did he hurt you?"

"It's hard to hit a Warmaster of my level if I'm expecting it. I'm fine. But he doesn't respect me as his commander, and he can't be allowed to attack a superior officer."

"Thunderation," Varoun said in a low voice. "You're right, of course, but replacing Hasanth is going to be difficult. I need you to be free to go where you're needed, not be mired in one place leading a division. If Chandar has completed his scouting mission..." He looked thoughtful. "I'm going to talk to Hasanth. You're to take command here until I reach Chandar and discover what he knows."

Aderyn pointed. "He's in there. He's not happy."

"And he will be even less happy when I get through with him." Varoun entered the tent without clapping and let the flap fall behind him. Moments later, Hasanth's servant came scuttling out. He avoided Aderyn and Owen and soon disappeared from sight among the tents.

The murmur of voices within the tent became audible, though not intelligible. "I... think we should leave," Aderyn said. "I don't need to hear this."

"We should see what Livia has arranged," Owen said. "There's nothing else you can do until morning, except receive the reports of the retrieval teams, and you can do that from anywhere."

Aderyn nodded. She felt so weary, spiritually, she was ready to lie down where she stood and sleep. But that wasn't practical, and besides, she was sure if she started moving, she'd feel more alert.

That turned out to be true. By the time she and Owen returned to their campsite, she felt invigorated. Some of that was curiosity. The knowledge that no one had been able to *scry* into the orcs' camps filled her with a desire to figure out a solution—well, see if *Livia* could figure out a solution. On the other hand, if a level seventeen spellslinger wasn't high enough level to break through [**Obscure**] or whatever the orcs had on their camp, that worried her. She decided not to think about that until the time came.

Weston and Isold were gone, but Livia and seven soldiers sat around the little fire that burned by magic. Aderyn Assessed them as she approached: two Flamecrafters, two Windwardens, two Tidecallers, and an Earthbreaker. All of them were either level ten or level eleven. The soldiers shot to their feet and saluted when Aderyn neared them. Aderyn still wasn't used to being saluted, but she no longer rejected the gesture. They saluted the general, and the general showed reciprocal respect by receiving the salute.

"Thank you, veterans, sergeant." She addressed the last title to the Earthbreaker, Sentan, who wore rank insignia showing he was the head of a platoon. "Please, sit. Livia, where did Weston and Isold go?"

"Isold went to help with healing. Most of the Bonemenders are tapped out, and there are still a few injured who won't survive the night without immediate healing. Weston joined one of the retrieval teams, as protection, since he's got the <**Cat's Eye Goggles**>. In case the orcs send their people to do the same thing we're doing and there's a clash." Livia didn't sound nearly as tired as she looked. "We've been discussing possibilities."

"We've tried *scry* on the enemy camp, both here and in other battles," the level eleven Tidecaller, Noema, said. She looked too young to be level eleven. "I mean, not us—I've talked to other spellslingers who've fought the orcs elsewhere. And we all agree that *scry* is working. The orcs have done something that makes it seem like there's thick fog when we *scry* their camps. Obviously there isn't—scouts report clear weather, and while they can't get very close, they can get close enough that they'd see fog if there was any."

"Nobody has *greater scry*. Nobody in the army," the male Flamecrafter, Ambor, said. "I talked to some acquaintances at the university, high-level spellslingers, and the ones who can cast *greater scry* said they saw blackness rather than fog."

"Strange," Aderyn said. "Or, maybe it isn't. I don't have any idea what's normal. Livia?"

"I don't know anything about *greater scry* in practice, since I don't have it." Livia scowled like this was a personal failing. "What I do know is that *scry* works like human vision. Casting it on a given location shows what you'd see if you were there in person. That means the skill **[Obscure]** shouldn't conceal anything from *scry*, because **[Obscure]**, according to Isold, confuses locator spells and items like the <**Wayfinder**>. It doesn't actually block vision."

"So, whatever is blocking *scry* isn't **[Obscure]**?"

"Right. But we could have guessed that, because based on what we see the orc elementalists doing, their spells are totally different from ours. We understand the words they use, but they use single words or short phrases, and about half the time, we don't know what relationship the spellslinging words have to do with the spell they cast. At any rate, it means if they have a spell that does what **[Obscure]** does, it works in a completely alien way."

Aderyn frowned. "Are you saying the orcs share our language?"

"I—" Livia hesitated. "I don't know."

"We understand their spellslinging words," Ambor said, "but most of us didn't realize ordinary people don't understand what *we* say when we cast spells. So now we don't know if they speak our language, or if all spellslingers really do speak their own spellslinging language that we only think is ordinary speech."

"It's not important at the moment," Livia said, with a glare at the Flamecrafter that said they'd had this argument already. "The point is, *scry* and *greater scry* won't work, and if I had enough time, I could figure out why."

"We have *some* time," Aderyn said. "Isn't that worth the effort?"

Livia gave her a sardonic look. "By 'enough time' read 'a year or so.' It's not a viable hope. But I think, working together, we can achieve it. It means a sideways approach."

"We don't all agree," Ambor said.

"Agreement is irrelevant," Livia said. "It's the commander's decision whether to implement our plan."

"I don't know what the plan is," Aderyn said.

"It means she'll push past the limits of her reserves," Ambor said hotly. "We're not supposed to hurt ourselves, not when there are so many slavering orcs who want to hurt us too."

"Livia," Aderyn said.

"It's my choice," Livia said. "Here's the plan. We use *scry* to look at the orc camp—the whole camp and its surroundings, not trying to see inside. Their obfuscation doesn't conceal that. Then, with the help of that *scrying*, I summon an earth elemental outside the camp, and through it I cast *greater dispel magic* on the camp. It won't be permanent, but it will suppress the obscuring effect long enough for everyone else to *scry* what's there."

"You don't know if it will work on orc magic," Ambor said. "You could knock yourself unconscious for nothing."

"Then I'll sleep it off and wake refreshed and ready to try a new approach." Livia sounded perfectly confident, not at all as if she had secret reservations.

"That... actually, it makes sense," Aderyn said. "Wait. This is why you made Weston leave, isn't it? He won't be in favor of anything that burns through your resources so thoroughly."

Livia wouldn't meet Aderyn's eyes. "We couldn't find another magical energy rejuvenation potion. This is sensible. It's not like I wouldn't spend all night sleeping anyway. And it's true, I encouraged him to go, but now that I've thought about it, I won't do it until he's back and we've talked about it."

"That's a relief. You know he'd see it as a betrayal."

"I have trouble remembering we're married and that's the sort of thing married people do, share each other's burdens instead of doing stupid things for the other person's own good." Livia's mouth curved in a sideways smile. "At least he's as prone to doing that as I am."

Aderyn nodded. "All right. This is a solid plan, and if it doesn't work, we'll still have learned something important. Imagine if you tried *greater dispel magic* at a time when it was crucial and we only found out then that it doesn't work on orc magic?"

"General, are you sure?" Ambor asked.

"Ambor, I think it's great that you're concerned for a fellow spell-slinger's well-being, and you're right about us not doing damage to ourselves. But Livia understands her capacity, and she knows the effects of using her entire reserves of power. So I'm going to allow it. Are you going to be able to participate? Because if you're really opposed to this plan, you can leave and I won't hold it against you." Aderyn hoped that had sounded sufficiently confident. She remembered how awful Livia looked when she exhausted her resources, how limp and unresisting she was. It wasn't anything she ever wanted to see again. But she felt the rightness of Livia's plan.

Sure enough, Ambor sat up straighter. "I can help, general. I'm sorry I raised doubts."

"Don't be sorry. It's important we all work together, which some-times means objecting so all sides of a problem get addressed." Aderyn lowered herself to sit beside Livia, and Owen sat beside her. "Should I send someone to fetch Weston?"

"Weston is back," Weston said, striding into camp. He held the <Cat's Eye Goggles> carelessly in one hand. "Do you need me for something?"

Livia extended her hand to Weston so he could pull her up. "I have a plan you won't like, but you need to listen to the whole thing before you object," she said. "Let's walk."

When they'd disappeared into the camp, Aderyn said, "Is there anything else you need for this? Do all of you have *scry*?"

The spellslingers nodded. "We're all close to the edge of our reserves, too," Noema said. "Not enough that *scry* will push us over. But close."

"What worries me is the possibility that the orcs will try a nighttime raid," Ambor said. "Just because they haven't so far doesn't mean they can't. They might catch us unawares."

"I know, which is why we post guards." Aderyn didn't say what Varoun had told her, that the guards were as much to spot deserters as to watch for intruders or attacks. "It's a good concern, but you needn't worry."

"I really want to know what the orcs are so keen to keep hidden," one of the Windwardens, Jayna, exclaimed. "It must be something important, but then why haven't they used it against us yet?"

"Or maybe it's just a side effect of their spellslinging being different from ours," Ambor said. "It might not be anything important."

Ambor was starting to annoy Aderyn with his constant pessimism. That reminded her unpleasantly of Hasanth, whom she didn't want to think about anymore. "In half an hour, we'll know, one way or the other," she said, firmly enough to cut off the incipient argument. "Maybe less than that. See, Livia and Weston are returning."

The two walked close together, not touching, which worried Aderyn until Livia glanced up at her husband and smiled. "Weston's going to sit with me and make sure I don't fall into the fire."

"And take care of her when she succumbs," Weston added. "I have to say I didn't think I'd end up carrying an unconscious woman to my bed so soon after marriage."

Livia laughed and resumed her seat, with Weston sitting behind her. "Ambor, you'll *scry* the orc camp location for me. Everyone else, keep your mirrors focused on the camp. If this works, you'll know it immediately."

Ambor withdrew a largish silver hand mirror from inside his shirt. It looked like it belonged on a rich woman's dressing table instead of in an army camp, but with no self-consciousness Ambor held it where Livia could see it. Aderyn scooted forward, gripped by curiosity. It showed the edges of Livia and Ambor's faces and, beyond that, the darkness of the night sky.

Ambor spoke a sentence that nearly made sense. The mirror flashed bright silver, and the view changed. It showed a sea of black canvas tent roofs, too distant for people to be visible, surrounded by plains that looked just like the ones they'd fought on that day. Aderyn saw no gray fog or sheer blackness.

Livia began speaking. While her words weren't any more intelligible than Ambor's had been, they sounded harsher, like stone grinding on stone. In the *scry* image, near its edge, something moved. In the next moment, Aderyn identified the movement as stones rolling across the plain, gathering at a point some distance from the orc camp. More stones joined the first ones until the pile was visible as a roughly man-shaped pillar. Seconds passed. The elemental took a step toward the camp, then another. It didn't go very far before it came to a halt.

"All right," Livia said, somewhat breathlessly as if she'd been the one to lift and pile all those stones. "Let's hope this is worth it." She chanted a sequence of words that seemed familiar to Aderyn, not comprehensi-ble, but as if she'd heard the nonsense syllables before.

A ripple of thick air like heat haze radiated out from the stone elemental, washing over the orc camp and disappearing almost instantly. Cries of surprise and delight came from the other spellslingers, who suddenly became very intent on their mirrors. And Livia let out a sigh and slumped backwards into Weston's arms.

CHAPTER FIVE

Aderyn bit back a dismayed cry. She'd expected this, but it still frightened her to see Livia go completely limp. Weston held her carefully and checked her pulse. "Feels strong. She didn't do damage to herself. I'll put her to bed."

Aderyn nodded. When she turned back to Ambor's mirror, the man had tilted it toward himself and was frowning at it with an expression of extreme concentration. "Show me," Aderyn commanded, not thinking that it might be a distraction.

But Ambor switched places so he could sit between Aderyn and Owen and held the mirror up so all of them could see. The view looked the same as it had before, black canvas tent roofs at too great a distance for any detail. Ambor said, "Draw in closer," as if he was instructing a person instead of a spell effect. The view expanded like they were birds diving on the orc encampment, the tents growing rapidly larger and closer. A bigger mirror might have made that feel terrifying, like they were really there, but the small oval was more like a peephole.

The view dipped and shifted. Now the imaginary bird of their *scrying* flew between the tents, just above the heads of orcs walking through the camp. They looked so calm Aderyn couldn't believe these were the same creatures she'd fought all day.

Abruptly, the orcs' motion became agitated, and a crowd appeared, orcs jostling and shoving one another, their attention focused on the center of the crowd. *Scry* revealed two orcs pummeling each other with a ferocity made eerie by the silence, since *scry* didn't capture sounds, not of the fight and not of the bystanders crowded around, watching.

One orc drew a long, rusty-bladed knife and stabbed his opponent in the chest, making him stagger backward. The first orc pressed his attack, stabbing again and again until the second orc collapsed, covered in that inhuman charcoal-red blood. The orc tossed the knife atop the corpse and walked away. The crowd dispersed, leaving the body where it lay.

"That's disturbing," Aderyn said.

"It's no more than I expected. Didn't the Assessment of Drorg say orcs duel to the death?" Owen leaned forward to watch the *scrying* oval move on through the camp.

"That wasn't a duel, that was a slaughter—wait, Ambor, go left." Aderyn leaned forward as well, searching the image for whatever had caught her eye.

Ambor moved the *scrying* to the left, where a gleam of bright blue light emanated from one of the tents. Up close, it was apparent they were filthy and much mended with coarse threads that made the black canvas look scarred. The blue light, on the other hand, was a clear, brilliant radiance, out of place among the sullen tents.

With a series of quiet instructions, Ambor steered the view to the open tent flap and past it so the entire tent interior was visible. Four small, misshapen candles burned at the corners of a square whose outline was cut into the hard ground. A naked orc sat cross-legged in the center of the square. The blue glow emanated from a tattoo drawn on his left shoulder and upper arm, an abstract design Aderyn didn't think represented anything real. The blue brilliance outshone the candles, mingling with their warm light to cast odd shadows on the tent walls.

"What is that?" Owen whispered.

Aderyn felt the same impulse to keep her voice down. The *scrying* produced an image so clear it was like they were barely three feet from the orc. "I think he must be an elementalist."

"You can't Assess him?"

"Not through *scry*. I have to be there in person." Aderyn cursed softly. "I wish that wasn't true."

"Something's happening," Ambor whispered.

The orc's lips moved in soundless speech. It reminded Aderyn more of Livia casting spells than the orc talking to someone outside the range of *scry* or to himself. She looked closely at the orc's body. More tattooed lines decorated his chest and thighs, these black and lightless. Aderyn avoided looking at the dark area between his abdomen and upper thighs. That meant she was looking at the center of his chest when the tattoo there began glowing with a deep orange light that brightened until it cast a glow as intense as the blue lines on his shoulder.

"So strange," Aderyn said. "It must have something to do with their spellslinging, but I don't know what."

"I have some ideas, but I want to discuss with the others," Ambor said. "I'm glad Livia's plan worked, but it would be good to have her input."

"The lights are dimmer," Owen said. "No, wait, it's—"

Gray fog boiled up from the center of the scene, obscuring everything. Ambor sighed and lowered the mirror. "I hope that was enough."

"It means nobody died going into the orc camp," Aderyn said, "and, Owen, remind me to forbid Weston to consider it. I don't mind pulling rank on this. Nobody's come back from that camp, and Weston is good, but until we know how they discover us, he's staying put."

"I doubt he needs commanding, but it's a good point," Owen said.

Ambor rose from his seat and stretched. "Everyone, tell the general what you saw. One at a time, please."

Aderyn liked Ambor better when he took charge of the spellslingers and stopped being pessimistic. "We'll go around the circle. Starting with Jayna."

She listened to the spellslingers' observations without asking questions. Anything she might ask would either be irrelevant or take them on a tangent, given that she knew nothing of how spellslinging worked. Instead, she let their words build up a picture in her mind of how the orc camp functioned.

When Ambor finished describing what they'd seen of the orc elementalist, Aderyn nodded. "Thank you all. This is the best information we've gotten so far. To sum up: the orcs are as belligerent with each other as they are with us, in the sense of being willing to pick fights with other orcs. They don't spar the way we do—they seem to attack each other at random, and sometimes those fights end in a death and sometimes they don't, but no one saw anything that might tell us the difference. That's all right. We don't need to know everything. We also learned that there's no size or musculature difference between male and female orcs the way there is between men and women."

"And that they aren't shy about having sex in the open," Noema muttered. She was still blushing from having revealed what she'd witnessed in the moment before *greater dispel magic* ended.

"Yes, that too." Aderyn wasn't sure that was something they could use, tactically, and fell back on being grateful she hadn't seen that moment herself. "Sadly, we still don't know how they're generating that effect that blocks *scry*, and although we proved *greater dispel magic* works on orc magic, we also proved that it doesn't work against that particular effect for long."

"I have an idea about that, but I'll discuss it with Livia in the morning," Ambor said.

"Good. Now we come to the interesting part. Several of you saw orc elementalists apparently engaged in some ritual that makes the tattoos on their bodies glow. Any theories?"

"General, what do you know about human spellslinging?" Ambor asked.

"Not much. I know to you all, the words you speak seem like ordinary language, but to outsiders, they're gibberish. And I know spellslingers have reservoirs of power that increase with higher levels, and that each spell costs a certain amount of power that gets reduced as you gain levels." Aderyn couldn't think of more details, though she was sure Livia had mentioned them.

"That's all true. Specifically, our reserves increase as we gain the ability to cast higher-level spells, and the more we use a spell, the easier it becomes." Ambor didn't show any nervousness at lecturing his general. "It's not numerical, and it's different for everyone, but try imagining this. Say a spellslinger at level one has a reserve of, I don't know, twenty drops of power, and it takes five drops to cast *grease*. Maybe this spellslinger uses that spell often, and by the time they can cast second-level spells and their reserve becomes thirty drops, it only takes three drops to cast *grease*. Is that helpful?"

"It is."

"I think the tattoos on the elementalists are instead of spell reserves," Jayna said. "Some of the tattoos reminded me of spells I know, like *whispering wind*. I could be wrong, but the shape felt like the words I say when I use that spell."

"But why wouldn't they have spell reserves?" Sentan said.

"My Assessment of the elementalists says they draw power from their connection to the earth," Aderyn said. "Not the kind of connection an Earthbreaker has, more like 'the earth' in the sense of the natural world. So they might have an unlimited power reserve."

Several people groaned. "That's depressing," Ambor said.

"Not really," Jayna said. "If they can only cast the spells they tattoo on themselves—"

"We don't know that's true," Ambor said.

Aderyn's newfound patience with him dwindled. "They have a limitation of some kind," she said, "if only because their spellslinging slows down the longer a battle goes, like they're running out of power. If the limitation isn't a power reserve, couldn't it be, maybe, a limitation of knowledge? Because the other thing my Assessment told me is that they don't know as wide a variety of spells as humans do."

"That's true," Ambor said. "I've noticed they go for certain spells over and over again. I thought it was just that those were most useful in battle, but it must be what you said, that they don't know more spells than those."

"I'm not going to insist on my theory being right," Jayna said, "but I think we should talk about it and see what other possibilities there are."

"Then I'll leave you to it," Aderyn said, rising. "Thank you all for your hard work. This will make a difference."

When they were out of earshot, Owen said, "*Will* it make a difference? Really?"

"I hope so. I don't know. The more we know about the enemy, the better equipped we are to defeat them. Maybe Livia can make sense of it." Aderyn clasped his hand. "I'm so tired. Let's go to bed. I feel like I'm on the verge of understanding something important, but my brain is too weary for high-level thought."

"You have great ideas, general," Owen said.

The word *general* triggered a memory. Aderyn groaned. "I can't. I have to talk to Varoun, if for no other reason than that I need to know who Hasanth's subordinate officers are, since I'm in command now." She groaned again, more weakly. "You might as well go to bed. No sense both of us going sleepless. I'll be there soon."

She tracked Varoun down at the command tent. The commander general looked as tired as Aderyn felt. "I've sent Hasanth back to Ikharatia," he said before Aderyn could speak. "I meant to find you before I return there myself. I've summoned Chandar to take command again, but he isn't anywhere he can return from easily. It might be several days before he arrives. So you're in command of this division until you can turn things over to him."

"It's what I expected." Aderyn tried to make her words sound casual, but her weariness overcame her, and she yawned. "I mean—yes, sir."

"Can this division hold out until reinforcements arrive?"

"I hope so. Owl Regiment took heavy casualties. But Livia also worked out a strategy that weakens the orc riders' effectiveness, and that made a difference today. We'll deploy it more widely in tomorrow's battle." She didn't say anything about the orc elementalists. Whatever the spellslingers had discovered today, it wasn't yet anything the army could use.

"Excellent. Get some rest, Aderyn. Remember, you can't do what you're best suited for if you're exhausted. That might mean not engaging directly in combat." Varoun clapped her on the shoulder. "Keep me updated. The last word I had from Rajman is that Ox and Hawk Regiments are no more than two days from this position, and Colonel Sudiptar is less than three. You don't have to hold out much longer."

"I'll do my best, sir."

Aderyn waited for Varoun to wield his **<Wand of World Door>** and vanish through the ebony oval before trudging back to her tent. Owen was already asleep, lying sprawled on his back with his mouth slack, snoring. She watched him for about half a minute, reflecting on how strange life was that she, Aderyn of Far Haven, was married and fighting a war thousands of miles from her small hometown. Then she stripped down to her shift and drawers and cuddled up beside Owen, and was asleep in seconds.

———

"JAYNA IS RIGHT," Livia said. "They scribe spells on their bodies."

It was the following morning, and the team was sitting by the fire eating breakfast. Livia showed no sign that blasting through her reserves had hurt her. "I didn't put it together until now," she continued, "but during yesterday's battle I targeted elementalists, and I saw those lights. I didn't think about it because I was busy not getting killed whenever I got close, and the lights disappeared rapidly enough I had no time to analyze the patterns. But based on your description, that has to be what they do. Their tattoos glow when they've prepared a spell, and casting a spell expends the power and makes the tattoo darken."

"And they renew the spells at night," Weston said. "But if they have to do that, what's the point of the tattoos? Or do you think they need the pattern to give the spell a home, or something?"

"I could make up an explanation, but really, I'm just guessing." Livia looked more alert than she had at this hour of the morning in the few days since giving up coffee. Aderyn thought about drawing attention to it, but decided if Livia didn't know an intellectual challenge could take the place of, as Livia put it, "the bitter elixir of life," telling her might ruin the effect.

"The tattoos might be a way of storing magical energy. I'm pretty sure not all elementalists have the same tattoos, or even the same number of tattoos," Livia continued. "You said the lights were different colors, and I noticed that too. Blue, green, orange, and white. That could mean anything—amount of power, type of elemental power, level of spell... again, I can only guess. However, there's one thing I'm certain of. If they have to renew their spells after sunset, we can try disrupting that renewal."

"That's not possible," Aderyn said. "The only way to get close to the orc encampment is with a large force, and our soldiers are exhausted from fighting all day."

"We could go," Weston suggested. "Just our team. Though... no, just five of us might not be enough, even at our level."

"And no scouts who got close to the camp returned." Aderyn let out a hiss of frustration. "Stopping those spellslingers could be critical to our success. Let me consider it."

She rose from her seat. "I'm going to walk, see if inspiration strikes. No, it's all right, I need to be alone for this."

She walked through the camp, ignored by the soldiers because she wasn't wearing her coat and insignia. It would have been peaceful except for the tension in the air that said everyone was gearing up for another day's battle. That they kept fighting despite knowing they were in a desperate position impressed her. How many of them were from Shantos, she didn't know, but all of them were aware they were fighting for their homes, if indirectly.

She came to the edge of camp and stared into the distance. All that was visible of the orc camp was a bumpiness on the horizon. She imagined she had some magic item that let her see farther than her natural vision. What might she perceive? Something to guide her strategy for the day?

Turning her back on the orcs, she started walking again, this time traversing the perimeter. The elementalists had to store spells in their bodies—what about forcing them to release the magic prematurely, or against their will? Something to ask Livia. They already had a plan to thwart the orc riders, and that turned the terrain against all the orcs, but not in an organized way. She needed more information, and she saw no way of getting it.

They could fall back to Shantos. The defensible city could hold out until the other regiments arrived. Aderyn considered the possibility for a moment, then dismissed it. She couldn't guarantee the orcs wouldn't simply ignore Shantos and sweep past toward Ikharatia, which was barely defensible at all. And it grated on her, the idea of giving in to the orcs even a little. No. Her army would hold, she was sure of it. And she had a few ideas to make that more likely.

When she'd circled the camp one and a half times, Aderyn returned to her tent. Owen sat outside, already armored, his eyes closed as if he was meditating. He opened one eye as she approached. "Everything all right?"

"I'd be happier if we could get a few spies into the enemy camp, but I think I have a plan. Would you find Livia for me?" Aderyn ducked into the tent and put on her <**Gossamer Mail**>. It was comfortable and flexed like fine cloth, but not a single hit directed at it had gone through, and the worst damage she'd taken was a deep bruise from a javelin thrust at her side. Her uniform coat, which she wore over it, had taken a lot more damage and been magically mended by Livia more than once.

When she emerged, not only Livia but all her friends waited, all of them armed and armored for battle except Isold, whose <**Robe of Sprockets and Cogs**> was as good as armor. "Livia, how many of our spellslingers can cast *create pit*?"

"Maybe half," Livia replied. "You want us to do what we did yesterday?"

"I had another idea. What about concealing a pit? Making it look like the ground is solid, but there's a pit underneath?"

"*Hungry pit* does that already, but it costs more in resources." Livia chewed her lip in thought. "*Illusion* would do it, but I don't know who all can cast it."

"I need you to find out. I officially designate you commander of our spellslingers. I want a lot of pits—they don't have to be deep, maybe five feet? Anyway, I want them scattered on the ground between us and the orc army and concealed. Then we'll have you all shape the earth to defend against the orc riders the way we did before. Weston, you stay with Livia. Isold, didn't you tell me orcs are immune to [**Cause Fear**]?"

"Except for the grunts, yes," Isold said. "Though otherwise mind magic works as well as anything."

"I want to see if you can demoralize them the old-fashioned way, through mysterious attacks they can't predict. Putting groups of them to sleep would be great—you see what I mean?"

"I do." Isold nodded. "I have some ideas."

"Good. Owen, I need to talk to the regimental commanders. You and I will have to stay mobile so I can direct the fighting as best I can, given the limits of the battlefield. I'm sure eventually we'll be in the middle of the fighting." Aderyn looked at each of her friends in turn. "I hate splitting us up. I always feel like if we're separated, it weakens us, even though I know it's not true."

"We'll be fine," Livia said. "You know it's true if I'm willing to say it."

Aderyn hugged her. "I know. Stay safe, everyone, and good luck."

CHAPTER SIX

The sun was halfway to its zenith by the time Aderyn finished giving orders to each regiment and climbed atop her stool to address the army. The earth's surface cracked where rain had churned it to mud three days earlier, before the brutal sun had baked it hard and dried the upper layers to powder. Dust caked the boots of the soldiers she faced, and already some faces looked grimy, but all of them bore the resolute expressions of men and women prepared to give the orcs a really bad day.

"Remember your orders," she called out with **[Amplify Voice]**. "Don't venture too far ahead—we don't want anyone caught in the traps we've set for the orcs. Hold your ground as best you can. We only have to hold out for two more days, all right? Just two days. We've made it this far—let's show those orcs what humans are capable of!"

A roar of approval rose from the massed soldiers. Again, Aderyn tried not to despair at how few there were.

"Let them hear you!" she shouted, and hopped down from her stool as another roar echoed through the camp. They were brave, and they were strong. It would have to be enough.

She turned to Maranya, who at level twelve was the highest-level Deadeye in the regiments. Maranya was short and plump and to Aderyn didn't look any more like a soldier than she herself did, but she held herself alertly ready to take action. Aderyn handed her the four glass bulbs whose contents roiled like pale gray storm clouds shot through with occasional flashes of lightning. "How easily can you hit a moving target?"

"Easily enough," Maranya said, as if a moving target was no different from any other. "But it takes concentration."

"You'll have defenders and a high vantage point. I want you to focus on hitting Drorg, the one-eyed orc on the white goretusk. I doubt even four of these <Death Cloud> potions can kill him, but any damage will help. I'm hoping seeing him weakened will demoralize the others." Aderyn gestured to Livia. "Livia, we'll need a hill."

"I understand. Maranya, stay with me." Livia gripped Aderyn's hand. "We've prepared the ground with concealed pits, so we're as ready as we can be. Good luck."

Shouts resounded through the regiments, and the soldiers surged into movement. Aderyn took a moment to look at each of her friends in turn, and then she and Owen joined Leopard Regiment in its march to battle. Behind her, Emri followed with Leopard's banner. Aderyn had instructed him to stay well back, reasoning that she would move too fast for him to keep up. She could join him as needed, and <Amplify Voice> would take the place of the banner signals.

Their boots kicked up small clouds of dust as they walked, nothing that interfered with sight—for now. Aderyn glanced back once to observe how the dust obscured the bodies of those following some distance behind. Sweat sheened her face and the nape of her neck beneath her ponytail, pooled beneath her arms and under her breasts. When she wiped the sweat from her forehead, her hand came away smeared with thin mud. This was going to be a grueling, filthy day.

After a few minutes, they reached a wide blue ribbon tied to a stick wedged into the ground. The ribbon marked the end of the safe territory. The orcs hadn't begun to move yet. Aderyn was confident they wouldn't interpret the humans' eagerness to join battle as a sign that trickery was afoot. She walked to the head of the army and waited.

The sun blazed down on them, and despite its heat it was welcome for the first time since Aderyn had arrived in the south—its brilliant light would put the orcs at a disadvantage. She clung to that knowledge as a counter to how miserably humid the day was, the air sticky and wet and clinging to her exposed skin like a caul. Every breath felt like it was coming through a damp cloth. She was never going to complain about summer in Far Haven again.

Finally, she saw movement. She readied her shield and shouted with [Amplify Voice], "Hold fast!" She walked rapidly along the line, Owen trailing her, until she reached the point she'd chosen, close to the trailing edge. Anticipation made her heart beat faster, and she breathed slowly to calm herself.

With a rumbling roar, the earth on the other side of the army surged upward into a hill shaped like an ocean wave, sending up billowing clouds of dust. As if responding to that signal, arrows filled the sky, arcing toward the oncoming orc horde. "Hold!" Aderyn shouted again, stopping the few foolish soldiers whose eagerness had almost taken them into the dangerous territory.

More arrows flew, and now the orcs returned fire. Arrows fletched with red thudded into the regiments, and cries of pain were lost in the pounding of oncoming goretusk riders. Aderyn made herself watch the rest of the orc army, the orcs on foot. Closer... closer...

In the center of the orc line, ten orcs flung up their arms as they stumbled and fell into an invisible pit. The orcs behind them tried to stop and were bowled over by the ones coming up behind them. Aderyn swallowed a laugh. It was funny, but the battle wasn't won yet.

The orc advance faltered as more monsters discovered the pit traps the hard way. Aderyn swore softly. "What?" Owen asked.

"Just thinking we should have put spikes at the bottom of the pits."

Owen chuckled. "Missed opportunities. Maybe next time."

"I was hoping there wouldn't *be* a next time." Aderyn drew her mystery sword. "Remember, our side needs to fight to engulf the orcs on this front. *Keep the pressure on their left!*" she added with [Amplify Voice], though she didn't think anyone heard her given the tremendous noise of the orc advance. It didn't matter. They knew the tactics. She hoped her strategy would hold past the first ten seconds.

Despite the now-ragged advance, the orcs lunging for them didn't look as if the surprise pits had distracted them at all. Roaring, they bore down upon the waiting defenders. Aderyn stepped up to meet the first raging monster and with [Compel] she dragged its attention from her to Owen, making the creature falter as it involuntarily switched targets. Owen sidestepped, putting Aderyn in a position for [Outflank], and in seconds they finished the orc and were looking for a new target.

This time, Aderyn and Owen fought only for a few minutes before Aderyn disengaged and moved back, hoping to get a sense of the battle-field. It was impossible. Everything was chaos. She couldn't see more than a few feet in front of her. Once again, she wished for *fly*. A screaming orc cut a soldier in front of her down, and she blocked its attack on her half a second before Owen spitted it from behind. The brilliant light of the <Sunsword> turned pinkish-gray with orc blood.

**Congratulations! You have defeated [Orc Masher].
You have earned [6500 XP]**

"We need to reach Livia!" Aderyn shouted. "I can't see anything!"

Owen nodded and took the head off another orc. Aderyn blinked the system message away and retreated, fighting defensively until she and Owen were behind the front line and could move rapidly eastward. Aderyn cursed again, this time silently. She had no business being in battle, not when her Warmaster's vision was the most important thing she could contribute.

Finding anyone in this mess was impossible. Aderyn considered using the <Wayfinder> and discarded the notion immediately. Even if she could concentrate in the middle of a battle, there was no way she could follow its guidance without either getting killed or getting Owen killed as he protected her. Finally, she made for Livia's first hill. Sheathing her sword, she clambered up its steep slope until she could crawl to the top. Maranya still crouched there, peering over the edge.

"I hit the white goretusk twice," she said in her high, fluting voice. "It didn't look like it or its rider took much damage, because both times they rode out of the cloud effect fast. The lightning struck the rider, though."

"Crap," Aderyn said. "I forgot how fast those monsters are."

"I can try again—"

"No, don't waste the <**Death Clouds**>. In fact, I'll take them. You shoot from here." Aderyn tucked the two remaining bulbs into her <**Purse of Great Capacity**> and surveyed the battlefield. To her delight, the left flank had crept up the side of the orc army and was putting pressure on the monsters there, neatly enclosing them between the soldiers and the field riddled with holes. The situation was less optimal on the side with the orc riders. Drorg had directed them to avoid most of the traps, and he rode at the head of their cavalry, making charges that trampled soldiers and then withdrawing before the humans could retaliate.

"Can you hit him?" Aderyn asked. Momentarily, she considered whether someone else killing Drorg would invalidate the [**Fated One's Destiny**] quest, then decided she didn't care. Drorg was responsible for enough human deaths it mattered more that he be eliminated than that specific people did the eliminating.

Maranya made a face. "I've hit him three times and his goretusk twice. He just yanked the arrows out like they were nothing. I'm starting to think he's immortal."

"He's not," Owen said. "And it's past time we proved that. Aderyn?"

"One moment," Aderyn said, scanning the area a second time and letting her instincts take over. Time for her second plan. With <**Amplify Voice**>, she called out, "Owl Regiment, fall back/*Make ready to close the trap.*"

There hadn't been time to do more than verify that at level seventeen, <**Secret Message**> could be conveyed to multiple listeners. So much could go wrong: the recipients might not hear either part of her instructions due to the noise of battle, or they might not remember what she'd told them about which message to listen to. For that matter, the orcs might not speak the same language and wouldn't understand the false message to be fooled by it. But despite all their clever tactics, the army was getting hammered, and Aderyn was ready to take a chance.

Owl Regiment started to fall back in some disarray, though from Aderyn's vantage point she could tell most of the disarray was faked. She thrilled to the sight of the orcs pressing forward, steadily shoving Owl's soldiers back. They didn't notice that they were being carefully funneled to where they were surrounded on both sides by Leopard and Eagle Regiments until it was too late. With a cry of defiance, the two flanks closed in on the orcs, cutting the orc army nearly in half.

Behind her, Maranya said, "Shit. General! General!"

Aderyn looked where Maranya was frantically pointing. A cloud of dust, coming up fast from the east. "Our reinforcements?" she said, though her heart told her no.

"It's more orcs, general." Maranya shielded her eyes from the bright sunlight. "Another two... I don't know if they call them regiments, but two more groups of orc warriors."

Aderyn couldn't make out anything at that distance, but a Dead-eye's vision was always going to be superior to hers. "They're going to turn that flanking maneuver on us. We have to withdraw and regroup."

"Those orc riders won't let us do that easily," Owen said. He was scanning the battlefield below. "I see Livia!"

"Take me to her!"

"We'll never make it before she moves again." Owen grabbed Aderyn's wrist. "What about those steel vials?"

"What—oh!" Aderyn fumbled in her purse until she felt the cold metal surface of the <Zap> potion. Owen was already holding his. He put his hand on Aderyn's chin and turned her head until she saw Livia, fighting back to back with Weston. Aderyn uncapped the steel tube by feel, never taking her eyes off Livia. "Go now!" She tipped the contents of the vial into her mouth and swallowed.

Her body imploded, shrinking rapidly in on itself until everything that made her Aderyn was compressed to a single point. In the next instant, she exploded past the bounds of her human body and rico-cheted off the air itself until she regained her usual form. Owen was beside her, looking disoriented. Aderyn shook her head and focused on Livia, now only two feet away.

"We have to withdraw!" Aderyn shouted. "Orc reinforcements are coming!"

Livia chanted something incomprehensible, and an orc lifted off the ground and slammed into two others, knocking them all flat to where the next orc rider that passed through trampled them without slowing or veering aside. That rider jerked and fell off his goretusk with Weston's thrown dagger in his throat. The goretusk fled, trampling more orcs as it went.

Congratulations! You have defeated [Orc Rider].
You have earned [6250 XP]

Livia stepped back, breathing heavily. "Where?"

"North and east. Right where they can trap us like we trapped the others. *Withdraw!*"

The last word, hurled with **[Amplify Voice]**, drew the attention of all the soldiers nearby. They began to retreat, and Aderyn saw her mistake—not everyone had heard or understood her, and the retreat was a messy shambles, with some soldiers standing their ground and others running and being cut down. Now Aderyn regretted leaving Emri at the rear. She hadn't realized how much more effective visual signals and the bugle calls were, and that mistake would cost lives. She pushed the thought aside. Time for recriminations when they'd all survived.

Chapter Seven

Gradually, the soldiers who'd understood the order passed it on to others, and Leopard Regiment formed up into a more graceful withdrawal. Aderyn couldn't see Drorg anywhere. With her luck, he was controlling his forces to unite with the cavalry of the orc reinforcements and intended to bear down on their unprotected flank. The soldiers needed to regroup if they were going to survive this new assault.

She pushed through the mob until she reached Emri, who stood his ground but whose wide eyes told Aderyn clearly how he felt about being abandoned. Which she'd done. She'd really screwed up.

The banner dipped slightly when Emri saw her. "Signal 'withdrawing retreat,'" Aderyn told him. "We're moving back."

Emri looked relieved to be included in the moving back. Surrounded by Owen, Weston, and Livia, they headed for the fallback position. The air was full of screams and shouts and moans of pain all choked with dust. The sounds twisted the knife in Aderyn's heart deeper. So many lost lives, so many injured— She made herself stop thinking about it. All she could do was try to rescue as many as possible from her mistake.

After a few minutes, having jogged south and west with the troops,

Aderyn told Livia, "I need to see how things stand. Can you take me up?"

"I'm running low on resources," Livia warned. "I can't do this more than maybe three more times, and it will be all I can do."

"This will be the last time," Aderyn promised.

Livia took her arm, and the ground lurched and rose beneath them. Aderyn cast her gaze across the battlefield. With the dust and the movement of many bodies, details were impossible to see, but they had put a quarter mile of ground between themselves and the orc horde, a distance that was widening as the original orc troops moved back to join their reinforcements. Aderyn's heart sank at the sight of so many orcs. Her army had done well that day, but those new forces more than made up for the orcs they'd killed.

She surveyed her own forces, noting the position of the regimental banners. The movements were orderly enough that it wasn't a rout, but the general milling about told her they were waiting for her orders. Aderyn did a quick, rough count, compared it to her Assessment of the orc numbers, and with [**Amplify Voice**] said, "Emri, bring the banner here."

By the time Emri scrambled awkwardly up the steep slope, Aderyn had come to a decision. "We have to fall back to Shantos," she told him and Livia. "By the time our reinforcements reach us, it will be too late for our regiments. We have to take a chance on stopping them at the city. Emri, what's the signal to tell them to retreat to shelter, or something like that?"

"It's 'retreat to quarters,' ma'am," Emri said. "That's the one you want?"

"Yes. Start signaling, and when everyone's moving, we'll follow." She glanced over her shoulder at the orcs again. "It's late enough in the day, and we gave them enough of a pummeling—*damn*. We had them, I'm sure of it."

"You couldn't know they had reinforcements nearby," Livia said.

"No, but I should have planned for the worst, and that was definitely the worst." Aderyn shaded her eyes against the setting sun. Eagle Regiment's banner had picked up the signal and was relaying it to the nearby soldiers, and Owl Regiment's banner followed a moment later.

The milling movement became purposeful as the soldiers marched rapidly southward.

By the time Aderyn and Livia and Emri descended the earthen hill, the bulk of the army had moved on, but Weston and Owen were waiting for them. The realization that she hadn't seen Isold all day struck Aderyn a sharp, terrifying pang. "Where's Isold?"

"We don't know," Weston said grimly. "He's still on the team roster, but his health keeps going up and down, or did while we were fighting. So he's around here somewhere and he was in the middle of the fighting."

"All right," Aderyn said, calming herself. "He'll find us. At the very least, he'll come to the banner. Let's move. It's only a couple of miles to Shantos."

She stayed near the rear of the army, her feeling of obligation about protecting her soldiers from stray orcs trumping her belief that the banner ought to be more readily visible. She'd already made enough mistakes today that one more wasn't going to tip the balance any more against her. Dust kicked up by hundreds of booted feet choked her, and eventually she pulled her coat up to cover her nose and mouth as her friends did the same.

Gradually, the plains gave way to hills, and Aderyn's legs strained gently at the incline they walked up. Yellow-green grasses covered the hills, shaking in the stiff southerly wind that came up with evening and blew away the remaining dust. In the distance, the sprawling bulk of Shantos behind its wall made a dark blotch on the landscape. Though it stood at the top of a rise, the terraced hills surrounding it rose higher still. The scene reminded Aderyn of a giant flower, with Shantos at the center and the petals of its hills unfolding around it.

"I hope everyone left," she murmured. "That doesn't look terribly defensible. All those terraces will be overrun."

"They're farms," Owen said. "I don't know what the growing season is here in the Southlands, but the orcs will destroy what they don't take for themselves."

"Resupplying," Aderyn said. "Crap."

She examined the territory again, this time forcing herself to forget about self-recrimination and let her Warmaster's vision work. "This route we're taking is the easiest and most direct. That doesn't mean the orcs might not approach from a different direction. About the only advantage we have is that the bowl Shantos sits in, those terraced hills, are too steep on the far side to allow an army through. That narrows their options. I think we can work with that. But we need to move quickly."

She broke into a run, followed by the others. The mass of soldiers parted for the banner, though not readily since it came from behind them. Moving quickly, she hurried to the front of the army and had Emri signal a halt. "We did our best, but we were outnumbered," she shouted. "Now our goal is to hold Shantos until the other regiments arrive. We have some time to rest and be healed, and time to lay a few traps for our orc friends."

A murmur went up. Aderyn thought it sounded more pleased than angry, which relieved her mind. She wasn't sure she was good at what Owen referred to as a "pep talk," inspiring words that would stir demoralized soldiers to greater bravery and commitment.

"But we'll need to take advantage of the remaining daylight to put these plans into place," she went on. "I have to ask you to push on just a little longer, but I can promise you'll sleep in real beds tonight."

A ragged cheer went up from the crowd, followed by more murmurs of conversation that grew into loud demands for information. "Steady on," Aderyn shouted. "All sapper platoons, to me, along with Colonel Viyan and his bannerman. The rest of you will follow Owl Regiment's banner to the city, and Colonel Thilar will give you your orders. Now, five minutes' rest." She turned to Livia and in her normal voice said, "Can you *scry* the orc army? Not closely, just to know if they've decided to follow us after all."

"Sure." Livia pulled out her mirror and spoke a few nonsense words.

In less than a minute, the colonels of Eagle and Owl Regiments arrived at Aderyn's side. To her relief, Isold followed them. He was battered and bloody, but he moved easily, and a quick glance at the team roster showed he wasn't badly injured. Aderyn hugged him quickly and then turned to her colonels. "We're going to see what the sappers can do to make this hazardous terrain for the orcs coming after us. Viyan, you're going to relay these orders to the sapper captains and supervise their work. We'll see how much they can accomplish before sunset. Thilar, take command of the remaining soldiers of all regiments and discover what it will take to make Shantos defensible. There shouldn't be many people left in the city, but we'll need to do what we can to protect them. Understood?"

"Did you have specific instructions for the sappers?" Viyan asked. He was a lean, angular man in his middle thirties who was just near-sighted enough that he always squinted when he looked into the distance. It gave him an air of fierce concentration Aderyn considered useful in a leader.

"I was going to show them where to focus and leave the rest to their ingenuity. Did either of you have any suggestions? No? Great. Let's move quickly. Livia?"

"They're making camp," Livia said distantly. "It looks funny from this distance because the reinforcements have tents of dark red canvas and they're not mingling with the black ones. I don't know if that means anything, but to me, it looks like a black blister popped open and oozing."

"Oh, *ergh*, Livia."

"Well, it does. Sorry, but I've been killing orcs all day and I'm in a bloodthirsty frame of mind. Is there anything else I can tell you?"

"Do you know how far away they are?"

"Give me a minute." Livia drew the mirror closer to her face. "I'm going to say... between a mile and a half and two miles from where we are right now."

Too close. Aderyn didn't say it. Everyone undoubtedly knew the truth. "It's enough," she said instead. "Thilar, get the troops moving in five minutes. Viyan, signal the sappers to join us." One of the few things she knew about the banner signals was that there was one for each type of soldier, to get those groups working together.

She showed the sapper captains what she had in mind, pointed out vulnerable points that would interfere most efficiently and fatally with the orcs' movement, but quickly realized that in their narrow specialization, they understood tactics as well as she did. So she ended by saying, "You know the goal. Make it happen, however you need to do it. I'm putting all our resources to your use. Let me know if anything has to change."

The captains saluted. If any of them resented her for putting them in this position, they showed no sign of it. Aderyn turned to Viyan. "I'll set watches in case the orcs change their tactics and come after us by night. You're to supervise the sapper platoons and send word if they need anything—or if the orcs appear. If they do, haul ass back to the city regardless of how much they've accomplished. Our people are more important than strategy, and they'll serve the kingdom more efficiently if they're not dead. Any questions?"

"None, general." Viyan saluted, a gesture that combined with his fierce squint made him resemble the eagle his regiment was named for.

The rest of the troops were tiny in the distance when Aderyn and her friends followed Emri across the hills toward Shantos. She made note of the roads they passed. There weren't many, but they were wide and well maintained and might as well have been arrows aimed at the city's heart. "We'll need the Earthbreakers out here in the morning. There can't be any easy routes for the orcs to move along."

"Already planning on it, general," Livia said with a grin. "Look, don't beat yourself up. Nobody could have predicted how things would go."

Aderyn grimaced. "I can think of a dozen things I should have done differently, starting with maintaining some kind of observation that would have told us about the reinforcements. And ending with us having fallen back to Shantos at the start. I was too cocky about our chances to defeat the orcs on their territory, but we had to expend so much magical energy on tearing up the terrain to stop the orc riders, and look at this!" She waved an arm at the hills. "This would have done two-thirds of our work for us."

"Are you telling yourself this so you'll learn for the future, or just wallowing in failure?" Owen asked.

His blunt question stopped Aderyn's rant short. "You're right," she said after a moment's consideration. "I guess I was thinking, if I don't yell at myself for what I did wrong, it's like I don't take responsibility. And I can't help thinking, how many people died because I made bad decisions? No, don't," she added, throwing up a hand to forestall

Owen's objection. "I'm not letting it get to me. War is unpredictable, and there's no way to know if things might not have gone worse if I'd acted differently. It's just my way of acknowledging their deaths and vowing to do everything I can not to let those deaths be meaningless."

"That's better," Owen said. He clasped her hand tightly. "What's our next step?"

"I need to see Shantos up close. Varoun said it had been mostly evacuated, and I really hope that's true. What I don't need is a bunch of non-adventurer, non-soldiers being in harm's way. The sappers will do what they can to force the orcs into a path of our choosing, we'll destroy all the other roads, and then... we hold out until the regiments arrive."

"Sounds uncomplicated," Weston said. "But that only means the complications won't arise until later. Isold, are you all right? I saw you bouncing up and down in health all day."

"I'm afraid I was overzealous in fighting," Isold said. "I set about doing as we discussed, using [Charm] and [Sleep] to manipulate our opponents. That eventually made me the de facto leader of a group of platoons, who surrounded me and took advantage of my various skills to kill the orcs thus manipulated. But it meant we pushed too far into the enemy line and were surrounded. It took great effort, and great sacrifice, to pull back. Speaking of feeling responsible for bad decisions."

"Oh, Isold, you shouldn't—" Aderyn shut up. "All right, I see the irony. If you shouldn't blame yourself, I shouldn't either. But you understand how it feels."

"I do. Far too many soldiers died today believing my skills went farther than they do." Isold sounded suddenly weary. "It's not something I want to get used to."

"What irks me is I never got a shot at Drorg," Weston said. "I swear by the end he knew what I was after and was taunting me."

"Same here," Owen said. "It felt almost as if he knew we have a quest with his name on it."

"You don't suppose that's true?" Aderyn asked, alarmed.

Owen shook his head. "It was just an illusion. Though, if orcs are capable of Assessing their opponents, he might know we're higher level than anyone else fighting him. That would tell him we're special, and then he'd know to watch out for us."

Aderyn groaned. "That's all I need. Orcs with human abilities. The system wouldn't do that, would it?"

"You'd know if anyone would," Livia pointed out. "What do *you* think?"

"All I know is the system is on our side, because it keeps mentioning how monstrous orcs are and how important it is that we kill them. But isn't it strange that the system would allow monsters like orcs to exist? Thinking creatures who are actively evil?"

"The system allows kobolds, and they're thinking creatures who aren't necessarily aligned with humans," Owen pointed out. "And the waspnettles had volition and consciousness. And what about the kaduvas? Those are even half human."

"The more I learn, the more questions I have," Aderyn said. "I mean, why does any of this exist? Levels, and skills, and monsters for adventurers to kill so they gain levels and boost their skills?"

"Aderyn, you're starting to freak me out." Livia laughed, but it had a nervous edge to it. "Those aren't questions we should ask, are they? The world is what it is."

"Yes, but aren't there reasons for that? If this is the prime world, that suggests it's exactly what the system wants—but then why were all those other human worlds created as imperfect reflections of this one?" Aderyn shook her head. "Sorry. This isn't the right time for an existential crisis. But these are the questions that keep me up at night, the closer we get to level twenty and to the resolution of the [**Fated One's Destiny**] quest."

Owen put an arm around her shoulders. "I didn't know it bothered you so much."

"It's not so much that it bothers me—I mean, I don't feel like not knowing is hurting us. More like I thought my connection to the system would give me answers, but instead it only makes me more curious. I promise I'm not lying awake fretting."

"That's good, because none of that matters when the orcs are on our doorstep," Livia said.

CHAPTER EIGHT

The sight of noncombatants thronging the great gate in the wall of Shantos dismayed Aderyn. She'd expected an abandoned city, but at first glance nothing seemed out of the ordinary for a city that wasn't threatened with attack and ruin. A few soldiers guarded the gate, looking like ordinary city guards in their poses and alertness, with only their uniforms and the insignia of Eagle Regiment to set them apart. Aderyn approached them. "Where's Colonel Thilar? What are all these people doing here?"

The two guards, both female Swordsworn of levels seven and nine, glanced at each other. "He said you'd be pissed off," the level seven Swordsworn said, more candidly than Aderyn expected from a soldier. "The colonel is meeting with the city council in that building down the road, the one with the green roof."

"City council?" Aderyn didn't think Janesh, duke of Shantos, had a city council.

The guards exchanged meaningful glances again. "The colonel says it's complicated. He asked us to ask you to join him as soon as you arrived."

"Oh, most certainly," Aderyn breathed. City council, far too many noncombatants still here... somebody had better have an explanation.

She ordered Emri to find a place to rest and went with her friends down the main street to the house with the green roof. It wasn't a comfortable, calm green like the depths of a forest; it was blindingly bright even at sunset, with paint chipped and scratched with years of wear. Aderyn acknowledged that she didn't know much about southern cities, but she'd seen their torrential rains and she didn't think paint on a roof was the kind of thing that lasted. Whoever was responsible for this had to repaint frequently, which struck her as the kind of conspicuous display of wealth only a fool would make. She reminded herself not to make snap judgments. Maybe the house belonged to someone who was expected to have a showy roof.

The house was actually a business of some kind, judging by the wooden plaque hanging from two chains above the front door. The ornate script on the plaque read DEBRAN, ARBITER, which told Aderyn exactly nothing. She pushed the door open and entered without knocking.

The spacious room they entered took up what seemed to be most of the ground floor of the house and was filled with comfortable, over-stuffed chairs upholstered in gaudy tapestry fabrics, turquoise and pink and more of that awful green. Stairs led out of sight to an upper floor, and raised voices came from upstairs, two people arguing over each other. Wary, Aderyn climbed the stairs, eavesdropping in hopes of learning the subject of the disagreement.

"You have no authority here," an unfamiliar man was saying. His voice was loud and relatively high-pitched, and rose higher as his words grew louder. "You will defend the city as I tell you."

The man's words annoyed Aderyn. He clearly wasn't Janesh, so who was he to demand anything?

"It's you who has no authority," Colonel Thilar said. "This is not up for argument. You should have left the city—"

"We don't recognize the remit of military force," the stranger cut in. "You can't make us leave our homes."

Aderyn had heard enough. She ascended the remaining stairs at a measured pace, stomping hard to make sure she was heard. The voices cut off. The stairs ended not at a landing, but in the middle of another large room nearly the size of the one below. A long wooden table shining like a polished chestnut occupied half of the room, with several chairs drawn up around it. No one sat at it; instead, a group of men surrounded Colonel Thilar on the opposite side of the staircase. To Aderyn's surprise, two of them had the pale skin of northerners, and one of those was a redhead.

Colonel Thilar, who had his back to her, turned at her approach and saluted. "General. This is Debran. He claims to be head of the city council supposedly ruling Shantos in the duke's absence." He indicated the redhead with a brief gesture.

Aderyn looked Debran up and down before Assessing him. Despite his complexion, he dressed like a Southlander, and his red hair was longish and caught up at the nape of his neck with a gold clasp in a southern style.

Name: Debran

Traits: intelligent, proud, determined, shortsighted

"Debran," she said. "Janesh put you in charge?"

"The duke has abandoned the city," Debran said. "I was elected to this position by a group of civic-minded individuals. We refuse to be frightened from our homes by children's tales."

"Children's—you mean, orcs?" Aderyn frowned. "You think they don't exist?"

"Certainly they exist, but they aren't the terrifying monsters Duke Janesh claims. Orcs can easily be overcome by human resistance. They've never done more than steal livestock and harass small settlements, and they're no match for city walls."

Aderyn gaped. "You're kidding."

Debran sneered. "Who are you, to talk so rudely to your betters?"

Owen, standing behind Aderyn, shifted his weight as he put his hand on the basket hilt of the **<Sunsword>**. Debran's gaze flicked to him and then away, clearly dismissing him as a threat.

Aderyn's weariness had begun to catch up to her, making the situation feel surreal. "I'm General Aderyn. Second in command to Commander General Varoun. And you are extremely mistaken about the threat the orcs pose. You and all the rest of the citizens still in Shantos need to leave immediately."

"As I told this one—" Debran jerked his head in Thilar's direction—

"you don't have the authority to order us to leave. If you want us gone, you'll have to exercise force against your fellow humans." He smiled, the self-righteous, smug expression of someone who thinks he has the moral high ground.

Aderyn controlled her temper. Yelling would likely do no good, given Debran's certainty and dismissal of her military rank. "All right. You say I don't have authority. Duke Janesh doesn't have authority. Who *does* have the authority to get you out of danger?"

The smug smile deepened. "I take my authority from the voice of the people. Those of us courageous enough to face this challenge refused to obey the demands of an autocratic puppet of the queen. They look to me as their natural leader."

"Janesh? A puppet?" Aderyn laughed. Debran's smile faltered slightly, as if her reaction was unexpected. "Wow. Did you say that to his face? I'm guessing not, because he would have had you arrested and dragged out of Shantos in chains. You sound like the type to talk big in private and cower in public."

"I do not cower!" Debran shouted, making the men around him shift uncomfortably. "Once this is over, I will petition the queen to have the cowardly duke removed from his position and myself installed as the true ruler, the one chosen by the people. I do not recognize your authority and I defy you to force any of us against our will."

Aderyn rolled her eyes. "Colonel Thilar. Debran is clearly mad. I authorize you to organize five platoons to round up the remaining citizens and escort them from the city south to Ikharatia. Anyone who resists will be bound and carried out. Any questions?"

"None, general," Thilar said with a grin.

"You can't—" Debran sputtered.

"I absolutely can," Aderyn said. "You need to get over your delusions. I don't know much about the Southlander government and nothing at all about how a northerner came to claim rulership of Shantos, but I'm sure as thunder it doesn't work the way you imagine. You, and your friends—" She nodded politely at the other men, who now looked extremely nervous. "You have until tomorrow morning at nine o'clock to gather what possessions you care about and present yourself at the gate."

"And if I refuse?"

The look on the face of this petty, selfish, small-minded man made Aderyn's temper snap. "Maybe I didn't make myself clear. You don't get to refuse. You can walk out of Shantos a free man, or you can be dragged out in chains, but either way, *you are going*. And if you continue to defy me, I'll make an example of you no one will forget for a hundred years. Because, Debran, I'm going to have to send good soldiers as escort to you fools who thought it was smart to ignore the evacuation order of your sworn duke, and if this city falls because they weren't here, I'll make sure everyone in the Southlander kingdom knows who to blame." Aderyn turned her back on Debran. "Colonel, spread the word. Every noncombatant in Shantos is to meet at the gate tomorrow at nine o'clock."

Thilar saluted. "Yes, general."

Debran, who'd turned a shade of red that didn't match his hair, sputtered, "Why—you—how *dare* you speak—"

Aderyn rounded on him, but Owen got there first, drawing and activating the **<Sunsword>**. "She's being generous. I, on the other hand, will have no trouble making an example of you right now. You're the kind of petty bureaucrat who makes others' lives difficult and pretends it's all in the rules *you* made up. People like you make me sick because you get other people killed and claim no responsibility."

"Who are *you*, boy?" Debran's shaking voice gave the lie to his confident words.

"Someone who killed a hell of a lot of orcs today and saw a lot of soldiers die at their hands. You want to dismiss that threat, fine. It's on you if your idiocy kills you. But you've convinced a lot of innocent people they're in no danger, and if Shantos is overrun with them still here, their deaths will be on your head."

Debran closed his mouth. His lips were shaking, either in fear or anger. Aderyn didn't care which. "Thank you, Owen," she said. "Gentlemen, you have your orders. I expect to see every one of you at nine o'clock tomorrow morning." She gestured to Thilar to join them and strode down the stairs, not hurrying.

Outside, she said, "What in *thunder* is wrong with these people?"

"They really don't believe the orcs are a threat, general," Thilar said.

"What that Debran told me before you arrived is that according to them, this 'war' is all a plot cooked up by Janesh to make everyone depend on him despite him not being a good ruler. Or maybe as a distraction from him not being a good ruler. The story wasn't consistent."

"That's ridiculous," Livia said.

"There are always disgruntled people who look for any reason to claim they don't have what they deserve," Owen said. "I'll take charge of the soldiers corralling citizens if you want, Aderyn."

"That's an excellent idea, but tomorrow. Tonight we have a lot to do, if you all don't mind helping?"

"Of course we don't," Isold said. "What do you need?"

It was nearly midnight before Aderyn trudged across the plaza south of the main gate to the empty house Major Revi of Leopard Regiment had selected for her and Owen to use. She'd felt slightly uncomfortable at taking over someone else's house, but it was either that or sleep in the street, and ultimately she'd recognized the necessity. She resolved to keep the house in the condition she'd entered it in, which wasn't difficult; the owners had left everything in disarray when they fled Shantos. Aderyn avoided the sink with its small pile of dirty dishes.

Owen was upstairs in the larger of the two bedrooms when she entered and called his name. She found him putting the final touches on the bedding. "I know, it's stupid," he said, "because we're just going to mess it up, but making the bed before lying in it myself makes me feel less like I'm sleeping in someone else's bed."

"I agree. Maybe it's not as odd as you think, since I feel the same." Aderyn hung her uniform coat over the back of a wooden chair and wriggled out of her mail shirt. "I'm too tired to bathe. Drawing water from the well, then making a fire to heat the water over... I'm sorry I smell like battle."

"So do I." Owen indicated a bucket of steaming water in the corner. "I figured we could at least sponge off."

The idea was so satisfying Aderyn laughed. "I feel happier about that bucket than I did about the bathing room in Elkenforest. And that had a full-size tub with four levels of heated water. That seems like forever ago."

"Funny how our perspective changes. Undress, and I'll scrub your back."

The warm water sluicing over Aderyn's body relaxed her. She accepted the rough cloth from Owen and rubbed his bare back and shoulders clean. For once, the sight of her husband's body didn't arouse her desires. She was far too tired for sex. By the way Owen's hands didn't stray while scrubbing her back, he felt the same. They dried off, and Aderyn, cringing at the feel of dirty clothes on clean skin, put her shift and drawers back on while Owen tipped the water out of the window.

The bed felt cool and comfortable despite the lingering heat and humidity. Aderyn was accustomed now to the Southlander method of bedmaking, one sheet fitted over the mattress and a thin blanket over that, no extra sheets, no heavy quilt. It suited the climate well. She snuggled close to Owen briefly. "I think we're as prepared as we can be, except for all the last-minute things that have to be done in the morning. Thunderation, but I'm tired of talking to people. I had to tell the story of our rout to Varoun, then to General Rajman, and finally to General Ananyi, who had the nerve to criticize my failed strategy."

Owen yawned. "You're the one who blamed yourself for that."

"Yes, but there's no point anyone else rubbing it in. Plus I don't have much respect for Ananyi's abilities. He couldn't keep Ishan or Sudiptar in line—oh, which reminds me that Sudiptar might be closer than the others coming to reinforce us. Not close enough to make a difference before tomorrow, but close. Ananyi tried to make it sound like he was all foresighted and so forth about sending Sudiptar ahead, but it was obvious Sudiptar was insubordinate again."

"That could be bad, if he's in charge of a regiment."

"It *is* bad. Sudiptar alone can't take on the orc army, so there's no point him arriving in advance of the others." It was Aderyn's turn to yawn. "Anyway, Rajman's two regiments should arrive sometime day after tomorrow, Major—I mean, Colonel Kavish by that same night, and Colonel Sudiptar anytime between tomorrow evening and morning of the following day. We don't have to hold out long. My worry is that the orcs will ignore us and proceed toward Ikharatia. If we can hold them here, great, but if they don't stop..."

"The orc reinforcements had some siege weapons," Owen said. "Chances are good they'll want to use them."

"That, and I think they want to kill as many humans as possible. If they leave us alone here, we can come on them from the rear, something not possible if they've destroyed us." Aderyn shuddered. "I just jinxed us, didn't I?"

"I don't believe in jinxes, love." Owen drew her into his arms and kissed her forehead. "And there's nothing left to do, as you point out, except sleep. You need to lay those burdens down."

"I keep going over lists in my head, checking and double-checking. My mind is too busy for sleep."

"Then tell me your lists, and maybe that will let you set them aside."

"All right." Aderyn breathed in deeply and let the air out in a slow, steady stream. "Talk to the other generals for their positions. Give instructions to the captains so their platoons know where to go in the morning. Make sure the regimental majors know what they are and aren't allowed to do while billeting all our soldiers in the city. Send messages to the citizens—no, you did that."

"I did. We had them pass word of the evacuation to their neighbors as well."

"That's a relief." Aderyn yawned again. "Where was I? Evaluate the surrounding terrain trying to figure out where the weak spots are. Do you suppose [Improved Assess 4] will do that? I wonder if I get it at level eighteen. I could really use it now..."

Between one word and the next, Aderyn drifted off to sleep.

CHAPTER NINE

Aderyn woke just before dawn when Owen got out of bed to relieve himself. She sat up, feeling energized and awake. Her previous day's aches still bothered her, but mentally, she was clear.

The sounds of crockery clinking drew her downstairs to where Private Isman, her personal servant, was washing dishes. The kitchen was spotless as it had not been before and smelled deliciously of sausage and eggs. "The food is on the table, general, under covers, and I brought new beer from the tavern down the street," he informed her.

Aderyn took back every criticism she'd ever silently directed at Isman for not being Private Nandi. "Thank you, private, I appreciate your service." She sat at the table and ate quickly, barely tasting the food in her awareness that the clock was ticking again and she only had a few hours before the orcs would appear on the horizon.

Owen joined her when she was almost finished. "I'm meeting the platoons in the plaza soon," he said, tucking into his meal with a neat urgency that mirrored hers. "They're prepared to escort the civilians to safety through the mountains. It's not the fastest route, but it keeps them away from the orcs."

"Civilians... do you mean citizens?"

Owen cast a quick glance at Isman. "It means citizens who are not soldiers. People who don't fight. Anyway, the citizens will be there at nine, which should be well before the orcs arrive, based on our previous battles."

"Good." She kissed him quickly. "I'm going to see about our defenses. Come to me once the civilians are on their way, all right?"

She found Livia just exiting the house across the street from hers. The Earthbreaker looked remarkably alert, given that the sun was just peeking over the housetops. "I hate orcs," Livia said cheerfully. "Making me rise early. Total bastards."

"I'm sorry about—"

"Don't say the word. I've about convinced myself it doesn't exist. Which is a good point—what if we were somewhere we couldn't get any, and I was dependent on it?" Livia shook her head. "Which I'm not. And I'm going to keep telling myself that until it's true and I've replaced this spell."

They walked together to the front gate, where soldiers had already gathered. "Do you know what spell you want instead?" Aderyn asked.

"Haven't decided. If I knew, meditation would be easier, because I'd have something to focus on. But there are enough seventh-level spells that appeal to me nothing stands out as obvious. I've got most of two weeks before I have to make the decision. Soldiers!" She addressed this last word to those gathering nearby who all wore the double-barred circle insignia of a military spellslinger. "General Aderyn would like to see our preparations. Aderyn, come up on the wall and take a look."

From the wall, Aderyn looked out across the hills leading up to the city. Those straight, smooth roads she'd worried about had disappeared. In their place, the sappers had dug trenches and piled stones to ruin the easy routes. Now, only one road remained, the one that ran across the hills directly to the front gate.

"I'm guessing that road isn't as good a route as it appears," Aderyn said.

Livia grinned. "It's got traps and hidden ditches all along the way. The orcs won't have an easy time reaching us. And, in case they get any bright ideas about circling the city, we set rock falls all the way through the mountains on both sides to discourage them."

"But not the rear."

"No. Owen said the refugees will go that way. They should be safe, or at least as safe as we can make that journey. Those idiots."

"No kidding." Aderyn surveyed the landscape again. If their work was unsuccessful, she'd just come up with another plan, that was all. "What else?"

"Our last-ditch tactic is something our Tidecallers came up with." Livia gestured at a group of seven men and women lined up along the battlements. "Working together, they drew up groundwater into a hidden reservoir above the city. If the fighting gets too fierce, Letha there will break it open and the water will flood the plains. But that's only for if they've forced us into a retreat. Obviously."

"I love it." Aderyn nodded at Letha, the lone Earthbreaker among the Tidecallers. "For the rest of our spellslingers, I want them positioned on the wall where they can have cover. You know their capabilities better than I do—the idea is to have each of them do their magic for a while and then pull back for a rest while others take their place."

"I understand, Aderyn. Don't worry about us."

"Where's Weston?"

Livia's smile vanished. "He went out with the sappers to finish the traps they couldn't set after sundown. He planned to stay until he caught sight of the orcs and then return with word. I hate it, but it was too sensible an idea to argue against."

Aderyn hugged her friend. "He'll be fine. He never takes stupid risks."

"It's the smart risks I worry about," Livia said.

Aderyn descended the stairs, leaving Livia behind, and met Isold heading up. "I intend to stay on the wall," he told Aderyn. "The sound of my voice carries far in this valley, and with a better vantage point, I believe I will be more effective."

"It's too bad [Amplify Voice] isn't a Herald skill," Aderyn joked.

Isold let out an exaggerated sigh of despondency. "Too true. I could control armies if that were the case."

That idea didn't terrify Aderyn the way it once would have. "Watch out for orc arrows, then."

"As always," Isold replied, and continued upward.

She met with her colonels to confirm they knew the plan; sent all the Deadeyes to the wall, where they would see the oncoming army sooner than anyone; checked the barricade at the gate, though she didn't know what a good barricade looked like. The heavy wood furniture set to either side of the gate in preparation for the return of Weston and the other sappers looked frighteningly weak despite its size. Aderyn wished for several long pines, or even gnarled olive trees or oaks, but few trees grew on these hills, so it was furniture or nothing. She trusted the skill of the sappers to make what they had work.

The cry had just gone up that Weston and his trap-setting teams were returning when someone grabbed Aderyn's arm. "We have a problem," Owen said. "Debran didn't come to the meeting point. No one knows where he is. And some of the civilians say there are others missing."

"Missing?" Aderyn swore, causing two passing soldiers to pause in alarm. "Hiding, you mean."

"That's exactly what I mean. I sent soldiers to Debran's house, and to the houses of a few others their neighbors hadn't seen, but those houses are empty. Debran and his friends have gone to ground."

"This is a big city. They could be anywhere. Damn them." Aderyn squeezed her eyes shut. "We can't do anything about it now. The sun is well up and we are prepared for an attack at any moment. Those citizens need to get moving."

"I already sent them and their escort on their way. If Debran is so hell-bent on staying, fine. The best we can do is make sure he doesn't endanger all the others."

"Yes. I don't have time for this." Aderyn cursed again, less violently. "But the others are gone?"

"Out the back gate, which has been sealed and barricaded. Which worries me. If we have to bug out, that will slow us down."

"There's no helping that. Let's just hope we don't have to... bug out? Do I want to know where that comes from?"

"Probably not." Owen kissed her lightly. "Where is everyone? Our team, I mean. It's superstition, but I want to know where we all end up, since we're separating today."

They ended up gathered together on the battlements directly above the gate. Weston had an arm around Livia's shoulders, but his gaze was fixed on the horizon, which bulged and teemed with movement. "They're not moving like they're in a hurry. They know they have us at a disadvantage."

"At least they won't be able to use their cavalry." Aderyn stopped as her own words rang a warning song in her head. "And if they can't use their cavalry... what will they do with it... *Livia.* I need you to *scry* the enemy army. Right now."

Livia didn't ask questions. She pulled out her mirror and murmured a few nonsense words that made its surface shimmer before showing rapidly moving forms. "The orc army is enormous," she said. "I can guess at the size—"

"Don't bother. Find the orc riders. Where are they?"

"Um..." Livia gestured, and the view receded rapidly until most of the right side of the army was visible. "There, on the right flank. Their left flank."

Aderyn moved closer, edging in on Livia so her friend had to move her shoulder. "Then they're still there. Are they at the extreme right, or are there orcs beyond them?"

The view shifted again. "The extreme right."

Aderyn gazed at the orc riders ambling along, their slow, deliberate pace chilling her. "Weston, how far away are they?"

Weston shaded his eyes and looked out over the hills. "Two and a half miles. Aderyn, what's wrong?"

Aderyn didn't answer. She surveyed the hills, made a guess as to where the valley bowl with its mountainous terraced guardians began, and said, "They're going to divide their forces. Drorg will lead his cavalry and I don't know how many other units away to circle around, and the rest are coming here."

"Then we'll have to protect our rear," Owen said.

Aderyn shook her head. "Drorg isn't coming here. He's bypassing Shantos entirely and heading for Ikharatia."

Nobody asked if she was sure. Isold said, "Do you suppose they know where our reinforcements are?"

"We have to assume they do. Based on what I can see, that division of forces means they want to trap our army here, allowing Drorg's cavalry to move freely." Aderyn slammed her fist onto the stone of the wall and winced as pain shot up her arm. "Change of plans. Owen, get all the Spellcrafters to the gate. Livia, find out how great a range our Flamecrafters have, and then I want everyone capable of casting *illusion* at any level at the gate as well. Weston, I need you and the sappers to double the traps and pitfalls you've set within a quarter mile of the gate —no, forget that, we can't afford them seeing you. Gather the sappers at the front gate instead for instructions, then meet me at the back gate with any other Moonlighters and Pathseers you can find."

"And what should I do?" Isold asked.

Plans formed in Aderyn's head so rapidly she felt dizzy. "I need to know how far away you can [**Coerce**] someone."

HALF AN HOUR LATER, Aderyn again stood on the battlements, this time at the far left where the wall-walk came to an end at a stone tower riddled with arrow slits. The orc army still wasn't close enough to be more than a ripple of movement across the hills, with the occasional glint of sunlight reflecting off metal. Orcs didn't care enough about polished armor to wear much that would reflect light. Drorg's riders and other soldiers had broken away fifteen minutes before, but what was left of the horde would have intimidated Aderyn if she wasn't buzzing with anticipation.

All around her, the terrace crops smoldered where the Flamecrafters had ignited them. The necessity angered Aderyn more than anything else. Shantos needed those crops. But denying the orcs their bounty mattered more, in the end. It still pissed her off that they were destroying their own people's things. Of course, what she intended to do to Shantos would probably have Janesh cursing her name, and there wasn't anything she could do to make up for it. She told herself at least he'd have a city to return to. Eventually.

Beside her, Isold said, "You have more confidence in me than I do."

"Don't worry. Your contribution is meant for extra security—my plan doesn't depend on it succeeding." Aderyn let out a deep breath. "Sergeant Avor, distance?"

"Another ten minutes will bring their forces within range," Avor said. The Deadeye sergeant was willowy, with long arms and legs, and to Aderyn this meant for once the system had given someone a class that matched their physical attributes.

"I want the first volley to go out in fifteen minutes. Remember to make it look good." Aderyn received the sergeant's salute and gestured to Isold to walk with her. The wall-walk teemed with Deadeyes armed with longbows. A third of them saluted Aderyn as she passed. The others, who to Aderyn's [Truesight] looked wispy and incorporeal, stared rigidly ahead. One of them rippled as her hand incautiously swept through its waist, but the illusion immediately firmed up again.

Aderyn paused to look at the strange contraption near one of the deep crenellations of the battlement. A young Spellcrafter was adjusting one of its many metal rods, all of them quivering under tension. "It's only going to be good for twenty shots, I'm afraid," the man said. "I'm sorry we didn't have more time, general."

"That's entirely on me, private, and whatever you can do, we're grateful for," Aderyn told him. She refused to dwell on what might have been. If she'd been able to get someone into the camp—no, it was too dangerous when they didn't know how their scouts kept getting spotted, and she wasn't going to risk Weston's life for the dubious benefit of possibly learning the orcs' plans. She'd found out in time, and that was all that mattered.

She and Isold continued walking until they reached Colonel Viyan and Livia. Livia leaned against the battlements with the tenseness of someone who wished she could fly, against everything Aderyn knew and loved about her. Unlike the Deadeyes, she was focused on a point halfway up one of the hills where the hidden reservoir was located.

Viyan was helping a Spellcrafter with another odd-looking device that looked like a Deadeye skeleton. Aderyn reflected on how strange it was that, given the instructions to come up with a magic item that shot arrows independent of someone operating it, every Spellcrafter had come up with something different. For the first time, she wished she knew more about that class. What little she'd learned from her grandfather Marrius and from the few Spellcrafters she'd met in her journeys told her Spellcrafting was more art than design, and these soldiers proved it.

Viyan came to meet them. "This is only rudimentary," he said, holding out a pair of spectacles with lenses painted black. "Fortunately, distance viewing isn't that complicated, so even with limited materials, I was able to produce these <Lenses of Farsight>. Push the button on the right corner to activate them."

"Thank you, Colonel." Aderyn put the glasses on and pushed the button. Immediately, the black paint disappeared, and her vision seesawed wildly for a moment, dizzying her. She grabbed Isold's hand to steady herself, but then the moment passed and she realized the distant orcs weren't so distant anymore. Thanks to the glasses, she could see them as clearly as if she were five feet away.

"All right," she murmured. "Where are you..."

She surveyed the horde, looking for its commander. She was certain her Warmaster's vision could identify the orc, or orcs—she hoped it wasn't orcs, plural. This plan would work better if they had a single leader Isold could sway.

Her eye fell on a tall, gaunt orc, completely bald and with very pale skin tinged with only a hint of green, and she stopped, aghast. The orc was mostly naked, wearing only a loincloth, and his body and head were *covered* in glowing tattoos. Aderyn's heart lurched. Swiftly, she Assessed him, though she didn't know if [Improved Assess 3] had distance limitations on monster Assessments.

Apparently not.

Name: Zothemza
Type: Monstrosity (orc elementalist)
Power level: 15
Attack(s): spellcasting, special
Immune to: none
Resistant to: all elemental attacks
Vulnerable to: bright light, *daylight, sunburst*
Special attacks: elemental blast
As you've already guessed, orc elementalists draw their power from the natural world, though the natural world resists their unnatural magic. I won't bore you with the details of how

elementalists gain the spells tattooed on their bodies. **All you care about now is that Zothemza is the most powerful elementalist of the orc horde, not only because he knows many, many spells, but because he is adept at wringing power from the earth to give potency to those spells. He keeps his troops in line by threatening to loose his magic against them and has made good on that threat often enough that no one challenges him.**

Zothemza's favorite attack is an elemental blast that channels the raw power of earth, air, fire, or water with immense destructive force, but he has many, more subtle spells at his disposal. The one thing he and all elementalists are incapable of is mind magic. See what your Herald friend can do with that.

"Crap," Aderyn whispered. She glanced at the orcs surrounding Zothemza and then handed the <**Lenses of Farsight**> to Isold. "Look for the naked, heavily tattooed orc elementalist near the banner with a bloody fist painted on it. Zothemza."

Isold stiffened. "I see him. Their leader?"

"The system says yes. He's not immune to mind magic, so we have a chance."

Isold lowered the glasses. "This attack will be most potent if I do it after the first volley of arrows."

"Then I'll stay with you. Spellcrafters, thank you for your service. Please go join your platoons now."

The noise of boots scraping across the stone stairs filled the air as the Spellcrafters ran for it. Aderyn looked over the edge of the wall-walk at the courtyard and the inner side of the gate. The barricade didn't look flimsy now; it looked virtually impregnable, which Aderyn guessed meant it would hold out for maybe five minutes. More than enough time.

She reviewed her revised plan mentally. The only ones left at the front gate were herself, Isold, Livia, ten spellslingers of level fifteen or sixteen, and thirty Deadeyes. In only a few minutes, those Deadeyes would shoot into the oncoming horde, and the spellslingers would activate the *major illusions* to triple the Deadeyes' apparent numbers. The Spellcrafters' arrow shooters were timed to start shooting with the Deadeyes' first volley. Livia would crack open the reservoir with *move earth* and flood the valley. And Isold would [Coerce] Zothemza into believing that assaulting the gate was his life's greatest ambition. That should keep him from being distracted if anyone noticed Aderyn's army bugging out through the back gate. Bug out. The phrase had a strange appeal.

Aderyn paced restlessly, waiting. Isold held his flute in one hand and spun it in a lazy silver circle. When the nearest real Deadeyes straightened and raised their bows, Aderyn stopped pacing. "You still see him?" she asked Isold.

Isold nodded. He handed her the glasses. "[Coercion] induces the victim to obey the command I give him without realizing his new desire is externally imposed. If it's something he's already inclined to do, the command becomes nearly irresistible. I will know immediately if it worked."

Aderyn wiped her sweaty palms on her trousers. She wished that wasn't her nervous habit. It made her look so uncertain, plus it wrinkled her trousers.

Thirty bows drew back. Thirty arrows pointed at the sky. Then, as if every Deadeye had [Bonded Mind], a hail of arrows arced through the sky and thudded audibly into the horde. Screams and guttural shouts rose up from the massed orcs. All the spellslingers called out nonsense words, and the illusory Deadeyes solidified and took aim. "Again," Aderyn shouted. "Spellslingers, run!"

This time, it was the spellslingers clattering down the stairs. The nearest arrow-shooting magic item shuddered and let fly an arrow almost in time with the illusion covering it. "Now, Isold," Aderyn said.

Isold raised his flute to his lips. A simple melody wrapped itself around Aderyn's spine and floated outward into the sunny day. For a moment, she thought about following it off the wall. Then she came to herself and raised the <Lenses of Farsight> to her eyes.

In a second, she located Zothemza. He was screaming at his troops. If [Coercion] had worked, it wasn't obvious. A tattoo like a white spider at the hollow of his throat glowed, and he floated into the air.

Isold lowered his flute. "Got him," he said with satisfaction. "That will last at least ten minutes."

"One more volley," Aderyn shouted. She looked down the line of

Deadeyes. In that moment, brilliant, hot yellow light blossomed to her left, and she turned to see a ball of fire the size of a cargo wagon bearing down on her.

"Aderyn, *duck!*" Isold shouted. He grabbed her around the shoulders and bore her painfully to the ground as the fireball engulfed the battlements.

CHAPTER TEN

Flames roared above Aderyn for what felt like an eternity. Then, as abruptly as they'd struck, they died away. Aderyn lifted her head and surveyed the battlements. Three of the Spellcrafted arrow shooters were on fire, their stocks of arrows blazing, and they had stopped moving. The Deadeye illusions continued to shoot, while the nearest two Deadeyes picked themselves up off the ground, beating out tiny flames.

"Time for a distraction," Livia said. She was already standing, pressed against the shelter of the crenellations. She cautiously peeked out and started chanting. A low rumbling began, well to the side of the city. Aderyn's first fear that Zothemza was unleashing another terrible attack died as she got to her feet and peered around the side of the battlements.

The slope of the nearest mountain on their right shook, the earth groaned, and then an entire shelf of rocks and debris exploded over the orc horde. A flood of dirty water followed the explosion, rushing down the slope and slamming into the orcs. Some of them stood their ground, but many were knocked over and sent crashing into their neighbors, who also fell.

Zothemza, hovering over the horde, did nothing but stare at the city like it was his worst enemy. Aderyn stared back at him, rooted in place as she willed Isold's [Coercion] to work. Isold's assurances aside, it didn't look like the elementalist was affected.

The howls of injured orcs filled the air. Zothemza ignored the cries of the stricken and bellowed something, pointing at the gate in an imperious "attack" gesture.

"Time to go," Livia said.

She and Isold grabbed Aderyn's arms and hauled her to the stairs, down which the Deadeyes were already pelting. Aderyn regained her senses and ran after Livia down the stairs.

Livia stopped at the foot of the stairs and dug each foot into the earth, so deeply she might have been rooted there. "Run! You have to outrun me!"

Aderyn took off, following Isold, who soon left her behind. She was grateful he didn't think he needed to wait on her. They all needed to reach the back gate as fast as possible.

She pushed herself to the limits of her endurance, listening for Livia's progress. At first, she heard nothing, and the memory of Zothemza hovering menacingly in front of the city stirred her fears. After all, Livia was no runner.

Then she heard more rumbling from behind as Livia cast *earth glide*. The spell moved Livia through the earth, plowing up anything in its path, faster than a galloping horse. Aderyn ran faster. The rumbling was joined by the crash of stones and timber splintering as the foundations of the nearest buildings were torn up so the buildings collapsed on each other and across the street. Aderyn had never known the spell to be so powerful.

She shrieked as hands grabbed her around the waist. "Hang on!" Livia shouted over the noise of destruction. Aderyn hooked her arms around Livia's neck and wrapped her legs around her waist, and Livia sped up, tearing a groove through the stone-paved streets. It was actually exhilarating, moving at such speeds, swerving around corners along the route they'd planned. Sprays of gravel and dirt struck Aderyn's face, and she pressed her lips closed and squeezed her eyes shut. That made her feel like they were going faster.

After a few minutes, Livia slowed to a halt, and Aderyn released her.

Livia's eyes were bright and her cheeks ruddy. "That was great!" she said. "Let's get moving."

They'd reached the smaller gate, located on the far side of the city but not exactly opposite the main gate. Owen approached them. "Everyone all right? Isold was singed!"

"An elementalist," Aderyn gasped. She was more out of breath from their rapid flight than Livia. "He's powerful. Nobody died, so let's run."

"We need to get at least a hundred feet from the gate for the last thing," Livia said. "And I'm going to be nearly tapped out afterward."

Weston scooped her up in his arms. "How about you conserve resources, then?"

"You'd better run fast, dearest," Livia replied.

The gate opened on a valley between two terraced hills, nicely placed for defense. Any army attacking from this side would be funneled neatly into a position where they couldn't bring the full force of an attack against the gate, and the defenders could pick them off easily. Ahead, some distance away, the valley opened up, and Aderyn's army waited. They were too far away for her to see details, but she told herself not to worry about them.

Aderyn ran, letting [Keep Pace] carry her along beside Owen, until Livia said, "This is far enough." Weston set her down, and she walked back a few paces to face the city. Taking a strong stance, arms wide, fists clenched, she bowed her head and began speaking long, ponderous syllables that sounded like stones rolling downhill.

As she spoke, another rumbling became audible, this one deeper and more terrifying. The ground beneath their feet shook so Aderyn and Owen had to hold on to one another to stay upright. Then, with a titanic roar, the mountains on either side of the gate broke apart into huge boulders that tumbled down their slopes, crashing into the wall and piling up on both sides. The collapse continued, with smaller and smaller stones thudding into the piles of rubble, until the gate and most of the wall to either side were completely covered in the remains of the mountains. Now the wall was twenty feet higher.

Livia lowered her fists. She was breathing heavily. "Don't anybody expect anything more from me for a while," she said.

"That was magnificent," Weston said, picking her up again and kissing her.

"You did more than I expected," Aderyn said. "Now, let's get back to the army. There's a lot for the rest of us to do today."

They marched, double time, until everyone started to flag, getting as far from Shantos as possible. It wasn't as far as Aderyn had hoped; the route out of the valley took them through mountainous hills, none of them terribly steep, but enough to make the journey long and difficult. Finally, as the hills began to flatten out, Aderyn called a halt and sent a runner to bring Ambor to her. "We'll rest for a while, get something to eat, and then decide on our next steps," she announced to the army.

Ambor, with his *scrying* mirror, confirmed that Zothemza's troops had broken through the gate and were searching the city, moving slowly and checking every house. "They think we're hiding," he said triumphantly. "That was a good plan."

"I couldn't guarantee they wouldn't just skip over Shantos and come after us," Aderyn reminded him. "This was always one of the possibilities, but only one. And we're not going to take chances." In fact, the orcs' caution worried her. Why not destroy houses where they believed the humans were hiding? Searching implied they were looking for something else, possibly prisoners—

"Oh, *shit*," she whispered. "No, don't worry about it," she told Ambor when he looked concerned. She'd totally forgotten about Debran and his recalcitrant friends in the hurry to implement her plan. All her irritation with the man disappeared in her horror at what the orcs might do to him.

She sent Ambor back to his platoon and turned to Owen. "Debran's still in the city."

Owen grimaced. "I wish I was callous enough to say 'it's his own damn fault if orcs kill him.' But—come here." He wrapped his arms around Aderyn. "If he'd obeyed you, he'd be safe now. Or safer, anyway. There's nothing we can do for him now. Don't let this eat at you."

"I'll try not to." She wiped stupid tears from her eyes. "I need to talk to some people, but—stay with me?"

"Of course." He let her go, but kept hold of her hand.

Aderyn pulled out the <Farspeaker> and General Rajman's coin.

When the general's gruff face appeared in the oval, she said, "General, the orc army has divided, and one half commanded by the orc riders' leader is headed for Ikharatia. Where are you?"

Rajman didn't make any stupid, unnecessary exclamations of wonder or fear. "Southeast of Shantos. Can you be more specific about their location, general?"

"They left Shantos this morning to circle eastward around the mountains, possibly looking for an easier spot to cross. They move rapidly, but they weren't in a hurry last I saw."

"We will be able to intercept them. Is Shantos under siege?"

Aderyn winced inwardly. "We had to abandon the city. It was evacuated days ago and it became a trap rather than a strategic haven. I'm afraid our regiments took a beating in its defense."

"I'm sorry we couldn't reach you sooner. What of the Ikharatia regiments that were meant to reinforce you as well? Colonel Sudiptar and Colonel Kavish?"

"I don't have a way to contact them directly. I'll speak to General Ananyi after this, though. And to Commander General Varoun. But given our relative positions, my plan is to bring my remaining troops around to attack the orc riders from behind. We should be able to contain them, between the two of us."

Rajman nodded. "I'll have someone *scry* out their location, and I'll speak to you later. Good fortune, general." The mirror cleared.

Aderyn sighed and put Rajman's coin away. "Ananyi. Want to bet he's going to criticize?"

"He did last time," Owen said. "I vote you put him in his place. It's not like he's done better."

"Tempting."

This time, the mirror took longer to clear. When Ananyi's plump face finally appeared, he looked annoyed. "General Aderyn. What is it?"

Aderyn decided to start polite. "General, Shantos has fallen, and orcs are on their way to Ikharatia. You need to—"

"Shantos, fallen?" Ananyi sounded appalled. "How could you have let that happen?"

"General, focus," Aderyn commanded. "We need to head off the orc army. Rajman is already on his way, and my remaining regiment will join his, catching the orcs—"

"What do you mean, your remaining regiment? Listen, young lady, if you are so careless as to let your troops be destroyed, I'm disinclined to take orders from you."

"And I choose to pretend you weren't insubordinate just now," Aderyn snapped. "The Shantos regiments were nearly destroyed because your supporting forces failed to arrive in time. Since we're talking about carelessness. Remember I am your superior, and the only person who gets to criticize my skills is Commander General Varoun. Now, I have orders for you. Let me know right now if you intend not to obey them, and I'll see you replaced with someone who will. Understood?"

Ananyi's dark face grew positively apoplectic the longer she spoke. "Don't you dare—"

"Enough," Aderyn said. "Kingfisher and Raven are almost to Shantos, at last report. Have them alter their course to head northeast, using *scry* to locate the orc army. Once Zothemza—the other orc leader— shakes off **[Coercion]**, he will bring his troops south to join the rest of his forces. We must destroy the advance force of orc riders before the two groups reunite."

"**[Coercion]**? What are you talking about? How do you know an orc's name?"

"Ananyi, do you always ask this many irrelevant questions? Send word to your regiments. Then I suggest you contact Commander General Varoun and tell him all about my shortcomings. You'll find a listening ear. That's all." Aderyn popped the coin out of the **<Farspeaker>**, cutting off Ananyi before he could complain again.

"That was great," Owen said. "But Varoun's not going to be happy with him."

"I said Varoun would listen. I said nothing about how he'd respond." Aderyn put the **<Farspeaker>** away. "Hasanth, and now Ananyi. I should be grateful so few of the army's commanders are hostile, but right now I'm still annoyed at being talked down to."

"I don't blame you." Owen clasped her hand briefly. "Come on. You need to eat. And then, I was thinking we could have several spellslingers *scry* the location of Drorg's cavalry, and combine what they see to give us a visual guide to where we can intercept them."

"That's a great idea. Individually, none of them are high enough level to give us a good view, and Livia is tapped out. But if they work together..." She stretched aching muscles and added, "I think this might actually work."

She ate rations scavenged from Shantos, stale bread and preserved meat and bottled jams that made the bread tasty, then found a quiet corner to speak to Varoun. The old general looked irritated, deep lines furrowing his brow and dragging down the corners of his mouth. "I'm sorry you had to deal with Ananyi," he said without preamble. "He's a conservative thinker and hasn't fought more than a handful of actions in the field, so most of his experience is theoretical. I told him, as I once told you, that abandoning Shantos was always a possibility. It's not destroyed, is it?"

Aderyn thought uncomfortably of the wreckage Livia had left in her wake. "Not all of it, sir."

Varoun smiled grimly. "It's irrelevant now. Explain to me how things stand."

Aderyn described the positions, as best she knew, of the various forces in play. "I'm afraid the Shantos regiments are so reduced I've had to combine them into a single regiment called Leopard under the command of Colonel Thilar. Colonel Viyan supervises the Spellcrafters now—he's a level nine Spellcrafter himself, and he has some ideas about magic items our people could create. We're about to start our march again, with the intent of catching the orc riders in a pincer with Hawk and Ox regiments."

"You'll need to move fast, so I won't keep you longer." Varoun's lips thinned. "Kingfisher and Raven will join you, though based on *scrying* it's likely we won't catch up until battle has been joined, if that. I'm sorry to say Ananyi's reluctance has been a problem there, that and Colonel Sudiptar taking initiative in a way that put him well out of position. I've set Ananyi to supervise the remaining Ikharatia regiments, and I will take direct command of those in the field."

"I see." Aderyn didn't ask questions about Ananyi's fate. In her opinion, he deserved to be allowed to gracefully retire, and that was the generous option. "Then I suppose I'll see you in the flesh in a couple of days."

"Indeed. Keep me informed, general."

Varoun's face vanished, leaving Aderyn looking at her own face instead. Behind her, Owen said, "I've spoken to the spellslingers with *scry*, and they've worked out a path. Do you want to see the map?"

"Owen, is it just me, or does it feel like we've done nothing but scramble to catch up to the orcs?" Aderyn asked.

Owen hugged her from behind. "You're not wrong. But that won't always be the case. Once Drorg's riders are dealt with, it's Zothemza who will be playing catch up."

Aderyn sighed. "Ah, optimism. I needed that."

CHAPTER ELEVEN

A day later, Aderyn perched atop Livia's column of raised earth and stone and gazed into the distance with the <**Lenses of Farsight**>. She'd come to love the awkward, ramshackle device, confounding Colonel Viyan with her request to keep the glasses. "If I had time and materials, I could construct something more fitting your rank," he'd said, but Aderyn assured him she didn't care how they looked because they worked so well and were so perfectly what she'd wished for.

The lenses showed her the battle taking place a few miles away as if it was at arm's length, which made it eerie in its silence. The magic item couldn't do anything about how confused and chaotic the movements were, or how impossible it was to see patterns; she was at the wrong angle for that. But it did let her know the important things.

"All right," she called to Livia, who brought her back to earth to join her friends. "Battle has been joined, and all I can tell is that our regiments intercepted them almost exactly on schedule and they haven't been fighting long. The way they're oriented, we're at the orcs' back, which is again ideal."

"Are we trying to catch them by surprise?" Weston asked.

"Not really. Not in the sense of an ambush. We will be unexpected, but unless we're really lucky, they'll have enough warning to get some of their fighters in position to take us head-on." Aderyn tucked the <**Lenses of Farsight**> away in her coat. "We just start marching and be prepared for them to receive us."

In the flurry of activity that followed, officers getting soldiers into position, giving final orders, Livia cleaning up the camp by deactivating the <**Soldier's Friend**>, Aderyn didn't at first realize Owen hadn't said anything since before she surveyed the battle. Once she'd spoken to the troops and they began marching, she said, "What's wrong?"

"I'm struggling with a decision."

"What decision? Do you want to talk it out so I can help you choose?"

Owen shook his head. "It's a decision I've made that you won't like."

That chilled Aderyn. "Aren't we supposed to decide these things together? It sounds ominous."

"Yeah. That's the struggle. Aderyn, when battle is joined, I'm going to hunt down Drorg and kill him."

"Oh." Aderyn didn't know what to say.

"You're technically my commander," Owen went on. "I should let you make the decision. But this isn't about the battle. It's about our quest. And when it comes to our quest, I'm still our leader. But you're also my wife and my partner, and I shouldn't boss you around. You can see how I might be conflicted."

"Owen, I never want either of us to think of ourselves or of the other as in charge," Aderyn exclaimed. "We're a team. But I think there are times when one of us is going to make the decision, because we each have different strengths. So I get it. You're asking, am I your commander right now, or are you our team's leader?"

"That's it." Owen let out a deep, relieved breath. "You understand."

"I do. Let me think about it for a bit."

They walked in silence. Aderyn, contrary to her words, didn't think about what Owen had said. Instead, she listened to Weston and Livia bicker lovingly about some topic she hadn't heard, listened to Isold hum an unfamiliar melody, and listened to Owen's footsteps in tandem with hers. Her team. Their fates were intertwined with the army for now, but she couldn't let that interfere with their actual quest. The army would save the Southlands; their quest might, dramatic as it seemed, save the world.

"You're right," she finally said. "You need to kill Drorg. I've been thinking like a general, but the whole point of me leading the army was to put us in a position to succeed at our quest. So that was one thing I've forgotten."

"Is there more?"

"I also forgot that the quest requirements imply that killing those five leaders and destroying their stronghold will force the orc army to retreat. So, even though it's not strategically essential to the war, we need those leaders dead, and that should be a primary goal of my battle plans." She took Owen's hand. "Thank you for sharing your dilemma. You've given me perspective."

Owen squeezed her hand in return. "I love you. And I love seeing you use your skills on behalf of the army. And giving orders and telling those other leaders what to do."

Aderyn laughed. "You don't think that makes me look bossy or arrogant?"

"Not at all. It's actually sexy as hell. And someday we'll be in a position where I can do something about it."

He spoke his last words in a low, intimate growl that made Aderyn shiver with delight. "I'll hold you to that."

They walked in silence after that, over the last of the hills and onto plains covered with thin grass only barely winning the battle against the dust their footsteps kicked up. Aderyn again covered her mouth with her coat and breathed shallowly. Her mind turned to strategy, going over possibilities depending on how the orcs reacted, and then how the humans countered, but after only a few moves, the possibilities were endless, so she stopped doing that and focused on the battle, not so distant now. Figures at the edges were distinguishable as orcs and humans, not blurs of motion.

Aderyn had Emri signal a general stop. "This is it," she called out with **[Amplify Voice]**. "You have your orders. Press them hard and keep them contained. We will have vengeance for our fallen dead!"

A roar sounded throughout the army, and Aderyn shouted,

"Advance!" as Emri signaled the same. The soldiers surged into motion, building speed until everyone was running, with Aderyn and her friends at their head.

To Aderyn's astonishment, the orcs had only begun to turn to face this new threat when her soldiers crashed into them. Hawk and Ox had been merciless in their attack, keeping the enemy's attention, and now dozens of orcs fell to human blades. She had time for one moment of elation before an orc masher was in her face, screaming, and she swept her sword's tip across the orc's throat and then impaled him on the backstroke. She blinked away the system defeat notice and let [Outflank] tug her into position opposite Owen, who made short work of their next opponent.

The battle stretched on, each little fight adding up to a long, long string of kills. Aderyn took a sword stroke to her left arm and had to pause to bind it up while Owen fought to defend her. It reminded her she hadn't seen Isold. As if by magic, she heard his battle song raised above the din and felt instantly stronger.

"This way!" Owen shouted.

Aderyn quickly surveyed her surroundings, but the melee was too crowded and chaotic for her to make anything strategic of what she saw. She followed Owen, hoping he knew where Drorg was. The other thing she hadn't seen was any orc riders, but she guessed they had been on the far side and Hawk and Ox Regiments were dealing with them.

Just as she thought this, she heard the high-pitched squealing of an animal in extreme pain, and [See It Coming] showed her a maddened, riderless goretusk charging straight at her in time for her to leap aside. It was moving too fast for her to stop it and kill it, so she ran on—but she'd lost sight of Owen, and it seemed the world was suddenly full of nothing but mounted orcs wielding short spears. She dodged a couple of blows, disemboweled a goretusk that dumped its rider at her feet for her to kill as well. *Where are you?* she said with [Bonded Mind].

Immediately, she realized that was a stupid question. It wasn't as if the battle had landmarks for Owen to identify his location. But his immediate reply, *Found Drorg*, invigorated her. It didn't matter that Owen was a powerful swordsman who didn't need help killing an orc, however strong; he was her partner, and she wanted to be there when he did.

She dodged attackers, not engaging unless she had to, and found herself on the outskirts of the battle. Taking a breath, she paused to survey the field. What little she saw cheered her. The two human armies pressed the orcs harder by the minute, in some places nearly meeting. Her instruction to her army—keep going until you find more humans—was working. Good thing, because there was no way she could transmit—

With that, she remembered Emri. She'd accidentally left him behind.

Aderyn frantically scanned the battlefield and saw the banner some distance away, still upright though grimy with dust. Her fear for her level two bannerman drove all thoughts of fighting Drorg out of her head. She ran, skirting the battle, until she was as close as she could get to the brightly-colored flag, then dove headlong into the fight, striking with her sword and kicking and punching, whatever it took to reach the banner.

With a final thrust and a final system defeat notice, she burst through the crowd. "Emri, sorry—who are you?"

The young woman gripping the flag turned a terrified look on Aderyn. "Emri's down," she gasped. "The orcs keep attacking me. It's like they know the banner is important."

Aderyn's gaze fell on a limp shape huddled near the woman's feet. Her heart, which had been pounding with her exertions, ached so sharply she felt she'd been knifed. For a moment, the huddled form was the dead Windwarden Kimay, killed while following her orders. Emri had trusted her, had gone on trusting her despite her many mistakes. Now this mistake had gotten him killed.

She realized now that there was a loose circle of soldiers surrounding the banner, never quite letting the orcs through, and that the fighting she'd thought she'd imagined to be particularly fierce here was as bad as she believed. "We have to leave him—"

"He's not dead, ma'am," the woman said. "I was scared to move in case they killed him. What do I do?"

Aderyn snatched the banner from her. "You carry him," she said.

"And follow me." So, the orcs were drawn to the banner, were they? That was the same as saying she could control where they went.

With a loud cry of, "Stay with me!" and an awkward signal to the nearest troops to form up around the banner—one of only three signals Aderyn knew how to execute—she made her way through the battle, gathering soldiers until the protective ring was three deep and no orcs were getting anywhere near. Aderyn knew the orcs were still with her, because she occasionally saw soldiers fall or be helped away by others, but she focused on dragging the fight across the battlefield to where the human presence was strongest.

Ahead, the orc cries grew louder, and through the melee Aderyn saw dozens of them throw up their arms as the ground dropped away from them. When *hungry pit* had done its job, Livia strolled up as if she wasn't surrounded by enemies. "That banner is like an inanimate [Compel]," she said.

"True! I hadn't thought of that, just that the orcs followed it." The battle was already less fierce now that she'd moved so many orcs to where there were a lot of humans to kill them.

She blinked away another system defeat message—they were coming fast enough she was used to ignoring them—but Livia startled, then grinned. "One more down," she said.

"One more—" Aderyn read back through the messages.

**Congratulations! You have defeated [Drorg, Orc Leader].
You have earned [12,500 XP]**

"Oh! I meant to be there!" Aderyn exclaimed.

"That ought to make the orcs run," Livia said with satisfaction.

"Once they know about it." Aderyn flourished the banner once more, signaling "forward," and followed the troops as they pressed the orcs hard. But after only a few minutes, the fighting lessened, and Aderyn had to signal again, this time "disengage." When the last orc rider had vanished over the northern horizon, Aderyn turned to the young woman whose name she'd never asked. "Is he…"

"Still alive, ma'am," the woman said.

"I'll get Isold," Livia said.

The woman laid Emri on the ground, and Aderyn checked him over. He had a terrible wound in his stomach that he clutched weakly, but appeared otherwise uninjured. Aderyn clung to her knowledge that gut wounds weren't usually fatal if treated soon enough. It was better than facing a crushing sense of guilt. She'd managed over time to stop seeing Kimay falling to his death—it was all her imagination, because she'd been nowhere near, which made it worse—but now she had a new terrible memory to eat at her. If Emri died...

Eventually, Isold arrived, and Aderyn stood back to let him use the **<Healing Stone>**. When Emri finally opened his eyes and blinked at her, she began, "I'm sorry—"

"It's all right, I was careless," Emri whispered before breaking out in a coughing fit. Aderyn helped him sit up out of the dust. "I tried to follow you."

"I forgot everything. There wasn't going to be any way for me to direct the battle, and I forgot—I'm sorry. I'm glad you didn't die."

Emri smiled, an unexpectedly cheerful expression. "Me too."

Aderyn laughed, relieved beyond measure. "You get some rest. I promise not to leave you behind again."

With Livia, she walked through the battlefield, her heart aching again at how many soldiers had died. That it wasn't nearly as many as they'd lost the first time they'd faced Drorg was small comfort. Isold left them to go help with the wounded, though he said, "I am running low on healing magic. I will have to return to Ikharatia tonight."

They found Owen and Weston standing together over the bloody body of an orc that lay near a white-painted goretusk corpse. Aderyn ran to hug Owen. "Which of you killed him?"

"I took him down, finally, after Weston stepped in front of the goretusk like a crazy person and let her nearly trample him so he could slit her throat," Owen said.

Livia gasped.

"It was nothing," Weston scoffed.

"Like a crazy person," Owen repeated. "He's angling for battle MVP. It's a good thing we don't count our kills. I don't want our relationship to turn into a gory feud."

"Count kills?" Weston said as he put his arms around Livia. "Is that a thing in—where you come from?"

"Well, there's this one movie," Owen said. "Anyway, it was a team effort, like always. And that's one step closer to our goal."

"Come with me," Livia told her husband. "I'm going to set up camp, and I want you where I can see you won't do any more crazy things today."

"Fair enough," Weston said.

BY NIGHTFALL, the battlefield had been cleared of human bodies and the wounded, and Livia's **<Soldier's Friend>** had set up enough tents to accommodate all the living. Little fires dotted the plains, one in front of every large tent, and although their heat wasn't needed thanks to the brutal climate, pots boiled with soup or water for tea over every one.

Aderyn sat near their own fire, her hunger sated, wishing she didn't feel so grimy. She could have gone back to Ikharatia when Isold had returned earlier to recharge the **<Healing Stone>** and gotten a wonderful bath, but it felt wrong to pamper herself when none of her soldiers could. She had enough benefits that that one seemed too indulgent.

"What's that?" she asked Owen, who was toying with something that sparkled in the firelight.

"Something I took off Drorg. I was hoping Isold might be able to identify it." He passed the bauble to Aderyn. It was a thick ring of steel, too large to fit any but the fattest finger even if it hadn't been covered on one side by a fine wire mesh that entirely filled the circle. An odd, faceted lump of glass capped the other side. Aderyn peered closer.

"It looks like it's filled with fine, straight wires," she said.

"That's what I thought. Isold?"

Isold accepted the ring from Aderyn. "How odd," he said. "I know nothing about it, not even the feeling I get of straining for half-forgotten knowledge that indicates an item is too high a level for me to identify. Perhaps it's not magical."

"No, it's magic," Livia said from where she leaned against Weston. "Here, let me see."

"Maybe we need someone who can cast *heritage*," Aderyn said.

"Maybe." Livia turned it so the facets caught the light and sparkled. "You say it doesn't seem familiar at all?"

"Not at all." Isold took the item back and peered at it as if intense focus might change the results. "Either it's *extremely* high level, or it was created by orcs."

"What makes you say that?" Weston said.

"We don't know anything about their magic aside from that it's elemental and requires a physical focus. It's possible they also have Spellcrafters, and the Spellcrafters' skills and the things they produce are too alien for my skill to recognize." Isold smiled. "Or I could just be reaching for an explanation as to why my [Identify Magic Item] skill failed."

"Well, I'm going to hang onto it," Owen said. "It can't be an accident that Drorg had this, and it's not safe to leave it where another orc might find it. For all we know, it's his badge of office." He put it away in his belt pouch.

"General Aderyn, ma'am?"

Aderyn straightened. "Yes, veteran?" She recognized the man as having originally belonged to Eagle Regiment, but she didn't know his name.

The veteran shifted uncomfortably. "There's some people who say they know you and want to speak to you. The perimeter guards stopped them. Ma'am, they're, um, they're high-level adventurers."

A prickle of apprehension stole down Aderyn's spine and vanished. "Did the perimeter guards Assess them? Who are they?"

The soldier nodded. "Their names are Ruan and Suveer."

CHAPTER TWELVE

They all hurried through the camp until Aderyn came to a stop out of sight of the perimeter. "We need to play this cautiously. I don't want Ruan thinking his arrival disrupted us, or worried us."

"That's a very good point." Owen gripped Aderyn's shoulder briefly in reassurance.

"I want to know what in thunder he's doing here," Livia said. "And yes, I realize we can ask him, but I'd wager a hundred gold he'll lie about it."

"That just means we don't take him at his word," Weston said. "I for one want to know why he thinks we'll greet him with any sympathy. Kanan was a traitor, and Ruan supported him."

"And we don't know why he left Kanan's employ, so we must be cautious." Isold held up a warning hand. "But we also have to consider that Ruan's appearance here is benign. He might have been unwilling to help Kanan kill a child. From what we know of him, he's a womanizer and possessed of a temper, neither of which condemn him as an unrepentant criminal."

"He also lied to Suveer about me," Aderyn pointed out, "probably to keep Suveer under his thumb. That's not nothing."

"True, but it also doesn't make him irredeemable. I'm just saying we need to withhold judgment. Don't trust him, but don't condemn him out of hand, either."

Aderyn wished Isold didn't make so much sense. "All right. Agreed. Do you want to do the questioning, Isold?"

"I think it should be General Aderyn, at least until we know what he wants." Isold usually smiled when he called her "general" so she would know he was teasing. Now, he looked perfectly serious.

"But we'll all be there to back you up," Owen said. "Let's go—and act like we're the ones in control."

"Because we are," Livia said.

They proceeded to the perimeter checkpoint, where soldiers barred two nearly identical men from entering camp. Aderyn controlled her shock at seeing Ruan and Suveer. Both men were grimy, their clothes stained as if they'd slept in them many nights, and Ruan's left sleeve was slit open to accommodate a bandage wrapped around his forearm. Ruan's long hair, normally well-kempt and tied neatly back at the nape of his neck, hung loose around his face, making him look haggard rather than handsome. Suveer's empty eye socket looked deeper and more puckered than usual.

In time, she suppressed a compassionate outburst and instead said, "Soldiers, stand down. Ruan. Suveer. What brings you to the army?" She was conscious that the two soldiers knew well that Ruan was a level fifteen Swordsworn who could cut them down faster than they could defend themselves. That they hadn't run impressed her. Some sort of bonus was in order—but later.

"Aderyn," Ruan said, sounding so relieved, so vulnerable, she almost didn't believe it was the same man who'd repeatedly hit on her despite knowing she was married. "We took a chance on finding you here. I doubt any other army commanders would be willing to listen to us."

"I don't know that we're willing to listen to you," Owen said. He spoke mildly, as if despite his words this was an ordinary meeting between acquaintances. "You know Kanan was executed for treason? Your former boss?"

"Kanan was never my boss," Ruan said scornfully. "We had similar goals for a while, and then our paths diverged. You can think whatever you like of me, Owen, but don't believe I'd ever go along with a plan to murder a child."

Owen shrugged. "That's noble, but it doesn't say why you're here."

"You wanted to speak to me, on military business?" Aderyn said. "Go ahead."

"Can we at least get a drink, and a place to sit?" Ruan said. "We've walked a long way, and I promise you'll want to hear our story. I understand if you don't want to extend us full hospitality. You're not Southlanders."

He didn't make it sound critical, but his words stung, like Aderyn's nationality made her inherently rude. But Aderyn didn't want to bring Ruan into the camp, implying trust, until she knew more. She glanced around. Here at the perimeter, not all the tents produced by the <Soldier's Friend> were occupied, and there was a fire with stools pulled up around it nearby.

"I'm sorry," she said automatically. "Let's sit over here. Private, please bring a couple of pitchers, and—are you hungry?" she asked Ruan.

"We would not reject food," Ruan said, flashing her a smile that for a moment made him look the way she remembered him.

"Bring a couple of bowls of soup and some bread," Aderyn added.

The two soldiers saluted. One of them returned to the perimeter, while the other hailed another private and murmured instructions. Aderyn pretended not to be embarrassed that she'd forgotten the perimeter guards weren't allowed to leave their posts, even if commanded. These two deserved a *big* bonus.

Ruan and Suveer had already taken seats. Suveer sat stiffly, though he looked as weary as his twin brother, and Ruan slouched and crossed his arms atop his knees. "Thank you," he said. "I know I haven't given you much reason to trust us, but I hope you'll set the past aside."

"You should stop being mysterious and tell us what brings you here," Weston said.

Ruan chuckled. "It's a long story, and I beg your pardon for that—it's just that you need to know the background to get the full import of what I have to say. And to be honest, I'm uncomfortable revealing some of it after spending so long keeping it to ourselves."

"That doesn't make you look good, if you've been concealing information," Aderyn said.

"It's only what we agreed on before—that the details of our quests as Fated Ones should be kept confidential, in case we ended up interfering with each other." Ruan didn't sound as if he felt guilty over this. Aderyn couldn't remember agreeing on anything, precisely, but she recalled the discussion where the subject had come up.

"All right, that's fair," she said.

A private hurried up, carrying two empty metal pitchers and a basket of dishes and assorted cutlery, followed by another private bearing a covered pot and a couple of loaves of camp bread. Isold served the soup in silence, and they all waited a few minutes as Ruan and Suveer ate. Ruan had made it sound like they weren't starving, but he and Suveer certainly consumed soup and bread like they hadn't eaten in a while. Livia summoned water into the pitchers, and everyone drank, even Aderyn, who wasn't thirsty. The shared water eased her tension.

"Thank you," Suveer said, startling Aderyn. His quiet voice was the same, bland and colorless, and he didn't meet anyone's eye.

"Yes, thank you," Ruan said. He set his empty bowl down and tore a small chunk from the half-loaf he still held. "I didn't realize how hungry I was. We've walked a long way."

"No more mystery," Aderyn said. She knew she sounded harsh, but she wasn't ready to accept Ruan at face value. "Tell us your story."

"This starts in Obsidian, or outside Obsidian," Ruan began. "With the Sarnok. I know you defeated it, or you wouldn't be here."

"Are you saying you killed the Sarnok? Just the two of you?" Owen exclaimed.

"There were more of us," Suveer replied, and subsided back into silence as if he'd exhausted his stores of information.

"We were a four-person team. Jannas, Doria, Suveer and I." Ruan bowed his head. "Jannas and Doria died in the fight with the Sarnok. Suveer and I decided we weren't going to give up—that we could do the Fated One quests in their memory."

To her surprise, Aderyn's [Sense Truth] skill didn't rouse her suspicions about Ruan's veracity. He looked and sounded like he meant to play on their sympathies, but he wasn't lying about the facts. "When was this? Your fight with the Sarnok?"

"About two and a half months ago. What about you?"

Aderyn counted back. "It's been three and a half months."

"So we just missed each other." Ruan smiled, looking more like himself. "I'm glad. I don't like to think about what might happen if two Fated Ones are after the same quest."

"That was fast, getting here in two and a half months," Owen said. "I thought the ocean route took longer."

"We found someone in Obsidian willing to cast *world door*. It took nearly all our savings, too, so we needed a sponsor to support us once we got here. That's when we took up with Kanan. We brought him prestige, he paid for our clothes and food and housing. But you're wondering about our Fated One quest."

"We are," Aderyn said.

"The quest that opened up after we killed the Sarnok is called [**Free the Prisoners**]. There's not a lot of information, but you know that's typical of these quests. You have to work out what they refer to and what the victory conditions are." Ruan drained his tin mug and set it down.

Aderyn's skin quivered with the awareness that all four of her friends were holding back exclamations. She herself didn't know where to begin. Even if the information provided by the system with regard to the Fated One quests was unique to Warmasters, Suveer would be aware of it—unless he was more crippled as a Warmaster than her Assessment of his skills had indicated.

"I take it you did figure it out, though," she said.

"All we initially had to go on was that the prisoners, whoever they were, were held in the Blighted Range. That seemed fortuitous, because Tielana is our home. Or was, years ago. We don't have any family left there now."

Suveer shifted his weight, lowering his head so the firelight made shadows across his scarred face that deepened the marks. Ruan paused as if waiting for his brother to contribute, then said, "At any rate, we started in Ikharatia, asking around to see if anyone knew about any prisoners trapped in the Blighted Range. No one knew anything except what we all do: that humans can't survive in the high-risk zones, and if there *were* prisoners, they wouldn't last long enough to be rescued."

"But the system doesn't give out quests that are impossible," Weston said.

"Right. We figured we either hadn't met the right person, or we were looking at things the wrong way. Then the first news of orcs invading came to the city, and the queen announced that the historians at the university would host a challenge to decide on the army's commander general. I didn't think anything of it, but Kanan asked me if I would compete on his behalf. I didn't really like the idea of getting involved in politics, but he made a compelling offer that would have left us independent of him or anyone else after the war was over. And Suveer has some tactical skills—is that a Warmaster thing?"

Aderyn suppressed the urge to say *Don't you know that?* Instead, she said, "Yes. But it was you competing, not Suveer. Why?"

"I don't do well under pressure," Suveer said. "Ruan's the one who's good at leading."

"I don't know how good I am, but it's true Suveer wouldn't have managed it," Ruan said. "On the other hand, it was Suveer who saw the quest notice had changed, so we both had something to contribute." He sat up straighter and gestured to bring up the Codex. "I'll read it to you. 'Orcs have taken human prisoners to their stronghold in the Blighted Range. Locate and rescue the prisoners and return them to their homes.' We discovered that change the night after the first test by the history masters. Before, it just said human prisoners in the Blighted Range."

"Orcs took human prisoners? Ruan, why didn't you tell anyone!"

"I went to Kanan first. I figured this might be a reason for me to gain control of the armies, because then I could direct them toward a rescue." Ruan's fists clenched, though his voice was as smooth as ever. "Kanan convinced me not to speak, that the information should come from him, because if I was the one to reveal it, I'd look like a selfish glory-hound who was in it for the Fated One reward, not for the sake of the prisoners. I believed him, and I thought he'd taken his knowledge to the queen. Or to Varoun, once Varoun was the winner. It was a lie."

"You should have—" Aderyn didn't know what to say. Chastising

Ruan was pointless, though it would make her feel better. "Never mind. When did you find out Kanan lied to you?"

"At the same time we learned he meant to kill King Colan and take the throne. I told you Suveer and I wouldn't be party to murdering a child. Kanan flung the truth about the prisoners in my face, saying I was a failure as a Fated One and too trusting. I would have killed him if he hadn't been surrounded by a dozen of his paid adventurers. I'm good, but I'm not stupid. And I had Suveer to think about. He's no swordsman." Ruan gazed intently at Aderyn. "Any other questions? Have I convinced you we're not lying?"

Aderyn still didn't feel the twitching uneasiness that was [Sense Truth] warning her. "Where did you go after leaving Kanan?"

"We fled the city to get away from the battle. Went north along the coast, then cut inland, skirting Lake Dannis. We knew Shantos was threatened by orcs, so we hoped to find one of the Southlander armies and see if they'd be willing to tell us where to find you. This was a lucky coincidence." Ruan smiled, not at all flirtatiously. For once, Aderyn almost liked him.

"And you wanted to find me because you figured I, being married to the Fated One—to *a* Fated One—would believe you?" she asked.

"I hoped you would care about rescuing humans, and that as second in command you'd have the authority to make it happen. I realize our teams are at odds, and you don't want me to succeed. But it matters that those people be saved, regardless of whether it's a Fated One quest or not." Ruan leaned forward. "I don't know what else to tell you. You wouldn't believe me if I said I'd give up this quest. I think I'm just as deserving of being the Fated One as Owen. But Suveer and I can't do it alone."

Aderyn matched him gaze for gaze. His intensity didn't move her; she knew Ruan well enough to remember he had a powerful presence. But she had responsibilities that mattered more than one man's desires. "Was the Sarnok the first Fated One quest you fulfilled?"

Ruan blinked. "Of course. Why, wasn't it yours?"

"It was. How did you kill the monster? Were you all level fifteen?"

"All of us except Suveer were level fifteen Swordsworn, and I had the advantages of a level fifteen Warmaster partner. And this." Ruan drew the greatsword at his hip out a few inches, revealing a black blade that glittered with golden specks in the firelight. "It's the <**Galling Blade**>. The wounds it causes don't heal naturally."

"Which means the Sarnok wouldn't have regenerated damage," Owen said.

"Suveer told us about the regeneration ability, yes," Ruan said. "It was still a difficult fight. I wish Jannis and Doria had survived. They were strong Swordsworn, but nothing survives a direct hit with that burning vision the Sarnok has." His jaw clenched as if he was controlling a strong emotion, and this time Aderyn felt sure he was putting them on. He wasn't as torn up about his teammates' deaths as he implied. All her sympathy for Ruan vanished.

"I'm sorry for your loss," she said. She was willing to play along. What mattered was that she knew Ruan wasn't being completely forthcoming, and that gave her an advantage. "So, you intend to carry out the next quest. What specifically did you hope I would do for you? Do you have a plan?"

"The plan is to sneak into the orc stronghold and free the prisoners." Ruan smiled, somewhat sheepishly. "I realize that's more of an intent than a plan, but until I see the place, I can't be more specific. What I do know is Suveer and I need allies. Obviously, we'd like those allies to be you all—you're high-level, experienced adventurers, and this is something we all care about. But if that's not possible, I thought maybe you'd let us ask for volunteers, spare fifteen or twenty soldiers to accompany us."

"I can't abandon my post," Aderyn said automatically, but her mind had already latched onto the idea of staging a daring raid on Charnel Keep. Defeating that dungeon *was* one of their quest requirements, and who said it had to happen only after the orc leaders were dead? And if they had to go there eventually, why not now?

But it was madness. She had a responsibility to the army, particularly now that Zothemza would go on the attack soon, speaking of quest requirements. She couldn't walk away from that. And there remained the fact that Ruan wasn't telling the whole truth. Going into danger with him might mean trouble for her and her friends.

"You wouldn't be abandoning your post so much as attacking on a different front," Ruan said, as if he'd heard her thoughts. "Who knows what effect raiding their stronghold will have on the orc army? You might change the course of the war."

"It's called Charnel Keep," Owen said. "You telling us you didn't even know that?"

Suveer ducked his head so his chin nearly brushed his collarbone. Ruan glared at Owen. "Suveer does his best. Understanding the quest requirements is difficult. Besides, what difference does knowing its name make?"

"You're right, it doesn't matter," Aderyn said. "Ruan, I can't leave my command right now. But you're also right that rescuing human prisoners is important. Let me think about your situation tonight, discuss it with my team, and we'll talk further in the morning. You're welcome to sleep here—these tents are unoccupied."

"That's as much as I can hope for, that you'll take me seriously," Ruan said. "Thank you, Aderyn." He extended his hand and gripped hers firmly, his gaze meeting hers with calm directness. Aderyn was sure he was full of crap, but she pretended she believed he was as noble as he presented himself.

CHAPTER THIRTEEN

The five friends walked back through the tents, but they hadn't gone far before Weston said, "I'll meet up with you later. I've got some eavesdropping to do."

"On Ruan?" Livia said. "You think he was lying?"

"He was definitely lying about some things." Weston kissed his wife and added, "I'm betting against learning anything incriminating, because Ruan is a clever bastard, but it's worth trying." He hurried silently back the way they'd come.

"Thunderation," Livia groused. "This is why I'm a cynic. I can never tell if someone's lying, so I assume the worst so I won't be surprised."

"He was not unhappy about his teammates' deaths," Isold said grimly. "I didn't get the sense that he had a hand in killing them, just that they were an obstacle he was now rid of."

"I sensed that too. Not the second thing, just that he wanted us to believe he was broken up about it." Aderyn glanced over her shoulder in the direction of Ruan's borrowed tent. "Let's go. We do need to talk about this."

Back at their own fire, Aderyn paced rather than seating herself beside Owen. "It might not be anything sinister. Maybe they just weren't good friends, and Ruan didn't mourn them more than you would a casual acquaintance who died. If he thought we'd consider that heartless, he might have put on a show to make himself look, well, not heartless."

"That is certainly a possibility," Isold said. "The important thing is that I am certain he didn't betray them. That would verge on evil behavior. Opportunism and heartlessness are not crimes."

"I don't like it," Owen said. "He's never shown himself to be worthy of trust. He tried to hit Aderyn, he thought flirting with her was acceptable, he was pals with Kanan—"

"You have a personal grudge against him," Aderyn said. "And I think he was telling the truth about why he left Kanan."

"Of course I have a personal grudge against him!" Owen rubbed a hand over his face. "I take it personally when someone attacks my wife, however they do it."

"And I love that about you." Aderyn paused in her pacing to hug him. "But if Ruan is right that there are human prisoners in Charnel Keep, we can't ignore that. I'm not sure about the ethics of our most obvious course, though."

"Ethics? We're rescuing prisoners. How is that unethical?" Livia said.

"She means because the best course of action is to take a regiment and invade Charnel Keep," Isold said, "denying Ruan and Suveer their quest."

"Oh." Livia chewed her lip in thought. "Couldn't they join the army and take part in the raid?"

"We don't know whether indirect action qualifies as a quest completion," Owen said. "So far, the orc leaders have all been killed by us. Maybe if another soldier takes out Zothemza, we won't get the credit and the quest will be invalidated."

"And we have no way of knowing short of taking a chance and letting it happen," Aderyn added. "Since we only know about the prisoners because of Ruan and Suveer, that would be treating them pretty shabbily."

"But you're right that we can't leave the troops to go off on a side quest, even if it would technically be a main quest. We *do* have to destroy Charnel Keep, after all." Owen dug a furrow with the toe of his boot as if it was the beginnings of a tactical map.

"That's what I thought, too." Aderyn sat on the stool next to him. "I don't know that letting him take volunteers is a great idea. I don't think we have any soldiers who are higher than level twelve, and Charnel Keep is in the high-risk zone. Even if they could fight off orcs, there are other dangers there that won't be as survivable."

"That's true for us, too," Livia said. "We're higher level than Ruan, but that doesn't make the Blighted Range safe. We'll have to be careful when we make the assault on the stronghold."

In the light of the nearest fire, a huge shadow loomed over the tents. "No luck," Weston said. "That is, Suveer and Ruan are sharing a tent, and when Suveer started to say something, Ruan shushed him and said 'we don't know who's listening.' Which at least confirms they're hiding something."

"It's becoming harder for me to come up with an innocuous reason for their behavior," Isold said with a smile. "Not that I want to. I dislike Ruan's attitude about women and I hate feeling like I should advocate for him."

"You're not advocating for him, you're helping us consider all the possibilities so we don't make foolish, unreasoned choices," Aderyn said. "Am I right that we all agree Ruan can't be trusted?"

"There's no thundering way I'd trust him with anything except maybe acting in his own interests," Livia said.

"We also can't trust that he won't interfere with our Fated One quest, just to give himself a leg up," Owen said. "Though we're ahead by one, did you notice? We're on the third quest and he's only on the second. We didn't reveal that, either. At any rate—no. I was going to say our quest is more important than his, but that's only in the personal way. Obviously saving people matters more."

"But you're right that we can't let him take precedence." Aderyn sighed. "And we're back to stealing the quest from them. Why do I feel so guilty about that?"

"Because you're a good person with a generous heart who knows how you'd feel if our positions were reversed." Owen clasped her hand.

"I'm guessing you're trying to figure out a way for everyone to get what they need."

"I am." She sighed again. "Strategically, we're not in a position to go to Charnel Keep with the army, not with Zothemza's forces right around the corner and who knows how many other orc armies coming to reinforce him. So we couldn't take the selfish route even if we wanted to."

"And Ruan and Suveer can't do it alone. Can't do it even with a group of volunteers. They'll just get killed," Owen said. "I hate saying this, but those prisoners are going to have to wait."

"I agree on both counts," Aderyn said.

"So what will you tell Ruan?" Livia asked.

"You won't think it's good news," Aderyn told Ruan the following morning at sunrise. "We can't go with you to Charnel Keep. I'm needed here, and the army's needs have to take precedence over the fate of a few prisoners."

"I understand," Ruan said, surprising Aderyn. "I imagine it hurt you to say that."

"It did. But command is about making the hard choices." Aderyn held up a hand when Ruan would have spoken again. "As to asking for volunteers, well, I could certainly do that. But most of our soldiers aren't any higher level than twelve, and while I'm sure they don't care about personal risk, it's still true that you intend to enter the high-risk zone, and I won't throw their lives away."

Ruan's face stilled. "I see."

"Maybe not. Ruan, your quest is important, not just to you but to me and to everyone imprisoned in Charnel Keep. So I have a different proposition for you. Stay here, fight with the army, and as soon as the strategic situation isn't so dire, my friends and I will go with you so you can accomplish your quest."

"You want us to join the army?"

"You'd be a powerful addition to our forces, Ruan, especially since you have a Warmaster partner. Think of it as working toward reaching your goal. The sooner we kill Zothemza and destroy his army, the sooner we'll be free to risk Charnel Keep." Aderyn held out her hand. "What do you think?"

Ruan hesitated only a moment before clasping her hand. "It's not what I expected, but I can't say I'm not eager to kill orcs. We'll do it."

Aderyn extended her hand to Suveer. "Suveer? Are you in?" she asked, pretending she hadn't heard Ruan say "we."

Suveer looked at her hand, then at her face. His one eye was closed nearly to a slit, and the way he stood, slightly turned away, suggested he thought he was about to take a blow. Then he took her hand briefly and as quickly pulled away. "If Ruan says so."

For a moment, Aderyn wanted to slap Suveer. How could he be so hesitant, so cringing, when he ought to have the confidence a Warmaster with a competent partner had earned? If she slapped him, and he struck back at her, at least he'd show some backbone.

She controlled her impulse and instead smiled politely at Suveer. "In two hours we march out. Zothemza—"

"Sorry, who is that?" Ruan asked.

"He's an orc elementalist, a powerful one, in charge of the army that attacked and occupied Shantos. Our spellslingers confirmed last night that he left that city behind and headed this way. We're going to see about cutting off his progress." Aderyn turned as someone hailed her. "Veteran Joshi. News?"

"General, the lookouts see movement to the south," Joshi said. She was a short, plump Swordsworn whose small size frequently threw orc attackers off. Aderyn knew from Colonel Thilar's reports that she had racked up quite the kill count despite being only level ten.

"The south? Is it our people, or theirs?"

"Colonel Viyan says it's Kingfisher and Raven, ma'am." Joshi grinned. "Those orc bastards won't know what hit them, right, general?"

"Don't be overconfident, veteran. And... yes." Aderyn accepted Joshi's salute and returned her attention to Ruan. "Varoun's at the head of those regiments. I've got to speak to him. Do you need any equipment? You've got a sword, but what about armor for both of you?"

"We'd appreciate that, yes." Ruan smiled, again without any sensual meaning. "Can I say I'm glad I didn't win command of the army? You are far better at it than I would ever be."

"Technically, I didn't win either. But thanks for the compliment." Aderyn gave him directions to the supply tents, directed one final look at Suveer as he slouched along in his brother's wake, and then pulled out the <**Farspeaker**> and Varoun's coin.

"I hope we're not too late, general," Varoun said when the mist cleared. He'd been so quick to respond Aderyn guessed his spellslingers had seen their army, too.

"Not at all, sir," Aderyn replied. "I was just about to check in with the scryers to get an idea of the tactical situation. As of last night, the orcs were east of Shantos. History suggests they won't be on the move yet, but I don't take chances. I can give you a better idea of when we'll clash in twenty minutes."

"No need. Those of us with *scry* mapped out the situation before we broke camp thirty minutes ago. The orcs hadn't yet moved out. You are ten miles southeast of their position."

"That's farther than I thought. You want us to stay here until we can join forces?"

"Yes, and no. I want us united when we attack, but you have time to choose a better location for a battle. *Scry* out the terrain, get into position, and contact me again. I have a Tidecaller assigned to watch your movements, but I may have further instructions."

"Understood." It felt so good not to be in ultimate command. Probably that made her a poor general as far as career soldiering went. How fortunate that wasn't what she wanted out of life. "Everything else all right?"

"Running smoothly, which always makes me nervous." Varoun smiled.

"Oh! Guess who showed up at our camp. Ruan and Suveer."

Varoun's smile disappeared. "Ruan? What does that thundering waste of air want?"

"He brought word that the orcs have been taking prisoners back to Charnel Keep—oh. That's the orc stronghold in the Blighted Range. I, um, guess I forgot to mention it because the attack on Shantos—"

"Never mind that. Prisoners? How many?"

"He didn't say." That she hadn't thought to ask embarrassed Aderyn. "But more than a few. Ruan's Fated One quest is to rescue them. And ours is to destroy Charnel Keep. So we both have reasons to go there. But I told him it was impossible right now, given the imminent attack."

"You're right." Varoun fell silent. Aderyn waited for him to finish his train of thought. "It's something we'll have to discuss later. Right now, we focus on taking out this orc army before it's reinforced again. Understood?"

"Yes, sir. I told you I wouldn't let the Fated One quest interfere with my duties."

Varoun grimaced. "I'm sorry I sounded like I doubted you. For my part, I know you came south for your own reasons, and I don't intend to abuse your generosity. So—we'll talk. I'll be waiting for your message." His image vanished, leaving Aderyn looking at her own reflection.

"Varoun trusts you," Owen said, startling Aderyn into giving a little shriek and spinning around. He grinned. "Sorry."

"I didn't hear you there." Aderyn put away the <**Farspeaker**> and let Owen hold her. "It's going to be a difficult battle today."

"I'm having trouble imagining an orc elementalist as powerful as Zothemza. Your description of his fireball was unbelievable." Owen's arms tightened on her. "I think Livia took it as a challenge. I'm worried for her."

"She has to be at least as powerful as he is. Maybe more so, because he's only power level fifteen." Aderyn hesitated. "On the other hand, orcs do magic so differently, maybe the power level isn't equivalent to our class levels, and he *is* more powerful?"

"Don't tell her that."

"You don't think it would intimidate her?"

"No, I think it would make her even more determined to kill him herself, and she might run through her reserves faster than he does." Owen grimaced. "I don't know. I'm jinxing us again."

"You said you don't believe in jinxes, so I don't either." Aderyn hugged him tightly and then stepped away. "I need to talk to the scryers for information. And then it's time to move."

CHAPTER FOURTEEN

Two hours later, Aderyn waited at the front of her army, surveying the northwestern horizon with the **<Lenses of Farsight>**. The orcs had become visible half an hour before, and they weren't moving fast, but Aderyn couldn't help herself; she watched them until her neck was sore from being held so rigidly, then she paced for a while, stretching. Then it was back to watching again.

Someone put a hand on her shoulder. "You're making everyone nervous," Owen murmured. "They need to relax. And so do you."

"I'm not nervous."

"You sure look like you are."

Aderyn lowered the glasses and blinked against the hot sunlight. "It's mesmerizing, watching them approach. Like watching ants carry sugar crystals to their nest. All right, I'll stop." With **[Amplify Voice]**, she called out, "Everyone stand down and get something to eat. We've got another hour before they're on us." She wasn't totally sure about the timing, but it would be close enough.

Soldiers settled on the ground by platoon, and some of the low-level noncombatants ran about with loaves of bread and baskets of dried meat. Aderyn let Owen lead her back through the troops to where Isold was passing out grapes and beef jerky from the **<Forager's Belt>**. She accepted a cup of icy cold water, so refreshing in the heat, and made herself relax. "I should prepare to welcome Varoun's regiments."

"Take a break, general," Livia said. "Varoun knows where we are. He doesn't need guiding, and he's not going to expect you to be right there when he arrives."

Aderyn sighed. "I hate this part. The waiting. I'm always afraid I'll lose my edge."

"Don't worry about it," Weston said. "Even if that happens, you'll find it again when you kill your first orc." He held out his tin mug for Livia to refill and shivered when the gout of water splashed his hand.

"That's true." Aderyn straightened as Suveer walked past, several feet away. Instinct got her on her feet. "I'll be back."

Suveer didn't stop until she'd called his name twice. He didn't turn around right away, so Aderyn walked a little faster to put herself in front of him, in case he changed his mind and fled. Though his chainmail was bulkier than her fine mail shirt, it fit him surprisingly well. She was used to him looking like he'd been dragged backwards through a hedgerow.

Suveer looked up when she reached him, but he didn't meet her eyes, keeping his head lowered slightly in his usual "please don't hit me" manner. His diffidence annoyed Aderyn, and she had to swallow her first three comments as being hostile. "Are you prepared?" she finally said. "Do you need anything else?"

Suveer shrugged. "Light armor is enough. I need to stay agile so I can distract Ruan's opponents with [Draw Fire]."

"I don't use that one often," Aderyn said. "Or maybe I do, and [See It Coming] obscures the effect."

"I don't know how to use that one." Suveer shifted like he was going to walk away.

"Don't know—Suveer, I know you have [Improved Assess 3]. You can figure out how any skill works by Assessing it. Is that not something you do?"

Suveer's head jerked up, his mouth slack with astonishment. "What are you talking about?"

All Aderyn's instincts tingled to the point she couldn't tell which skill was warning her or what it was warning her about. All she knew for sure was that she should be very careful in what she said next, or she'd lose a major opportunity. She wished she knew what. "I didn't figure it out for a long time. In fact, I'm pretty sure I had the ability long before I finally tried. It was mostly an accident. I don't remember whether it was one of my skills, or one of Owen's, but I was curious about it and on a whim I Assessed it. And that prompted a system message describing the skill."

"That can't be true," Suveer said flatly.

Aderyn suppressed her irritation at him effectively calling her a liar. "You can see for yourself. Are there any other skills you couldn't figure out? Try Assessing them."

Suveer's one eye narrowed, making the scar tissue over the other eye socket bunch and crinkle. He raised his hand to his left temple and snapped his fingers to bring up the Codex. Aderyn watched his lips move as he silently said, "Assess." Then Suveer stilled completely. His eye focused on the middle distance, and his lips moved again as he read the Codex.

When he finally focused on Aderyn again, his lips were trembling, but his voice was clear, if quiet, when he said, "So that's what [Compel] does. Why doesn't Assess say how to use it?"

"It's only available when you're in combat—well, technically it's available any time you're at odds with someone." Aderyn tried to sound casual. "When the battle begins today, use [Discern Weakness] on an enemy and see if there's anything different."

"So you don't want to help me," Suveer said.

"What? I just helped you!"

"You won't tell me how it works. Ruan's right, you can't stand the thought of anyone being a better Warmaster than you."

Aderyn had never heard Suveer speak so forcefully. It astonished her so much it took her a moment to understand the meaning of his words. "Suveer, that is *not* true. I don't know if all Warmasters see their skills the same, and I'm afraid if I tell you what [Compel] looks like to me, and it looks differently to you, you won't be able to use it. Ruan is mistaken. I want nothing more than for you to be a great Warmaster!"

"And that's why you didn't want us to meet, back in Ikharatia?"

"Didn't want us to meet?" Aderyn sputtered. "Ruan was the one who kept coming up with reasons to keep us apart, Suveer. Not me."

"He said you'd say that." Suveer lowered his head again. "Don't bother trying to be my friend. I don't need anyone but my brother." He brushed past her.

Anger surged through Aderyn, but that same mysterious impulse turned her anger into, "Suveer? There's something else. If you practice, you can access the Codex without words or gestures. You squinch your right eye until you see the lines. It takes time to learn, but it makes you faster."

"Why are you still lying to me? That's impossible."

"It's not a lie. I want you to believe that I mean you well. Good luck fighting today."

Suveer hesitated for a moment. Then he hurried away.

Aderyn watched him go. Slowly, she made her shoulders and fists relax. Then she walked back to join her friends, who'd all been watching their interaction. "I don't understand him. At all."

"What's to understand? He's emotionally stunted and unable to communicate well," Livia said.

"But I'm now certain that's not natural. Ruan made him that way. Suveer said Ruan told him I don't want anyone to be a better Warmaster than myself, and that I was the one who didn't want to talk to Suveer in Ikharatia. Those are both flat-out lies."

"Ruan clearly wants to keep Suveer under his control," Isold said. "He must have lied to him for years for Suveer to be that limited."

"All right, but how does that help Ruan?" Aderyn heard her voice rising in pitch and calmed herself again. "Ruan's hurting himself by controlling Suveer's skill development. Suveer said he didn't even know what [See It Coming] is, but he's good at [Draw Fire]—well, using those two skills together makes [Draw Fire] more effective as well as safer for the Warmaster! Does Ruan not care if Suveer gets hurt?"

Weston pointed at his eye. "Obviously not, if he got that scar in battle."

Aderyn shuddered. "That's horrific. It's his own *brother*."

"It's not like we care, though, right?" Livia said. "I mean, beyond the abstract caring that Suveer is a human being who doesn't deserve to be treated like dirt. We can't fix Suveer and Ruan."

"I can't bear the thought of a high-level Warmaster—of a Warmaster of any level—being so convinced he's useless," Aderyn declared.

"Watch out," Owen said. "You can't save everyone."

"I don't want to save everyone, Owen, I just want Suveer—"

"I'm serious, Aderyn." Owen put his hands on her shoulders and turned her to face him. "This isn't like Jessemia. She was just hampered by pride and foolishness. Suveer has been under Ruan's thumb for years. I'd bet on Ruan's bad treatment of him starting in childhood, even. That's not the sort of thing that heals easily, if it heals at all."

"But—"

"Your compassion does you credit," Isold said. "And we've all seen you grow as a Warmaster despite everything that said your class was worthless. It's understandable that you'd want someone who shares your class to be a true equal. But you said it yourself. Jessemia chose to change. You can't impress change on someone, particularly not on someone who doesn't believe he needs to change."

Aderyn glowered at Isold. "What's so wrong with me showing Suveer a different way?"

"Nothing, except you won't be satisfied unless that leads to him choosing that different way." Isold faced her down implacably. "You have to be willing to accept that Suveer may choose differently."

"But that's like giving up before I begin!"

"No. It means acknowledging that Suveer isn't your puppet. Or did you want to take over Ruan's role?"

Aderyn flinched. "Isold!"

"Isold, enough," Owen said.

Isold's lips pinched tightly together. Then he said, "There's only so much you can do, Aderyn. That's all."

Aderyn turned her back on him and walked away.

She didn't pay attention to where she was going until she realized the cloud of dust in the distance was growing larger. For a moment, fear thrilled through her that the orcs were nearly upon them. Then she saw banners, and the glint of sun on steel, and stopped where she was so when Kingfisher and Raven Regiments came to a halt, she was there to greet Varoun.

"Eager, aren't you?" Varoun said with a smile. The elderly general wore half-plate armor similar to Owen's and a helmet with no visor. "Everything all right? The orcs are still some distance away?"

"They'll be on us in less than an hour. We've established ourselves as I described and prepared the ground with pitfalls to funnel the orc army onto a battlefield of our choosing." Aderyn wiped her sweaty forehead and wished for cloud cover, though in the Southlands, cloud cover meant rain, rain meant a deluge, and a deluge meant swampy, muddy conditions that were terrible to fight in.

"Excellent. Have you decided on the disposition of troops?"

"I thought I should leave that to you, sir, since you know your regiments better than I do."

Varoun nodded. "Show me the battlefield."

They returned to Aderyn's army, where she flagged down a spell-slinger to cast *scry*. She and Varoun looked over the terrain and checked the position of the orcs. Aderyn pointed out where their army's traps were; they were obvious from above, but she had seen them in person at ground level and knew they were more or less invisible from that vantage point.

"Here, and here," Varoun said finally. "To attack that weak flank. Hawk, Ox, and Leopard to maintain position—let's see if we can't fool the orcs into believing you have no reinforcements."

"I agree." A little of Aderyn's good cheer returned. "Then I'll rejoin my forces, and—good luck to you."

"And to you." They clasped hands, and parted.

Aderyn found her friends where she'd left them. They sat around the magically burning campfire in silence, each of them staring into the fire or drawing lines in the earth with the sticks they used for cooking meat in the evenings. She'd forgotten her fight with Isold for the moment, but seeing them so uncomfortable brought it all back, along with embarrassment and guilt and a trace of anger at Isold for being so heartless.

"Varoun's here," she said. "We should go. His regiments are positioning themselves now."

"Aderyn," Owen said.

"Are you going to criticize me again?" she exclaimed. "How am I the bad one for wanting to help someone who's suffering?"

"You're not bad," Owen said. "Just..."

"Well? Just what?"

Owen glanced past Aderyn's shoulder. Aderyn turned to face Isold, whose face was deathly still. "I don't want to fight," Isold said.

"Are you sure? It sounded like a fight to me," Aderyn shot back.

"Aderyn!" Livia exclaimed. The Earthbreaker looked so horrified it brought Aderyn back to herself.

"You don't understand," Aderyn said, her throat aching with unshed tears. "You're my friends. I depend on you, and I trust you. But you're not Warmasters. Nobody is except me and Suveer, and Suveer is broken. I can't bear the thought that I'm the only one, don't you see that? If I can help Suveer, I will."

"At what cost?" Isold said. "Let's say Suveer is redeemable. How much of yourself are you willing to give for that redemption? Your life? Your heart?"

"That's too dramatic."

"It's entirely likely. You were nearly killed for the sake of saving Jessemia. What makes you think saving Suveer will come at less of a cost?"

Isold's point hit home. Aderyn, her mouth open, found she couldn't think of a retort.

"Aderyn," Isold said, this time gently. "We love you. We love that you have faith in people beyond what they have in themselves. But I think I speak for all of us when I say that if your quest to redeem Suveer means losing your life, we'd kill him ourselves to save you."

Aderyn's chest ached along with her throat. "I," she began, swallowed, and continued, "You don't—do you really think it could come to that?"

"Somehow it doesn't seem to have occurred to you that changing Suveer means taking him from Ruan," Isold said. "Do you think Ruan will be happy about losing his hold on his brother? What do you think *Ruan* might be willing to do to stop you?"

"Oh." Aderyn turned back to Owen. His grim expression told her he'd thought of this, too. "You're right. I didn't think."

"It's not that you shouldn't try to help Suveer," Owen said. "It's that you need to acknowledge that you have limitations. I know to you that feels like giving up, but the alternative is that you sacrifice things you can't afford to lose for the sake of someone who won't give a damn that you've done it."

Aderyn nodded. "Isold, I'm sorry. You saw things more clearly than I did. Thank you for persisting."

"I understand." Isold hugged her. "As I recall, you did the same for me once."

Weston cleared his throat. "I'm glad we didn't go into battle with that hanging over our heads, but the corollary to that is—we are about to go into battle, and we should get in position."

"I have an elementalist to fight," Livia said, cracking the knuckles of her stone hand.

Aderyn caught Weston's eye. Weston nodded slightly, as if he'd read her mind. Someone was going to have to defend Livia during the battle, because neither Aderyn nor Weston believed she would stop before she reached her limit.

"All right," she said. "Then let's do this."

They all clasped hands for a moment, then walked through the empty camp to where the soldiers were regrouping by platoon, by specialty, and by regiment. When Aderyn reached the head of the troops, she didn't need the <Lenses of Farsight> to see how close the orcs were; they were moving fast, and Aderyn's blood thrilled with the anticipation of a fight. No bannerman today; her plan required other arrangements, and worry for Emri would only slow her down.

She stood balanced on Weston's shoulders and with [Amplify Voice] called out, "This is it! Remember your part in the plan, and when that falls apart, kill as many orcs as you can!"

A roar of eager anticipation rose from the assembled troops. Aderyn dropped to the ground, checked the positions of the soldiers nearest her, and shouted, "Go, go, *go!*"

CHAPTER FIFTEEN

Arrows darkened the sky like a veil sweeping across the clouds. The orcs' front line shuddered, but didn't disintegrate. Another volley of arrows passed, and then the orc archers returned fire. Aderyn covered her head with her shield. She'd already determined **[See It Coming]** wasn't proof against a dozen arrows all aimed at different places. Nothing struck, though an arrow drove a groove through the ground near her and shuddered briefly before falling over. Around her, soldiers streamed past, running in silence now rather than waste breath shouting defiance at the enemy. Why Owen wasn't with them, she didn't know; all she knew was **[Keep Pace]** hadn't taken effect.

Then Owen grabbed her arm and shouted, "This way!"

She ran with him, pausing to defend against another stream of orc arrows, until they closed with orcs who cringed away from the light of the **<Sunsword>**. Owen fought like a demon, his sword cutting through the orc line, and in the speed of his attack Aderyn found her own attack was less valuable to defeating their opponents than **[Compel]** or **[Outflank]**. She darted back and forth, controlling Owen's targets, nearly blinded by the system defeat notices that never stopped appearing.

All around her, men and women closed with orc warriors. Aderyn couldn't afford to watch their battles, and she didn't dare notice when her soldiers died at the notched, heavy blades of orc grunts or mashers. The time to mourn was later, when they'd won.

Someone shoved her, and she shoved back, only then realizing it was a soldier's dead body an orc had pushed into her. Surprise became fury, and all her resolutions vanished as she reflexively went for the orc.

**Congratulations! You have defeated [Orc Masher].
You have earned [6475 XP]**

Snarling, Aderyn stabbed the monster repeatedly with the mystery sword until Owen dragged her away from its corpse.

"Don't," was all he said, but Aderyn knew what he meant. Don't take it personally. That could get her killed. Aderyn nodded, wiped charcoal-red blood off her hands, and returned to providing Owen with **[Outflank]**. Together, they surged through the orc army.

She realized they'd reached the dangerous right flank, where the Earthbreakers had turned the terrain into a death trap for orc riders, only when she stumbled and nearly fell into a gaping pit. With that at her back, she wiped sweat out of her eyes and surveyed the battle. None of the orc riders were visible, but she didn't assume that meant they'd all been neutralized. The furious motion of the fighting meant nothing more than a few feet away was clear.

Except for the whirling cyclone near the center.

Zothemza, lanky and pale, hovered seven feet above the battlefield, his bare feet dangling like a child's. His mostly naked body glowed with colored lights, white and green and orange and blue, their brightness almost as great as the <**Sunsword's**>. With a wave of one hand, he guided the cyclone to sweep a tight circle in front of him, tossing orcs and humans alike into the air and clearing a space. Aderyn couldn't tell what the point was until a spar of rock shot out of the ground, fast as a fist, punching Zothemza back.

"Owen!" Aderyn shouted. "Owen, that's Livia!"

Owen finished his opponent and stepped back into a defensive stance, breathing heavily. Aderyn waved at the cyclone, which now spun erratically out of control across the battlefield, and Zothemza, who pressed a hand to his chest as if that strike had really hurt. "Livia's fighting him," Aderyn said. "We have to back her up."

"Stay close, then," Owen said.

The two of them again fought their way across the battlefield, Owen turning attacks aside rather than engaging closely with most of the orcs in his way. Aderyn searched the crowds ahead for Weston, who would be more visible than Livia and would definitely be at her side. She skewered an orc seconds before someone else's sword took the creature's head off and nearly slit her throat on the backswing. "Sorry!" Ruan shouted.

Aderyn took a step back. Ruan faced off against another orc, a big, green-skinned monster that towered over him. His greatsword looked like a slash of night glittering with stars, the dark inverse of Owen's slim, curved blade. Beyond him, Suveer scuttled past into an [Outflank] position and awkwardly stabbed the orc elite a blow that glanced off the orc's rough-cured hide armor. The orc shouted and whirled to strike Suveer.

In the next second, the orc screamed in pain as Ruan's greatsword cleaved his sword arm off. Blood spattered Suveer, who didn't wipe it away. He held his ground against the screaming orc elite in a determined way that didn't at all resemble the Suveer Aderyn thought she knew. Ruan shouted and brought his sword around in a great sweeping arc that ended with the blade deeply embedded in the orc's back. The orc elite shuddered and collapsed.

The whole thing had taken only a few seconds, but it was long enough for Owen to shout Aderyn's name in panic. Startled, Aderyn turned and found herself face to face with a marauding goretusk ridden by an orc intent on running her down. She threw herself to the side, rolled, and came to her feet in time to see Ruan bring his greatsword down on the goretusk's neck, severing its head. Then Owen was there, grabbing her free hand and shouting, "Stop gawking! Zothemza's striking back!"

That brought Aderyn to her senses. She ran with Owen, this time taking the lead and letting [See It Coming] guide them between combatants. Ahead, the fighting seemed less fierce, but then she realized she was looking at an empty space that grew gradually wider as humans and orcs fled the magical battle raging there.

Livia, shrouded in the ever-shifting slabs of stone that constituted her armor, wielded an enormous stone hammer that glowed with the radiance of *stone fist*. She shouted, and the earth beneath her feet bulged and lifted her to meet the levitating Zothemza. With another cry, she slammed the elemental hammer against her foe's side, knocking him back.

Tattoos on Zothemza's wounded arm glowed orange, and the air between him and Livia shimmered with heat haze. Livia dropped back to earth and called out a few words, and a dome of earth rose up, surrounding her and Weston and Owen and Aderyn. Seconds later, the air shook with a titanic blast, and fierce heat dried Aderyn's eyes and nostrils.

"*Mass protection from fire,*" Livia said. She didn't sound winded or even a little tired. "He sure does love that attack. Fireball, or cyclone—any of those elemental blasts."

"How can you hurt him with earth attacks? He's got protection against elemental magic," Aderyn said.

"That's true. But it turns out what he does *not* have is protection from an ordinary attack that happens to be made of stone. Like the hammer. Or my fist." Livia grinned. "I'd punch him in his thundering stupid face if he'd hold still long enough."

Aderyn glanced over her shoulder as the earth dome cracked and shattered into a million ceramic pieces. Isold had just [**Coerced**] two orc grunts to fight each other and was approaching rapidly. "What if—"

Wind rose up around her, whipping faster and faster until she couldn't breathe. She fell to the ground, pressing her face into the earth with her arm curved over her head, searching for a pocket of still air. Then the cyclone was gone. Gasping, Aderyn said, "What if Isold uses [**Hypnotize**]?"

"I tried," Isold said. "It didn't last long. And the problem with [**Hypnotize**] is—"

"Watch out!" Livia shrieked. She threw herself bodily at Isold, knocking him out of the way of a sickly green blast of what looked like liquid fire. It hit the ground two feet from Isold and began smoking and emitting a stinking cloud of acid gas. Livia rolled to her feet and flung out one hand, chanting, and a hail of iron spikes flew at Zothemza, who dodged all but one. Shrieking in pain, Zothemza levitated higher.

"[Hypnotize] stops working if the victim has shrugged it off before," Isold finished. "And anything I can reasonably [Coerce] him to do will take him away from this fight and force us to chase him down."

"We've got five seconds before he recovers," Weston said. His whole attention was on the hovering elementalist. "Livia?"

"I'm fine," Livia said. "I still have half my reserves. You all watch to make sure nobody comes to his rescue." With a shout, she rose into the air atop an accelerating pillar of stone.

"I'm watching her," Weston immediately said.

"Then we'll guard you," Owen said. "I'm going to regret saying this, but we haven't seen many other elementalists today, have we?"

"Regret—"

A crack of thunder preceded the cloudless sky opening up above them. Aderyn shrieked in surprise as a fist-sized hailstone struck her shoulder. She raised her shield to protect her head and cast about frantically for the elementalist who'd created the hailstorm. Owen was ahead of her. He threw down his shield and ran through the storm to tackle an orc whose tattoos mostly glowed blue. Aderyn tossed aside her shield and ran, dodging the stones, to stab the elementalist through the heart where Owen had knocked him down. "I see," she said, panting. "More jinxes?"

Another crash of thunder startled them. Rain took the place of hail, hard, stinging, hot raindrops that sizzled when they touched the earth. Aderyn's face burned as if a thousand tiny coals scored her cheeks. She scrambled to pick up her shield as Owen did the same. Several feet away, Isold began singing, a soporific melody Aderyn recognized. She'd heard it often enough that it no longer made her feel even a little sleepy, but across the cleared space, ten or twelve orcs sagged in sleep. The burning rain stopped.

Weston shouted, "Livia!"

Aderyn tilted her head back cautiously, not wanting to take a chance on a few burning raindrops lingering. She couldn't see Livia's combat clearly, what with the pillar of earth in the way, but colored lights flashed as Zothemza unleashed the magical energy from his tattoos, and the irregular thumping as Livia landed blows with *stone fist* told Aderyn her friend was still upright.

Weston sheathed his sword and ran at the pillar. Though it wasn't perfectly vertical, it did have a steep slope and was only a couple of feet across. Weston ran up it like it was a garden path and hauled himself over the edge to where Livia stood. Seconds later, a tremendous *boom* shook the air, and Livia's pillar crumbled. Aderyn darted out of the way of the rubble. Weston landed amid the falling wreckage with Livia's body in his arms.

"She's not dead," he panted. "Ran through her reserves. And Zothemza is still up there."

Owen pushed him aside. "He's not up there. He's here."

Zothemza crouched a short distance away, in the remains of the pillar, his shoulders heaving with his heavy breaths. A few tattoos still shone, but most of the markings across his body were dark like soot. He rose, slowly, like a snake uncoiling, until he faced the friends. Aderyn took her position at Owen's side and drew her sword. Isold moved to stand on his other side so the three blocked the way to Weston and the unconscious Livia.

Zothemza's eyes were solid black from edge to edge, but he turned his head as he surveyed the five so it was clear he was examining each of them in turn. Owen drew his sword as well. "Come and take us," he snarled.

Isold took one step forward and drew breath to sing. Instantly, the tattoos on Zothemza's face blazed a brilliant green, and with a crack, the earth split open beneath them. Aderyn lost her balance, reflexively grabbed Owen's shoulder, and then all five of them tumbled into the rift.

Dust and a shower of stones struck Aderyn in the face, choking her. She scrabbled at the sheer walls of the rift, trying to slow her descent, and finally managed to embed the tip of the mystery sword into the wall and press her feet against the opposite wall, bringing herself to a halt. The earth groaned as if it was trying to close on her, but aside from a couple of tremors, nothing moved.

Above her, the sky looked like an X, one fat bright bar of sunlight crossed by a thinner one. Aderyn blinked dust out of her eyes and realized it was Owen's <Sunsword> wedged between the walls, with Owen clinging to the hilt with his feet pressed against the tiniest ridge beneath him. Again, the rift trembled, and the <Sunsword> quivered. Aderyn bit back a cry of fear. If the <Sunsword> was the only thing keeping the rift from closing on them—

—actually, that was a good thing, because with [Weapon Mastery], Owen's sword was unbreakable. They probably weren't about to die. Still, getting out quickly was a good idea.

Aderyn told herself she was not about to be crushed and carefully craned her neck to look past herself. Isold was just below her, tucked into a smaller crevice and cradling his arm like it was injured. Lower down, Weston had his back pressed against one side of the rift and his feet jammed against the opposite side. Livia sprawled across his lap, still unconscious.

"Is everyone all right?" Owen called down.

Everyone but Livia responded with some kind of "yes." Owen went on, "The battle's still raging, so we have to be smart about this. We need to get Livia out, but someone else has to be there to defend her. Aderyn? Aderyn, are you all right? Don't freak out!"

Aderyn made herself breathe normally. She glanced around again and forced a lighthearted reply. "You don't still have that rope, do you? Not in a battle?"

"Sweetheart, ever since Gamboling Coil I carry rope everywhere. Hang on."

Owen wriggled a bit, and then a length of rope dropped past Aderyn's face to dangle loosely in front of her. She tugged on it and discovered Owen had tied it to himself. "I'll go first," she said. "Then send Livia up. Then Weston, Isold, and Owen. Otherwise Weston can't give a hand to the rest of you. Don't remove the <Sunsword> until everyone's out." Her voice shook saying those final words, visions of being crushed by the closing rift fogging her mind. No. She wasn't a coward, and the rift would only kill her if she panicked.

With Owen's help and the aid of the rope, Aderyn maneuvered around her husband and climbed to the surface. To her surprise, no one had entered the empty space where Livia and Zothemza had dueled.

The fighting didn't seem as intense, either. Zothemza had vanished. Aderyn told herself none of that mattered if they all didn't escape the rift.

She helped haul Livia up and settled her safely beside the rift, then drew her sword and paced, glaring fiercely at any orc that threatened to come near. Again, none did, though a few snarled and bared their teeth at her before backing away. One more mystery she couldn't solve at the moment.

Shortly, Weston clambered out of the rift, knelt on its edge for a few seconds as if catching his breath, and then wrapped one length of rope around his massive fist and braced himself. "Isold says his arm isn't broken, but he can't put much weight on it," he told Aderyn. "Is Livia all right?"

"She's going to be pissed off about missing this."

Weston let out a bark of laughter. "She'll be pissed off Zothemza turned her own element against us." He began drawing the rope in, hand over hand.

Isold eventually rose out of the rift, one hand clutching the rope, and then Weston repeated the maneuver for Owen. Aderyn continued to pace the confines of their defended space while the men stared into the rift. "If I remove the sword, the rift will close, and that will probably happen faster than I can pull it up," Owen said.

"It's less than a foot from the surface," Weston said. "We should chance it. At worst, we'll have to dig it up, or wait for Livia to recover and shape the earth out of the way."

"If it was an enemy, I could use [**Reposition**] on it," Aderyn said.

"Let's be glad it's not an enemy," Owen said. "All right. I'll tie the rope to the hilt and... oh. I have an idea."

Aderyn listened to the sounds of Owen clambering into the rift and back out again. "Ready? On my mark—three, two, one, *mark!*"

The rope swished, and with a thump, the rift closed. Aderyn looked just long enough to see Owen cradling the hilt of the <**Sunsword**>, its glowing blade vanished.

"Ever since level seventeen, I've been able to activate and deactivate the blade with a thought," he said. "I figured, if the blade was dismissed, the hilt would be lighter and might move faster. I'm glad I was right."

The noise of battle was greatly diminished now. Aderyn sheathed her sword and hugged Owen. "We survived. But we didn't defeat Zothemza."

"No, but it looks like we might have won the battle," Owen said.

"Let me talk to Varoun. He probably knows more than I do about what happened."

But the <Farspeaker> remained clouded. After ten minutes passed, Aderyn put it away. "I hope that means he's busy with chasing stragglers. It really does look like we won."

They hurried back to the encampment, which was already busy with healing the wounded. Weston carried Livia to their tent, while Isold, who had already healed his own arm, left them to assist the Bonemenders. Kingfisher and Raven Regiments hadn't set up camp, since they'd arrived so close to the start of the battle, and Aderyn had no idea where to find Varoun.

She and Owen crossed the battlefield again, occasionally running into scouting parties searching for the wounded or retrieving human bodies. None of those attached to Varoun's regiments had seen him. Eventually, Aderyn put on the <Lenses of Farsight> and scanned the horizon. Whatever orcs had survived—and the scouts assured her it had not been a total defeat—they had retreated past the range of that magic item.

They walked to the limit of where the bodies lay, orc and human. Aderyn couldn't believe it was barely midafternoon. She gazed into the distance with her unaided eye, then took out the <Farspeaker> again. "He must be busy," she said as the mirror again clouded over and didn't change.

"There's a lot to do," Owen said. "Even if the price of victory wasn't as high as it was outside Shantos."

"Yes. We have to find some way of tracking Zothemza—"

The mirror cleared. For a moment, Aderyn thought saying Zothemza's name had her imagining his gaunt visage everywhere.

Then she realized she really was looking at him.

Zothemza's black-eyed gaze fixed on her. The tattoos on his cheeks were dull charcoal-gray and shifted as his jaw clenched. Then he let out a roar that shattered the stillness.

Aderyn shrieked in surprise and dropped the <**Farspeaker**>. It bounced once and landed face down. With trembling hands, she snatched it up, not knowing whether she feared breaking it more than seeing that vicious face again. She turned it over. Zothemza was gone. Only her own image stared back at her.

"He's got Varoun," she whispered.

CHAPTER SIXTEEN

"We don't know that," Owen said. "Maybe he stole Varoun's <**Farspeaker**>."

Aderyn gave him a sardonic look. "Varoun keeps his as close as I do. If Zothemza has it, Varoun is either captured or—" She closed her mouth tight shut on the word "dead."

"All right," Owen said. "Then we need to search for him. If we can't prove he's dead, we should assume he's a captive."

"Right." Aderyn put away her <**Farspeaker**>. "Right. I—oh, Owen, I don't know what to hope for. I don't want him to be dead, but being a prisoner of the orcs can't be much better than death and might be worse."

Owen hugged her. "Let's worry about finding out the truth first. Damn it, I wish Livia was awake. We need someone to *scry* the orcs' position."

"It's all right," Aderyn said. "We have help."

ADERYN HATED that there were fewer of the scrying spellslingers that evening than when they'd all worked together to see into the orc camp outside Shantos. Somehow, that brought home their losses more than seeing the rows of bodies lined up for honorable cremation outside the camp. She determined not to let her sorrow infect the others. She already needed them to do the impossible.

"I know seeing inside the orc camp is unlikely," she said. "But we've searched the area and we definitely have soldiers unaccounted for whose bodies we didn't find. Including Commander General Varoun. So at the very least, we need to know where Zothemza's army went, but if possible, we need to verify that our people are still alive."

"It could be that it was just Drorg's encampment that was impenetrable by *scry*," Ambor said. "There's no reason to give up before we try."

"Thank you, Ambor, that's the kind of thinking we need." Aderyn gestured to them all to sit in a circle. "Can you start by locating his army?"

The twenty-some spellslingers pulled out their scrying mirrors, all of which looked different, like they'd each found something they liked and stuck with it instead of being issued a standard mirror at the company store. Their varied mutterings conjured flashes of light here and there as they cast the spell at their own pace. Aderyn peered over Ambor's shoulder discreetly, not wanting to disturb him.

The view Ambor's mirror showed was of a darkening plain Aderyn didn't recognize. That was heartening, actually, given that the plains to the north didn't have distinguishing features and that was in itself a distinction. The view swayed as if they were looking through the eyes of a bird who'd just dived on prey, and suddenly the dark smudge of many moving bodies filled the mirror's oval.

"Anyone?" Ambor called out.

"We're looking for landmarks," a woman Bonemender said.

"They're headed northeast," said a man Aderyn couldn't see.

"I have it!" the Windwarden Jayna shouted. "Where's a map?"

Aderyn rushed to Jayna's side with a map. Jayna traded Aderyn her mirror for it and patted her sides searching for a pencil or a stub of charcoal. Aderyn looked at the mirror, but it had cleared to merely reflective silver when it left Jayna's hand.

Jayna held up a pencil triumphantly and held it hovering over the map's surface. "This is Shantos," she muttered to herself, "this is Adhiraj, this is that ridge that divides them... and here is where Zothemza's forces are." She marked a small but definite X on the map, right at the base of a line of mesas making a plateau that eventually merged with the Blighted Range.

Aderyn blinked. "But we're here," she said, putting a finger east of Shantos. "There's no way they could have gotten that far."

"I'm not mistaken, general," Jayna said, not sounding insulted. "I can't explain it, but I'm sure that's where they've made camp."

"I still need confirmation." Aderyn nodded at a stocky Flamecrafter. "You've found them, too? Where?"

"Not right there," the Flamecrafter said. Aderyn's heart sank when he placed his X only a fraction of an inch north of Jayna's. "But it's close enough."

"Thank you both," Aderyn said, cutting off the argument between Jayna and the Flamecrafter she saw erupting in the near future. "Now we need to see if we can get a look inside their camp."

But her hopes were dashed when the depressing black fog boiled up in each mirror. "Don't worry about it," she told the disappointed spell-slingers. "We know Varoun is there. This was just for confirmation."

"And to see how we can attack them," Ambor said. "That's important."

"It's not as important as locating them, which you did. Thank you all for your help." Aderyn bade them goodnight and slouched back to her team's campsite. She indulged in a little disappointment of her own. They couldn't leave their own in orc hands, and they certainly couldn't abandon the commander general of the army. But if the orcs had a way of traveling faster than humans, how could they do anything to rescue them?

Owen rose to greet her when she neared their campfire. He handed her a stick with chunks of beef spitted on it. It smelled delicious, rousing Aderyn's appetite. "I don't think I could bear to eat anything more complicated than this," she said around a mouthful of meat. "I'm hungry, but I'm too impatient for real food."

"I feel the same. Here, sit." Owen gestured to one of the little stools, and Aderyn sat and devoured her meal. Neither of them spoke. Aderyn was still mentally going over plans. The orcs had gotten farther away than ought to have been possible, but not as far as *world door* would take them, so either they didn't have Varoun's <**Wand of World Door**> or couldn't operate it. No. That mystery didn't matter now. What mattered was working out what to do next.

Weston emerged from his tent and sat opposite Aderyn. "She's sleeping. Isold wants to go back to Ikharatia in the morning, once Livia can cast *world door*, to replenish the <**Healing Stone**> and find a magical energy potion. We both agree Livia can beat Zothemza if she can extend her reserves."

"I thought those were dangerous."

"Dangerous if you drink them before you're close to your limit. Livia now knows better how to be cautious." Weston didn't look happy. "Zothemza's power is unbelievable. It could just be because his magic is different, and he's capable of different things, but watching Livia fight him... I don't know if I've ever actually felt afraid during a fight before."

"He must be going elsewhere to regroup," Aderyn said. "That look he gave us, just before opening that rift... it felt like he knew we were close to defeating him, and he chose that attack to give himself time to get away."

"I'm sure he wanted us dead, too," Owen said.

"Yes, for him that would be best, but he could have hit us with *fireball* to do that. I think he was running out of options and had to cast something that would keep us occupied if it didn't kill us outright." Aderyn set her empty skewer aside and accepted a mug of water from Owen. It wasn't icy cold, which reminded her that Livia was still unable to help them. They had no way to penetrate the fog that magically shrouded the orc camp. Which meant she should avoid any plans that depended on gaining extra knowledge.

"We have to rescue our people," she said. "But if the orcs can continue to outpace us, we'll just exhaust ourselves running after them, not to mention potentially running into their reinforcements."

"We could go," Weston said. "Just our team."

"I can't leave the army without leadership." Aderyn propped her chin on her hand and stared into the fire. She had a few competent generals who could implement strategies planned by her, but none of them were anywhere near. Rajman, for instance, was defending Tielana and he couldn't be pulled away from it. The same thing was true of General Tamil at Adhiraj. Chandar was on his way, because Varoun had said he'd contacted Chandar days ago, but Aderyn had no idea when he would arrive. And she needed to make the decision before Ananyi found out Varoun was missing and tried to pull rank to take over. They didn't need another internal battle.

"I have to find out where Chandar is," she said. "He's got to be close." She pulled out the <Farspeaker> and Chandar's coin. The surface fogged over only briefly before Chandar's face appeared in the oval. "General Aderyn?"

His voice echoed oddly, coming from the oval as well as from somewhere beyond their tents. Aderyn looked up, searching. "General Chandar, where are you?"

"Closer than I thought." The voice came more strongly now, and in seconds, Chandar himself strode through the gap between Aderyn and Isold's tents.

Aderyn put away the <Farspeaker> and went to meet him, holding out a hand in greeting. "This is the best coincidence. How did you know to come here?"

The Pathseer general clasped Aderyn's hand and nodded to her friends. "General Varoun ordered me to return about a week ago. My men and I have traveled a long way, all the way from the Blighted Range on the northwest, to find the army. Where is he? He's not responding to my communications."

"I have bad news. Varoun was captured by orcs today. They took him and several other prisoners north. It's why I contacted you. Sit, let's talk."

Chandar took a seat just as Isold entered the campsite. "The <Healing Stone> is nearly out of charges," he told Aderyn.

"Weston said you want to go back to Ikharatia in the morning."

"I do, if it won't interfere with your plans."

"Having that magic item is more important." Aderyn settled back on her stool. "General—"

"Just Chandar, when it's just us," Chandar said. "It's military tradition." He gave her a lopsided smile. "Though most military traditions are a matter of 'let's see what we can get away with.'"

"All right. Chandar, what have you learned? All of it. Varoun didn't tell me much about any reports you made. Sorry if that feels repetitive."

"Not at all. Some of what I learned recently makes my earlier observations moot, so I'd have repeated myself to Varoun as well." Chandar cleared his throat, then thanked Owen for the mug of water he handed him. "My scouts went northwest from Ikharatia to follow up on the disappearances of other scouts and smaller forces. We discovered—and killed—bands of orcs, nothing big enough to qualify as an army unless they united, which none of them did. We learned they're mostly interested in large cities, based on the pattern of their attacks."

"But there aren't any large cities out west," Aderyn said, reviewing her mental map of the Southlands.

"None as large as Adhiraj or Shantos, but there are a few that are bigger than villages. The orcs raze those if they can. Sometimes. Sometimes they leave them alone, and I didn't know why at first. But the important thing is they focus on the cities even when they're not strategically important."

"Which means Tielana could be in danger next," Aderyn said. "All right. What else?"

"We knew right away I had an opposite number. An orc who was directing their scouts and raiding parties. She's elusive—"

"*She?*" Weston exclaimed.

Chandar grinned. "We didn't think the orcs had any female leaders. In fact, we didn't know this scout commander was female until we finally had a run-in with her, on our way here. She barely looks like an orc—not bulky, not tall, more like one of those will-o-wisp monsters—have you heard of those?"

"Will-o-wisps look like female humans, slim and winged and semi-corporeal," Isold said.

"Well, she's like that, except not so tiny. Just like a small, dainty woman." Chandar grimaced. "Though no woman any man would be attracted to. She files her teeth to points and they're permanently stained with blood. I got right up close to her, close enough to smell her rank breath, and then the next moment she was gone and I was bleeding from a gut wound inflicted by her knife. Nearly didn't make it." Chandar put his fingers through a wide, bloodstained gash in his shirt for emphasis.

"She's that fast on the attack?" Owen exclaimed.

Chandar shook his head. "I mean literally gone. Like I passed out for a few seconds and lost time."

"That sounds like a Herald's skills," Isold said. "**[Hypnotize]**, or **[Fascinate]**."

"That was what Veteran Thayara thought," Chandar said. "Commander of my scout platoons. She's a talented level ten Spider and smarter than me. She hung back in that fight and watched the orc leader, learning her moves—it's something Thayara is good at. Watching, and then going for the throat."

Aderyn, watching Chandar, thought he looked more self-conscious when he talked about Thayara than made sense, but when he added, "I'd back her observations anytime, without question," the sincerity in his words told her Chandar was sweet on his scout commander. Not having any idea of whether this was acceptable in the Southlander army, she opted not to say anything.

"Once I was healed, Thayara reported what she'd seen," Chandar went on. "This orc woman is light on her feet, true, but sometimes she seems to *skip* from place to place like she has the spell, though we didn't see her use any other spells. Some of the platoons reported seeing colors and hearing bells that distracted them momentarily, and these aren't soldiers who are prone to being swayed by anything. Thayara noted that the orc had what looked like a stick she occasionally raised to her lips, like it was a pipe or flute, but she never heard a sound."

"If she's got Herald-like skills—" Owen said.

"That could mean **[Obscure]**," Aderyn finished. "But that's a skill, not magic."

"For Heralds, the line between magic and not is sometimes very fine," Isold said. "All my skills have magical effects, even though they are not spells. **[Obscure]** does not create a physical effect, but as we've seen today, orcs don't do things the way we do. It's not at all a stretch to imagine an orc Herald, so to speak, whose skills are adjacent to mine and have different effects."

"So it's possible the thing that keeps us from seeing into the orc camps is a Herald skill," Aderyn said. "How can we make use of that?"

"We did not try [Break Enchantment] on the effect," Isold pointed out. "I'm not sure it works at a remove, just as [Improved Assess 3] doesn't work on a *scry* image. But it's worth trying."

"Okay, but let's not go racing off yet," Owen said. "Was there anything else, Chandar?"

"We killed most of the orc Herald's companions before she fled. She took out far too many of my men." Chandar's grim expression made him look villainous, not at all like himself. "But meeting her gave me greater understanding of what we'd seen in our scouting up until then. Before, I'd told Varoun there was no pattern to the settlements and towns the orcs struck. Sometimes they'd raze a town completely and leave one five miles distant completely untouched. Once we knew this orc Herald existed, things became clearer."

"Was she responsible for choosing targets, then?"

"Yes, but it went further than that." Chandar had his empty mug in his hands and turned it over and over in a restless motion. "She wanted them to eliminate towns with high-level retired adventurers."

He said this so straightforwardly Aderyn felt another chill. "High level?"

Chandar shrugged. "Not by your standards, maybe. I don't know what it's like in the north, but Southlanders generally retire no later than level fourteen so they can have children before they're in their thirties. I know my parents always said they wanted to be young enough to have the energy to chase toddlers." He smiled, and looked more like himself. "So that's what I would consider 'high level'—maybe level eleven and up. I'm sure of the information. I don't know what it means."

"It means those were advance forces clearing out the serious threats," Aderyn said automatically. "They left the ones who can't defend themselves as easily for the main body of the army to destroy later."

"That's sick," Weston said. "Sensible from their perspective, but sick."

"It is." Aderyn stared into the fire, thinking. Orcs killing the bigger threats to make sweeping through the area a second time easy. Orcs taking prisoners—taking them into the Blighted Range, based on the direction Zothemza had gone. Orcs claiming cities and clearing them out for settlement.

Then it came to her in breathtaking, horrible clarity.

She held up a hand gesturing Chandar to silence. "I get it now," she said. "The orcs are looking to settle. They don't want to destroy the territory they conquer. They want to occupy it."

CHAPTER SEVENTEEN

"Settle," Owen said. "As in, *settle*? Farming and trading and living in houses?"

"Or whatever it is their society does. I doubt it's that tranquil, after what we observed in their camps." Aderyn shot to her feet, knocking over her stool. "The system said orcs hate humans for taking what they perceive as their rightful territory. This is their way of righting that supposed imbalance. And—thunderation, they don't want prisoners. They want *slaves*."

"But they can't want to enslave Varoun," Weston said. "He's a high-level retired adventurer. Shouldn't they see him as a threat?"

"I don't know. This is all coming from instinct. There's a lot of questions I want answers to. But I'm certain of these conclusions." Aderyn turned to Isold. "It's just become vitally important that we see what's going on in Zothemza's camp. Will you find the scryers and bring them here? If this works, we'll want as many on hand as possible."

Isold nodded and hurried away.

"Chandar, I didn't think to ask—are your people taken care of? Anyone injured? We have plenty of spare tents." Aderyn cringed inside at the thought of why that was.

"Yes, I noticed." Chandar looked like he wanted to know why they'd wasted time setting up tents no one would use, but either native politeness or a reluctance to interrogate his commander stopped him speaking. "If you don't mind, I'll check on them now. We have a few wounded still, nothing serious, and I'm sure a hot meal would not be rejected."

"Yes. Return here when they're settled, please? I will have new orders for you."

When Chandar was gone, Owen said, "You can't possibly have new orders unless [Break Enchantment] works. Unless—"

"I don't know yet," Aderyn said. "But I'm increasingly convinced my hunch is right, and we'll be heading into the high-risk zone come morning."

"Don't think I'm opposed to that idea, because it's exactly the kind of risk I like," Weston said, "but Owen is right. If we don't know for sure those prisoners are still alive, it turns into the kind of risk I hate."

"I agree. That's why it's still just a hunch. But Chandar showing up just when I need him? Prisoners we know we need to rescue, and not just the abstract possibility Ruan presented? The fact that we still have to kill Zothemza, and—actually, what does the [Crush the Horde] quest say now?"

They all fell silent as they read the Codex.

An army of monstrous orcs has emerged from the Blighted Range, intent on conquering the southern human lands. Destroy their leaders and push the army back into the mountains.

Victory conditions:
Death of Glasha, orc commander general
ACHIEVED Death of Ornok, second in command
Death of Zothemza, orc elementalist
ACHIEVED Death of Drorg, orc cavalry commander
Death of petite orc chanter
Destruction of Charnel Keep
Orc army retreats

Reward: [75,000 XP] plus any XP gained through actions taken to complete the quest.

"What is a chanter?" Weston murmured.

"It sounds like 'enchantment,'" Aderyn said. "Maybe it means someone who specializes in mind control skills. Or it could be literal, and she chants her magic."

"Either one fills me with dread," Owen said. "But I was serious about not making decisions until after we see if **[Break Enchantment]** works. If we do have to go into the Blighted Range soon, I want as much knowledge as possible."

Aderyn almost protested that Owen wasn't the commander general before remembering that her plan meant their team going in alone, without the army, and that made him the leader. Though "alone" wasn't exactly right, was it? It meant Ruan and Suveer as well. That thought left her conflicted. Extra hands meant greater safety, probably, but if it was Ruan and Suveer's hands, how sure could she be that they were united in intent? If Ruan had the chance to fulfil his Fated One quest, she wasn't confident he would weigh her party's needs in his decision.

Isold returned with all the scryers in tow. "I explained the plan to them," he told Aderyn, "or at least, it's my assumption that they will *scry* the camp, and I will attempt to use **[Break Enchantment]** through that *scrying*."

"I guess it's simple when you put it that way," Aderyn said. "Let's give it a try."

Owen and Weston gave up their seats so all the spellslingers could have places to sit. Even then, a few of them had to sit on the ground. None of them looked disgruntled about this. As before, each pulled out a mirror and cast the spell, and light flashed in scattered bursts until all the mirrors showed the roiling black fog.

Isold knelt in front of Jayna and gripped her mirror's frame with both hands without taking it from her. "I sense something," he said immediately. Aderyn grabbed Owen's hand and squeezed it so she wouldn't say anything distracting. "It is... actually, very like fog, but filled with corruption. Touching it will be unpleasant."

He bowed his head, though his eyes remained open. "It resists my touch the way the poles of two magnets repel one another. It feels like a game in a fog-walled maze, each of us searching to be the first to find the heart. Intriguing." His breathing was labored like he was running. "And yet you don't seem to know I am here, or if you do, you are far more clever than I imagine..."

The entire campsite was silent. Distantly, Aderyn heard the murmur of voices at other fires, a laugh, the sound of a fiddle at the edges of her perception so she almost couldn't tell if it was real or a mental trick. Isold breathed heavily through his mouth, and when he spoke, there was a rasping edge to his voice that worried Aderyn, so used was she to how melodic his voice was. "Let us see... this way, or that? I think—*hah*."

Jayna's mirror cleared, showing a close-up view of battered, filthy black canvas. The other scryers each exclaimed as their mirrors cleared as well. Isold let go of Jayna's mirror and sat back on his heels. "That is not something I want to repeat," he said. He held out his hands palm outward. Aderyn hissed. Red stripes like rope burns, some of them oozing with popped blisters, crisscrossed his hands.

"The **<Wand of Healing>**, I think," Isold said, examining his injuries. "And then I am off to bed. My shoulders and back ache as if that battle was real."

"Everybody, quick, let's see if our people are alive," Aderyn said.

Isold shook his head. "No need for quickness. **[Break Enchantment]** is a permanent effect, and after what I experienced, I am certain that barrier will not be restored until the chanter is physically present in Zothemza's camp to use her skill again."

"Then you saw the quest changed," Owen said.

"I did. I was curious." Isold drew the healing item from its sheath and passed its tip over his left hand. Thick, phosphorescent green light dribbled from it to bathe his hand in healing power. "I'm fine, Aderyn. You need to see what they *scry*."

Aderyn dragged her attention from the mesmerizing healing and stood where she could watch over Jayna's shoulder. The Windwarden had her lower lip caught between her teeth, though she was intent enough on her mirror she might not realize it. Despite what Isold had said about not needing to be fast, the view from *scry* swayed and sped along the "corridors" made by the orc tents like a hawk hunting prey.

"Check the tents," Ambor said. "We don't know where our people are being kept."

"'Check the tents,'" Jayna murmured irritably. "Flamecrafters. Always bossy." But her bird's-eye view dipped inside a tent and flew out as fast when it turned out to be empty.

The motion made Aderyn feel queasy, but she stuck close beside Jayna, her heart pounding with excitement. Isold hadn't said if the chanter, or even Zothemza, knew the protective obscuration was gone, but it wasn't hard to imagine they were sneaking through the camp invisibly.

"Wait," she said, gripping Jayna's shoulder. "It's Zothemza. I want to get a closer look at him."

Jayna nodded and returned the view to the last tent, which wasn't any bigger or more elaborate than the others. Candles like lumpy apples burned wanly at the corners of a square gouged into the earth, nearly filling the tent. Zothemza, totally naked now, sat cross-legged in the square. His lips were moving, and pale green light glowed on the tattoos across his cheeks. Aderyn couldn't tell if the glow was intensifying, but when she looked away to examine his other tattoos and then looked back, she was sure the green light was brighter.

"He's helpless," she said. "He can't possibly interrupt his, I don't know what you'd call it, his restoration? He can't interrupt that to cast a spell. Can anyone do a spell through the *scrying* mirror?"

A chorus of "no" went up from the group. Aderyn cursed. "We've got one spellslinger who could kill him through the mirror, and she's asleep." She immediately felt bad about maligning Livia, even indirectly, when she'd given her literal all that afternoon fighting the elementalist. "All right. No dwelling on what we can't do. What *can* we do?"

"I found the prisoners!" an Earthbreaker shouted. "Everyone look to the north, the big open space between a ring of tents."

The rustling of people shifting, as if searching meant doing it physically, filled the air for a few seconds, then all was still again. Aderyn nodded to Jayna, who sent the hawk flying high until the view showed the whole camp. It was smaller than it had been before, smaller by a lot, Aderyn noted with satisfaction.

Her eye was drawn to the empty space the Earthbreaker had referred to, and then the hawk plummeted and jerked to a halt ten feet above the ground. Except it wasn't empty. There were no tents or other structures, true, but it was full of people. Humans. All the ones Aderyn could see had their hands bound in front of them and wore collars attached to ropes tethered to a makeshift picket fence marking the boundary of the prison camp, as Aderyn thought of it. None of them were armored, but the orcs hadn't stripped them naked, which Aderyn counted as a blessing. If she was right, and the orcs intended to take their prisoners into the Blighted Range, every bit of protection helped.

The view tilted crazily, and then Jayna focused in on Varoun. He was bound and tethered like the others, but he knelt instead of sprawling in sleep. He was clearly awake, though his eyes were closed; his whole body was tense with concentration. Aderyn realized why. "[Escape Artist]," she said. "He's trying to free himself."

"I don't know what he can do even if he's free." Weston loomed over Aderyn, watching Varoun. "Did you see the guards?"

"No." Aderyn started to ask Jayna to move the view, but Jayna didn't need to be prompted. The hawk flew backward, expanding the view, and Aderyn sucked in a horrified breath. There were guards, yes, at least twenty orcs with much-notched swords patrolling the area, occasionally kicking any of the humans who moved more than a twitch.

There were also corpses.

Spiked poles rose at intervals along the picket fence. Each one impaled a human body, the end of the spike emerging from chest or belly. The terrible agony on each face made it clear they'd been alive for this. Blood spattered the ground around each and streaked the hair and faces of the living prisoners tethered nearest.

"By thunder," someone said weakly. "That one's moving."

Someone nearby let out a little scream, and there was a flurry of movement as the woman collapsed and others rushed to help her. Aderyn's stomach revolted. "Jayna," she said quietly, "show me."

Jayna nodded. The hawk circled the prison camp, showing Aderyn each of the tortured bodies in turn. **[Improved Assess 3]** didn't work through *scry*, so Aderyn couldn't learn the names of the dead, but in her heart, she committed each distorted face to memory. When they came to the one that wasn't yet dead, Aderyn made Jayna pause until the man's body stopped twitching. It was all she could do for the soldier.

She wiped tears from her eyes and said, "Show me Varoun again."

Varoun had stopped straining against his bonds and leaned back against the fence in an exhausted pose. "That's right," Aderyn whispered. "You know what they'll do if you make an escape and fail. It won't even be you. Watching them die in agony will be the punishment." Varoun wouldn't try to escape until the odds were better. For now, he was depending on her.

"Is she all right?" she called across the campsite.

"No," Ambor said. "That was her husband."

Aderyn closed her eyes to contain hot tears. There was nothing she could say to make that better. "Help her to her tent, and someone stay with her," she heard herself say. "We've seen enough. I wish—" She pinched her lips shut. Wishing wouldn't make it better, either. "Thank you all for your service. Rest now, and don't worry about the morning."

When all the spellslingers were gone, Owen took Aderyn in his arms and held her tight. "I'm sorry."

"For what?"

"You shouldn't have witnessed that. You're going to let it eat at you, what you failed to prevent. Aderyn—"

"I love you, Owen," Aderyn said. "But this time, you're wrong. It's true that sight was nearly unbearable, but I'm not going to let it stop me. We are going to rescue those prisoners, and we are going to kill every orc we meet. It's not about the quest anymore. It's about justice."

CHAPTER EIGHTEEN

Aderyn was alone when Chandar returned. Isold had gone to his tent looking weary, Weston had said something about checking on Livia, and Owen had gone to find Ruan and Suveer. Chandar hadn't looked haggard before, but he'd clearly gotten something to eat and his step was lighter. "Where did these tents come from? They're not military issue."

"They're produced by a magic item called the <**Soldier's Friend**>. We got it in the north, so maybe it draws on some northern design. Here, have a seat." Aderyn gestured at the stool next to hers. "We've verified that Varoun is alive, along with most of our people who were captured."

"I don't love the sound of 'most of,' but war is brutal."

Aderyn couldn't stop herself recalling those tortured bodies. "It is."

"Then, what's the plan, general?"

It was so nice to work with someone who didn't fight her on everything. "Based on your information, it's now essential we protect the cities and larger towns. We don't have the numbers to defend every small village that happens to have high-level adventurers, so I want you to work with the spellslingers at the university in Ikharatia to find ways to communicate with every town out west for evacuation."

"That's a lot of towns, and a lot of evacuation," Chandar said, scratching his beard, which looked like it hadn't been trimmed in a while. "Won't that leave those towns open to orc occupation? Since you've identified that as their purpose."

"If those townsfolk don't leave, odds are the orcs will kill them all and occupy the town anyway," Aderyn replied. "But those orcs won't want to leave a contingent in every small town they claim, because that will reduce the army's numbers. I believe if the orcs come across an abandoned town, they'll ignore it."

"Sound logic," Chandar said. "So. Get those towns evacuated. Next?"

"We reinforce our cities and the largest of the towns. That's where the orc armies will go. We can't afford to waste our energy chasing them around. Instead, we fortify places and have the spellslingers with *greater scry* watch for the orcs, then the human commanders will communicate this information with each other via <**Farspeaker**> so everyone is aware of how the battles go."

Chandar scratched his beard again. "Begging your pardon, but that's a defensive strategy."

"It is. And this is the part you're not going to like." Aderyn fixed him with her gaze. "I am going after Varoun."

"You can't," Chandar exclaimed. "Who will command—oh."

"Oh, exactly," Aderyn said. "I'm making you temporary commander general while Varoun and I are gone. You just have to execute my strategy and not flinch, and I believe you can do that."

"But it makes more sense to attack the orcs."

"I know it seems that way, but the orcs appear to have nearly unlimited reinforcements, and if we can't fight them from a strong position, they'll just pick us off in the field until we have to flee to our cities anyway. And there's more."

"What more could there possibly be?" Chandar's voice rose in pitch.

"Calm down, general. You know I'm here with my team, and my husband is the Fated One? Our quest is to defeat the orc army, and the system information suggests that if we can defeat the orc stronghold and kill key leaders of the army, we will end this war."

Aderyn glanced up at the sound of footsteps. Owen entered the camp, followed by Ruan and Suveer. "We weren't going to do it before, because I promised I'd commit to my role as second in command. But Varoun has been taken, and I believe my friends and I can rescue him and do significant damage to the orcs in the process. At the very least, we will weaken the orc armies, and then we'll need a new strategy. But for now, I need to know I can count on you."

Chandar nodded. "Of course. I'm still not sure I see how it all works, but I will carry out your orders." He smiled unexpectedly. "Fortress defense is something I'm good at."

"I'm glad. I know it seems strange, but I assure you it's the best plan." Aderyn rose, prompting Chandar to do the same. "In the morning, we'll go over things in more detail. I'll want you to have a list of cities and towns that should be fortified so we can decide on where to send troops."

"I will. Thanks for having faith in me, general."

"Call me Aderyn. And thanks for having faith in *me*."

When Chandar was gone, Aderyn sank back onto her stool and scrubbed her tired eyes with the heels of her hands. "That went well. Ruan, Suveer, did Owen explain things?"

"He did." Ruan settled on a stool opposite Aderyn, and a second later, Suveer sat slightly behind him and to his left. "Thanks for including us."

"Well, this is your quest, too."

"That you could have resolved by taking a regiment to Charnel Keep and rescuing the prisoners without us. Don't think I didn't realize that was an option."

Aderyn reddened. "I wouldn't have."

"You might. You care about others, and I know to you, people matter more than quests. But you didn't, and here we are. Owen didn't say anything about the specifics."

"There aren't many specifics right now. We know Zothemza's orcs traveled farther than marching alone would take them, but we don't know how. I'm hoping Livia can provide insight in the morning. Then, if it turns out they can keep outpacing us, we'll need something to let us catch up. That could be *transport*, or it might be <**Potions of Speed**>, or there could be something I'm not aware of." Aderyn looked at Owen. "Am I missing anything?"

"We can't get too close to the orc camp unless we discover how they keep spotting our scouts," Owen said.

"Maybe the scouts are too low a level." Suveer spoke in his usual dull way, but his speaking at all was unexpected enough it startled Aderyn as if he'd shouted.

"It could be that," Owen said. "Or it could be an elementalist spell we don't have. Or maybe it's the chanter I mentioned, the one who hid the camp interior. Whatever it is, we have to figure it out, because even at level seventeen and level fifteen—"

"Level sixteen, after that battle," Ruan said.

"Really? That's great. Anyway, even at those high levels, enough orcs can overcome us." He sat beside Aderyn. "We may end up following them to wherever Zothemza is going."

"Isn't he going to Charnel Keep?" Ruan asked.

"I... don't know," Aderyn said. She hadn't given the prisoners' destination much thought; she'd assumed her team would intercept Zothemza's army and rescue them then. "They're heading north, but I thought that was so they could join forces with another orc army and then return south. But it's true they won't want to haul prisoners with them all that way. And Charnel Keep is the one place we know the orcs have as a stronghold in the Blighted Range."

"They might split up forces," Suveer said, "send a detachment to guard the prisoners and the rest return to fight humans." He was looking at the ground, not at Aderyn, but her Warmaster instincts told her his comment made sense. She stopped herself before she could praise him. It was true, Suveer needed to gain confidence, but her condescension wouldn't achieve that.

"I think you're right," she said instead. "It might be something we could perceive with *scry*, keep track of Zothemza's progress and whether his army splits up or is joined by another. But that's another thing for the morning."

"Sounds like morning will be busy," Ruan said.

"It will. We won't be able to head out until nearly noon, I imagine. So if there's anything you need to take care of, there will be time."

"Nothing, unless you have a way to get us back to Ikharatia quickly." Ruan adjusted the lie of his sword, resting at his hip. "I would dearly love a bath."

"Sadly, that's a luxury we'll all have to forgo, since it's beyond Livia's abilities." Aderyn thought again of the <**Wand of World Door**>. She hoped it was merely captured and not destroyed. "But Livia will take Isold there to gather supplies, so if there's anything you want, let him know."

"I will, thanks." Ruan stood and nodded politely to Aderyn and to Owen. Suveer, rising half a second behind his brother, kept his head bowed as if none of them existed. "And thanks again for including us. I know this is deadly serious, but I'm looking forward to the challenge."

"So am I," Owen said.

He took Aderyn's hand and pulled her into his embrace after Ruan and Suveer left. "That was polite," he murmured. "Maybe traveling with them won't be a nightmare, after all."

"Or maybe Ruan is just waiting for his moment," Aderyn said, then giggled. "Where did that come from? I'm never the pessimistic one."

"If you're as tired as I am, it was your weariness speaking." Owen guided her to their tent. "Sleep, now. Tomorrow comes early."

"Six o'clock in the morning," Aderyn said with a yawn. "Just like always."

IT WAS JUST past eleven the following morning when Livia and Isold returned, one at a time via *world door*. Livia didn't look worn out despite having now cast the spell four times in one morning. "My resources have expanded," she said when Aderyn commented. "*World door* is still a strain, but I can feel I've got about a third of my reserves left. Just don't ask me to *greater polymorph* anyone."

Aderyn indulged the passing whim of Livia turning Ruan into a ferret and then dismissed the amusing thought. "Did you discuss our options for traveling?"

"We did. I'm sorry, but I have no idea how the orcs move that fast. Maybe it's not even magic. Maybe they just have amazing powers of endurance." Livia looked cranky, as if the orcs had personally offended her.

"And I asked about non-magical transportation for us, wagons and the like," Isold said. "There's no transportation that goes faster than a human running, at least not where there are no roads. That leaves us with magic."

"Those speed enhancers?" Aderyn asked.

"The ones we used before only last for three hours," Isold said, "and that might or might not be enough. I opted for <**Potions of Alacrity**>, which are more expensive, but last twice as long, and give the drinker greater speed than their lesser cousins. They also replenish your stamina as you run, leaving you refreshed rather than exhausted at their expiry." He handed out bulbs of thick lemon-colored liquid to everyone, including Ruan and Suveer. He also gave Ruan a few other potions and a small money pouch. "I took the cost of yours out of the money you gave me to buy what you requested. Weapon oils to enhance the damage your sword does, two <**Potions of Healing**>, and a <**Potion of Strength**>."

"We'll share our healing with you, Ruan," Aderyn protested.

"Is it wrong for me to say I assumed that?" Ruan grinned. "These are for emergency use, in case Suveer or I are out of reach of Isold and it's a critical situation." He gave one of the pale green potions to Suveer and put the others away in his belt pouch.

Aderyn wanted to ask why Suveer didn't rate extra weapon damage or a strength boost, but Isold was already speaking again. "I've also recharged the <**Healing Stone**> to full, and I sold one of the <**Everburning Logs**> we found in the Enchanterium for a surprisingly large sum. Which was good, because I needed most of it to pay for Weston's new weapons."

He unslung the narrow-bladed sword with the plain grip hanging over his shoulder and handed it to Weston. "They didn't have exactly what you were looking for, and I was told an invisible weapon that remains invisible after striking is beyond the scope of every Spellcrafter in Ikharatia."

"I knew I was likely asking too much," Weston said. "What did you find instead?" He withdrew the sword from its sheath a few inches to examine the metal.

"This is a <**Quivering Blade**>, imbued with an illusion that makes it seem to an enemy like six blades constantly shifting. It's a rapier, not a short sword, and the woman I spoke to said it is a favorite of Moonlighters and Lightfingers when paired with thrown weapons." Isold smiled, an expression that made him look ready to spring a wonderful surprise on Weston. "And, speaking of thrown weapons, I found this."

He withdrew a folded leather parcel from his knapsack and handed it to Weston. Weston weighed it in one hand, then opened it. Five throwing knives with hilts wrapped in dull red leather fit neatly in a row along the leather sheath. Weston eased one out and held it up to the light, which was dim thanks to an oncoming storm but still bright enough to make him squint. The matte-black surface of the spatulate blade reflected none of the sunlight and looked to Aderyn like it might be sucking the light into the metal.

Weston balanced it on one huge finger and nodded. "It's perfect for stealth, and the balance is odd but not unworkable. But you've got a look that says there's more."

Isold's smile became wicked. "Try throwing it at something. Not something we care about."

Weston's eyebrows raised, but he gripped the knife lightly and with a flick of his wrist sent it flying at one of the stools. "Too much spin," he grunted. "I've never—"

The spinning blade burst into flame. With a quiet *thwack*, it bit deep into the stool, which started to smoke and then caught fire.

Weston gaped. "Thunderation."

"<**Fire Dancer's Knives**>," Isold said. "I'm assured the spin is part of the weapon's balance. I hope that doesn't make them ineffective."

"Not a bit." Weston walked over to the stool, then hesitated. "How do I..."

"The Spellcrafter said just to take hold of it." Isold looked uncertain. "Now I'm not sure these were a good idea."

Weston shrugged and wrapped his hand around the hilt. The fire went out, and Weston let out a hiss of pain. "It's fine," he said when Livia exclaimed and extinguished the burning stool with *drench*, splashing Weston. "It hurt, but more like touching a hot pan than fire. Look, I'm not burned. And now that I know what to expect, it will be easier in future." Weston clapped Isold on the shoulder. "I knew letting you look was the right idea. I wouldn't have found these on my own."

"It was my pleasure." Isold closed his knapsack. "Now comes the difficult part. Tracking our foe."

"Will your map help at all with that?" Owen asked.

"Yes, and no." Isold looked pensive. "Living creatures do not show up on my system map. Natural formations do, and cities, and places within cities. But there's no way for me to identify a person, Varoun for example, and track him on the map. That would take a level twelve Path-seer, and General Chandar is needed here."

"But you said there's a way," Aderyn said.

"We have two possibilities. One is the <Wayfinder>. Since I'm sure your heart's desire is finding and rescuing the prisoners, it will easily lead us there."

"Of course!" Aderyn's face fell. "But not if we're running at high speeds. I'd trip after the third step."

"You see the same difficulty I did." Isold held up a finger. "But we have another option. My skill [Find Object] works at long distances just as the <Wayfinder> does and is only limited by my awareness of the object I seek."

"But who knows what objects those orcs have?" Livia said. "It's not as if you've seen them. I guess I could *scry* and show you something."

"No need. They will have the <Wand of World Door>, which is a thing I have observed many times." Isold smiled again. "And the item [Find Object] focuses on *does* appear on my map, so not only will I know where it is, I can plot a course that avoids any hazards or natural features that might be in our way."

"Fantastic," Owen said. "Is there anything else anyone wants to do? Then, Isold, how about you do your thing. Let's at least find out how far away Zothemza is before we swig down these potions."

Isold already had the inward-turned expression he got when he was looking at his system map. "The scryers marked Zothemza's position thirty miles northeast of here, at the base of these cliffs that run east-west, the beginning of a series of... you could call them steps leading deeper into the Blighted Range. That was last night. They have moved since then, and again they are farther than such an army should be able to move. They are now at the top of the tableland and another ten miles on in the same direction."

"Okay, we can handle that," Owen said. "The <**Potion of Alacrity**> doesn't let us leap like gazelles, does it? We'll have to climb the cliffs the usual way?"

"Sadly, it does not." Isold pulled out his bulb of yellow liquid and uncorked it. "And I believe we should go. Delay is not our friend."

Aderyn gulped down the contents of her potion bulb and gagged on the sour-bitter taste of soap and lemons. The second the liquid hit her stomach, her entire body quivered with the urge to run. "Oh, this feels strange," she said. "Like if I don't run, I might burst."

"Let's not do that," Owen said. "Go!"

CHAPTER NINETEEN

When Aderyn's foot hit the ground, it accelerated her into another, involuntary step, and then another. Suddenly she wasn't running, it was the ground flying past her as her legs kept her upright and balanced.

She barely dodged a tent and then bounced to the side to avoid running into a couple of soldiers. She had no idea where her friends were. The tents blurred in her vision as she sped past them, and only [See It Coming] kept her from tripping. How that skill continued to work when she was sure she was moving too fast for her reflexes to adjust, she didn't know, but she was grateful.

In seconds, she was out of the camp and accelerating again. Awareness that she might have left everyone else behind made her dig in her heels against the demand of the magic that she run, run, run until she reached the horizon. Slowly, she came to a halt. Fighting the quivering desire to keep going, she turned around. The others were coming up behind her, not very fast, and by the time Owen reached her, he was walking, if stiffly.

"My body wants me to run," he told her. "It's almost painful to resist."

"And I ran into several tents and knocked at least one person down," Weston said. "Thanks for stopping for us."

"That was astonishing," Ruan said. "You were a blur. Is that a Warmaster skill?"

"It's [See It Coming]. Suveer, did it work for you at all now that you know how it works?"

"Sometimes," Suveer muttered. "I didn't run into anything."

"I can't believe we didn't know about it." Ruan clapped his brother on the shoulder. "Something to practice, eh?"

Suveer shrugged. "When there's time, I guess."

Aderyn almost suggested ways they could help Suveer practice, but the urge to run had grown until it was an ache in her calves and chest. "Isold, you need to run ahead. We're following you."

"With pleasure," Isold said, and took off.

Aderyn watched him for a few seconds, letting him get a solid lead. His body did blur, though it didn't look like his legs were moving any faster than usual. It was more like his stride covered more ground, and even that wasn't a totally accurate description of the fluid grace with which he sped.

"Go!" Owen shouted, and Aderyn gave in to the desire to move.

She ran effortlessly, with no weariness or strain except the familiar tug of [Keep Pace] on her calves. Even that didn't weary her the way it usually did. Isold continued to outpace them all, which belatedly reminded her that he was the fastest of all of them under normal circumstances. Maybe they should have considered that, as well as the fact that Livia, who could run when she had to, still wasn't very fast. Aderyn thought about turning around to see if Livia lagged behind, but the sense of balancing on a narrow rope warned her she would fall if she did.

The sky darkened as they proceeded north, filling with rainclouds pushed in from the west by strong winds. The terrain where they ran was plains bordered by tall, fern-leafed trees the soldiers called palms, possibly because the leaves looked like spread-fingered hands. Bushes and tall grasses flourished across the plains, rustling loudly where the seven runners dashed through. It was impossible to see the ground, so

Aderyn hoped there wasn't anything that might trip them. Falling at these speeds would hurt.

She saw the rain falling then, a great sheet of water approaching from the left faster than they ran. Outrunning the rainstorm, that would be a story to tell around the campfire, but it wasn't going to happen. In a few more seconds, the leading edge of the storm hit, and raindrops hammered Aderyn's head and stung her face like hailstones. Instinctively, she put up an arm to protect her eyes. She took two more steps, overbalanced, and flailed with both arms, her eyes closed, to keep from falling.

Then the rain was gone, the cloudburst continuing past them eastward. They had run past the storm in seconds. Aderyn swiped water from her face. No one had fallen, though Isold had run a great circle around them as if that was the only way he could return to check on them. With a shout, Owen accelerated, and they were off again.

The speed at which they ran messed with Aderyn's sense of time passing. Had it been minutes, or hours, since they'd left the camp behind? Surely it hadn't been hours, and yet now they were approaching the tree line miles from camp and no one had slowed. Aderyn let herself run and analyzed the trees. They were widely spaced, so maybe it was possible to run at speed between them... or maybe they'd crash into the tree trunks and end their journey quickly.

Ahead, Isold had nearly reached the first of the trees. He seemed to be slowing, but it might have been an illusion, a trick of the eye created by Isold's moving form against the backdrop of still, tall trees. When he passed between two of them, he was running as fast as ever. So it was a risk he meant all of them to take.

For [See It Coming], it wasn't much of a risk. To Aderyn, the trees came at her with a surreal slowness, as if the world had slowed instead of her speeding up, and then whipped out of sight after she dodged them. And she'd been right about how widely spaced the trees were, given that she didn't hear any shouts of pain or cries for help. This was an amazing way to travel. How many miles would it take them?

She started doing the math in her head, but then someone did cry out, a shout of pain rather than fear or warning. With effort, Aderyn made herself turn and found the maneuver took her in the same wide circle Isold had run earlier, the effect of moving sideways at the same time as forward.

Suveer had fallen and lay at the end of a short groove in the earth, like his body had plowed up the ground until his momentum gave out. His eyes were closed in pain, and he gripped his ankle like holding it would make it stop hurting. Gradually, everyone returned to the spot. Isold brought out the <**Wand of Healing**>, but Suveer waved him off. "Wait a minute."

"Wait? Why?" Isold asked.

"I just—need a minute." Suveer rocked back and forth, his teeth bared. To Aderyn, it looked like he was wrestling with himself. Finally, he opened his eyes and let go of his ankle. "All right."

Isold looked as if he thought Suveer was crazy, but he activated the wand and passed it over the injured ankle. Aderyn caught the look on Ruan's face and was even more confused. Ruan looked like he was satisfied, like Suveer had done something good. So whatever that had been about, it was a thing the brothers were used to. Maybe. Or Ruan was a total bastard who enjoyed seeing people be hurt—no, that was too much even for her dislike of the supposed Fated One. She let it go. There was nothing she could do to figure it out, if there even was something to discover.

Ruan gave Suveer a hand up. "What happened?"

"I tripped."

Aderyn waited for more of an explanation, but Suveer, having said those two words, fell silent. Owen cleared his throat. "I'm amazed this is the first fall we've had. Isold, isn't there any way to control how fast we run? That could have been much worse."

"I'm afraid not. However, the speed at which we run gradually decreases over the course of the six hours. Possibly not enough of a decrease to be perceptible." Isold's eyes focused on his system map. "This belt of trees ends a few miles from here, and then it's all plains and hills until we reach the first tableland. We will simply have to take care."

"I guess if there weren't drawbacks, people would use these potions until they got addicted, right?" Owen looked like he was trying to find a bright side and didn't believe his own words.

"Using too many <**Potions of Speed**> eventually damages your internal organs, according to Mother," Aderyn said. "I imagine these are even worse."

Owen shuddered. "I'll stick to having internal organs that haven't been turned to jelly, thanks. Let's move on. We have until an hour before sunset before these wear off."

They ran through the trees with no more incidents, but Aderyn still worried about the others who didn't have her advantages. Except for the other Warmaster. She thought about Suveer as she dodged tree trunks. He'd tripped—all right, that wasn't unexpected, but as a fellow Warmaster Aderyn knew what happened if you concentrated on a skill while you were doing something else. Her guess was he'd been experimenting with [See It Coming] and missed his step, but why wouldn't he admit to that? Nobody would think less of him. If anything, her friends would be pleased that he wanted to improve his skills.

And then there was that odd insistence on not being healed right away, and the look on Ruan's face. Aderyn had no ideas about those mysteries. The brothers' relationship was too weird for her to fathom.

They all sped up after leaving the trees behind. Though the clouds occasionally thinned so the sun was brighter, it was impossible to see exactly where it was in the sky. It felt like midafternoon, though, and when she saw the distant rise of the cliff marking the tableland, it was with a sense of relief that they'd make it up the first step before sunset.

The escarpment ran for miles in both directions, its base shrouded in shrubs and bushes, its top overgrown with trees and more greenery. Aderyn slowed to a stop before she ran into it and was relieved to find stopping was easier than it had been. She looked up the cliffside, which rose a good sixty or seventy feet. "There's a bit of an overhang. Is that going to be a problem?"

"It's fine. Everyone stand back." Livia walked away from the cliff, counting paces under her breath. When she was satisfied, she took a solid stance facing the escarpment and began chanting. The words rolled off her tongue like a landslide, and then the sound of earth moving drowned her out. The ground hunched like a wave rising to meet the top of the cliff, making a massive pile of stone and dirt that backed against the escarpment. As if shaped by an invisible hand wielding a giant straightedge, steps appeared one by one, marching down the side of the hill.

Livia drew in a deep breath when the last step formed and the earth stopped quivering. "Don't run," she said. "It's sturdy, that's not the problem. But you can see how relatively narrow the steps are. Nobody fall."

"That was amazing." Ruan looked human for once, utterly astonished without a trace of arrogance on his handsome face. "I've never seen anything like it. Doria was a Tidecaller, and she was getting powerful, but nothing like that."

"I'm sorry you lost your friend," Livia said. "I've never seen what a high-level Tidecaller is capable of."

"Thank you." Ruan still looked stunned, but Aderyn had the sudden impression again that he wasn't being completely forthcoming. "We should move on. How much time do we have left? Any guesses?"

Livia pulled out her pocket watch. "A little under three hours."

"Isold, where are the orcs?" Owen asked.

"Let's get to the top and regroup," Isold suggested.

At the top, they waited for Livia to reshape the earth— "We shouldn't make it easy for the orcs to get to the bottom, if they come this way," she said—and then Isold consulted his map.

"Another twenty-five miles," he said. "They are still moving, but not faster than is reasonable."

"I did the calculations as we ran," Weston said. "We're running at more than three times our walking speed, and we haven't needed to stop for rest breaks. We can cover twenty miles in two hours, and however far the orcs move beyond that point, we'll still have a good hour to put ourselves in reach of them."

"Then let's move." Owen nodded to Isold. "You'll need to stop us before we're in sight of the orcs."

"Don't forget our speed will decrease soon, if it hasn't already," Isold warned.

"Noted. Thanks. Let's go!"

This time, Isold led them eastward along the tableland, not along its edge but close enough that the land below was visible. Aderyn marveled at the sight of the fields and forest they'd already run through. They were so tiny and perfect she couldn't help imagining herself visible at that distance. Then she considered whether orcs had anything that let them see great distances, and her pleasure died at the thought that they might have been spotted by orcs who now tracked them as they ran. It was unlikely, but she started watching the terrain around them and tensing every time they reached a spot where an ambush would be effective. But [Sense Ambush] remained dormant.

The clear terrain of the tableland became spotted with copses of trees and bushes taller than Aderyn. If any of them sheltered monsters, the monsters were intimidated by the seven humans, because nothing leaped out at them as they ran. Knee-high grass slapped at Aderyn's legs, leaving faint green streaks on the gray cloth of her uniform trousers. She'd left her coat and insignia behind, opting for a thin tunic under her mail that didn't make her sweat despite its long sleeves, protection against insect bites.

Gradually, the copses became large enough to be called groves too thickly forested to run through. In dodging the trees, Aderyn realized she had better control over her speeding body, which would have been a relief if she hadn't also realized she was slowing down. She pushed herself harder. If they couldn't find the orcs before the effect wore off, they might never catch up.

With the persistent cloud cover, darkness came early, and the sun hadn't yet dropped below the horizon when Owen waved everyone down. "We shouldn't run in the dark, especially with all these trees around," he said. "Isold?"

"We are within four miles of the orcs." Isold's body was tense but not quivering with the urge to run. "They stopped moving half an hour ago. I assume they have camped for the night."

"Livia, how much time is left?"

"Between fifteen and twenty minutes." Livia held her watch close to her eyes.

"If we run fifteen minutes, we can halve the remaining distance," Weston said.

"That might be too close," Aderyn warned. "The scouts who disappeared got at least that close."

Owen nodded. "Okay. We run another ten minutes and see where that puts us. Then we make a plan."

It was less than ten minutes before the quivering in Aderyn's legs and chest slowed and stopped. She still ran fast, but when she caught sight of Isold halted in front of her, she was able to stop without difficulty. Eventually, everyone gathered around Isold. There was almost no sunlight left. Aderyn heard nothing but the night birds calling and the whine of the insects and the rush of the breezes that always picked up in the evening.

"I hear them." Weston raised his hand as if he expected to silence the birds. "Not clearly. Shouts and the occasional laugh and some screams, cut off."

"How close can you get?" Owen asked.

"As close as you want." Weston's grin in the dimness showed white teeth against his dark beard. "And, not to brag or anything, but I'm a much higher level Moonlighter than anyone in the army. I'm not worried about being spotted."

"Let's get a little closer," Owen said. "If anything goes wrong, we'll need to rush to the rescue."

"I'm not so confident I'll turn that down." Weston gestured. "Follow me. Stay low to the ground, and stop when I do."

They crept after Weston, not very quietly. Owen in his half-plate and Ruan in his hardened leather brigandine creaked when they walked. Enough trees surrounded them now that Aderyn watched her surroundings closely, worried about stumbling across an orc sentry Weston had missed. Even orcs had to know camping near thickets of trees gave cover to the enemy. But no orcs shouted a warning.

The noise of the orc camp soon became audible, a terrible melody of harsh laughter and cries of pain Aderyn couldn't help imagining reasons for. If they were torturing their human prisoners... knowing they wanted live slaves didn't stop her picturing tortures that would keep them alive but docile.

Finally, Weston held up a hand. He beckoned them all close. "Two guards over that way," he whispered, pointing in two different directions. "Easy enough for me to pass through the gap. You stay here. I won't go far." With that, he put up the hood of the **<Cloak of Mists>**.

To Aderyn, nothing changed, but without [Truesight] his outline would have become insubstantial, not quite invisible, but difficult to see.

She watched him creep closer until he really did vanish, or appeared to—that was his skill [Hide in Plain Sight]. Then she sat back on her heels and tried to calm herself. Her body might no longer be under the influence of the <Potion of Alacrity>, but her mind still jittered as if the speed had affected her brain rather than her body. Suppose Weston did find a way into the camp? They needed a plan for rescuing all those prisoners. There were a lot of orcs in the camp, not to mention Zothemza, and Aderyn was sure Livia's reserves were too low for a fight.

More to the point, what if they rescued the prisoners now? Ruan and Suveer's quest was to rescue the prisoners from Charnel Keep, not from the orc army. She wasn't sure she could justify leaving Varoun and the others to make their way back to the camp while they went on to the Blighted Range and the orc stronghold. She mentally shook herself. Those were problems for after they'd succeeded here.

Beside her, Livia hissed. "Weston's health is dropping."

Aderyn swiftly brought up the team roster. Weston's health bar was not only at three-quarters of its normal length, it was cherry-red instead of a nice calm blue. "He's hurt. Why haven't we heard anything? If they caught him—"

"They couldn't have caught him," Owen said. He, too, was looking at the team roster, his whole body rigid as if he could will Weston to recover. "Someone would have raised an alarm."

"It's not weapon damage," Isold said. "Look at how regular that is. It's some other effect. Something that does steady damage over time."

A heavy weight landed on the ground near Aderyn. Gasping, she yanked the cloak hood off Weston's head so he was visible to everyone. His face in the fading light was red, and blisters formed all across his skin and the backs of his hands. "Hot," he murmured, and sagged in unconsciousness.

CHAPTER TWENTY

"Quick, Isold," Owen said.

Isold already held the **\<Healing Stone\>** pressed to Weston's face. "It's barely stopping the damage from progressing. Possibly he's been poisoned like Livia was in Finion's Gate."

"It's not poison," Livia said. "It's magic. Shit." She took Weston's hand and added, "He's burning up. Maybe literally."

"What do we—" Aderyn began.

"There's only one thing I have, and if I'm wrong..." Livia closed her eyes and murmured a long string of words that almost made sense. Weston began shivering as if despite the evidence he was freezing cold. Livia never stopped speaking. Her words grew more urgent, like she was arguing with some unseen person—or arguing with the magic that had Weston in its grip.

Aderyn, watching Weston's contorted red face, whispered, "It's working!" The blisters had begun to fade, and his face was more pink than red. When she checked the team roster, Weston's health bar was frighteningly low, but it was back to blue.

Livia gasped and swayed where she sat, but remained upright. "I almost didn't have enough," she murmured. "That was vicious."

"What was it?" Owen asked.

"No idea—or, rather, there's no spell that would cause it, and I still don't understand how orc spellslinging works." Livia wiped tears from her eyes. "His blood was too hot, almost boiling. He needs healing, because I doubt that's something he can naturally recover from."

Isold nodded and passed the <**Healing Stone**> over the back of Weston's neck, lifting his long hair out of the way.

Ruan was watching the still-unseen orc camp. "Those guards look like they hear something. We need to be quieter."

"They're not moving, though," Suveer said. "They take a few steps forward and then back, like there's a wall."

Owen nodded. "We need to get out of here. Is Weston conscious yet? Let's carry him."

With more noise than before, they hauled Weston for a short distance until the giant Moonlighter said, "Stop. I'm fine. You people make more noise than a herd of tessobelas." He got to his knees, looked around, and stood. "We're out of sight of the camp, but let's go a little farther. Those orcs make my skin itch."

Once they were far enough for Weston's satisfaction, Livia summoned four tents, and they all sat around the small fire Weston assured them the orcs wouldn't see. "And I'm not sure they'd chase us if they did," he said. "That was the strangest thing I've ever seen. I got right up close, close enough I could have taken out both guards without anyone noticing, and I saw they don't move. They don't walk the perimeter and they don't get too far from camp. That's all I saw before I started feeling sick."

"What did it feel like?" Livia asked.

"Like a fever, except it was painful as well as hot." Weston touched his forehead. "Painful like a burn, and inside rather than on my skin. It didn't take long to realize it wasn't my imagination, and then I hurried back as fast as I could."

"Whatever magic it was, it heated your blood," Livia said. "And the temperature kept rising. It would have cooked you from the inside if *greater dispel magic* hadn't worked."

"If it's an effect they always place on their camp perimeter, that would explain why none of our scouts came back," Owen said. "Can you dispel the effect, Livia? The trap, or whatever it is?"

"If you mean, can I do it now, no. My reserves are too low." Livia's eyes moved as if she was scanning invisible text. "If you're asking if it's possible, then yes. Probably. Since *greater dispel magic* worked to suppress the obfuscation on the other camp, it's likely it works on any orc magic. But it wouldn't be quiet or unnoticeable. We'd bring the whole army down on us."

"I hate to say this, but we have to let it go for tonight." Owen met Aderyn's eyes. "We're going to need magic, and Livia's already cast four *world door* and some other powerful spells today."

"There's no point in me scouting again, either. The prisoners are being held away from the edge of camp, so I can't even locate them for us to *transport* in." Weston ran one huge hand over his face. "The best I can tell you is there seems to be a zone affected by that blood-heating spell, and my guess is it doesn't distinguish between human and orc."

"They'd risk killing their own people?" Isold said.

"Our army sets a perimeter guard to watch for deserters in addition to enemies," Aderyn said. "I guess it's not too much to imagine the orcs would be more punitive about it."

"Then we wait until sunrise, and try again," Owen said.

ADERYN'S mental agitation followed her into her dreams, where she saw rows upon rows of impaled men and women, all of them struggling to speak to her. She woke grateful for her turn at watch, and at its end almost asked Weston if she could stay to watch with him, afraid of what awaited her in sleep. But she decided that was the act of a coward, and in the end, she slept peacefully.

In the morning, they ate cold rations. "We don't know how good an orc's sense of smell is, and the wind is blowing in their direction," Weston had said. Aderyn didn't mind. She was eager to be on the move, whatever that ended up meaning, and cooking took too much time.

She didn't let herself dwell on how many orcs were in the camp. There was no way her team could attack directly. What she hoped for was seeing something in daylight that would suggest an alternative. Livia *burrowing* up into the middle of the prisoners' space, or Isold putting a dozen orcs to sleep, for example. Surely a better view would give her Warmaster's vision ideas.

Once they broke camp, they walked back toward the orcs' encampment, stopping when Weston said, "This is as far as you should go. I'll scout around and see if there is a better hiding place elsewhere."

"I'll *scry* to make sure our people aren't—" Livia cut herself off and pulled out her mirror.

Aderyn watched Weston go instead of looking at the *scrying* mirror, but when the others began muttering, she whispered, "What?"

"All the elementalists are gathered in one place," Isold said. "There is a line gouged in the turf, and they are spread out along one side of it."

Aderyn maneuvered to get a glimpse of the mirror and ended up between Suveer and Ruan. The view from *scry* showed a line of nineteen elementalists standing with their backs toward Livia's viewpoint. Colored lights outlined the tattoos over their bodies. None were as heavily tattooed as Zothemza, who was not part of the line, and every one bore an identical tattoo that glowed with white light, brighter than the others. Though they were naked except for loincloths, Aderyn couldn't tell if any of them were female. It didn't matter except to satisfy her curiosity. Male, female, they were all viciously intent on destroying humanity.

One thing Isold hadn't mentioned was that there weren't any tents pitched. The ground was disturbed as if there once had been structures to flatten the grass, but nothing remained.

"Draw back farther," Owen said, but the viewpoint was already moving, backing up to show more of the space. More orcs became visible, all of them armed and armored as if ready for battle. "Why are they all behind the elementalists?" she murmured.

"It's like they're waiting for something," Ruan said.

Before Ruan finished speaking, the air along the groove in the earth shimmered, and a second line of orc elementalists appeared. Aderyn gasped. "Did they just *transport* reinforcements here?"

"I don't think so," Isold said. "Those are reversed images. I believe they turned the air into a mirror."

Distantly, Aderyn heard the high-pitched whine of a mosquito, but too loud to be just one. The sound grew in intensity until it hurt her ears. "What *is* that?"

Isold tilted his head. "It sounds like a child crying."

"No, it's that sound you hear when everything is totally still," Ruan said.

"I hear insects whining," Aderyn said.

"Hush, everyone." Owen's head was tipped back, and he was searching their surroundings. "It's coming this way, whatever it is."

With a titanic crack like the snap of a gigantic whip and a boom that shook the trees, a wave of sound struck them, knocking everyone but Livia down. Livia's feet were half-buried in the soil, anchoring her, and her attention never left the mirror. "Something else is happening."

Aderyn got to her feet and looked at the mirror over Livia's shoulder. The air mirror was more obvious now, extending twenty feet above the ground. It still reflected the elementalists, but the reflection was skewed sideways, as if some force had shifted the mirror a foot to the left and taken the reflections with it.

All the elementalists stepped back. The white-glowing tattoos had turned charcoal-dark. One of the elementalists suddenly swayed and fell in a heap beside the line. The others ignored him. Aderyn held her breath. Something else was about to happen, she was sure of it.

Zothemza came into view from the right. He wasn't levitating this time; he walked with a slight limp, and his long arms swung loosely from his shoulders. A loose drape of patchy fur hung around his neck, obscuring his back, but Aderyn remembered it was as tattooed as the rest of him.

The orc elementalist leader walked along the line, ignoring the others, who all stood at attention until he was past and then relaxed as if they'd survived an ordeal. When Zothemza reached the fallen orc, he stood over him for a few seconds. The orc twitched, then reached out a shaking hand to Zothemza, who gripped the male's wrist rather than his hand.

The fallen orc jerked, his back arching like he was trying to get away from some terrible pain. Then he went into spasms, jerking and twisting and kicking. Zothemza never let go of his wrist and didn't react to the thrashing orc, not even when the orc's foot caught one of Zothemza's skinny, bare legs. Gradually, the orc's tattoos glowed brighter, all of them becoming so bright Aderyn had to shield her eyes, until with a flash the lights pulsed once and then vanished. The orc slumped motionless, all his tattoos dark. Zothemza cast the orc's arm away contemptuously and continued his slow march along the line of elementalists.

"His tattoos are brighter now," Suveer said. He didn't sound as if he cared much about Zothemza's tattoos one way or the other.

"Like he drew the power out of that other orc," Owen said. "That could be a problem."

"You mean, if he can regenerate his power during battle?" Livia sounded annoyed. "We might end up fighting forever."

Aderyn didn't point out that Livia only had one magical restoration potion. "We can't worry about that now. What was the point of that spell, or whatever you call the orc magic?"

"I'm calling them spells because orcs aren't worth the mental space it would take to come up with something original," Livia said. "And— huh. Look at that." In the scrying mirror, Zothemza had finished his "inspection" and his lips moved in speech. With a lurch, all the elementalists stepped forward, into the mirror wall—and vanished.

"Oh," Livia said. "Oh. I think I see—no, wait, look at what the others do."

More orcs surged forward. Aderyn couldn't Assess them through scry, and the orcs didn't have anything so formal as uniforms, but she'd begun to be able to recognize the subtle distinctions between grunts and mashers and elites. These were grunts, and they moved without hesitation into the mirror wall. They, too, vanished.

"I have a very bad feeling about this," Owen said.

"Me, too," Livia said. "I think we just found out how they move so fast."

"How far can they go using that... that spell?" Ruan asked.

"No idea." Livia shrugged. Her attention was still on the mirror.

"We may not learn that until the <**Wand of World Door**> is taken through," Isold said.

Another wave of orcs passed through the mirror wall, then another, and finally— "There they are!" Aderyn exclaimed. The human prisoners were now roped together in a long line, and their hands were still bound and they looked like they'd slept rough, but none of them appeared seriously injured or walked slowly. Varoun was in the middle of the group, his head held high as he surveyed his surroundings. He had a black eye, and traces of blood matted his white hair, but he, too, seemed otherwise unharmed.

"I suppose it was too much to hope they'd leave them behind," Livia muttered.

"If they left them behind, they'd leave corpses," Owen said bluntly. "Where is Weston? He's got to have seen this."

"Probably observing from a different vantage point." Aderyn watched until no more prisoners passed through the mirror wall, and more orcs took their place. She counted until the number became depressingly high, then waited until everyone but Zothemza had vanished. The elementalist leader slapped the wall three times, sending shuddering ripples through it like it was water and not magic, and stepped through. The moment he was gone, the wall shattered with a shriek like a baby's cry of extreme pain, the shards scattering in every direction.

Livia dismissed *scry* and put the mirror away. "Weston! Come on, there's no one left."

They joined Weston on the far side of where the orc encampment had been, near a tangle of earth and broken tree limbs. "This is where they were keeping the prisoners," he said.

"How can you tell?" Ruan sounded skeptical.

Weston knelt and dug at the base of one of the tree limbs that was embedded upright in the earth. "This is what's left of the, um, corral where they kept them, and *this* is what Varoun left us." He displayed a coin-sized emblem that glinted like gold.

"His general's insignia," Aderyn said. "I'm amazed he was able to hide that. I didn't think Moonlighters had that skill."

"No, but we are a sneaky lot, and Varoun is a wily old Moonlighter who knows more than just the skills his class grants him." Weston beamed as if the compliment was directed his way.

"That means he knows someone would come after them," Aderyn

continued, "and in case they couldn't *scry*, this would tell them he, at least, is still alive."

"But we don't know where they are," Ruan said. "Do we? Where's the wand now?"

Isold examined his map. "They are ten miles east and north of here, and on the move."

"If they do that every day, we'll never catch up," Ruan said.

"We are not giving up," Owen said. "It will mean a long day with few breaks, but we can catch them. And while we walk, everyone's going to think about ways to rescue our people, okay? This isn't impossible."

Ruan looked like he wanted to argue the point, but he subsided. Aderyn glanced at Suveer, who didn't seem to be paying attention to anything but his boots.

"Look at this," Livia said. She stood some distance away, examining a blackened strip of earth. A dead orc lay curled up beside it. "This is the fellow Zothemza killed, or sucked dry, or whatever. And this is what happened when they cast their spell." She looked about three seconds away from vomiting.

"What is it?" Weston asked. "You look almost as bad as this fellow does."

"You can't sense it. The earth is dead," Livia said. "Worse than dead —more like it's been violently stripped of every living part of itself. No wonder it screamed. I can't—" She turned away, covering her mouth.

"The system said orc magic is unnatural, like it hurts the earth," Aderyn said. "I didn't realize that was literal."

"I wonder," Owen said. "None of the orc armies we faced did this. It wasn't until Zothemza had to bug out—I mean, flee, that his elemental- ists pulled this stunt. If it's not something they can use regularly, we might not be as bad off as we thought."

"We need to go after them," Livia said. "They can't be allowed to do this. No evil should persist this long. I want all of them dead."

"I have a path to where they are," Isold said. "We should start walking."

Aderyn looked once over her shoulder at the remains of the orc camp. Livia was right about not letting evil walk free.

As an experiment, she tried to summon up a different perspective, seeing things the orc way. They were banished to the Blighted Range, which couldn't be easy; everyone hated them; they just wanted to settle like humans did. None of it could overcome her memories of the men and women murdered cruelly just to keep the other prisoners cowed. It couldn't stop her remembering how brutally orcs had killed soldiers in battle. For once, her famed compassion had a limit.

CHAPTER TWENTY-ONE

Compared to the ease with which they'd traveled the day before, this morning felt like slogging through mud. The ground was clear enough, and the rainstorm they'd encountered the other day hadn't reached this far north, but moisture saturated the air and the sun beat down on their heads with unrelenting pressure. After a few miles Aderyn bore an irrational resentment of the sun. It was doing this on purpose to slow them.

Around noon, when they stopped for a short rest and something to eat, Isold said, "We are not making good progress. I think we should alter course to take us more frequently beneath the trees' shelter. It will make the route a mile or two longer, but we will move more rapidly."

"I love this idea." Owen pushed his sweat-darkened hair back from his face. "Do I want to know how far ahead the orcs are now?"

"Fifteen miles or so in a direct line." Isold focused on his system map. "They are not moving rapidly. After that initial leap forward, their progression has been normal for a large body of men—orcs, that is. We can still catch up to them by nightfall if we press on."

"And do what?" Ruan asked. "Do we have a plan? I'm not really the cunning sort."

"We either have to deal with that spell barrier, or bypass it,"

Weston said. "If they continue to put the prisoners in the same general area within their camp, it's close enough for Livia to *transport* in."

"But there are at least fifty prisoners," Livia said. "I can't take that many all at once. I'd need at least six *transports*, and that's not counting taking myself back in every time. I could do it, but I wouldn't be good for anything else."

"I could use [**Sleep**] to clear a path, but that still doesn't resolve the issue of the trap," Isold said. "Livia, you said you could neutralize it, but it would be noticeable."

"Specifically, those elementalists would sense it," Livia said. "It's not a situation like when I cast *greater dispel magic* on the orc camp before. Then, they noticed it, but it didn't matter because we weren't trying to sneak in. And, speaking of noticeable, *transport* is loud."

"I think we're going about this the wrong way," Owen said. "We've established that we can't do this without alerting the camp. We need to forget about sneaking. We should make an attack while they're on the move."

"Did you see how many orcs there are?" Ruan said. "I don't know about you, but I'm not so confident in my ranks in [**Superior Weapon Proficiency**] that I'm willing to take on even part of an orc army, even with all of you going along."

"We're not going along with you, you're going with us," Weston said irritably. "And I'm not sure it's a terrible idea. If we're going to make noise anyway, it should be when we have the greatest advantage. Alerting the orc camp when Livia dispels the blood-boiling magic is like throwing that advantage away."

"Aderyn? What do you think?" Owen asked.

Aderyn nodded. "You're right. We need to ambush them. But based on what Isold said, we won't be able to catch up to them before they make camp. Right?"

"That's my estimate, yes."

"Then how are we supposed to ambush them?" Ruan asked.

Aderyn looked at Suveer, who for once seemed to be paying attention. "We keep going until we're past them, and set our ambush along tomorrow's march route. Right, Suveer?"

Suveer shrugged. "It makes sense. Otherwise we just keep chasing them."

"But they're going to leap forward in the morning," Weston said. "I'm all for setting a trap, but there's no way we can travel that far and still be functional the next day."

"Then we keep going after them and make a new plan," Aderyn said, "but I have a feeling they won't try that trick again, because they think they have a lead no one can overcome. They don't have any reason to believe someone's following them, so they aren't in a hurry. I think this will work."

"Then we'll do that," Owen said. "And we'd better speed it up."

"Hold on," Ruan said. "Shouldn't we all agree?"

Owen met Ruan's gaze and held it. "You're not a member of our team, so I'm sure to you that makes sense. But the way it works is, we discuss, and I decide, because the thing *we* agreed on is that I'm the leader. And as long as you're traveling with us, I expect you to abide by that. We can't afford to have us all haring off in different directions. If you're not okay with that, you should leave now, no hard feelings."

Ruan returned his steady gaze. For a few seconds, he said nothing. Then he said, "That makes sense. But I expect to have an equal say in the discussions."

"You and Suveer both. Fair enough," Aderyn said.

"If we're agreed, then—let's move," Owen said.

Their route took them through terrain bumpy with rises that weren't tall enough to be considered hills. Despite the constant up and down motion, the afternoon's trek was easier, though Aderyn thought that was as much because they had a clear plan as that Isold's new path kept them under the trees' shade almost all the time. A breeze picked up in the late afternoon, cooling them further, and by sunset Aderyn was as close to comfortable as she'd yet been in the Southlands.

She spent the afternoon running through possibilities for ambushes, though there wasn't really any point to doing that when she hadn't seen the terrain. It gave her something to focus on. So when Owen said, "Am I turned around, or have we been going south?" she was surprised to discover the setting sun was on her right and not her left.

"The orcs turned south at midafternoon." Isold focused on his system map. "I took us in a diagonal path to shorten our journey, and then south to parallel their progress. We are now a short distance ahead of them and a mile to their right. I judged it better for us to stay well out of range of any scouts they might have."

"That's great," Owen said. "Aderyn, how far ahead should we go?"

"We need to find a place between these hills that's narrow but doesn't obviously look like a trap." Aderyn surveyed the land ahead. "Somewhere with plenty of trees for concealment. I really wish [Improved Assess 3] could Assess terrain!"

"Don't worry about it. Between you and Weston, we should be in a great position." Owen took her hand. "Let's go until we lose the light, then set up camp. It might not be our ideal spot, but we can always find that in the morning."

"If I cast *darkvision* on everyone, we can go until we find what Aderyn described, and no worries about the light," Livia said.

"That's better. Okay, let's find a good camping spot."

Another thirty minutes of walking brought them to a copse halfway up a hillside. Livia set up camp to the south of the copse as Weston suggested, putting the trees between them and the orcs, "just in case," Weston said. No one argued with him.

Aderyn spent her turn at watch again going over possibilities, considering her teammates' skills and spells and her own abilities. Since *darkvision* had worn off before her watch, she even tried using the <Lenses of Farsight> to look at the terrain ahead. The world remained as dark as ever. Suppose she used those with the <Cat's Eye Goggles>? When she woke Weston for his turn at watch and proposed it, Weston eagerly agreed. Sadly, wearing the two together just produced a lot of green lines scattered across Aderyn's vision like a loose handful of straw. She conceded defeat and went to sleep.

Weston woke everyone before dawn, even Livia, who was surprisingly alert. With the wind in their favor, they had a hot breakfast of porridge with honey. Aderyn ate rapidly, not really tasting her food. She didn't love porridge at the best of times, but now it was welcome fuel for the task ahead.

The sun had barely risen when they broke camp and headed south. "Not too far," Isold warned, "because they might still change direction.

We can't take things for granted and be unable to adapt to new circumstances." Aderyn took his words to heart. She noted three possible ambush locations and pointed them out to the others. "Suveer? Do you agree?"

"I'm not that good at analysis," Suveer said in his usual dull way.

Aderyn's patience snapped. She made herself take a calming breath, then said, "If you don't practice, you never will become better. Take a look and let your instincts work for you."

Suveer tilted his head to look directly at her. She'd noticed over the days they'd spent together that this was his habit, turning his one good eye to focus on whoever he was addressing. In the corner of her vision, she caught Ruan watching them both, but she didn't want to lose Suveer's attention by seeing what Ruan thought of this.

Suveer looked past Aderyn at the hills and trees. "I don't know what's good," he began, but before Aderyn could lose her temper completely, he added, "because I don't know everyone's skills. If the Moonlighter can use [Hide in Plain Sight], that's a different strategy than if he has to find a hiding place."

"That's right," Aderyn said, as straightforwardly as she could so she didn't sound patronizing. "If you Assess each of us, you can start to put a plan together. We can work on strategy, you and I."

Suveer shrugged. "I don't like to Assess people without their permission. It's rude."

Aderyn didn't agree, since Assessing people without them knowing had saved her team's lives more than once, but she decided not to react as if Suveer had called her rude as well. "I think everyone here is fine with you Assessing them, given that we all have to work together. Start with me, and we'll go from there."

"The orcs still have not moved," Isold said. "We have some time."

An uncomfortable silence fell as Suveer stared at everyone in turn. Ruan sat on the ground and went over his greatsword, examining the blade for flaws. Owen straightened his armor across his shoulders like it didn't sit right. Finally, Suveer said, "You all have a lot of skills. [Combat Momentum], that's where your damage increases if you keep hitting targets, right?"

"That's right," Owen said, glancing at Aderyn in a way that [Read

Body Language] said wanted to know if Aderyn had told Suveer this. Aderyn shook her head, the tiniest movement.

"Sounds powerful," Suveer said, and lapsed back into silence.

When it became clear Suveer didn't have anything else to say, Owen said, "Isold?"

"Still no movement. Perhaps Aderyn could go over the strategy?"

Aderyn cleared her throat. "We'll want to take them from behind. Start with Livia's attack—*hungry pit*, or *move earth*, whatever suits the terrain. Then Isold uses **[Mass Sleep]** to eliminate more orcs. The idea is to clear a path to the prisoners. Do you agree, Suveer?"

Suveer shrugged. "That will work. The prisoners will either be near the rear or toward the middle, because driving them out in front would be stupid even for orcs."

"I understand," Weston said. "We make it possible for them to flee. They're all adventurers, and unless some of them are severely wounded, they won't hesitate to take advantage of a distraction. Especially since I'm betting Varoun has prepared them for some kind of break for freedom."

"Exactly." Aderyn pointed at the narrow space between the two closest rises. "Let's say this is where we attack. Livia and Isold, up here, then Weston, Ruan, and Suveer on one side and Owen and me on the other."

"All right," Ruan said, "but the orcs aren't going to stand still for us, and that Zothemza is definitely not going to wait around to be attacked. Then what?"

"Then I kick his ass," Livia said. "I know his preferred spells now, and I'm ready to renew my resources. I'm not superstitious about saying he is going down today."

"Like Weston said, we focus on clearing a path for the prisoners," Aderyn said. "We help anyone who can't move quickly and encourage the others to run. Get them away and to safety, and discourage the orcs from following us. If Zothemza is dead, that should be easier, so if you get a chance at him, take it."

"Right. I'm not going to be put out if I don't deal the final blow," Livia said. "Not much, anyway."

Isold stiffened. "They're moving. And they're headed this way. No great leaps forward, either. Good guess, Aderyn. By my estimation, they'll pass, hmm, almost directly through here. Perhaps a quarter mile to the left."

"Move quickly, then," Owen said

It took almost no time for Aderyn to choose a good place for an ambush and for Weston to conceal all of them. Then they waited. Aderyn, for once, didn't have sweaty palms. In the shade of the tree where Weston had put her, she didn't even feel overly warm. Tension gripped her, but it was a good kind of tension, the anticipation of doing something exciting and dangerous. She watched the northern approach through the <**Lenses of Farsight**> and occasionally spoke to Owen with [**Bonded Mind**]. He was just far enough away and out of sight for the skill to work.

Still nothing, she told him.

Relax. They'll come soon enough.

I am relaxed. That's not true, I'm tense, but in a good way.

I get that. Do you think Suveer is getting better? At his class?

The abrupt change of topic startled Aderyn. *I'm not sure. He seems more willing to use his skills, but he's still reticent. I don't know if that's an improvement.*

And he still looks to Ruan all the time. Did you notice? He glances at Ruan every time you tell him to do a Warmaster thing.

Aderyn hadn't noticed this, but then she never looked at Ruan if she could help it. He might have changed his behavior, but she remembered him swinging a heavy stick at her face and wasn't totally convinced. *I wish—never mind.*

I know. It's all right. You wouldn't be who you are if you didn't want the best for others.

Aderyn smiled. *I love you. Thank you—oh! I see movement.*

She leaned forward, though this did nothing to bring the orcs into clearer sight. All she saw was a small cloud of dust and purposeful movement, not the randomness that would mean a herd of animals. In a few minutes, small figures became clear, and soon Aderyn had to remove the glasses because they were confusing her sense of distance. *Another five minutes,* she told Owen.

Understood. We're ready.

Aderyn loosened her mystery sword in its scabbard, thankful for dry palms. She didn't have any way to tell time, and "five minutes" was a guess, but her plan didn't depend on exact timing in that way. Soon, the sound of marching boots was audible, and then the first wave of orcs had reached Aderyn's hiding place and was passing without any sign they knew something was wrong.

She continued to watch, this time looking for Zothemza. He marched near the front, as heavy-footed as the others despite being barefoot. His body glowed with brilliant colors, white, orange, blue, and green, and despite his near-nakedness and the slump of his shoulders, Aderyn would never have taken him for anything but their leader.

More orcs passed. Aderyn Assessed the group as soon as she could see most of it all at once. Five hundred forty orc grunts, three hundred and seven orc mashers, eighty-two elites, thirty-three elementalists. It was still a good thing her group didn't intend to fight this lot, but their numbers were far smaller than she'd anticipated. Her army had done some serious damage before Zothemza had retreated. No orc riders, though?

Aderyn's first feelings of gratitude that they wouldn't have to deal with cavalry were overridden by suspicion. All her instincts told her something was wrong. Where were the orc riders? They hadn't dispersed when Owen killed Drorg, because she'd seen them in the later battle, so it wasn't as if they wouldn't fight without their leader. And she was sure Zothemza had had orc riders when he retreated.

She surveyed the army, searching for clues. Small numbers, no riders...

And then she realized what else was missing.

Owen! she called out with **[Bonded Mind]**. *Owen, we have to—*

A tremendous *thump* of moving earth filled the air, and at the rear of the orc army, dozens of orcs shouted or screamed in terror as *hungry pit* devoured them. The high, soporific voice of Isold's flute soared over the noise, and another few dozen orcs sagged in sleep.

Aderyn shot to her feet and stumbled down the hill, waving her hands even though it was too late. "No!" she shouted. "The prisoners are gone!"

CHAPTER TWENTY-TWO

"What?" Owen shouted. "Aderyn, come back!"

Aderyn glanced over her shoulder. Owen raced from his hiding place, stumbling along in a way that told her [Keep Pace] was working. "No prisoners!" she shouted. "We need to fall back—"

The earth swayed and rose in a giant wave, and Livia rode down its side to reach Aderyn. "What did you say?"

Aderyn wanted to scream with frustration. "The prisoners are gone. They left them, or killed them—I don't know, but we need to get out of here!"

Livia pushed Aderyn down, and suddenly the sun was gone, blacked out by a dome of dark earth that shuddered as something struck it a powerful blow. Dry heat made Aderyn's eyes itch. "It's too late," Livia said. "I can't get us all out of here with *transport*. The only way out is through. Go find Owen—I'll take care of this thundering bastard!" The dome cracked, and Livia rose out of it on a pillar of stone, chanting words that made her stone fist glitter with magical force.

Aderyn got to her feet, staring at Zothemza. He once again floated above the earth, his tattoos glowing with unearthly light. Livia shouted again, and [Elemental Hammer] appeared in her right hand. She swung a mighty blow at the elementalist's head that bounced off an invisible barrier that shimmered green when the hammer struck it.

Someone grabbed her around the waist. "You're going to get killed," Owen exclaimed. "We have to stop the other elementalists from joining in the fight. Killing Zothemza is the only way out now."

Aderyn drew her sword. "I'm with you!"

Together, they waded through the melee. The other elementalists glowed as Zothemza did, though not so brilliantly, and the light made them excellent targets. As she and Owen fought their way through the orcs, the part of Aderyn that was always watching and evaluating her opponents noted that each orc fought independently, no group tactics, no fighting back to back. It was something she could tell the others to make use of later, but for now, all it meant was that none of the fighters defended the elementalists, and when she and Owen avoided their magic, they were easy to kill.

She stopped noticing the system defeat notices after a while, ignoring them in favor of keeping an eye on her team's health bars, which dropped and rose and dropped again. In her preoccupation, she shrieked when Weston grabbed her arm and said, "Livia's flagging."

Owen continued to fight the orcs that approached, but Weston and Aderyn stood in a rare pocket of quiet in the middle of the battle, as if the orcs didn't want to get too close to their leader even when he wasn't turning his power on them. Livia hadn't stopped pounding on Zothemza, but Weston was right; she looked tired.

"Drink it," Weston urged quietly. "Don't wait. Drink it now."

"She can't," Aderyn said. "He's waiting for a crack in her defenses. If she stops to drink a potion, he'll kill her."

Weston cursed. He drew a red-hilted knife from the sheath across his chest and took aim. As the <Fire Dancer's Knife> spun away from his fingers, it caught fire and flew like a tiny star to carom off Zothemza's spindly chest like bouncing off stone. Zothemza glanced after it contemptuously. "No!" Weston shouted.

Aderyn kept him from racing up the pillar of stone Livia stood on. "It worked! He's distracted!"

An empty glass bulb, tinted pink from the remains of a red potion, landed on the ground at Weston's feet. Livia stretched, apparently ignoring Zothemza. The orange tattoo on the elementalist's belly grew blindingly bright, and heat radiated from it strongly enough that Aderyn felt it from fifteen feet away. "Livia, watch out!"

Livia chanted something and waved a hand, a dismissive gesture. The familiar dome of earth bulged upward, but instead of protecting Livia, it surrounded Zothemza in a sphere of earth and stone.

A muffled *thump* shook the sphere, which turned briefly glassy like brown ceramic. Seconds later, it cracked into a million shards, and Zothemza, blazing with white light, emerged from the ruins. Wisps of smoke from the contained *fireball* rose from his body, but he looked furious rather than afraid. The look lasted for a fraction of a second. Livia's [**Elemental Hammer**] struck his head so hard Aderyn heard bone crack.

For a moment, Zothemza hung in midair, his head lolling as if he was unconscious. Then he dropped, landing amid the shards of the earth dome without trying to stop himself. With a rumble of earth, Livia's pillar retracted, and she stepped off, cautiously approaching her enemy.

"Livia, let me finish him," Weston said.

Livia waved him off. "He's dead." She raised her stone left fist as if despite this assertion, she wasn't sure.

White light surged across the top of Zothemza's bald head, and Livia took a step back, clutching her throat. Her eyes bulged, and her mouth opened and closed, straining for air. Weston leaped forward, but Livia released her throat and waved him off. She made a quick motion with both hands, drew in a deep breath, and suddenly it was Zothemza grabbing his throat like he couldn't breathe. Livia stood over him, watching his thrashing grow steadily weaker, until every tattoo on the elementalist's body went dark.

Congratulations! You have defeated [Zothemza, Orc Leader]. You have earned [18,750 XP]

"[**Counterspell**]," Livia said. "I didn't know it worked like that."

"It saved your life," Weston said, gathering his wife into his arms.

"I know. I'm grateful. That gives me ideas." Livia hugged him briefly, then stepped away, hefting her [**Elemental Hammer**]. "Dearest, lift that body where they can see it, all right? And Aderyn, get their attention."

Weston made a face, but he grabbed Zothemza's body around the neck and held it high. Aderyn shouted with [**Amplify Voice**], "Your leader is dead! How long do you think you'll last against the one who killed him?"

Stillness spread like a wave flowing outward from Aderyn and washing over the melee. An elementalist threw a diffuse fireball at Ruan, who brushed it aside like it was nothing. Then the remaining orcs scattered in every direction, most of them heading back they way they'd come, all of them clearly panicked.

Before the last orc had vanished, Owen said, "We need to get out of here before they regroup. They may be cowards without their leader, but there's no guarantee they might not decide they should kill us so their cowardice is hidden."

"Wait," Isold said. "I know what happened."

He removed something strapped to Zothemza's spindly thigh that Aderyn had thought was a scar and brandished it. "Here is the <**Wand of World Door**>. It's the object I was following. It didn't occur to me that they might split their forces. I apologize. That mistake could have gotten us killed."

"None of us thought of it either," Ruan said.

"Suveer did," Aderyn said, struck by memory. "It was a possibility, but I forgot in the heat of chasing Zothemza. I'm sorry, Suveer, I should have taken it seriously."

Suveer shrugged. "We didn't know what they'd do. It doesn't matter now."

"And we got the wand back, right?" Ruan exclaimed.

Isold eyed him as if suspicious of Ruan's sudden burst of positivity. "That's a good way to look at it."

"Yes, and I knew this army was smaller, but I didn't put it together that it meant half of them took the prisoners elsewhere," Aderyn said. "We don't have to blame anyone, we just have to fix the mistake."

"Okay, good, but let's talk on the way," Owen said. "I'm guessing the point where Zothemza's forces headed south is where they sent the prisoners onward, probably north."

"Can we use the wand to take us there?" Aderyn suggested. "We all know how to activate a wand."

"The <**Wand of World Door**> doesn't have the same limitations the spell does," Livia said. "But I'll need to *scry* where the prisoners went, and that will take time, because I have no idea where to look other than 'north of here somewhere.'" She accepted the wand from Isold and found a sheath for it on her knapsack. "Let's get out of here first and figure it out later."

They walked rapidly northward, too rapidly for speech, sticking to the trees when they could and hurrying across the open ground when they couldn't. They saw no orcs, either lone ones fleeing the battle or groups moving purposefully to rejoin the army. At noon, Owen called a halt, and they all settled in the shelter of a thicket of trees for food and rest. Livia refilled their waterskins, Isold handed out food from the <**Forager's Belt**>, and they ate in silence.

Eventually, Isold said, "Did anyone see the level up notice?"

"The *what?*" Aderyn and Livia exclaimed in unison.

Isold smiled. "I thought not. It was quite the melee for a while there, but we reached level eighteen shortly before Livia killed Zothemza."

Silence fell again, but it was the tense silence of five people all reading the Codex.

Name: Aderyn

∞ **Jacob Owen Lindberg**

Level: 18

Class: Warmaster

Skills: Bluff (17), Climb (14), Conversation (16), Intimidate (12), Sense Truth (19), Survival (10), Swim (3), Knowledge: Monsters (18), Knowledge: World Lore (10), Knowledge: Demons (2), Unite

Class Skills: Improved Assess 4 (31), Awareness (21), Knowledge: Geography (17), Spot (18), Discern Weakness (30), Dodge (19), Improvised Distraction (18), Outflank (24), Draw Fire (14), Keep Pace (23), Amplify Voice (20), See It Coming (26), Basic Weapon Proficiency (Swords) (16), Read Body Language (17),

Basic Map Access (8), Compel (11), Spot Weakness (9), Secret Message (6), Bonded Mind (10), Sense Ambush (5), Reposition (5), Truesight (2), Darkvision (0)

She sucked in an excited breath. "[Improved Assess 4]!"

"Does it do what you hoped?" Owen asked.

"I don't—" She laughed, feeling embarrassed. "You know, it's never once occurred to me to Assess that skill for more information? I guess because it's the thing that lets me do that, and it would be like trying to use your eyes to look at your eyeballs, or something." With another laugh, she Assessed the skill.

[Improved Assess 4] is the third upgrade to the [Improved Assess] skill. In addition to refining on previous upgrades, [Improved Assess 4] unlocks the [Terrain Analysis] feature. This skill upgrade is available only to the Warmaster class. And it's about time you figured that out, Aderyn.

Aderyn's embarrassment deepened, but only for a moment. The system's message struck her as ruefully amused at Aderyn's mistake rather than critical. "It says [Terrain Analysis]. I wonder..." She sat up from where she was leaning against a tree and gazed over the hilly expanse, fields and tropical forest that extended as far as she could see until it all merged into a bluish haze. "Assess," she whispered, snapping her fingers. It felt fitting to do this the old-fashioned way.

Bright green intersecting lines sprang up across the terrain, making a grid of squares five feet across that distorted to rise or fall wherever hills or valleys changed the landscape. The lines curved and disappeared wherever they met a grove of trees, but when Aderyn looked more closely, it was as if they simply plunged into the earth, like the trees represented holes in the landscape. She stared at it all in wonder. Whatever it meant, it was beautiful.

She noticed a smudge at the base of the nearest hill, like something had smeared the green line. As she focused on it, it enlarged, revealing tiny words that became big enough for Aderyn to read.

Terrain object: hill, height 4 feet
Slope: shallow

Analysis: provides neither cover nor heightened vantage

"Wow," Aderyn breathed. "This is amazing!" She focused on another hill, then on a grove of trees. Each gave her a few lines of text related to the strategic usefulness of the terrain feature. "I could have used this earlier today—but I'm not going to complain. The system will get sarcastic with me if I'm not properly grateful."

"What do you mean, the system will get sarcastic?" Ruan asked.

Aderyn glanced at Suveer. "Well, my Assessments are sort of chatty now. Like the system has a personality. You don't have that, Suveer?"

Suveer shook his head. "I've never heard of that."

The tingle of [Sense Truth] made the hairs on Aderyn's arms stand up. Suveer was lying, and in addition to lying to her, he was lying to Ruan. Aderyn's conviction of this shook her with its certainty. She could understand Suveer lying to her, if Ruan had convinced him that she had selfish reasons for not helping him, but lying to his brother? And if Suveer did actually have communication with the system the way she did, why would he conceal that?

"[Crippling Strike]," Owen murmured. He was lying back with his head pillowed on his folded arms, looking into the foliage. "I can guess about that one."

"Yes, it does what it says," Aderyn said after Assessing it. "Swifthands get it at a lower level. It's more of a paralyzing blow, but it leaves the victim unable to use whatever limb you used the skill on."

"I don't know what [Coup de Grace] does," Weston said. "I've gone well past the level my mother was when she retired, so this is all new to me."

"That's—wow, it's deadly," Aderyn mused, reading the Assessment. "It combines [Advanced Sneak Attack] with [To the Heart] and [Improved Bluff] to allow you to conceal where an attack is coming from and turn that attack into a kill shot."

"I hope that means it's instinctive, because that's a lot of skills to juggle." Weston stretched out full length like Owen had.

"My new skill is a more powerful version of [Coercion] called [Compulsion]," Isold said. "I no longer find these terrifying now that we are fighting monsters with intelligence enough to shrug off the lesser versions of these skills."

"Does that mean we're ready to try the **<Wand of World Door>**?" Owen asked.

"I'm still choosing spells," Livia said absently. "Give me a minute."

They waited for more than a minute until Livia stood and stretched. "I got a ninth-level spell. I chose *stone prison*, which encloses a group of people in a stone chamber that persists as long as I want it to."

"You mean, until they suffocate?" Aderyn said.

"No, magic maintains the atmosphere inside. They'd be more likely to starve—don't look at me like that! You know I wouldn't seal even my worst enemy into death by starvation." Livia grimaced. "What I was actually thinking is it could be a protection for us, if we needed some-place safe that no enemy could penetrate."

"Clever," Owen said. "Any other spells?"

"Well, you and Weston might like this one," Livia said with a grin. "It's called *launch,* and it lets me fling an ally across a battlefield to a place of my choosing. Sadly, I can't use it to toss monsters around, but imagine you getting into position in seconds without fighting your way through a crowd."

"Um, what will that do to **[Keep Pace]**?" Aderyn asked.

Livia's mouth fell open. "I didn't think of that."

"Nothing," Owen said. "We have to be running or walking for that skill to take effect. Didn't you notice? Like, when we were in the Enchanterium and Akdukhur sent us up that chute? You didn't come flying after me."

"Oh. You're right, I didn't notice." Again, Aderyn tried not to feel embarrassed. It was all right to miss things, even for her, and now she had **[Improved Assess 4]** as well as—

"**[Darkvision]**! I almost missed it. It's like having a permanent set of **<Cat's Eye Goggles>**. I wonder what the **<Lenses of Farsight>** will do now?" Aderyn resisted the urge to vocally wish for nightfall already.

Owen hugged her. "I think we all needed a boost. But it's time. Livia, what do you need?"

"There's no point walking, since *world door* when cast with the wand goes as far as I know to open it. So it won't help us to go farther now. Let's just sit here while I *scry*. It might take some time." Livia resumed her seat leaning against a tree and murmured something under her breath that made her mirror flash once before showing a barren plain.

Aderyn watched Livia cast *scry* five times before growing—not bored, exactly, but Livia wasn't doing anything interesting except mutter to herself and repeat the spell. Why Livia couldn't cast it once and do what she had looking at the orc camp, making the viewpoint fly like a hawk, Aderyn didn't know, but she wasn't a spellslinger and there was no point telling Livia how to work her magic.

It was midafternoon before Livia said, "I found their trail. Thunderation, but that was harder than I expected." She looked as weary as if her spellslinging had been physical exertion.

"So you know where we should go?" Owen asked.

"Not quite. I found their trail, but I haven't seen them yet. I want to prove the prisoners are with this group before we go racing after the wrong thing—sorry, Isold, that wasn't a criticism."

"I understand." Isold didn't sound insulted.

"One more time," Livia said, mostly to herself, and murmured the almost-intelligible words of the spell. Again, the mirror flashed, and this time everyone crowded around to watch the *scrying*. Aderyn ended up opposite Livia, which meant the scene was upside down to her, but there wasn't anything to see yet, just more barren territory. She idly attempted to Assess the terrain, but got nothing, as expected.

It did strike her that the landscape looked drier than where they stood, with fewer trees and withered scrub growth instead of lush, leafy bushes. Well, northward lay the Blighted Range, and Isold had said the ground began rising in steps or plateaus almost immediately from where Shantos was, so if the elevation increased markedly on the northward journey, maybe that meant the climate changed, too. Or it could be proximity to the high-risk zone caused the blight to spread farther than the mountains. Either way, it looked grim and unpleasant.

In the mirror, a moving dark mass filled the oval and was gone. Everyone let out cries of dismay, and Livia said, "I know, it's fine, everybody shut up and let me do this."

The viewpoint reversed, moving more slowly, and again the dark mass was visible. "Lower," Livia said, and the mass drew closer until they could distinguish individual bodies. Orcs, marching stolidly northward behind a banner on which was painted a crude half-lidded eye weeping tears of blood. Aderyn's hands clenched hard enough to hurt as her nails cut into her palms. No one spoke.

The viewpoint slowed further, sweeping across the orc army, until it centered on a darker patch of bodies to the left and rear of the army. Aderyn caught a glimpse of white hair. "It's Varoun. They're there."

"Still fifty-odd prisoners," Weston said. "And they're positioned exactly where we hoped they'd be this morning. We can do that ambush again, if *world door* can drop us far enough ahead of their line of march."

"After that *scrying*, and the few spells I cast this morning after the potion, I'm at about three-quarters of my reserves," Livia said. "That's good enough for me."

"Then let's do this," Owen said. "We should arrive at least a mile ahead of them, since *world door* takes time even with the wand. Aderyn, you go first."

Aderyn reflected that Owen must be deeply committed to this action if he didn't insist on going first, and moreover was willing to let her go ahead without him. "I'll start preparing the ambush site. It should be simple now."

Livia already had the **<Wand of World Door>** out and was whipping it around in the familiar activation pattern. She paused. Her eyes moved as if reading invisible text. "We have a problem."

"Don't tell me only Varoun can use the wand," Owen said.

Livia shook her head. Once more, she activated the wand. Nothing happened. "There's a message," Livia said. "It says, 'Magical transportation into this location is prohibited.'"

"What's so special about that location?" Ruan asked.

Aderyn looked at Owen, who looked like he'd eaten something sour. "It means," he said, "the orcs have already crossed into the Blighted Range. They're in the high-risk zone."

CHAPTER TWENTY-THREE

"It makes sense," Livia said. "The system warns us about the high-risk zones so we don't stumble into them by accident. I can see how it wouldn't want people *transporting* in and getting caught in the middle of a dragon's den or something."

"But there's nothing stopping us from walking in, right?" Owen said.

"Of course not." Aderyn glared at him, willing **[Read Body Language]** to remind him that Ruan and Suveer were not privy to the knowledge that Owen was from another world. "We're allowed to choose. If we ignore the warnings, that's on us. But there *are* warnings, for our protection. You know that."

"Right," Owen said. "My point is, if we can figure out where the high-risk zone begins, we can at least use *world door* to get us that far."

"Sure," Livia said. "I noticed there was a point where the bushes changed dramatically. That might be a sign. But, again, it will take time."

"Don't worry about it." Owen sat down and beckoned to Aderyn to join him. "Everyone rest up. Might as well take advantage of the break."

Aderyn sat leaning against Owen's shoulder and closed her eyes. She wasn't sleepy, and she didn't think she could sleep if she were, but sitting and listening to the breeze through the treetops and the music of the birds soothed her anxious spirits. First discovering the prisoners were gone, then learning they couldn't use *world door* to get ahead of them for a rescue—it was discouraging if she let it be.

"Aderyn," Owen whispered, "you asleep?"

"No, just resting."

"What should I know about the high-risk zones? I don't want to give myself away to Ruan."

She sat up. "You're finally taking me seriously about that?"

Owen shushed her. "I always take you seriously." Aderyn gave him a sardonic look, and he amended, "All right, I forget sometimes. But I try, I swear!"

Aderyn settled back against him. "I believe you. Let's see... you know the high-risk zones are the places with monsters and dungeons too powerful for even level twenty adventurers. It's one of the reasons we know the level cap exists, because adventurers used to go there, long ago, and they had to be high level for that. At least, there are plenty of stories that say so. The details are probably mythical, but we know the journeys happened."

"And there are dragons there. Or is that mythical, too?"

"Yes, and no. There are small dragons in the high-risk zones, and sometimes they emerge and teams of adventurers have to work together to protect the nearby settlements. But the stories of the really big ones are just stories. No one's ever seen one, and even the tales from before the level cap don't prove anything."

"Well, what about Ymri in the Enchanterium? Wasn't it modeled on a real dragon? Because if it was small, I'd be terrified of meeting a big one."

"It could as easily have been modeled on stories of imaginary ones. My parents have several books—fiction books—about adventurers fighting dragons, and in those dragons come in varying sizes depending on how scary the author wanted to make them." Aderyn shifted to lay her head in Owen's lap. "There are enough real monsters in the high-risk zones I don't worry about the possibly imaginary ones."

"Understandable. What are the real ones?"

"There are monstrous versions of real animals, like dire hawks, only these are truly vicious predators in their normal versions. Panthers and tigers, giant snakes, giant spiders—"

Owen shuddered. "I told you, spiders creep me out."

"Let's hope we don't meet any, then. So, monstrous animals. Then there are larger, meaner versions of monsters you see everywhere, like how the deep delver was a giant chaos worm. And there are creatures that only exist in the high-risk zones. Dragons—the small ones—hydras, serpentfolk, cacayans, and probably lots of others we don't know names of because it's been hundreds of years since anyone entered the high-risk zones and returned."

"Which we propose to do. How dangerous is this, Aderyn?"

She'd been trying not to dwell on that. "Very dangerous. But we don't exactly have a choice if we want to rescue the prisoners, let alone complete the **[Crush the Horde]** quest. Our best strategy is to keep from encountering monsters, as much as that's possible. But, well, the monsters aren't the only problem. There's environmental challenges, pitfalls, strangler vines, acid rain—the list goes on."

Owen sighed. "I sort of thought this quest wouldn't send us anywhere too dangerous, but do you know what that tells me?"

"What?"

"That the system *doesn't* think it's too dangerous. Which means we have a chance. We've never faced anything that was impossible, even when it *was* impossible, like defeating the Sarnok at level ten."

Aderyn blinked up at him. "You're not suggesting the system made those victories possible, are you?"

"No. Maybe. I don't think the system does that, do you? What would be the point of adventuring if you knew how it would turn out?"

"Right." But Aderyn was already thinking of other possibilities. Could the system predict their capabilities, and steer them toward appropriate challenges? No, that couldn't be true. They'd stumbled on the Sarnok by accident, and Aderyn didn't think the deep delver had been part of the original Lonely Tor dungeon. And since the system gave out different quests as parts of the **[Fated One's Destiny]** quest, if it wanted to help certain teams, it could give them easy quests.

On the other hand, the system knew who she was. It knew about her teammates, or Owen at any rate. The more interaction Aderyn had with it, the more she thought of it as a friendly older sister. And maybe that was a bad thing, assuming the system cared about her in that way. Suppose she depended on its compassion when it didn't actually have any?

Idly, she opened the Codex and glanced over her skills. So many skills, and some of them hadn't been seen in the world for decades, maybe centuries. She didn't know how long Warmasters had been considered worthless—maybe before the level cap, people had known better what their capabilities were.

Remembering with some embarrassment what the system had said about **[Improved Assess 4]**, Aderyn Assessed **[Darkvision]**, though she knew what it did already.

[Darkvision]: Alters the eyes to perceive objects in all but completely lightless conditions. Initially this means gaining 50% of your daylight vision in darkness, with this percentage improving with additional ranks. Were you hoping for some unrelated conversation?

"I—" Aderyn stopped. Owen was playing with her ponytail, but his attention was on Isold and Weston, who were talking about monsters in the high-risk zones. Even so, he would notice if she started talking to the air. She tried subvocalizing, the way most people activated the Codex. "I don't know what I expected."

Nothing happened for about three seconds. Then lines of text formed across her vision.

If you know enough to speak to me, I have the capacity to answer. But I can't tell you your future. You would hate it if I did, too.

"I guess I would," Aderyn murmured under her breath. "Can you tell me if we're on the wrong path? Are we foolhardy to enter the Blighted Range?" She didn't know why she asked. Being addressed directly by the system had been unnerving. This conversation frightened her, this feeling that she was doing something not only unprecedented, but forbidden.

You accepted the quest. The path you take to complete it is your own. It always has been.

"All right," Aderyn whispered.

"What was that?" Owen asked.

"Nothing." A million other questions thronged her mind, but half of them struck her as inane and the other half prying. And she was afraid to ask the one question she really wanted an answer to: *Why me?* She feared the answer would change her life, maybe not for the better.

"All right, I think I've found a good place," Livia said. She looked up from her *scrying* mirror. "I don't know exactly how far it is from the high-risk zone, but then I've always heard the boundary shifts within half a mile one way or the other depending on the day. Or the hour, maybe. At any rate, this spot will put us close enough."

Owen helped Aderyn stand. "I should go first," he said. "Then Ruan, Isold, Aderyn, Suveer, Weston, and Livia."

"Is there a reason behind that remarkably decisive list?" Ruan asked.

"I always have reasons." Owen stared Ruan down coolly and said nothing more. Ruan's lips pressed tightly together, and he didn't object further.

Livia activated the wand, and Owen stepped into the ebony oval and appeared to freeze in place. Ruan said, "He must be something if you're all willing to go along with his orders."

"It's how good teams work," Weston said curtly. "You must remember that."

"We all worked independently," Ruan said. "You know, before half of us were killed." His sarcastic tone made Aderyn uncomfortable, but Weston just shrugged and went back to ignoring Ruan.

Abruptly, Owen vanished, and the *world door* oval shrank in on itself and disappeared. Livia prepared to activate the wand again. "I could get used to this. I probably shouldn't, and then be disappointed by having to cast the spell from my own reserves." She flicked the wand through its activation pattern.

This time, Ruan stepped through without looking back. His absence relaxed Aderyn. "You're lucky to have your brother as your partner," she told Suveer. "Imagine if he hadn't been in a position to adventure with you."

"I guess," Suveer said with a diffident shrug. He still wouldn't meet Aderyn's eyes. "I'm not a great partner. Ruan's nice about it, but I know I drag him down."

"I know that's not true," Aderyn exclaimed. "Ruan's skill ranks are as high as any Swordsworn with a Warmaster partner. You're doing something right."

Suveer glanced up from where he'd been staring at the ground. For just a moment, he looked surprised. "I don't know what his skill ranks ought to be. Ruan says he doesn't care."

Aderyn was certain that was not the case. She decided not to challenge him. "Why do you not use all your skills? Won't that make you a better partner?"

Suveer's one eye narrowed. "I do use all my skills. I'm just not very good at some of them. It's the ones Ruan and I can use together that matter."

She couldn't let that one go. "Who told you that? Ruan? What about the skills that benefit you?"

With a snap, the *world door* closed. Aderyn barely noticed. "Suveer, you're not useless. I don't know why you—"

"You don't know anything about it," Suveer said. "We're not the same."

"Aderyn," Isold said.

She glanced his way. Isold's grim expression brought her back to herself. He shook his head, the tiniest movement. Behind him, the *world door* stood ready for him to enter.

"All right," she said to Isold. To Suveer, she said, "You're right. We're not the same. All I want is for you to realize that you don't have a worthless class. You don't have to be like me to know that—you just have to look at everything you do for Ruan. That's all."

She looked back at Isold. He still didn't look happy, but he walked through the ebony oval without another word.

Suveer continued to watch Aderyn. "Why do you care?" he asked abruptly. "What do you want from me?"

"What do I—you mean, what do I want you to do for me? Nothing.

We're the highest-level Warmasters in the world, Suveer. I guess I hoped we could share experiences." Telling Suveer she wanted him to grow a spine was cruel, even though it was true.

"You hoped—" For once, Suveer looked puzzled, as if her answer made no sense. His shoulders relaxed from their tense, hunched position. Aderyn held her breath, waiting for... she didn't know what she was waiting for. For Suveer to realize the truth, maybe.

Suveer turned away and studied the ground again. "Our class is the only thing we have in common. Stop trying to be my friend. I know it's a lie."

It felt like a slap to the face. She knew she must look ghastly, because Weston said, "Aderyn doesn't lie about things like that. You should apologize."

Suveer ignored him. Weston opened his mouth, and Aderyn cut him off. "It's not important. Thanks, Weston, but Suveer can believe what he likes. It doesn't change the truth." She spat those final words at Suveer's back. He didn't react.

"He's a—"

"Can we not argue just before we go into dangers we might not survive?" Livia said. The oval closed on Isold, but Livia didn't activate the wand again. "Aderyn, you're next. You and Suveer can work this out another time."

Aderyn nodded, though she was still angry. She stepped into *world door*, welcoming the quiet stillness of its passage, the soft surface underfoot and the glassy clearness of the tunnel walls. Suveer had won this round, but she wasn't going to give up. She'd almost gotten through to him. She'd seen his surprise when she mentioned Ruan's Swordsworn ranks. He really hadn't known he made a difference. And she wasn't going to give up on convincing him that meant he mattered.

Chapter Twenty-Four

When Aderyn exited *world door*, the dryness of the air startled her, so different from the thick, humid, hot air of the Southlands. The trees were the same, thick boles with rough bark that rose eighty or ninety feet in the air before branching out into heavy limbs lush with enormous fronds or clusters of leaves shaped like giant hands. But a second glance told her these trees weren't as similar as she'd thought. They all looked dry, the bark peeling away from the wood, the leaves dull olive or yellowish green and drooping from lack of water. Even the ground was dry, the earth powdery with only a scattering of tall grasses or low, spindly shrubs clustering around the tree trunks trying to draw from whatever groundwater sustained them.

There was a road, though. Not the kind of road made intentionally, paved and clearly defined. This was a road beaten out by thousands of booted feet traveling back and forth, crushing any undergrowth out of existence. With its hard, uneven ruts, it was also the only evidence that rain ever fell here. Those booted feet had marched this way through the mud as well as during dry times.

Owen's hand steadied Aderyn as she stepped through. Someday she'd learn to do that gracefully. He held onto her hand for a few paces, which helped ease her anger over Suveer. Isold watched her in silence until Aderyn looked away, uncomfortable at his regard. Ruan had his back to them and was scanning the road ahead. "I don't think anyone's coming back," he said without turning, "but we want to watch the road to the south, in case some of those orcs we scattered return this way."

"I agree," Owen said. "Aderyn, how about you Assess the terrain while the rest of us keep watch?"

Aderyn nodded. She walked a short distance away from the road, avoiding the trees, and Assessed what clear ground she could see.

The green lines sprang up, overlaying the land with a grid of squares five feet on a side. To her left, they curved to sink beneath the trees; to her right, they covered the road and the bare ground to either side. She couldn't call them fields because practically nothing grew there, so "bare ground" would have to do.

The grid didn't extend to the horizon. Aderyn counted squares and discovered [Improved Assess 4] extended eighty feet from where she stood and forty feet in either direction. She guessed that range would increase as her skill ranks did.

Owen stood on the edge of a grid square, oblivious to the green lines. They ignored him as well, not distorting as they did when they passed over a terrain feature like a hill or a grove of trees. Since she already had the ability to Assess a human or monster, this didn't worry her, though she did briefly wonder about the possibility of seeing a creature as a part of a terrain analysis. Suppose she could use that knowledge in a strategic analysis?

With a snap, Suveer stumbled out of the *world door* oval. Aderyn had a moment of smug satisfaction that he was even less graceful than she. Then she felt bad about her smugness, but mostly because she didn't feel worse at the spiteful thought.

She turned her attention to the "road" heading north. It veered to the left to avoid a low rise and then disappeared around the hill's far side. So orcs had enough sense to take the easy way even though it was longer. The thought gave her a little twinge of uneasiness. Orcs were cruel, destructive, and violent even to their own kind, but they were also intelligent, and she didn't know why that disturbed her. She and her friends had killed humans who were trying to kill them, and that didn't bother her.

No, it was the idea that her team had killed other monsters that were intelligent without knowing they were. Like the kobolds, who'd turned out to be not hostile except in defense of their homes. She wasn't going to feel guilty over killing things that wanted her dead, but she couldn't help wondering if any of them could have been reasoned with. And *that* was what disturbed her: the possibility that she would hesitate in a fight, and she or someone she cared about would be hurt.

Before she could stop herself, she whispered, "Is that true?"

Immediately, she regretted asking the system anything. She shouldn't depend on being able to talk to it, or get answers to questions. Suppose she annoyed it by assuming a connection that wasn't there? And she was assuming the system knew her thoughts. If that was true, it was scary.

Aderyn, what does [Improved Assess 4] tell you about monsters?

Aderyn froze. "Um. Their attacks, their weaknesses. I don't know if this upgrade includes more."

I tell you enough to give you an advantage, if you're smart enough to take it. Think about the misthounds. Think about the kobolds. That's all I can say.

Aderyn called up the Monster Folio and reviewed the entries on the creatures the system had mentioned. The system had suggested the misthounds could be dealt with another way, hadn't it? And it had changed the kobolds' type from abomination to anomaly, meaning they weren't hostile. If she thought about it that way, the system always told her when a monster was dangerous, but it didn't always say whether it could be reasoned with. That wasn't exactly comforting, unless the comment about Aderyn being smart enough to understand was meant as reassurance. It might mean Aderyn should act on what she was told and withhold judgment until later.

"That's everyone," Owen said, startling her. "Aderyn, what can you tell us?"

Aderyn cleared her throat. "They went north through the hills, sticking to the easy ground of the lowlands instead of taking the direct route. Some of those hills are natural ambush sites, but it's unlikely they left anyone behind to take advantage of them. *Our* biggest advantage is they don't know we're following them, but we shouldn't get cocky."

"Then let's form up," Owen said. "Ruan, you want to take the lead with me? With Aderyn and Suveer in the second rank. Then Isold and Livia, with Weston bringing up the rear."

Ruan eyed Owen speculatively. "You know," he said, "we haven't discussed the problem of gaining experience."

"I've been thinking about that," Owen replied. "You mean because my team has more people, and the odds of us getting the final blow on a monster we're both fighting are good. Which leaves you and Suveer out in the cold."

"I don't have a solution. It's not as if it's safe for any of us to stand back so a particular person gets the kill." Ruan continued to watch Owen warily, as if expecting treachery. It annoyed Aderyn.

"Can't we just agree to work together, and see what happens in the first couple of fights?" she said. "After all, this is a dangerous place, and we're going to fight orcs eventually as well as whatever monsters live here. And it's the quests we both care about. Those are worth more experience than any monster."

Ruan nodded slowly. "That's true. All right. But if it turns out I'm not getting my share of the kills—"

"We'll reconsider," Owen agreed. "It's not fair for you to take on danger with no reward."

Again, Ruan gave Owen a long, considering look. Then he nodded again.

Aderyn took her position a short distance behind Owen and suppressed annoyance that they couldn't walk together as they usually did. Beside her, Suveer looked more alert than she'd ever seen him, scanning their surroundings with his head tilted in that odd way. She couldn't help trying to put herself in his shoes, at least as far as having only one eye went. Why hadn't they had his eye restored? She knew that magic was possible. Maybe it cost too much for them to afford.

They followed the orc road around the low rise to discover more curves ahead. While the heat wasn't as bad as in the lowlands, the dry air felt unexpectedly uncomfortable. Aderyn hated humidity, how the air clung to her body like a damp second skin, but this was a different kind of discomfort. The dryness sucked at her eyes and nostrils and mouth like a creature intent on drawing all the moisture out of her body. Her skin felt itchy and parched and stretched tight over her muscles. She resisted the urge to scratch.

The land looked as dry as her body felt. They soon left the trees behind for the unbroken hills, which seemed to rise out of the ground and push the trees and their undergrowth to each side until the tree line was a green-yellow smudge on the east and west horizons. Long yellow grasses drooped dispiritedly across the hills, without any wildflowers to break the monotony. Aderyn's feet kicked up puffs of dust with every step.

Abruptly, a system message appeared, bringing all of them to a halt.

**Warning! Warning! Warning!: You are about to enter dangerous terrain. Recommended minimum level for this area is [22].
If you choose to proceed, you will face hazards geared for high-level adventurers. Continue at your own risk.**

"I guess this is it," Weston said.

"Don't say 'it can't be that bad,'" Livia said.

"I wouldn't say that!"

"No, but I know you were thinking it. The [**Fated One's Destiny**] quest sent us here, so it's tempting to believe the warning doesn't apply to us. But we don't know that's true."

"Agreed," Owen said. "On the other hand, I don't think it's unreasonable to think that because the system sent us here, it's not impossible. So nobody lose hope, all right?" He turned to Ruan. "You still up for this?"

"More than ever," Ruan said. "Now it feels like a real challenge."

Owen nodded. He took a couple of steps forward, then three more, and stopped. "The message changed. Go ahead and cross the border. I know, it's not visible."

Aderyn walked forward. The warning message didn't disappear for a few steps, until all at once it flickered and was replaced by new words:

I told you once there was a fine line between daring and foolhardiness. You're still walking it. Take care, and remember: not all dangers come with warning labels.

Aderyn said nothing, though she was intensely curious about what everyone else saw. Obviously that wasn't a message that would appear to anyone but her. Suveer, though, might have seen something similar... and, again, it wasn't something she could ask. Couldn't really talk about anything, since with Ruan and Suveer there, conversation had to be constrained to avoid giving away Owen's origins. And she was sure Ruan would find a way to interrupt her if she talked to Suveer about being a better Warmaster. So she continued to trudge along, watching the road and occasionally using **[Improved Assess 4]** just to see the green lines flexing and curving along with the landscape.

"What does **[Improved Assess 4]** do?" Suveer asked.

Startled, Aderyn let the green lines disappear and focused on him. "It shows a grid over the terrain. Like bright green lines. And the different terrain features are labeled, with information about their strategic use."

"I see," Suveer said, and fell silent, as if he'd exhausted his conversational reserves.

"Do you use **[Improved Assess 3]** often?" Aderyn kept an eye on Ruan, but he didn't look inclined to intervene.

Suveer shrugged. "When I remember. I don't see much point in Assessing buildings. Monsters are more important."

"I agree," Aderyn said, though she didn't really. But she understood his point that adventurers were more likely to need to know about monsters than architecture. "And you said the system doesn't talk to you. That's interesting, don't you think?"

"Why would that matter? Assessing things is enough." Suveer finally looked at Aderyn, and she felt for the first time he was genuinely interested in her answer. It flustered her, the more so because she wasn't sure she had an answer.

"I don't know," she finally said. "It happened so gradually I didn't at first realize there was a difference to the system messages. So it wasn't like I wanted it to happen—I mean, it wasn't a thing I looked forward to and would have been disappointed by if it didn't. But now, it's like the system—" She stopped, feeling uneasy. "It's like it takes an interest, is all."

She didn't know what had prompted her to avoid telling Suveer the truth about her feeling that there was a personality behind the system messages that was interested in her. She only knew it would be a mistake, and a colossal mistake at that.

"I guess that would be interesting," Suveer said, and returned to watching the landscape. The tingle of [Sense Truth] prickled the back of Aderyn's neck. It convinced her, once again, that Suveer did know something about the system messages becoming more personal that he'd concealed from everyone, including his own brother. But if the system talked to him the way it talked to her, and she'd been open about it, why wouldn't he? Aderyn determined to figure out the truth. Maybe it was wrong for her to pry, but keeping secrets could be fatal when you headed into a dangerous situation. Then she remembered that she was keeping secrets, and Owen's origin was a secret... all right, maybe she should leave Suveer alone.

The road continued to weave between hills, but the strain in Aderyn's calves told her they were gradually rising. Small bushes now grew here and there on the hills, scraggly gray-green bushes with leaves the size of Aderyn's thumbnail in varying stages of growth. Most were full-grown shrubs with long, trailing branches, but some were small and spherical and others were dried-up skeletons that looked like a stiff wind would uproot them and send them tumbling across the hills. Aderyn watched them for a while, grateful to have relief from the monotonous landscape.

The chime of Owen activating the [Sunsword] drew her attention. She was about to use [Improved Assess 4] against whatever enemy he'd spotted when she realized there wasn't anything around. Instead, Owen brought the glowing blade around in a sweeping slash—at Ruan.

"What in thunder—" Ruan shouted, drawing his greatsword and blocking Owen's first strike. "Are you—" He stopped defending and went on the attack, forcing Owen back a step.

"Orcs!" Owen shouted, just as Ruan said, "The orcs have returned!"

"What are you talking about?" Livia exclaimed. "Stop!"

Aderyn swiftly Assessed the area, turning in place to cover more of a range, though she didn't know how orcs could have sneaked up on them or why that meant Owen and Ruan were fighting each other. Instead, she got a different response.

Name: Whisperweed [7]
Type: Abomination
Power level: 10
Terrain: wasteland, plains, low mountain ranges
Attack: special
Immune to: mind control magic and effects
Resistant to: weapons damage
Vulnerable to: elemental damage
Special attacks: telepathic blinding

Whisperweeds look like dry, skeletal bushes—in fact, you've probably seen them tumble across the landscape in a high wind. They are, in fact, clever telepaths who confuse prey into attacking their friends, then devour the bodies left behind. They're also the worst gossips you'll ever meet, though as you're not a whisperweed, you won't be able to hear their chatter. Consider yourself lucky.

"They've been mind controlled!" she shouted. "We have to stop them before they kill each other!"

Chapter Twenty-Five

Isold broke into song, a rapid, lilting melody that made Aderyn want to dance. She drew her sword, then hesitated. Both Owen and Ruan fought fiercely and with astonishing grace that almost disguised the fact that this was a duel and not a dance. If she tried to intervene, she'd either get herself killed or give one of them a fatal advantage. She hovered nearby anyway, balancing lightly on the balls of her feet so she could leap in if she had a chance.

She was aware of Livia chanting something incomprehensible just as Owen and Ruan disengaged and lowered their swords, breathing heavily. Then something punched her between her shoulder blades, an agonizing blow that knocked her to her knees. She rolled over to see Livia standing over her, her stone fist glittering with magic and drawn back in preparation for another punch.

[See It Coming] got Aderyn out of the way of Livia's *stone fist* the second time. She scrambled to her feet and backed away, keeping a close eye on Livia. "The weeds, the skeletal weeds!" she shouted. "They're attacking us with their minds! Destroy the weeds!" She dodged another blow. If she could keep Livia's attention on her, her friend wouldn't go after anyone less well equipped to stay out of her way, and maybe Livia wouldn't think to cast any other spells.

Isold's song grew louder. A thin, high-pitched screech joined it, discordant and eerie. Aderyn didn't dare take her eyes off Livia to see what made it.

Congratulations! You have defeated [Whisperweed].
You have earned [5275 XP]

Isold stepped behind Livia and gripped her head between his long-fingered hands. Livia shouted and tried to twist away. Aderyn dove in and wrapped her arms around Livia, pinioning the Earthbreaker's hands. Livia fought her like a madwoman, twisting and jerking. For a moment, Aderyn was sure she was going to break free. Then she realized Livia was muttering the words of a spell under her breath as she struggled. "Hurry, Isold," Aderyn gasped. She blinked away another system notice without reading it.

Livia's words cut off. She stopped struggling. "What was that?"

"Whisperweeds," Aderyn said. "Those dry ones that look like skeletons. We need an elemental attack!"

"On it," Livia said. She began chanting again, something long and sonorous. Aderyn took a moment to look around. Owen and Ruan were hacking at the whisperweeds, sending shards of dry branches flying. Ruan suddenly lowered his sword. Then he left his opponent behind and went after Suveer.

Suveer screamed and dodged the first blow, but only barely. Without stopping to think, Aderyn rushed to put herself between Ruan and the unarmed Suveer. "Isold, help!" she shouted. She blocked Ruan's next attack, which rang through her sword and up her arms like she'd struck an iron bar. Distantly, she remembered she didn't have [Weapon Mastery] and her sword was vulnerable to breaking as Ruan's greatsword was not, and instead of engaging with Ruan, she dodged to one side and let the sword whiff past her head.

"Hey!" Owen shouted. "Over here, you lunatic!" He swatted Ruan's legs with the flat of the [Sunsword]. Ruan turned on him in an instant, their swords clashing. Aderyn, her heart racing, couldn't help watching the fight for a few seconds, though she heard the sound of earth rumbling and knew Livia was on the attack. Owen had battled many formidable opponents in the Glory Games, but now he was up against a master easily his equal. Back and forth they moved, until Isold's song hit notes Aderyn would have sworn were outside his range, and Ruan lowered his sword.

Three system defeat notices occurred in quick succession:

Congratulations! You have defeated [Whisperweed].
You have earned [5275 XP]

"Where's the rest?" Livia shouted.

Aderyn surveyed the area, counting. Livia had uprooted three of the whisperweeds, revealing bulbous "roots" with roughly-carved faces, the eyes mere slits and the mouths turned down in frowns. Thready tendrils like tiny, limp arms sagged lifeless across the roots. They didn't inspire any sympathy in Aderyn. Two more whisperweeds had been hacked to splinters. She didn't see any more of the creatures nearby, even when she turned **[Improved Assess 4]** in every direction. "They're gone. What happened to the other two?"

"Ruan uprooted one, and I slashed through the base of another," Weston said. "They both rolled away with the breeze. What *were* those things?"

"Telepaths who confuse people into killing their friends. I think 'telepath' is another word for 'mind control.'" Aderyn straightened her mail shirt and fixed her ponytail, which had come mostly undone in the struggle with Livia. "Did anyone get hurt?"

"Not for lack of trying," Ruan said. "Sorry about that."

"Yeah, me too," Owen replied. "That could have been messy. Though I think we're almost evenly matched."

"Only 'almost'?" Ruan said with a grin. "I guess we'll never be in a position to find out, unless we run into more of those whisperweeds."

"I'd hate that," Owen said. "Let's keep moving. Aderyn, do you—"

"It's still better if you're in front. Suveer and I will pay better attention and Assess more frequently." Aderyn nodded at Suveer. "Is that all right?"

"Sure." Suveer shrugged. Aderyn was starting to hate his shrug. Every time he did it, she felt a terrible urge to slap him. Terrible, because she wanted to believe she wasn't the sort of person who reacted to mere annoyance with violence, but his ongoing diffidence went beyond annoying into dangerous. They were in the high-risk zone! Everyone needed to use their abilities to the fullest if they all wanted to survive, and that included Suveer—who seemed determined to believe he didn't have any.

She watched more carefully for the whisperweeds, but didn't see any others near the road, though in the distance she saw tumbling bushes blowing westward with the wind. Maybe the whisperweeds could control their movement. If they were gossips as the system said, that meant they could talk to each other, and it was likely those other whisperweeds knew what had happened to their fellows. Aderyn was just as happy not to face them again.

They stopped for a short rest an hour later. There were no trees for shelter, so they sat in the long grasses and had their meal. The relative coolness of the air felt good, though the dryness still made Aderyn want to scratch every inch of exposed skin. She ate the bread and cheese they'd brought from the regiment stores and thought about the future. She didn't know how far ahead the orcs and their prisoners were, but she and her friends almost certainly moved faster. Even so, it seemed likely they wouldn't overtake the orcs, which meant freeing the prisoners from captivity in Charnel Keep.

She reminded herself that it was a dungeon like any other—well, not like any other, but they'd faced many dangerous dungeons and survived, so there was no reason to fear it. Still, she couldn't help imagining a castle full of orcs, and fighting through waves of enemies, and they didn't know where the prisoners would be kept... No. She wasn't going to be defeated before they'd even tried.

"Aderyn," Isold said, "could you take a look at this? I would like to know what [**Improved Assess 4**] says."

Aderyn rose and dusted off her posterior. "Is it dangerous?"

"No. At least, I don't think so. I am simply curious about the different tactical advantages of the road ahead."

The hairs on the back of Aderyn's neck tingled. Isold wasn't telling the whole truth. And since he wanted to conceal his real interest, it was something Ruan and Suveer shouldn't hear, because he never kept secrets from his friends. Aderyn pretended his request was normal and followed him a short distance down the road, out of earshot of anyone except Weston.

"I think you should know," Isold said, in a low voice that definitely wouldn't carry, "that in their last fight, Ruan was free of the mind control several seconds before he lowered his sword."

Aderyn kept from looking back at Ruan. "How do you know? Does that mean you can feel it when [Break Enchantment] takes effect?"

Isold nodded. "At first, I doubted myself, so I continued singing. There's no question. Ruan attacked Owen on purpose."

"Do you think he wanted to kill Owen and pretend it was an accident?" It was a stupid question. Of course that's what Ruan wanted. "And he believes he got away with it."

"You were the only one of us I could think of a reason to speak privately with." Isold's expression was grim. "And you can tell Owen tonight."

"We should leave Ruan and Suveer behind." She knew that was wrong the moment she spoke the words. "Except we can't, because there's no way they'd survive here on their own. We might as well murder them ourselves."

"And Ruan was a powerful ally in the fight against the whisper-weeds," Isold said. "Things would have gone much worse if he hadn't been there."

"But we can't—" Aderyn realized her voice had become shrill and tried again, more quietly. "We can't watch our backs constantly for Ruan to turn on us. It's not safe."

"Based on what I observed, Ruan won't try anything overt. He'll only strike if he can make it look like an accident. And I could be wrong about his motives. He might only have wanted to test Owen's skills."

"Test them so he'd know what he'll face when he goes after Owen for real, you mean."

Isold sighed. "Yes. I hoped you might see a better solution."

Aderyn thought about it for a minute. "Kicking Ruan and Suveer out just means having them where we can't see them, which opens us up to an attack at a much worse time. It's better if we're able to keep an eye on them, and never give Ruan the opportunity to strike."

"That's reasonable," Isold said. "Now, tell me what you see about that hill. We should be able to give a good excuse for speaking privately."

But when they returned to the others, no one asked any questions or commented on their absence. Aderyn returned to Owen's side and leaned against him. He didn't say anything, but put his arm around her and hugged her. She loved those little gestures of his.

"We should move out soon," he said to the group. "Everyone ready?"

"Let me refill your waterskins," Livia said.

As she went around to each person, Owen whispered, "Something wrong?"

Aderyn nodded. "It can wait until tonight." She couldn't use [Secret Message] to convey anything this complicated.

Owen grimaced, but just helped her to her feet.

They walked on through the afternoon, kicking up enough dust they had to cover their mouths and noses to avoid breathing dirt. At one point, Aderyn noticed a shimmer across the ground ahead and called a halt while she Assessed it.

Name: Black Ooze [10]
Type: Formless
Power level: 13
Terrain: marsh, plains, low hills
Attack: special
Immune to: all weapon damage
Resistant to: none
Vulnerable to: elemental fire damage, sonic damage
Special attack: engulf

Black oozes, despite their name, are skilled mimics that look just like the ordinary ground surrounding them. It's not until some hapless creature steps on them that they discover why they're called black oozes: the ooze expands to engulf its prey, surrounding the creature in a thick, gooey black substance that forces its way into any orifice and... you know what? I think you get the idea.

Obviously an ooze won't be damaged by weapons, but elemental magic will hurt it, particularly fire. A sonic attack

disrupts its structure, freezing it in place long enough for the victim's friends to pull them to safety. You *do* have friends nearby, right?

Interestingly, the terrain also blazed with the green fire of a trap. Aderyn had never seen a monster that was also a trap. She was tempted to go ahead and see what it meant, but… "They're too much," she said after reading the message. "We should go around."

"Why not fight them?" Ruan said. "We could use the experience."

"You did hear the part about them being immune to weapon damage, right?" Owen said. "You wouldn't get any experience unless you have a fireball up your sleeve somewhere."

"Besides, there are ten of them, and I don't know if they can move," Aderyn said. "It's better if we walk around them. **[Truesight]** tells me where they are."

"Sure, all right," Ruan said. He made it sound like he had been the one to object, but Aderyn decided to leave him his pride.

They left the road and, with Aderyn in the lead, made their way around the patch of black oozes. The creatures covered several dozen yards to either side of the road, enough that Aderyn imagined anyone who managed to spot the ones covering the path might not realize just stepping to the side wasn't safe. **[Truesight]** still didn't reveal what was beneath the illusion of bare ground, but she caught glimpses of black on occasion and rejoiced at the expansion of her skill.

They were back on the road, well past the oozes, when a system message appeared:

You have received [2000 XP] for avoiding the [Black Ooze environmental threat].

"Two thousand experience!" Ruan exclaimed. "What's an environmental threat?"

"It's a trap that isn't set by a person or monster," Aderyn said. "Something that arises out of the landscape."

"Well, I won't argue with that," Ruan said with a grin.

Sunset came with no sight of the orcs or their stronghold. Owen called a halt when the sun dipped halfway below the distant horizon. "Do you want separate tents?" he asked Ruan.

"We didn't bring tents," Ruan said. "I thought the plan was to sleep in the open. Better visibility."

"That's a fair point, but shelter when we don't know what kind of weather this place has is smart." Owen gestured at the rutted road. "And we have tents. Enough that you and Suveer don't need to share if you prefer."

Ruan's eyes narrowed. "In that magic knapsack?"

"We'll share," Suveer said. It was the most assertive thing Aderyn had heard from him all day.

Livia walked a few steps away and, holding the <**Soldier's Friend**> at arm's length, pressed the side with four little V's. Ruan and Suveer backed away in alarm at the whirlwind of tiny creatures that surrounded her. In seconds, four elegant white tents stood in a square, facing a neat little campfire ringed with stones.

"Thunderation," Ruan breathed. "That's some powerful magic. I saw those tents appear in the military camp, but I didn't guess the activation looked like that."

"We'll want to douse the fire. It's too great a beacon," Weston said. "Unless we need it for warmth. The air's already a bit nippy."

Aderyn hadn't noticed while she was walking, since her exertions kept her warm, but Weston was right: there was a chill in the air now that the sun was setting. "It could also scare creatures away."

"I think we're more at risk from drawing creatures to our fire," Owen said. "Let's go without tonight and see what happens."

Livia gestured, and a gout of water fell out of the air to extinguish the fire with a great splash. Ruan dodged. Suveer didn't. "Sorry," Livia said, almost sounding like she meant it.

"Well, I for one am ready to eat," Ruan said. "Then we should see about watches."

"There are enough of us to double up, except for Weston, who doesn't need backup," Owen said. "Do you two have any preferences?"

"Just that I prefer to watch with Suveer. In case something attacks, and I need my partner." Ruan sounded so professional he almost wasn't the same person Aderyn disliked.

"Fair enough. Then Livia and Isold, Ruan and Suveer, me and Aderyn, and Weston." Owen sat on one of the little conjured stools. "And I'm hungry, too."

It wasn't a comfortable meal. Aderyn was used to these dinners at the end of a long day's walk being friendly and relaxing, chatting or joking with her friends. With Ruan and Suveer there, she felt awkward about making jokes or conversation that would exclude them. Ruan occasionally made remarks that someone would respond to, but they never turned into a longer chat. Suveer remained silent, the kind of silence that feels like hostility. Aderyn was grateful when she could retire to her tent.

As soon as the tent flap fell, Owen said, "I've been dying of curiosity all day. What did you and Isold talk about?"

Aderyn had almost forgotten, in the tension over the black oozes, what Isold had revealed. Remembering that tent walls didn't block sound, she drew Owen close and whispered, "Ruan was free of compulsion before the end of your fight. He went on fighting to test your skills or maybe looking for a way to kill you that he couldn't be blamed for."

Owen relaxed. "Is that all? I noticed—all right, I didn't know all that, but his style changed midway through. He stopped being so mindlessly aggressive and went deliberately on the attack."

"We can't leave them here. They'd follow us and attack when we're weak."

"Totally true. And I'm not sorry that that was my first thought and not that they'd die in the Blighted Range on their own." Owen hugged Aderyn closer. "We don't have any choice but to keep a close eye on him. And Suveer, I guess, though I have trouble imagining him taking the initiative in anything."

"I still feel sorry for him, but it's lessened now that I find him so annoying. How can anyone be satisfied with believing they suck? That is the right word, right?"

"It is the right word, and I don't get it either. Suveer must have been constantly emotionally abused throughout his life to be this convinced of his failings. And even that isn't enough to fill me with compassion for him." Owen kissed her. "Maybe it can be enough for you."

Aderyn kissed him in return, a slow, passionate kiss that warmed her all through her body. "I can't remember the last time we had sex."

"Well, it's not going to be tonight. Not even I can imagine being that vulnerable in the high-risk zone." Still, he returned her kiss, his hands roaming over her back. "This is less fun when we're both wearing armor."

"I know. It's like trying to cuddle a tin can."

Owen chuckled and released her. "Let's see how much sleep we can get before our watch."

Aderyn was sure sleep would be impossible. She wasn't afraid of the high-risk zone, not accompanied by her friends, but that just meant it was exciting, and who could sleep under those conditions? Still, she eventually drifted off to sleep. When Owen woke her for their watch, she quickly put on her mail shirt and left the tent, separating from Owen to walk the perimeter opposite him.

She hadn't known what to expect from her new skill [Darkvision]. She'd once worn Weston's <Cat's Eye Goggles> that let the wearer see in the dark, and she'd expected something like that. Instead, the world was in shades of gray, the sky charcoal, the tree line on the western horizon slate, the pale grasses and the white tents the color of dense fog. Everything within about twenty feet of her was sharply outlined, and beyond that objects had blurred edges, but she could see them. It was breathtaking.

She had to tell someone. This skill was too amazing not to share. Instead of calling Owen's name, she hurried along her path to join him. But when she came within sight of him, he wasn't alone. A slim, pale figure with short black hair had her arms around him, and the two of them were kissing. The woman's form shimmered, and briefly she looked like Aderyn before reverting to her other appearance. Shock stopped Aderyn in place, and for a fraction of a second, jealousy struck her. Then she realized how stupid that was.

"*Everybody up!*" she shouted with [Amplify Voice]. "We're under attack!"

CHAPTER TWENTY-SIX

Aderyn didn't wait for the scrambling of five people coming alert and leaving their tents to stop. She ran to Owen, drawing her sword. Owen hadn't reacted at her shout, but the pale woman drew a long knife from a sheath along her thigh. Aderyn screamed Owen's name. He continued passionately kissing the woman, right up until she drove the knife home deep in his belly, below his armor.

Owen gasped and staggered backward, his eyes wide, his lips bloody. The strange woman turned to face Aderyn. For a moment, she looked like Weston, but **[Truesight]** revealed her real form beneath the illusion. Aderyn screamed again in fury and despair and attacked.

The woman's long knife countered Aderyn's sword, but only barely. Aderyn registered the woman's distorted features, her prominent cheekbones and eyebrow ridges, her flared nostrils, and her bared teeth, filed to points. There was no time to Assess her, but the teeth triggered a memory. Something about a woman no man would want to kiss. She didn't have time to pursue that memory, either.

She fought fiercely, stepping over Owen's fallen body where he lay clutching the horrible wound in his stomach. Step by step, she forced the woman back. She didn't know why the woman kept smiling when Aderyn clearly had the upper hand.

Then the woman disengaged, leaped lightly out of Aderyn's reach, and began to sing.

Out of the darkness came the roar of guttural voices making a dissonant chorus with the woman's song. Aderyn saw them before they reached her: orcs, a dozen or more, charging toward her.

Aderyn backed up, unwilling to turn her back on the monsters but aware that she was too far away from her allies for safety. "Orcs!" she boomed out. "They're attacking!"

Ruan leaped past her, followed by Suveer. Ruan met the orc onslaught with a powerful blow of the <Galling Blade> to the neck of the orc in the lead, nearly decapitating it. Aderyn heard Livia chanting nonsense words from somewhere behind her. Light burst over the scene, turning everything bright as day. All the orcs cringed away, giving Aderyn a chance to Assess the strange woman.

Name: Ahda

Type: Monstrosity (orc chanter)

Power level: 16

Terrain: any

Attack(s): special

Immune to: none

Resistant to: mind control attacks

Vulnerable to: bright light, *daylight, sunburst*

Special attacks: confusion, hypnotism, illusion, empathic drain

Orc chanters aren't exactly the counterparts of human Heralds, but their skill sets overlap significantly. Ahda is, for lack of a better word, the leader of the chanters; they don't obey her except by coercion and fear, and she rarely demands their obedience, preferring the chaos that rises when undirected chanters enter a combat. Ahda's favorite attack is to take the form of her victim's friend or loved one before stabbing the victim in the chest or belly—preferably a wound that won't kill instantly, so she can enjoy their emotional and physical pain.

Note that Ahda, like all chanters, is resistant to mental

attacks and not immune. This is a result of being not quite a Herald's counterpart—oh, you don't care about the details. The point is that if a chanter has a vulnerability—not the literal kind—it is in underestimating what human Heralds are capable of. I suggest you take advantage of that. And don't look her in the eye.

In the time it took Aderyn to read the system message, Weston had leaped past her, flinging knives with deadly accuracy before finishing his target off with his rapier. Aderyn made herself turn her back on the fight and hurried to kneel beside Isold at Owen's side. Isold held the <Healing Stone> against Owen's side, preparing to activate it. Distantly, *thunderstomp* rumbled the earth.

"Isold, the woman—the chanter—the system says she won't know how to fight against you," Aderyn gasped. "We don't have much time. We're seriously outnumbered."

"Owen may die if I don't treat him now." Isold looked past Aderyn and clearly didn't like what she saw. "You'll have to do it. I showed you before."

"Yes, but I—" Aderyn stopped complaining. It was true, she hadn't been able to consistently activate the <Healing Stone> when Isold had demonstrated, but there wasn't time for her to whine about what she didn't know. She accepted the stone from Isold. "I'll do it."

Isold hurried away. Aderyn squeezed her husband's hand and felt like crying when he turned out to be unconscious. No more wasting time. She pressed the stone against the terrible wound in his abdomen and closed her eyes.

Can you hear me? she thought, mentally speaking the words. *I need your help.* She told herself not to be embarrassed, but she still cringed inside.

The stone didn't respond. This was the same problem she'd had before, feeling stupid about talking to an inanimate object. And now Owen might die for her ridiculous embarrassment.

She tried again. *I need you to work, or my husband will die. That's important to me, and I think you care about healing people.*

Consider where all power comes from, Aderyn. You touch the face of power all the time. This is no different.

Aderyn gasped. The message vanished just as she finished reading it. It had never occurred to her that magic items might tap into the power of the system. They were just magic items. But it made sense. Their power had to come from somewhere.

Gripping the <Healing Stone> more tightly, she thought, *It's time for you to work. Please.*

The stone glowed bright green. Owen's skin became translucent with the same green glow. Aderyn let her mind unfocus and watched Owen's internal organs knit back together, followed by muscle and then skin. Owen let out a gasp and tried to sit up. Aderyn pushed his shoulder down. "Just wait."

"You stabbed me," Owen said, sounding so bewildered it broke Aderyn's heart. "Aderyn, why did you stab me?"

"It wasn't me, it was the orc chanter Ahda." The green glow faded, and Aderyn dropped the <Healing Stone> into the <Purse of Great Capacity>. "She made you believe it was me."

"That bitch," Owen snarled. This time, he made it to his feet. "Where is she?"

"We need to fight the orcs. Ruan and Weston will be overwhelmed, and I don't know where Livia is." She hadn't heard *thunderstomp* again, which meant Livia was out there punching orcs, unless she'd been overwhelmed.

"Let's go," Owen said.

The fighting hadn't yet reached the tents, but thanks to *daylight*, the orcs didn't have the advantage of concealment. Aderyn and Owen passed Ruan fighting an enormous orc two feet taller than he, with Suveer darting around to provide [Outflank], and Owen sped up to [Overrun] another orc attempting to take Ruan from his weak side.

The orc fell, and Aderyn took advantage of his prone position to stab him, finding a gap beneath his arm where his armor didn't meet. The orc shouted, rolled to his feet, and met Owen's <Sunsword> coming the other way, shearing the orc's arm off and cutting deep into the orc's chest. Owen deactivated the blade briefly rather than wasting time pulling it free, then activated it again to slit the orc's throat.

Congratulations! You have defeated [Orc Elite].

You have earned [8050 XP]

Aderyn stepped back as the orc fell at her feet. When she looked around for another foe, she realized about half the orcs she'd noticed were dead—and in the hottest part of the fight, Isold and Ahda faced off as if completely unaware of the battle raging around them.

An orc reared up in Aderyn's face, screaming defiance. She barely got her sword in place to deflect the blow from the orc's heavy, notched blade. The tug of [Outflank] warned her Owen was in a position to attack, so she held her position, her heart hammering at the orc's nearness and the stink of its breath and body odor.

Something brilliantly white burst through the orc's chest. Aderyn recognized the <Sunsword> just as Owen withdrew the blade from behind and the orc collapsed.

Aderyn searched the battlefield again. Two of the orcs had disengaged from Ruan and Weston and were headed Isold's way. Isold still seemed rapt in concentration. Dread terror struck Aderyn like a blow to the chest. That didn't look like he was winning. It looked like Ahda had mesmerized him.

Fear, and the feeling that it was her fault for telling him to go after Ahda, propelled her into motion, racing to intercept the orcs and leaving Owen behind. She threw herself between Isold and the orcs, not having any idea what she would do to stop them.

The enormous monsters paused at Aderyn's sudden appearance. They looked at one another, then back at Aderyn. Both laughed, a terrible, choking sound that didn't sound like they found her funny.

Suddenly, one staggered into the other, nearly taking both of them down. Livia stood behind them, her stone fist glittering with magic. "Wake up, Aderyn," she said, aiming another blow at the first orc. "We haven't won yet."

Aderyn slashed at the second orc's legs as Livia's punch landed, and this time, both fell. They revealed Owen racing toward them, swearing loudly. "Do *not* go running off like that!" he shouted. "[Keep Pace] isn't great over short distances. Did you want to get yourself killed?"

"Finish them!" Aderyn shouted back. "I have to help Isold."

She approached Isold and Ahda, both of whom stood very still.

Neither spoke, but the rigidity of their bodies said a silent battle was raging. Aderyn reached for Isold, thinking to shake him out of the hypnosis Ahda wielded over him. But before she could touch him, Isold lifted a hand and touched Ahda in the center of her forehead. In a quiet voice that nevertheless resonated with power, he said, "*Die.*"

Ahda reversed her long knife and gripped the hilt in both hands. With a single powerful thrust, she drove the blade into her belly, angled upward to reach the heart. She stood unmoving for a moment, her expression almost peaceful. Then her face crumpled in agony, and she dropped, keening her pain.

Aderyn stared at her, her mind blank. Isold had—

She realized Isold was folding at the knees and got herself under his shoulder to keep him from falling. "What was that?"

"[Compulsion]." Isold's voice, normally so beautiful and compelling, was almost too faint to hear. "It is more powerful than [Coercion]—well, obviously so. It was the only attack I had that surpassed her powers. And to my surprise, I feel no guilt over using it."

"She was evil. I can tell you how evil, if that would help."

Isold smiled. "Not necessary, but thank you."

The sounds of battle were quieter now, and when Aderyn looked around, only Ruan and Owen were still fighting opponents. Neither of the orcs appeared to be aware that Ahda had fallen. "She's not dead yet," Aderyn said. "Maybe I should—"

Congratulations! You have defeated [Ahda, Orc Leader].
You have earned [23,575 XP]

The orc fighting Ruan broke and ran. Ruan chased after him, with Suveer dragged along in his wake. Owen's opponent saw his companion flee and turned to do the same. Owen hamstrung him and buried his sword in the orc's back when he fell.

Congratulations! You have defeated [Orc Elite].
You have earned [8050 XP]

"Somebody go after Ruan!" Weston shouted. "We can't let that orc get away to fetch reinforcements!"

They all ran then, even Livia, but they didn't get far before they met Ruan and Suveer coming back. Ruan was cleaning the glittering black surface of the **<Galling Blade>** with a ragged, dirty cloth torn from some orc's clothing. "Good fight," he said. "Anybody hurt?"

"I took a cut to my arm," Weston said. "Starting to feel it now."

"Owen is healed," Aderyn said. She handed the **<Healing Stone>** to Isold.

"You figured it out," Isold said. He drew the **<Wand of Healing>** and used it to heal the deep slash across Weston's left forearm.

"I did." Aderyn didn't want to share the system's message to her. She still felt mixed up inside when she thought about it. The system's communications were so personal now, she felt shy about exposing them to the world—and yet what if the knowledge could help her friends? She didn't have a good answer for that.

"That's good, because I feel better knowing more than one of us can use it," Isold said.

"We should move camp," Ruan said. "That's a lot of orc bodies I really don't want to sleep near."

"Of course. Everyone gather your things. Aderyn, how about you and I scout for a different location?" Owen gestured to Aderyn to join him. Normally, she didn't like it when he assumed she would agree to something that wasn't a given, but after seeing him nearly die, she was too happy and relieved to care.

They walked a short distance down the road. Aderyn searched the terrain, hoping for something that could provide them concealment, and when Owen spoke, it startled her. "I thought I was kissing you."

"Oh! I know. She specialized in fooling people into thinking their friends or loved ones attacked them."

"No, Aderyn." Owen's voice was almost too quiet to hear. "I really thought I was kissing you. And I didn't care about anything else. Not our safety, not the possibility that we might be attacked. I can't forgive myself for that."

Aderyn stopped. "Owen, what are you saying?"

"I'm saying it was so real, and I let myself be fooled. That's not safe for any of us."

Aderyn took a calming breath so she wouldn't shout at her beloved for being an idiot. "Owen, the same could have happened to any of us. Are you saying you're so special you should have been invulnerable?"

"No! I'm saying I should have—"

"Sweetheart, you're taking on too much guilt. I know it feels humiliating. Remember the Beguiler in Finion's Gate? You don't think I should have been able to fight that [Coercion] off, do you?"

"Of course not." Owen gripped her hand. "No. I just... I just can't bear the thought of any of you being hurt because I was weak. Least of all you."

"You weren't weak. And it was chance that Ahda went after you. She might have attacked me, and if I'd been near death, I couldn't have learned her weakness. So in a sense, you protected all of us by being her target." Aderyn put her arms around him and kissed him. "I was so afraid I wouldn't be able to make the <Healing Stone> work. I couldn't bear it if you were dead. Even knowing there's one more gemstone in the <Ring of the Cat> doesn't change that fear."

Owen returned her kiss. "I'm sorry, sweetheart. I shouldn't have fallen into despair like that. You're right, I'm not so special as to be invulnerable."

"I'm glad you didn't die. And we achieved another quest milestone!"

"Who is Ahda? The orc chanter?"

They paused to review the [Fated One's Destiny: Crush the Horde] message.

An army of monstrous orcs has emerged from the Blighted Range, intent on conquering the southern human lands. Destroy their leaders and push the army back into the mountains.

Victory conditions:
Death of Glasha, orc commander general
ACHIEVED Death of Ornok, second in command
ACHIEVED Death of Zothemza, orc elementalist

ACHIEVED Death of Drorg, orc cavalry commander
ACHIEVED Death of Ahda, orc chanter
Destruction of Charnel Keep
Orc army retreats

Reward: [75,000 XP] plus any XP gained through actions taken
to complete the quest.

"We are making some serious progress," Owen murmured.

"With just the really big things left. I wonder what Glasha is like. Do you suppose he's bigger than the other orcs?"

"I'm not looking farther ahead than Charnel Keep," Owen said. "The rest can wait."

CHAPTER TWENTY-SEVEN

They walked for hours the following day with no sight of orcs, prisoners, or Charnel Keep. The deeper they went into the Blighted Range, the drier and angrier the landscape became. Aderyn didn't know why "angry" was the word that came to mind when she Assessed the terrain. There were no more trees and barely any scrub growth to soften the stark, rocky lines of the landscape or provide shade from the burning sun. The hills the road skirted had gone from being low rises to tall, ruddy cliffs through which the road now ran straight as a furrow. Marks in the high cliff walls some twenty or so feet up indicated someone had hacked their way through, as violently as if the cliff had fought back.

Even the dust had changed, becoming gradually redder until their boots looked dusted with flakes of blood. They again covered their mouths and noses, but this time Aderyn felt superstitiously as if inhaling this dust might contaminate them, infect them with whatever poison had made this the Blighted Range. She couldn't imagine every high-risk zone was this awful.

The road was wide enough for an orc army to pass easily, but they kept to their marching order rather than group up together. Aderyn's calves again felt the strain that told her they were walking uphill, which was a different feeling than the tug of **[Keep Pace]**. Usually that skill didn't take effect if she and Owen were both walking at the same rate, but separated. That was fortunate, because much as she loved Owen, she didn't want to be lock-stepped with him.

Owen and Ruan stopped abruptly at the top of a rise. Aderyn slowed before joining them. She immediately saw what had brought them to a halt. The sheer cliffs came to an end some fifteen feet from where they stood, not sloping into shallower inclines, but sheared off with the same marks Aderyn had observed before. Beyond that, a dusty chalk-red plain extended into the distance. Nothing grew there; no roads were visible.

In the distance, a fortress rose atop a cliff, dusty red against the slate-colored mountains surrounding it. Though it was at least a mile away, it still looked enormous, blocky and bold with tarnished metal roofs that met at odd angles. It looked like a child's block castle with a pile of scrap metal dumped atop it.

Everyone else gathered around. No one spoke. The enormity of the fortress took Aderyn's breath away. Finally, she drew in a deep breath and immediately regretted it as she sucked in a lungful of dust. Coughing hard, she waved off her friends and finally got herself under control. "All right. It's a big building. It looks impregnable. But I doubt that's true." She wiped her watering eyes and Assessed the fortress.

Name: Charnel Keep
Type: Standard timed, huge, victory condition variant B
Power Level: 17
Inhabitants: abominations, magical beasts, monstrosities, vermin
Traps: rare
Environmental hazards: rockfall, terrain hazards
Reward: miscellaneous magical and mundane objects worth a total of 1,218,039 gold at current rates of exchange
Charnel Keep is a remnant of an earlier monstrous race who, weakened by infighting, were destroyed by orc raiders. Until recently, the orcs were scattered throughout the Blighted Range, settling where they could, and had no interest in the fortress of their victims. When Glasha took over by ruthlessly killing most

of the other orc leaders, the orcs rebuilt Charnel Keep at their commander's orders. Now it is a well-defended stronghold from which Glasha plans the invasion of the human lands.

You can see the entrance, which is heavily guarded from the outside and within. Take a look at the base of the cliff, where those gates are. Charnel Keep sits atop a warren of subterranean passages, dug out centuries ago by chaos worms burrowing through them, then extended by that earlier race. Don't worry, the worms are long gone. It's the other inhabitants you'll need to be concerned about. There are entrances to the underground passages the orcs aren't aware of, as well as a few they do know about. It's up to you how you approach it.

As to the dungeon type, this is the first timed dungeon you've encountered. From the time you enter Charnel Keep—this includes its underground network—you have twenty-four hours to accomplish the goal, which is the death of Glasha. Failure to do so in the given time means you will have to exit and re-enter the dungeon to try again. Orcs don't respawn, but there are hundreds of them, and the dungeon resets itself on a failure. This means you'll not only have to fight those battles again, but Glasha and the orcs will be aware you tried once and will be on high alert. I don't need to warn you further, do I?

Just a few more hints: avoid the obvious conclusions, don't run headlong down any blind passages, and greed is your enemy. Good luck, Aderyn. You're so close.

She didn't read aloud the last two sentences, but it didn't matter, because Weston was saying, "Over a million gold in treasure? I'm glad for the warning about greed, because anyone would have their head turned by that much."

"I wonder where it all came from," Isold said. "That's an astonishing pile of treasure, if it's all in items rather than coin."

"Yes, that's great, but why didn't the Assessment say anything about the prisoners?" Ruan said. "That's the important part, and I'm not saying that because it's my quest."

"With the Ivory Palace, we had two possible victory conditions," Aderyn said. "If rescuing the prisoners isn't one of Charnel Keep's victory conditions, that must be because it's a quest reserved for Ruan. Suveer, you should Assess the place. **[Improved Assess 3]** will tell you if that's true."

Suveer nodded. They waited while he stood, very stiffly, staring at the distant keep. After a while, he trembled as if from full-body goose-bumps and blinked several times. "It says killing the commander is the victory condition. It didn't say anything about the prisoners."

"That's enough to convince me," Owen said. "Aderyn, do we need to get closer to find these entrances the Assessment mentioned?"

Aderyn brandished the <**Lenses of Farsight**> at him. "Not anymore." She put the glasses on, closed her eyes briefly against the disorientation, then surveyed the keep's foundation. With the glasses, it appeared to be about five feet away. She immediately saw two of the gates the system had referred to. The one on the left was a single iron slab almost as wide as the main entrance, but it wasn't tall; it might have been seven feet tall, if that. The one on the right was an ordinary set of double doors sized for the average orc. Those doors were made of iron, too. She was about to use **[Improved Assess 4]** again when it occurred to her to check the guards the Assessment had referred to.

The iron gate, blackened with age and dented in places as if a battering ram had tried and failed to gain entrance, could easily admit a column of orcs six wide. Round towers flanked it, not very tall—in fact, now that she saw it closer, Aderyn realized the keep was only two stories tall, though they were very high stories. If she hadn't known better, she would have thought giants inhabited it.

Movement atop one tower caught her eye. An orc masher came into view, armed with a heavy crossbow. The orc paused, surveyed the ground surrounding the gate, and then walked away. Aderyn relaxed out of the frozen position she'd involuntarily taken when she saw the monster. A glance at the other tower revealed two orc grunts, similarly armed, strolling around the top of the tower. Both towers had clear lines of sight to each of the gates in the cliff base.

"I can't tell what's inside, but it doesn't matter, because we can't go that way," she said. With **[Improved Assess 4]**, she swept her gaze across the foundation. The green lines looked even more vivid against the reddish earth. All three gates bore the reddish haze of "danger" that said they were a bad idea as entrances.

"Just a minute," she said when Owen addressed her. She scanned the cliffs where they stood. The cliffs encircled the plain about two-thirds of the way around, when they joined the slate-colored mountains that rose higher and higher until they loomed over Charnel Keep. Rather than looking like they meant to engulf it, they looked like sentinels, warning anyone fool enough to attack it that doing so would be fatal.

"All right." Aderyn removed the glasses and blinked to clear her vision. "The entrances on this side aren't accessible without those guards on the towers seeing us. We're going to need to make our way around, staying concealed, and see about a different entrance. I doubt those orcs can see very far in the sunlight, but we don't take chances."

Making their way around meant backtracking to a place where they could climb the cliff. From above, the stony expanse rose and fell in a series of shallow inclines and slopes, not enough to give cover from anything passing by, but enough to conceal their movement from the observant eyes of the orc guards. At least, Aderyn was reasonably sure this was true.

Even so, they sidled past open areas so quick movement wouldn't draw the eye, and clung to the steeper surfaces to stay out of sight. The sun gradually dropped lower and then fell behind them. Sweat and red dust caked Aderyn's neck and hairline. Livia's *drench* had increasing appeal, but it would only turn the dust to mud and make things worse.

They were too far from Charnel Keep for [**Improved Assess 4**] to reach, but [**Spot Weakness**] had a much longer range and was probably better for identifying entrances than [**Terrain Analysis**]. Aderyn turned that skill on the dungeon every time they passed a wider gap in the hills. Nothing appeared until they were a quarter of the way around the plain, halfway to the mountains, and the smoothly sloped hills had become more jagged and less red. Aderyn froze briefly, then came to her senses and dropped to lie flat with her head lifted just high enough to see Charnel Keep past the hills.

"I see an opening. It's barely visible," she said. "In fact, I'm not sure whether it's an opening or a crack. Meaning a weakness in the wall."

"It's still too light for us to risk crossing that plain in the open," Owen said. "Will *mass invisibility* cover all of us?"

"All but one, but Weston has the [Cloak of Mists]," Livia said. "Still, we ought to wait for sunset. The moon's only a few days from full and should give us enough light for a straightforward walk like that one."

"Fair. Let's rest and eat something." Owen settled against one of the stone walls and tilted his head back. "I haven't been drinking enough. Too tense."

Aderyn handed him a newly-filled waterskin. "It was nerve-wracking, I agree. Though I feel certain those guards don't look this way. They seemed concerned about the obvious entrances."

"I'm tense about the timed dungeon." Owen took a long drink and tilted his head back again. "Twenty-four hours isn't much."

"We've cleared dungeons in less time than that," Weston said. "Dungeon Spiteful. Winter's Peril."

"And some have taken a lot longer." Owen squeezed his eyes shut as if protecting himself from blinding light. "Sorry. You're right, it's not impossible. If we think like it is, we're working against ourselves."

"And remember I have the <**Wayfinder**>," Aderyn said. "That should make finding the prisoners easy and cut down on our time."

"You have a <**Wayfinder**>?" Ruan sat up. "You can't use it."

"Why not?"

"Because my quest says *locate* and rescue the prisoners. What if you doing the locating invalidates it?"

Ruan's intensity reminded Aderyn of his furious attack on her during the wargames, and she controlled a flinch. "Aren't their lives more important?"

Ruan, about to say something else, closed his mouth. He looked like he was working through responses. Finally, he said, "People's lives are important. But so is this quest. And it doesn't have a time limit. Maybe this means we have to split up once we're inside."

"Is that safe?" Isold said. "A fortress full of orcs is going to be difficult enough for seven of us to defeat. Even if you use stealth to get the prisoners out, one mistake and you might all be dead."

"I've come too far to give up on this quest now." Ruan was as dust-covered and weary-looking as all of them, but he held his head as proudly as if he was addressing the queen. "If it means this is just Suveer and me going it alone, that's what has to happen. And it would certainly prove my worthiness."

Out of the corner of her eye, Aderyn saw movement. She glanced that way, fearing an ambush her skill hadn't noticed in her distraction over Ruan, but it was just Suveer, who'd lowered his head and was playing with the ties attaching his belt pouch to his trousers. Realization that Ruan kept saying "I" in regard to the Fated One quest prompted her to say, "Suveer's Warmaster skills could make that possible. But he has to believe he can do it."

Suveer shrugged. "I make Ruan stronger. That lets him defeat monsters and succeed at quests."

Aderyn opened her mouth to argue, and a hand closed on her knee painfully tight, a clear warning to her to shut up. Owen said, "That is part of what a Warmaster does, and I'd be lying if I said I didn't appreciate what Aderyn's skills do to boost me. But it's not everything she does."

"Suveer is good at what he does," Ruan said. "Between the two of us, I'm sure we can figure this out."

"At least stick with us until we find a way into the upper levels," Aderyn said. "There have to be doors leading up into the keep itself, or the system wouldn't have pointed to the caverns as an entrance. I can use the <**Wayfinder**> that far, and then we'll split to carry out our separate quests."

"That's reasonable." Ruan loosed his hair from its tail and shook it out before tying it up again. "The sun's nearly set, and it occurs to me that anyone looking in this direction will be looking right at it. I think now is the time to go."

They clambered down to the plain, staying as concealed as possible. There wasn't a lot of cover, and Aderyn's nerves were wound to snapping by the time they all reached the bottom and gathered around Livia. Livia swiftly chanted a series of oddly echoing words, and the air grew thick around them, like they were surrounded by clear jelly.

With Weston ahead, barely visible by the ripples in the air he made, the other six walked rapidly across the plain, staying close together. The moon, which was a flattened orb directly above, cast Weston's shadow but not those of the invisible team members, so as the sun sank behind the hills, he became easier to follow. Not even Aderyn's paranoia could imagine orc guards noticing the moving pale blotch of gray, or realizing a human caused it if they did.

Aderyn didn't steer them directly, in case there were unseen observers who might hear her, but she had aimed Weston and Livia at the point [Spot Weakness] had identified. As soon as they reached the keep's stony foundation, she left the group and walked to the hole, or crevice, or crack to see more accurately what her skill had identified.

She found it was a little of each. It was a gaping hole into the foundation, but not a round one; instead, it was a tall triangle no bigger than five feet wide at its base and six feet tall at its height. But the narrowness of the triangle meant that only four of those feet were accessible by humans, the rest being not much more than a crack, and Weston was going to have a hard time of it. Aderyn regarded the hole, and this time, she couldn't help herself; she shuddered, picturing stone closing in around her, the weight of Charnel Keep bearing down on her—

Arms encircled her. "You can do this," Owen whispered. "It's an entrance, so it opens up farther on. You can bear it that long."

Aderyn clung to his arms and closed her eyes. "I hate being weak."

"A weak person would turn around and leave. You're the strongest person I know."

"I'll go first," Livia said. "I can sculpt the stone around me and widen that passage some without bringing the keep down on my head." She sounded grimly pleased at the possibility.

"Wait," Isold said, grabbing Livia before she could dive into the passage. "We should use the <Wand of Epic Bounty> first. I cannot imagine any other twenty-four hour period that is more potentially deadly."

"What's that?" Ruan asked.

An awkward silence fell. Aderyn was sure all her friends were thinking the same thing: the wand produced six Miracle Meals that gave protection from damage for a day, and there were seven people in their group. Finally, Owen said, "It's a powerful buff, but one of us will have to go without."

"Well, Suveer doesn't go into danger the way I do, so it should be him who doesn't use it," Ruan said.

"What are you talking about?" Aderyn exclaimed. "You expect him to use [Draw Fire] all the time, and he—"

"He's right, Aderyn," Suveer said. "It's important Ruan take less damage so he can kill monsters before they kill us. I don't need that buff."

"Suveer!"

"Let it go, Aderyn," Owen murmured. "It's Suveer's choice, remember?"

Aderyn reddened. The memory of being chastised by Isold burned. "Fine."

Ruan looked skeptical when Livia's wand produced a small jar of capsules instead of a huge meal, but he swallowed his without comment. Livia made as if to toss the wand away, then stowed it in her knapsack instead. "It's useless now, but I don't like throwing it away."

"Maybe a Spellcrafter can renew the charges," Owen said.

"That's my thought. All right, it's time." Without a backwards glance, Livia dove into the opening, sending up showers of cracked stone from the now-wider entrance.

A system message appeared.

WARNING: A timed dungeon instance has begun. You entered Charnel Keep at [5:58:04 p.m.] You must complete the dungeon victory condition in 24 hours. Failure to do so will reset the dungeon and require you to exit and re-enter if you wish to attempt it again.

Below the system message, a counter reading 23:59:03 glowed in white. As Aderyn noticed it, it ticked over to 23:59:02. With a gesture, she dismissed the system message, but the counter shrank to small numbers in the center of the upper limits of her Codex display.

"Well," Owen said. "I guess it's begun. Who goes next?"

"Me," Aderyn said. "I want it over with."

"You're not afraid of small spaces, are you?" Ruan said.

He hadn't sounded dismissive—much—but Aderyn's tension made her respond with, "You want to talk about what *you're* afraid of?"

She didn't know what she'd meant by that, but Ruan raised both hands defensively and said, "Sorry, I didn't mean anything by it. If you're willing to go in there and you're afraid, that's brave by my standards."

His rapid backing down surprised Aderyn. She said, "All right," but silently she wondered what he thought she'd meant. It almost sounded like he thought she knew a secret about his weaknesses. If he believed Warmasters could discern that sort of thing... well, she wasn't so noble that she'd tell him it was impossible. She still believed she needed every defense against Ruan she could get.

After about ten minutes—Aderyn could have calculated the exact number from the counter, but that felt like paranoia—Livia returned. "It's a long passage that widens out after about twenty feet. Sorry that took so long, but I heard noises and I had to move quietly in case they were monsters."

"Did you see any?" Owen asked.

Livia shook her head. "It might have been my imagination. Sound echoes in there—you'll see what I mean. Let's move. We want to save time wherever we can." She disappeared back into the tunnel. Aderyn took a deep breath and crawled after her.

CHAPTER TWENTY-EIGHT

She had to remind herself to be grateful to Livia for widening the passage. At the very least, the roof and upper walls were smooth like rough-modeled clay, and they didn't cling to her clothes or pluck at her hair. But Livia was comfortable surrounded by stone, and her idea of "wide enough" still terrified Aderyn. The sense of being buried alive, of being slowly ground down by the weight of the stone, accompanied by the complete lightlessness, brought her close to panic. Only her awareness that the person close behind her was probably Owen kept her from freezing and staying there until she was crushed.

She didn't know why Livia hadn't created *orbs of light* and had no idea whether seeing her surroundings would be better or worse. She made herself focus on crawling, one hand, one knee at a time, and to distract herself imagined the kind of creatures that might live in these caverns. Sightless mole rats. Burrowing worms that spat acid. Black oozes that clung to the ceiling. Spider swarms. Owen might have trouble with the last, if he was as freaked out by spiders as he claimed. In passing, it occurred to her that thinking of bigger fears might be a bad idea, but she could fight mole rats and spiders. There was no way to fight claustrophobia with a sword.

Just as she thought that, she realized that the roof of the tunnel was rising, and there was a small glimmer of light in the distance. Gratefully, she crawled faster until she could rise to a crouch and then stand upright. Livia stood a short distance away, watching the passage as it extended out of sight around a curve. She hugged Aderyn when Aderyn staggered up to her. "I'm sure that was terrifying."

"I thought about monsters instead," Aderyn said, hugging her back. "I assume you haven't seen any."

"Not yet, but I won't summon more light until we're all through, just in case something out there notices."

Owen emerged from the narrow passage and put his arms around Aderyn. "Good job."

"Maybe someday I'll get used to small, enclosed spaces," she replied. "When I'm three hundred."

Owen chuckled and released her. "If you plan on living to three hundred, I'm sure you'll find other things to be afraid of." He walked a short distance down the passage, not quite to the curve. "I hear that echo Livia mentioned. It's going to be hard to tell where creatures are coming from."

"I'm not worried. **[Sense Ambush]** doesn't care about echoes." Aderyn joined him. The walls of the passage, in the faint light of Livia's one *orb of light*, were bumpy and black and gleamed wetly, though when Aderyn touched them, they felt dry and smoothly rounded against her fingers. She sniffed her hand; it smelled unpleasantly of rot and fungus.

Owen rested his hand lightly on the <**Sunsword's**> hilt. "You want to use the <**Wayfinder**>, see if it leads us to an exit?"

"Oh! Yes. I like to examine my surroundings first, in case there's a danger the <**Wayfinder**> doesn't lead us around. It understands about walls, but I don't think it's aware of monsters. Besides, there's really only one way to go for now." She drew the magic item out of her purse and cupped it in both hands. She was experienced enough in its use after all these months that not knowing exactly what the exit looked like didn't interfere with it finding that exit.

She focused on her heart's desire, and the orb's rings began spinning, turning pink when she faced down the passage. Wanting to be thorough, she turned slowly in a circle. When she faced the entrance through which Weston was now emerging, the rings sped up, turning bright cherry red and becoming warm to the touch. "Well, crap," she said.

"What's wrong?" Owen joined her. He looked at the glowing <**Wayfinder**>, then at the entrance. "Crap."

"It will be fine," Aderyn said. "It does know there's another exit. It just can't distinguish which one we want. It's like I said—it tells us where my heart's desire is, but it won't mention the ogre guarding it."

"Okay, but that's going to slow us down." Owen's lips pinched shut. "No, you're right. It will still move us faster than if we had to wander around searching the hard way."

Ruan and Suveer came closer, staring at the orb. "I've never seen a <**Wayfinder**>," Ruan said. "Here's a thought. What if you loan it to me, and I'll return it once my quest is complete? In fact, that might make things go faster, since there's probably only one group of prisoners in here."

Aderyn's heart thumped once in painful warning she didn't need. "It's harder to use than you think, and there's not a lot of time for you to learn. Also, this was a gift from my grandfather, and I don't risk losing it. Probably you'll be fine, but what if the orcs defeat you?" She wasn't about to say there was no thundering way she would give Ruan anything more important than a handful of rations.

"Oh, right. Too bad." Ruan nodded. "So, how *does* it work? It looks like it glows more when you point it at the entrance we came in by."

"I'm trying to find another exit, and it indicates there's something down that passage, but it resonates more strongly with the closest one. I'll just have to be careful." The others had gathered around now, and Aderyn held up the <**Wayfinder**> so they could all see when she faced down the passage. "Weston, you're up here with me. The Assessment said very few traps, but there are potential terrain hazards that I think referred to this level of the dungeon. Everyone else, you know where to go."

"Ruan and Suveer, that means you're watching behind us," Owen said.

Ruan didn't protest, but he did draw his sword. That was all Aderyn saw before she turned her attention back to the <**Wayfinder**>.

The passage ahead curved smoothly until it was pointed the opposite direction from the way they'd entered. The floor was as bumpy as the walls, not flat, but rounded as if the passage was a near-perfect oval in cross section. It made for insecure footing, and Aderyn had to walk even more slowly than she usually did when using the <Wayfinder>. Occasionally, her foot slipped, and she lost focus as she kept herself from falling. Refocusing didn't take much time, but it was time Aderyn resented losing. She didn't let herself look at the counter with its white numbers. That was just as much a distraction.

Her foot came down on something pearl-gray, and instinctively she braced herself against slipping. Instead, her foot stuck there with the slightest adhesion. She pulled away from the substance with no trouble and looked around. Strands of the pearly material clung to the walls, some of it crossing the passage. Weston, a few steps ahead, was poking the stuff with his dagger.

"It's webbing," he said.

That sent a chill down Aderyn's spine. "It's, um, really big for webbing."

"Webbing?" Owen said.

"Don't freak out, sweetheart," Aderyn quickly said. "We haven't seen any spiders."

"I'm not going to freak out," Owen said disdainfully.

Aderyn was sure if she had been looking at her husband just then, [Read Body Language] would have given him the lie. But she knew what it was like to fear something you had no control over, and she sympathized with him. Spiders you hadn't seen yet were far scarier than the ones in your face you could kill.

Weston walked a short distance down the passage. "It branches off here. Heads back the way we came, I think. I can't really tell because the new passage is choked with spiderwebs."

"Let's hope it's not where we need to go," Aderyn said, and walked forward to join Weston. The webbing became thicker the farther she went, but when she walked through it, it still didn't cling to her feet or her arms strongly enough that she couldn't easily pull free.

Weston had been right when he said the new passage was choked with webs. Masses of the pearly-gray strands filled the space, seeming to glow the more there were of them collected in one place. From where she stood, the webs looked like a solid mass. "It's not our route," she said in some relief.

"The webbing gets thicker ahead," Weston said. "We might still have a problem."

"Let's worry about that when it happens," Owen said.

Aderyn glanced over her shoulder. Owen walked stiffly, like he was trying to avoid contact with any webbing even though it wasn't much of an impediment. Her heart went out to him, but she didn't say anything. He would be humiliated if she made a fuss over something he probably wasn't all that scared of. Owen wasn't afraid of any monster or dungeon they'd ever faced.

She and Weston continued down the hall. Their passing tore strands of web loose from their moorings so they floated lightly in the breeze made by their bodies. Aderyn couldn't help ducking away from the ones hanging from the ceiling that brushed her hair and her face. Still, nothing attacked her. What was the possibility that these were old, abandoned webs? They looked too fresh and, yes, even pretty to be cobwebs.

They drew near to another junction, this one offering four other passages. Aderyn was about to examine all of them when Weston said, "Did you hear that? It sounded like rain on a metal roof."

Aderyn listened. "I don't—wait." In the distance, she heard a rapid tapping. It did sound a little like rain on a roof, fast and echoing in the passage. "Where is it coming from?"

The echoes made it impossible for her to distinguish, but Weston immediately said, "That way." He pointed at the right-hand passage, which was narrower than the others and as choked with webbing as the one they'd passed.

Aderyn stared into the whiteness. It trembled slightly, like something was shaking it. Before she had time to use [**Improved Assess 4**], the pearly masses bubbled like foam, and a tide of white, scrambling, many-legged creatures poured toward her.

Aderyn shrieked and backed up, letting Weston get ahead of her so she could Assess the monsters.

Name: Skitterling [31]
Type: Vermin
Power level: 8

Terrain: subterranean, forest
Attack(s): bite, special
Immune to: none
Resistant to: none
Vulnerable to: elemental attacks, bludgeoning damage
Special: venom
Skitterlings are giant spiders—no, not that giant. They're only the size of large dogs, but they look bigger because their legs add to their size. Their white carapaces provide them with concealment in their webs, but they stand out against dark subterranean passages. They get their name from the skittering sound their sharp legs make against stone. Their bite, which does minimal damage as their mouths are small, delivers a mild venom, barely anything to worry about so long as you're only facing one skitterling. It's your bad luck that they travel in packs.

"They're dangerous as a group!" she called out, not using [**Amplify Voice**] for fear of drawing more enemies. "Separate them! Their bite is venomous, so watch out for that, and if you've got a bludgeon, use it!"

"I love the sound of that," Livia cried, and spoke a couple of indistinct words that made her stone fist glow with magical power.

There was a magical staff in the <**Knapsack of Plenty**>, but with how fast the skitterlings were moving, Aderyn didn't dare risk going for it. Instead, she took heart that the creatures weren't immune to edged weapons and went for the nearest one threatening Weston just as Owen appeared at her side. "We need to drive a wedge," she told Owen. "Break up their formation."

"Got it," Owen said. He pushed past her and into the mass of skitterlings, beating about with the <**Sunsword**>. Aderyn hurried after him, cursing silently. She hadn't meant throw himself into the middle of danger!

Something flashed past Aderyn's head, burning like a tiny star, and struck a mass of webbing clinging to the wall. The <**Fire Dancer's Knife**> blazed into furious flame that curled the webbing with its heat and then burned lines of light across the tunnel as it set more webbing on fire. Skitterlings scattered. Two weren't fast enough. Fire engulfed their white bodies, and they shook with helpless spasms until their legs curled in and they lay still in death.

Congratulations! You have killed [Skitterling].
You have earned [2675 XP]

The first two system defeat notices had barely faded before Livia's exultant shout and the sharp crack of stone shattering exoskeleton preceded a third. Aderyn fought back to back with Weston now, with Owen opposite her. The skitterlings darted fast as fire out of range and back again, and it took Aderyn a moment to see the pattern to their movements and match it. More defeat notices popped up.

Then Suveer screamed. "There's more of them coming from behind!"

Aderyn whipped around. Suveer, backing away from the web-choked passage they'd bypassed, was waving wildly at another flood of skitterlings, dead silent except for the eerie clicking of their sharp-tipped legs on stone. "Another forty-seven!" she called out after Assessing the horde.

Isold let out a low, pained cry. He wielded one half of the <Skeleton Ladder> like a club and smashed the skitterling clinging to his leg. "It bit me," he said. "Not very painful, but with forty-seven of them—"

"Sixty-three in all," Aderyn shouted. "We need to retreat! Find a place where we can control the fight!"

"Weston, what's ahead?" Owen called out.

"Two right-hand passages are full of webs—shit, there's more of them coming!" Weston grabbed his fallen knife and sheathed it. "Straight ahead is wide, left is narrow, neither of them—shit, shit, *shit!* They just keep coming! Neither of those passages have webs!"

"To the left," Aderyn said. She could barely see that opening from where she stood, but as Weston said, it wasn't wide and it looked like it might make for a good chokepoint. "I said *left!*" she repeated with **[Amplify Voice]**. "Go! Go! Go!"

She followed her own instructions and disengaged from the skitterling she was fighting with a final blow that didn't quite kill it. The thick, barely sticky webbing covering the floor gave her good traction, and she hurtled to the opening and backed into it, sweeping the combat with her gaze and adding frantically. Ninety-seven skitterlings. If they had the right tactical advantage, even ninety-seven power level eight vermin wouldn't overwhelm them.

She beckoned frantically to the others to join her. Ruan and Suveer were last, fighting a rearguard action to keep from being bitten. Bitten *more*, Aderyn amended; their clothes bore small tears in places, and the cast of their dark skin was greenish as if they were poisoned.

"All right, let's back up some more," she said when they were all together. "We need to find the narrowest spot—"

"Aderyn, they're leaving," Owen said.

Aderyn stopped going farther down the new passageway and looked over her shoulder. Then she turned around entirely. The flood of white skitterlings had become a barely-moving tide, as creature after creature backed away from their group.

"They must be smart enough to know we have the upper hand now," Livia said.

Aderyn shook her head. "No. Vermin can't reason that way. They act on instinct." She looked around again. The passage where they stood was completely free of webbing. "They never come here. They never come here because—"

Livia held up her hand for silence. "Something's approaching. I feel it in the stone."

Something moved farther down the passage, out of range of Livia's lights. Something big.

"They never come here," Aderyn finished, "because there's something here that scares them."

The sound of hissing filled the air, not a snake's hiss or the hiss of air escaping a bladder but the hiss of something breathing out, long and low. An enormous black shape emerged from the darkness. Eight monstrous multijointed legs, longer than Weston was tall, that terminated in sharp pointed claws supported a bulging black abdomen, shiny and streaked with red. A dozen lidless black eyes that shone like oil focused on the humans cowering below. Mandibles clashed, dripping a viscous, clear substance that stank of decay.

The giant spider paused in front of them, its terrifying eyes as focused as if it was capable of Assessing. It worked its mandibles again, once, twice. It hissed again, and pounced.

Everyone scattered. The spider landed where Aderyn had been, hissing and dribbling gouts of stinking saliva that spattered the stone and intensified the stink. Aderyn hadn't needed [See It Coming] to know to get out of the way. She pressed her back to the wall and Assessed the monster.

Name: Darkshroud

Type: Abomination

Power level: 20

Terrain: subterranean

Attack(s): claw x4, bite, stinger, special

Immune to: poison, acid, [Outflank]

Resistant to: mind control magic and effects, bludgeoning weapon damage

Vulnerable to: none

Special: venom, acid, shadowstep

Run, Aderyn. Run now.

CHAPTER TWENTY-NINE

"*Run!*" Aderyn screamed. "Follow me!"

She scrambled away from the wall seconds before a sharp-clawed limb struck where she'd been, sending up a spray of sparks and chips of stone. Darkshroud hissed and darted after Aderyn, forcing her to sidle along more slowly than she wanted. She didn't dare turn her back on the spider and lose the advantage of [**See It Coming**].

She heard the others scattering, and the thuds of weapons striking the skitterlings' bodies. She wanted to scream with frustration at how the small monsters were probably going to get her friends killed by Darkshroud. The spider aimed another spear of a limb at Aderyn, and in the moment after it missed, she took a quick look around. Ruan was fighting skitterlings with Suveer providing distractions. Livia and Weston were back to back, protecting Isold, who laid about with the <Skeleton Ladder>. And Owen was making his way around behind Darkshroud, trying to [**Outflank**] the creature.

Aderyn held back another scream. They couldn't fight this thing! But [**Read Body Language**] told Aderyn as clearly as if he'd announced it that Owen was terrified and was dealing with his fear the only way he knew how, by attacking the source. She couldn't communicate the need to flee without drawing Darkshroud's attention to her husband. So she stopped backing away and deflected the next strike with her sword.

She'd never been so grateful for [See It Coming]. Though this was the fastest thing she'd ever had to defend against, she knocked every blow aside and had enough time for [Discern Weakness]. The swollen abdomen shone red, warning of its resistance to attacks, and tiny blue specks shone at every joint of the terrible legs. Her arms were tiring from how rapidly she had to react, but she told herself this wasn't impossible.

"Aderyn!" Owen shouted. "[Outflank] isn't working!"

Aderyn silently cursed herself for forgetting to communicate what she'd read in the Assessment. She met the spider's many inhuman eyes, black and glistening like a dozen tiny oil slicks and malevolent as nothing else she'd ever seen. She slapped aside another blow, and let out a pained cry when the second followed the first too quickly and cut a gash in her thigh, just below the bottom of her mail shirt. "Owen, we can't fight this!"

Darkshroud hissed again and reared up, raising four black legs high in the air. Desperate and in pain, Aderyn bolted for the exit, staggered on her wounded leg, and fell to her knees. She rolled onto her back for what protection that would give. She wasn't going to die without facing her enemy.

Then Owen was there, putting himself between her and the spider. Darkshroud reared back again, this time apparently unsettled by the glowing <Sunsword>. It took a few steps backward, into the darkness. Then it vanished.

Owen didn't lower his sword. "Are you okay?"

"Just a minor wound. Where did the spider go?"

"I don't know. I think it retreated."

"It disappeared, Owen." Terror shot through Aderyn's veins. "It's invisible!"

"Wouldn't you see through that, with [Truesight]?" Owen backed up and then gave Aderyn a hand up. "Or at least know something was wrong?"

"That's right." Aderyn turned around. There weren't many skitterlings left. Most had fled, though a few crushed white bodies blended with the webbing. The others gathered around, and Isold exclaimed over Aderyn's leg and drew out the <**Wand of Healing**>.

"The big spider is gone," Owen said. Aderyn knew she was the only one who heard the tremor in his voice. "But it's not dead, and I'm sure it hasn't given up on killing us. We need to be especially careful. Aderyn, which way now?"

The orb's weight steadied Aderyn's hands, which were shaking with the aftermath of fear and adrenalin. "That way." Despite her conviction that Darkshroud wasn't in its cavern anymore, she was just as happy the <**Wayfinder**> directed her away from it, down the one clear passage.

She moved slowly, with Weston beside her, her skin crawling at every echo, every distant sound. The new passage was darker than the others thanks to being free of skitterling webs, and Aderyn was about to suggest Livia create more *orbs of light* when the back of her neck tingled with [**Sense Ambush**]. She stopped and grabbed Weston's arm. "Something's about to attack us."

Weston nodded. "There's not much we can do to avoid it. Prepare to attack?"

"Let's see what's up there," Aderyn agreed.

She took another step. The swollen black shape of Darkshroud lunged at her, its mandibles clashing.

Weston shoved Aderyn out of the way and raised his rapier, but it was too late—the spider's mandibles closed on his shoulder. Weston screamed. Aderyn recovered her balance and chased Darkshroud as it dragged Weston backward.

"I don't care if we can't fight it! I need to know more, *now!*" she shrieked, and Assessed the spider again.

She skimmed past the information about the creature's attacks and devoured the new text appearing below.

If you're going to persist in fighting this creature, I'll give you what help I can. What you've likely already noticed is that Darkshroud's shadowstep ability lets her teleport, short-range, between areas of darkness. Deprive her of those, and she's not so maneuverable.

Darkshroud's many eyes means [Outflank] will give you no advantage, but [See It Coming] is faster than her clawed legs. Remember the vulnerable spots revealed by [Discern Weakness]. Depriving Darkshroud of some of her attacks will make a huge difference.

Darkshroud's bite is laced with acidic saliva, which is strong enough to melt stone—oh, you noticed that? I'm glad you don't depend solely on my advice. Here's something you'd better not ignore: *Do not* get hit by that stinger. In addition to doing physical damage, it injects a poison that rots your body from the inside, liquefying it so Darkshroud can sip your remains at her leisure. Are you scared yet? Fear is a powerful motivator if you master it, and I believe you have.

The knowledge that as long as the light following her kept the darkness from being complete, Darkshroud couldn't shadowstep away with Weston, gave Aderyn fresh speed. Pounding footsteps coming up behind her sounded like Livia had discovered motivation to run. "Livia, we need *sunburst* now!"

The welcome sound of nonsense words were followed by a burst of light so brilliant Aderyn involuntarily closed her eyes. Darkshroud hissed again, and this time it sounded furious. The spider stopped moving. Its mandibles closed harder on Weston's shoulder, and he screamed again, this time weakly, as thick saliva coursed over his upper body.

Ruan ran past, shouting and wielding his greatsword, with Suveer hurrying close behind. "Don't bother with **[Outflank]**, Ruan, it's immune! Everyone, listen up—if we can cut off some of those leg joints, we stand a chance against it. The bite is acidic, the stinger is powerful poison, but keep the creature out of the dark places and maybe we won't all die!"

As stirring speeches went, that one wouldn't go down in history, but with Weston still in Darkshroud's grip, it was all Aderyn could manage.

She followed Owen and Ruan. Ruan had switched to attacking the leg joints, but he wasn't making much progress. She left him to it and hurried to free Weston, but Livia beat her there. The Earthbreaker wound up and punched Darkshroud in the middle of its small, many-eyed head. Two of its lidless eyes popped like blisters, and Darkshroud shrieked, a thin but penetrating sound. It dropped Weston and backed away, hissing.

"That's right, I'm coming for you," Livia growled. She punched again, but Darkshroud dodged the blow. Then it leaped over the four of them, nearly taking Ruan's sword with it, and landed near Isold. Isold reacted by taking a step back and holding a hand up, palm first. In a calm voice that resonated with compelling harmonics, he said, "*Sit.*"

Giant spiders aren't made for sitting. This one tried anyway.

Isold dodged the tangle of limbs and ran for Weston, pulling out the <**Healing Stone**>. "Take its legs while it's down!" he shouted.

Ruan slammed the <**Galling Blade**> against one leg like sectioning a chicken. "Hah!" he exclaimed as the joint neatly severed, and Darkshroud shuddered. "I can do that all day!"

Owen aimed for another leg joint, against which the <**Sunsword**> looked impressively brilliant. The leg snapped. Owen darted backward. "It's getting up! Watch out!"

Aderyn saw the rear of the abdomen for the first time. The stinger was barely noticeable against the black carapace, not very large compared to the hideous weapon the waspnettle queen had wielded. But the description of the stinger's poison did not leave her inclined to discount its danger. "Stay away—"

Darkshroud whipped around, almost too fast to see. Aderyn dropped, and the whiff of stinking air that blew past her head and the brush of hard exoskeleton against her hair told her she almost hadn't gotten out of the way in time. She aimed a blow at the abdomen and scored a hit that made Darkshroud hiss again. Rolling to her feet, she pursued the spider as it lurched from one side of the passage to another. Two of its horrible clawed feet were missing, but it still ran lightly, if awkwardly.

Livia chanted again, and the stone of the passage flowed like water to engulf two rear legs. The stone hardened around them in the moment before Darkshroud sprang again, this time aiming for Ruan. The grasp of *immobilize* met the force with which Darkshroud propelled itself. Darkshroud leapt, jerked, and shrieked again as it dislocated those rear legs. Owen scrambled up the stone pillars and slashed again and again at one of the dislocated joints until he severed it.

This time, the scream was weaker. Darkshroud struggled free of *immobilize*. Its head swayed, surveying its enemies. Then it leaped again, past Ruan, and tried to scramble away.

"Stop it! If it reaches a dark space, it can teleport away and this battle will never end," Aderyn shouted.

Ruan and Owen together pelted after the limping spider. Ruan dove beneath its abdomen, avoiding the stinger. Owen clambered one-handed up the spider's back, balancing carefully as its lopsided movement threatened to throw him off. He slid down the abdomen to the head, inserted the tip of the <Sunsword> into the gap between head and body as if he had all the time in the world, and drove the blade home.

Darkshroud's body contracted in a spasm that did toss Owen off, wrenching the sword from his grip. He landed neatly and ran back to try again, but Darkshroud jerked again and sagged. Ruan shouted and slid away from beneath the monster.

**Congratulations! You have defeated [Darkshroud].
You have earned [52,000 XP]**

Owen stopped moving, breathing heavily. His shoulders shook with what to Aderyn looked like residual terror, but he didn't otherwise look unnerved. "Sorry," he told Ruan. "I honestly didn't think about experience, just about killing that thing."

"It's all right." Ruan sheathed his sword. "Somebody had to get the final blow."

"Suveer's in trouble," Isold said.

Aderyn whipped around. She'd lost track of Suveer in the fighting, but he'd been near her when the stinger nearly struck. Now he lay on the rounded floor of the passage, breathing shallowly and trembling. Black veins pulsing with fluid threaded across his normally warmly-brown skin. Terrible foreboding filled her. "The stinger hit him. How long ago was that?"

"It's only been a few seconds," Isold said, palming the **<Healing Stone>**. "He'll be fine."

"No. The poison is stronger than that. Stronger than the one that nearly killed Livia." What were the odds the one of them who hadn't taken the Miracle Meal was the one Darkshroud had stung? Aderyn stripped off the **<Knapsack of Plenty>** and felt around inside. Isold had two, but she had one—

She pulled out the **<Potion of Life>** and uncorked it. "Help him sit up a bit, Ruan." Careful not to spill, she set the bottle's lip against Suveer's mouth.

Suveer shook his head. "Not yet," he whispered. "Not ready yet. Stronger."

"What?" Impatience replaced fear. "You have to drink this soon or you will die, Suveer!"

"Endurance breeds... stronger... more skills..." Suveer's voice grew fainter.

Aderyn lost her patience. She pinched Suveer's nose shut, then, when he opened his mouth to breathe, released his nose to grip his jaw. With a deft motion, she poured the potion down his throat, shaping his mouth so the liquid wouldn't dribble out. Suveer gasped, choked, and gagged the potion down.

Brilliant green light exploded from every inch of Suveer's skin. Suveer arched his back, wrenching out of his brother's hands and falling to lie on his side. Again, his breathing grew heavy, but the black veins shrank to thin lines and then vanished. Slowly, Suveer relaxed out of the tension that gripped him. One hand lifted to touch his face below the missing eye. Then he said, "What did that do?"

"It's a **<Potion of Life>**," Aderyn said, absently tucking the empty bulb into her knapsack. "Darkshroud's poison rots your insides. Liquefies them. I don't know what in thunder you were playing at, Suveer—"

"Don't yell at him, Aderyn, he gets it," Owen said. He gently rested his arm around her shoulders. He was still trembling, but his voice was strong. "I can't believe we survived that."

Suveer sat up, still lightly brushing his fingertips over his skin and then the scar tissue. His whole attention was on Aderyn. "You used something that powerful on someone not in your team? On me?"

"Like we're going to let a companion rot, no matter whose team he's on," Weston said. He was naked from the waist up and held a crumpled bundle of fabric and leather scraps. "That acid did a number on my clothing. Is there enough left for *repair* to work, dearest?"

"We'll see." Livia's voice was shaking. No one drew attention to it.

For a while, no one spoke except Livia muttering the *repair* spell under her breath. Aderyn watched the fabric and armor ripple into existence and let the magic calm her. *Repair* always looked as though it was revealing something that already was there, like removing invisibility, though when she'd asked Livia about it Livia had said it was a complicated thing even she didn't understand.

Finally, Livia tossed the clothing and armor to Weston and said, "We need to move on. This isn't one of those rapid-respawn dungeons, is it? Like the Ivory Palace?"

"No. Just the timer." Aderyn couldn't help herself; she looked at the counter with its white-light numbers. It stunned her how little time that had taken. "It hasn't even been an hour. Darkshroud felt like it took forever to kill."

"It had a name?" Owen shuddered. "I don't think I needed to know that. Aderyn, are we going the right way?"

Aderyn focused on the <Wayfinder>, which radiated red immediately. "There's another exit back there, I think down that second passage that didn't have webs. But the one ahead of us is closer. I'm—" She closed her eyes and compared her mental picture of the outside of Charnel Keep, what little she'd seen, with the picture the <Wayfinder> was building for her. "If this is as simple as I believe, then there are three exits for sure. One is the hole we came in by, and the other two are the doors in the base at the front of the keep. There might be other hidden exits, but my guess is we're headed for the smaller of those doors."

"I don't understand," Ruan said. "Wouldn't those doors lead to the main keep, and not to down here?"

"I'm not sure I understand it either, but it matches what I've seen." Aderyn brought the orb up to eye level and watched its rings spin. "It might not matter. We're searching for an exit, and I trust the <Wayfinder> to find one that will help us. So we need to keep going, and worry about what's there when we've reached it."

"Don't spread out," Owen said. "We don't need to risk being separated. Aderyn, go ahead."

With Aderyn once more in the lead, they proceeded down the new passage. No spiderwebs appeared; no giant black spiders leaped from the shadows. When the passage split into three smaller passages, the <Wayfinder> didn't waver in pointing at the one on the left. Aderyn rotated her neck swiftly, easing the tension, and kept walking.

The farther they went, the more the walls closed in. The passage was now half as wide as it had been and the ceiling was barely a foot over Aderyn's head. Weston, walking beside her, had to crouch. Aderyn swallowed and reminded herself she was walking freely and the walls weren't going to spontaneously crush her.

Then she stopped. Ahead, a rockfall brought the passage to an end. Aderyn checked the <Wayfinder>, which was deep red and whirring fast enough to hum. "Livia?"

"I would like to know," Livia said, walking forward to rest a hand on the pile of rubble, "why that thing knows a bunch of rocks aren't an impediment to us. Why doesn't it just steer us in a straight course? It's not like I can't use *pass through stone* freely." She closed her eyes and rested her forehead against the pile. Her lips moved, but Aderyn heard nothing, not even the muddled words of the spellslinging language.

In a minute, Livia straightened. "Everyone back up. This is going to be complicated, and it helps if I don't have to worry about hitting someone with a flying rock."

Everyone backed up. Ruan backed up farther. Aderyn had the spiteful feeling that he wasn't as great as he thought he was, if he was nervous about spellslinging.

She watched Suveer, who looked more alert than usual. Where had he gotten the ridiculous notion that enduring pain made your skills better, or gave you extra ranks, or whatever idiocy had nearly gotten him turned to a puddle of goo? Ruan, probably. Or it could have been Suveer's own stupid idea, something he'd internalized along with the belief that his class was useless even at level sixteen. Whatever it was, she wanted to teach him otherwise. Maybe saving his life would incline him to listen to her now.

Rumbling filled the narrow space, spreading outward and echoing until Aderyn felt the mountain really was coming down on her head. She made herself breathe calmly and didn't shriek when someone touched her hand. "Sorry," Owen said. "It's going to be fine."

"That's what I was going to tell you. Are you less freaked out by spiders now that you killed Darkshroud? Or—I'm sorry, maybe you aren't all that afraid of them, and you were joking when you said you were."

"No, spiders terrify me." Owen squeezed her hand. "I'm going to have nightmares about that thing appearing out of the shadows. And how it nearly crushed you like a bug. I'm so grateful for [See It Coming] and it's not even my skill."

"I guess it really is true that bravery is being scared shitless and doing the right thing anyway."

"That's well said. Did you come up with that?"

"No, it's something my mother always says." Aderyn chuckled. "And then Father says, 'Language, Lyzette!' and we all laugh. I miss my family so much!"

"We're getting close," Owen said. "I hope reaching level twenty correlates with the end of the Fated One quests."

The rumbling faded and then stopped. Livia stood next to a perfectly round opening in what was now a solid wall of stone, rippling as if it had flowed like lava. "Sorry it's not bigger, but there are tradeoffs —never mind, it doesn't matter."

"I'll go first," Aderyn said. "We've got to be close to the exit."

She ducked through the hole, which was barely four feet in diameter. It was more of a small tunnel than a hole, but it took her barely five seconds to make her way through, not nearly enough time for her to become afraid.

She emerged from the hole. With a gasp, she threw herself sideways as the ghostly shape of a fist-sized black stone flew at her head. A second later, the real thing impacted on the stone wall, sending rock chips flying.

Aderyn ended up in a fighter's crouch, Assessing the passage. No monster hordes burst from hiding, no white spiders came crawling from every crevice to attack. Instead, several dozen humans came to a halt a short distance from her. None were armed, though a couple of Flamecrafters and Earthbreakers had fists wreathed in flame or glittering with magic.

Aderyn's attention focused on the one figure her Assessment had targeted—a scruffy, white-bearded Moonlighter who held another fist-sized stone ready to throw. She exclaimed, "Varoun!"

CHAPTER THIRTY

Varoun lowered his arm. "Aderyn. You're not alone, are you?"

"We're all here." Aderyn hurried forward to clasp his hand. He drew her into a soldier's embrace, pounding her back twice for emphasis. "We thought this was the exit. What are you all doing here? I mean, in this part of the dungeon? We knew the orcs took their prisoners to Charnel Keep."

"This is what orcs use for cells." Varoun gestured. The place they stood in wasn't so much a passage as a large chamber with rough-hewn walls not as smoothly bumpy as the rest. Someone had hacked open the passage to make this room big enough to hold a hundred humans. Behind Varoun, Aderyn saw a dark, narrow tunnel with the same hacked-out look, down to the steps rising from it.

The sound of more people passing through Livia's tunnel drew Aderyn's attention back to her friends. "I guess we got lucky," she said. "Ruan doesn't have to search the whole keep."

"General Varoun!" Owen exclaimed. "Is everyone all right?"

"No one is badly injured, and of those they took prisoner—" Varoun fell silent, his jaw muscles tense. "There are still forty-nine of us here."

"We saw what the orcs did to the others," Aderyn said. "So they marched you here and isolated you all in this cavern? Not to be critical, but you have Earthbreakers—why didn't you escape?"

"We had guards who threatened to kill anyone who even looked like they intended escape or attack." Varoun pointed again. Aderyn hadn't noticed the dead orc lying on the ground nearby. The very dead orc, burned almost beyond recognition as humanoid. Two more dead orcs lay collapsed near the stairs. One was unmarked, and the other's head was crushed. "I assume it was Livia who manipulated the rock fall into a tunnel? That distracted the orcs enough that we were able to kill them. We were afraid something worse would come through the tunnel, though."

"Just us." Aderyn looked up the tunnel containing stairs. It was too dark for **[Darkvision]** to be effective, and as far as she could tell it went on forever. "Where does that tunnel go? To the outer door?"

"There's a small room at the top of the stairs where they bring prisoners through. It has a second door I assume accesses the keep itself." Varoun spoke as precisely as ever, though he was disheveled and filthy and moved more stiffly than usual. "When we were brought in, there were two guards waiting. I don't know if that is because they'd had word new prisoners were coming, or if it's standard procedure. But overcoming them should be simple, if your plan is to infiltrate the keep and kill the orc commander general."

"That's our quest," Owen said.

"Not mine," Ruan said. "My quest is to free the prisoners. Do you know if there are other humans in the keep, sir?"

Varoun gave Ruan a long, considering look. "We don't know. Chandar reported to me that orcs had captured humans before, but they might all be dead. There weren't any others in this chamber when we arrived."

"Then I have to search the keep." Ruan turned to Aderyn. "Are you sure you won't lend me the <**Wayfinder**>? No, you're right, you shouldn't do that. Sorry."

Ruan was being so reasonable Aderyn was suspicious. She didn't believe he was the altruistic type. On the other hand, this was a Fated One quest, and it had a sizable experience reward in addition to unlocking the next one. So Ruan wasn't being altruistic, after all. She hated that that gave her comfort.

"But what do we do?" she said. "It's important that you all are safe, so we can't have you following us into the keep. But it's not like the Blighted Range is any more safe than here."

"We can take care of ourselves if we work together," Varoun said. "If you guide us to where you entered, we can make our way back to the Southlands in relative safety."

"But—"

"He's right. They're not weak," Owen told her.

"And you should take this," Livia said, offering him the <**Wand of World Door**>. "You'll need it more than we will."

Varoun accepted it and sheathed it gracefully. "Thank you. That will make our journey easier."

"Is there anything else we can do for you, sir?" Owen asked.

"Some healing. We have a few too injured to move quickly." Varoun put a hand on Aderyn's shoulder. "It will be all right, Aderyn. I didn't get to be an old Moonlighter without learning a few tricks. And gaining twenty-seven ranks in [**Improvised Weapon**]."

"I know. I just feel as if I've taken on three quests that all demand my attention at once." Aderyn smiled. "Good luck, Varoun."

"Good luck to you, Aderyn. I wish I had more information I could give you about what awaits you above. Don't underestimate their general. We heard the orcs talk about him, always in terms of terrible fear. I believe he's the sort who will readily kill anyone for any reason, which makes him unpredictable and therefore dangerous."

"We'll be careful. Now, let me warn you about the dangers we met underground."

The counter read 22:01:28 when Isold finished healing the last of the wounded and Ruan and Weston had looted the orc bodies. Still plenty of time—though not so much that she intended to celebrate before they'd won. She clasped Varoun's hand in farewell and didn't wait for all the soldiers to exit before approaching the stairs. This time, Livia's lights illuminated it, and the light relieved Aderyn's mind that she might be climbing stairs into a closed-in, terrifying space. The stairs didn't rise more than about thirty feet, and the tunnel was high-ceilinged enough for even the biggest orc to pass.

Weston, in the lead with Owen immediately behind him, reached the heavy trap door at the end of the tunnel and ran a finger over the padlock. As Aderyn was going over plans for getting the orcs outside to let them through without revealing they were human, Weston withdrew a crude key from his belt pouch and whispered, "Be ready when I open the trap door. We need to move fast."

Owen rested his hand, not on the basket hilt of the deactivated <Sunsword>, but on his <Deadly Blade>. Aderyn silently agreed that the brilliant light of the magic sword would definitely give them away. Weston opened the padlock, not being stealthy about it. The lock ground open so loudly Aderyn didn't think stealth was possible, even for a Moonlighter.

Weston returned the key to his belt pouch and pushed the door open a fraction. The rusty hinges made even more noise than the lock had, but no one on the other side shouted an alarm. Aderyn couldn't see anything beyond the dim light of torches. Weston flung the trap door open to bang against the stone of the floor and leapt through the hole, followed by Owen. Aderyn rushed after him, tugged along by [Keep Pace].

Two orcs, one leaning against the wall, the other sitting on a crudely-built stool, looked up at Weston and Owen's entrance. Aderyn couldn't read orc expressions easily, but the way their eyes widened and their mouths fell slack, revealing canines nearly big enough to be fangs —of course they were surprised, but the important thing was that their reaction hadn't been to signal a warning. Weston finished the standing one in total silence; Owen's victim had time to grunt before the <Deadly Blade> laid open its throat and then stabbed it through the heart.

Aderyn caught the sitting one and lowered it quietly to the ground, just in case. She moved to the side to let the others enter. Though the torches burned low, [Darkvision] made the room's features clear. It was mostly empty except for two stools, the torches, and a pile of polearms leaning against the wall in one corner that looked like a messy, deadly haystack.

Aside from the hole in the floor leading to the cells, there were two exits. One of them was larger and much sturdier, made of blackened iron and barred with a slab of oak Aderyn wasn't sure she could lift. The other, opposite the first, was a more ordinary door, oak deeply pitted with small holes as if someone had used it for target practice. "That one," she said, not speaking too loudly, just in case.

She pulled out the <**Wayfinder**>. "What am I searching for?"

"Glasha," Owen said.

"The prisoners," Ruan said at the same time.

Aderyn scowled. "I can't do both at the same time. Owen?"

Owen glanced at Ruan. "Maybe it's time to split up. We don't have much time."

"I know you'll think it's self-serving, since it's my quest, but rescuing humans has to be more important than killing the orc general. Or at least should take precedence." Ruan addressed, not Owen, but Aderyn.

"I agree the safety of humans is important, Ruan, but if we rescue them first, we'll have to do something to protect them. Which means separating, probably." Aderyn closed her hand tighter on the spikes of the <**Wayfinder**>. She hated the idea of leaving prisoners in the orcs' hands any longer than they had to, but she had to be sensible. "And killing Glasha will cause confusion that will make it easier to get the humans out. We either need to find Glasha and kill him, or split up so we can pursue our separate quests."

Ruan nodded slowly. "All right. It's not like Suveer and I weren't prepared to go it alone if we had to. You're right."

Again, he sounded so reasonable Aderyn was suspicious. But she still didn't feel like he was lying to her. "I'm sorry we can't help."

"I know. But it really is all right." Ruan gripped Aderyn's shoulder briefly in reassurance. "And this way, you don't have to worry about what's happening to the human prisoners, right?"

Aderyn hadn't worried about that until he said something, but now she couldn't not picture those impaled bodies trembling on bloody stakes. "Right."

"There's no one in the hall outside," Weston said. "Let's move."

The door wasn't locked, and its hinges didn't squeal, but Aderyn still felt like they made more noise than a herd of goretusks. She followed Weston out the door, which opened on the corner of two halls. More torches burned in iron sconces at intervals down both halls, blackening the stone walls with soot ingrained over centuries. These torches gave off more light than the others, but still didn't illuminate the halls brightly. To Aderyn, [Darkvision] gave the scene an oddly doubled look, as if the level of illumination was right at the border where the skill would activate.

She oriented herself by her system map. It didn't provide her with a map of Charnel Keep, but it did show her which way was north in relation to the building. One of the halls ran north and the other ran west. Doors opened at random intervals along the western hall, which ended at another intersection. The northern hall had only two doors, both on the left. By Aderyn's mental calculations, the right side of that hallway was the outer wall of the keep.

Distantly, she heard a rising and falling sound that made her think of celebrations, or dances, and the occasional shriek that might have been excitement or terror. Something to stay away from. She swiftly brought up the Codex and glanced at the entry for [Fated One's Destiny: Crush the Horde], just long enough to re-read the line about Glasha. When she was trying to locate an unknown person or place, every piece of information helped. Then she closed her eyes and willed herself to locate Glasha.

She was facing the northern hallway, and when the orb warmed immediately, it heartened her. Maybe this wouldn't take very long, after all. To be thorough, she turned in a slow circle. The <Wayfinder> warmed again when she'd turned ninety degrees to the left. She opened her eyes. Its pink glow pointed her directly at the western hallway.

"Crap," she whispered. She rotated back and discovered the orb was just as certain the northern hall would take her to Glasha. "I guess we have to choose."

"Does that mean it's not working?" Ruan asked. His eyes were fixed avidly on the <Wayfinder>.

"It means Glasha is somewhere equally distant from both these paths," Aderyn said. "Or either path is a good one."

"Let's go north, then," Owen said. "Fewer doors for orcs to open unexpectedly."

"I'd like to go first this time," Ruan said.

Owen regarded him as if searching for secret treachery. "All right. Ruan and Suveer, Aderyn and me, then Isold, Livia, and Weston. Aderyn, let us know if anything changes with the <**Wayfinder**>."

The halls were wide enough for Owen and Aderyn to walk side by side. Ahead of them, Ruan moved with a graceful alertness Aderyn admired despite not liking him much. The torches flickered as they passed, little dancing flames that moved as gracefully as Ruan.

At the first door, Ruan hesitated, then motioned for Aderyn and Owen to join him. He cupped his ear and pointed at the door. Beyond the door, something clacked like wood on wood. The sound came at irregular intervals, *clack, clack, clack-clack... clack.*

Owen and Ruan exchanged glances. Ruan shrugged. Owen gestured him to continue. When Owen lagged behind, Aderyn slowed with him, but he gestured for her to proceed as well. "Going to get Weston to listen," he whispered.

Aderyn nodded. Ruan and Suveer were already farther ahead than she liked, though they weren't moving rapidly. She glanced back once at her friends, who were gathered around the door while Weston listened, then hurried to catch up to Ruan and Suveer. "Let's wait for them," she whispered.

Ruan nodded. "This place stinks."

Aderyn hadn't noticed a smell other than the tarry, hot scent of the torches. Maybe he meant a metaphorical smell. Ruan had just passed the second door. Whatever was behind it didn't make any noise. Or maybe there was nothing there. Aderyn was starting to feel nervous about not having encountered any orcs. The distant noise of celebrating, or whatever it was, had diminished but not disappeared, and the silence was so eerie Aderyn had to stop herself talking just to break it.

Weston looked past the others at Aderyn. He began walking their way at a rapid pace that turned into a run. Aderyn, surprised, glanced around for whatever had him so anxious.

Ruan yawned and leaned against the wall. "I think—"

Something went *click.* Ruan staggered as the stone he was leaning against retracted into the wall. Above Aderyn's head, metal groaned. She looked up and saw the ghostly form of a row of iron spikes hurtling at her face.

Aderyn gasped. She grabbed Suveer, who was standing beside her staring at the floor, and threw them both out of the path of the descending portcullis. The wall of iron bars slammed into the floor with a resounding crash, right where Aderyn had been standing. Aderyn picked herself up off the floor and tried to lift the portcullis. No result.

Weston jogged up to the portcullis and gripped it with both hands, straining. It didn't even quiver, though Weston's muscles bulged with effort. He released the bars after a few seconds. "I couldn't tell you from back there," he said, "but I noticed some of the stones are actually trap triggers. Livia neutralized the one we passed before—"

"Just a matter of shaping it so it can't depress." Livia flexed her fingers. "Give me a minute, and I'll carve us a tunnel beneath—"

Weston held up a hand. "Someone's coming. Whoever's in that room back there. This is going to get noisy."

Aderyn made a decision. "I'll find you. It shouldn't take long. There's a hall right here that heads back west. Let me know through **[Bonded Mind]**—"

Owen reached through the bars and gripped her free hand. "No talking. Just go!"

CHAPTER THIRTY-ONE

Ruan was already moving. Aderyn grabbed Suveer's hand and towed him along after her. Behind them, a door opened, and a guttural voice shouted something, but Aderyn couldn't make it out. Her heart ached at leaving her friends to face the enemy without her, but she was right: she could find them anywhere.

She passed the hallway she'd mentioned to Owen and kept going, following Ruan. A glance had showed her many doors, and doors were the enemy. Instead, she continued until they came to the end of the hall, another corner that turned west. This hall had only one door, or rather a set of double doors, on the left. A small hallway opposite the doors was completely dark.

Ruan stopped just around the corner, barely breathing hard. "We have to keep moving. If we can find a way that leads south, that should reunite us. It's a keep, right? Is that literal? Because a traditional keep is built in quarters around a central room or tower. I think we were in the southeast quarter."

"How do you know that?"

Ruan grinned. "I'm not completely ignorant of history. Do you want to use the <**Wayfinder**> now, or test my theory?"

Aderyn clutched the orb to her chest. It had gone dark and still during the terror of fleeing. "Let's go to the end of this hall first. There's obviously no other way to go, and wherever that dark hall leads, it's away from them."

Quietly, they walked to the end of the hall. Ruan strode nearly as silently as Weston, and took the lead like this was a walk down a tree-lined lane and not a trek through an orc-ridden keep. But his steps slowed as he neared the end. "It's open," he said. "Big empty space."

Aderyn joined him. It was partly true. The hall came to an end at what should have been a four-way intersection of halls. To the left, another hall headed south, but ahead and to the right, flagstones defined a big, empty space. The only structure was a flat, wide column of stone like the remains of a wall, but it was solid and terminated at the thirty-foot-high ceiling. In the distance beyond that, Aderyn's <**Darkvision**> revealed more walls on the far side.

"Shit," Ruan said, pointing left. "I think those portcullises come in pairs. Look at that."

Aderyn looked. The hall leading south had a couple of doors, including one very large and ornate one on the western side, and she could see the entrance to the hall they'd bypassed in their flight. But what drew her attention was the heavy iron portcullis dropped into place just past that second hall, blocking the way farther south. The way back to her friends.

A system message popped up.

Congratulations! You have defeated [Orc Elite].
You have earned [9000 XP]

Aderyn gasped. "They're in combat." As she spoke, a second, identical message appeared across her vision.

She turned around, and Ruan grabbed her shoulder. "We can't open the portcullis, and even if we could, we can't go back without running into who knows what kind of trouble, Aderyn. They'll be fine. We need to stay focused."

Aderyn closed her eyes. *What happened?* she asked Owen with **[Bonded Mind]**.

Training room. We surprised a couple of orcs. We're working our way back around, but there's another closed portcullis.

We saw it. Keep moving. We'll meet up eventually.

Moving west. Stay in touch.

Aderyn nodded, though Owen couldn't see her. "They're all right."

"Good. Now what?" Ruan said.

"You're asking me?"

"You're the one with the magic item that takes us anywhere. Of course I'm asking you."

"We should go after the prisoners," Suveer said.

Aderyn hadn't heard him make a single noise since she'd saved him from liquefaction, not even a grunt of protest or pain when she dragged him away from the falling portcullis. "The prisoners?"

"What Owen said made sense at the time," Suveer said. "But you know where your friends are—they're stuck back there. You don't need the <**Wayfinder**> for that. We should rescue the prisoners before time runs out."

"But—" Aderyn paused. Suveer sounded more focused than she remembered. "The prisoner rescue isn't on a timer. We should..." Her voice trailed off as she considered her next words. Searching for Glasha on her own was suicidal. Even the three of them together were probably no match for the orc commander general. And Suveer was right that there wasn't anything she could do for her friends that they couldn't do for themselves. If she went back, there would be two groups in that quarter, possibly rousing twice as many orcs and ruining their chances of reaching Glasha.

On the other hand, if they found the prisoners, she could help Ruan and Suveer get them moving to safety, and that would give Owen and the others time to extricate themselves. Then she could use the <**Wayfinder**> to locate them and Glasha, and she wouldn't be worried and distracted by the possible fate of the prisoners. She dismissed the passing thought that this was a justification to do what she'd originally hoped to do.

"Suveer makes a good point," Ruan said, looking faintly surprised. "We really only have three choices. You can go back and look for the others, which will take up time you could use to explore and maybe get a sense of where everything is in this nightmare of a keep. You can leave us to rescue the prisoners ourselves and try to find Glasha on your own, which is a terrible idea. I think Owen might kill me if I left you here without companions. Or you can help us locate the prisoners. I know what I'd choose, but I'm leaving it up to you."

Aderyn nodded. "All right," she said, holding up the <**Wayfinder**>. "Let's find the prisoners."

She focused on the magic item, which glowed pale red immediately as if it agreed with her deep desire to find and free any prisoners. "That's reassuring. There are humans up here." *We're going to find the prisoners,* she silently told Owen.

"So we aren't wasting our time," Ruan said. He pressed against the wall to the north and peeked around the corner. "Is it telling you to go that way? I can't see anything past that big empty space."

The prisoners? Are you crazy? Owen's frustration echoed through his immaterial voice. *We need to reunite first.*

Aderyn shook her head. "It's beyond that opening." She told Owen, *It's smart. You have to work your way northward, and if we free the prisoners, that gives Ruan and Suveer something to do that gets them out of our way.*

I hate it that you make sense. Okay. Just keep me notified, all right? And don't let Ruan put you in danger.

Understood. I love you.

A door somewhere to the north opened and closed with a loud bang. Aderyn dropped the <**Wayfinder**> into her purse and whispered, "We have to move. Follow me."

She headed west, skirting the flagstones. [**Darkvision**] revealed a drooping tree with limp branches like a dying willow and a tangled, messy garden, overgrown but not encroaching on the stones surrounding it. A swift glance upward told her the space was open to the sky, like an atrium. The idea of orcs doing anything so civilized as gardening was absurd, but she was curious about what they might plant. Strangler vines or blood-sucking tomatoes, probably.

Heavy footsteps approached from the north. Aderyn didn't have a Moonlighter's hearing to know how many enemies it was, and stopping to Assess was stupidly dangerous. She hurried faster. Ahead, a wall divided the passage in half down its middle, narrowing it, but not equally. The passage on the left was twice the width of the one on the right. It was also lit by more of the flickering torches. The one on the right was completely dark.

Aderyn gestured to Ruan and Suveer to follow her and ducked into the dark passage on the right, moving back far enough that she was completely in shadow. Ruan and Suveer passed her, but Ruan immediately turned around and came to her side. They both stood perfectly still, listening, watching.

A group of orcs came into sight on the far side of the atrium. The noise of their hobnailed boots striking the stone drowned out any quieter sounds. Aderyn relaxed when they continued south. Then she grabbed Ruan's shoulder. "They're going to find that portcullis lowered and know someone's here. We have to keep moving."

She snatched the <**Wayfinder**> out and stared at it, her hands trembling with tension. It glowed bright red immediately, reassuring her that at least they were close to their goal. When she turned in the fastest circle she could manage without losing her connection to her heart's desire, the orb brightened when she was facing west down the dark hallway. [**Darkvision**] showed her nothing ahead along the pitch-black corridor, and she heard no noises.

Behind them, someone shouted.

"That's it," Ruan said. "That way?" He ran down the hall without waiting for Aderyn. Aderyn cursed under her breath and followed him, with Suveer right on her heels.

Ruan hadn't gone far. He'd stopped at a side passage leading north. "This way, or go on?"

Aderyn still had the <**Wayfinder**> out. "We turn right. And you need to stay with me, Ruan. If there's no light the whole way through this hall, we might stumble over a monster that sees us when we can't see it."

"All right, I understand." Ruan's barely-seen shape was a darker shadow against the gloom.

Aderyn turned right. This new hallway was even darker than the previous one. The only light came from the <**Wayfinder**>, and it mostly only lit her hands and chest and face. But it was enough for

[Darkvision] to activate. The passage turned in a zigzag path, gradually curving around some central object or room. Wooden doors, some of them hanging ajar, appeared at intervals on either side of the hall, but none ever faced each other. Unlit torches in sconces gave off a faint smell of char and grease.

"That noise is getting louder," Ruan said.

"I think it's because we're coming out in the open again," Aderyn said. To her, the shouts were fainter than before, and they came from behind—right where she'd left Owen and the others. No. There had been no other system notices, and the team roster showed only minimal damage to Weston and Owen.

As if she'd jinxed herself the way Livia always claimed optimism would do, another system message appeared, followed by another. Both orc grunts, and Owen's health bar had dropped noticeably. Speaking to her husband while he might be in combat was a bad idea, much as she wanted reassurance. She clamped down on futile panic and kept walking, glancing from the <Wayfinder> to her surroundings and back again.

Ahead, a faint light glowed, the same dimly reddish light of the keep's torches. Aderyn came to a halt in front of two doors side by side. The light came from a cross-hall opposite the doors. "The <Wayfinder> points that way." She gestured with the orb at the barely-lit cross-hall.

Ruan stiffened. He vigorously waved a hand at the doors, one of which had started to open. Aderyn backed up around the corner, while Ruan, who'd been a short distance ahead of her, hurried to the next corner of the zigzag curve.

Two orcs emerged from the door. They were unusually short and looked more piggish than most of their kind, with sharp tusks protruding from their mouths and broad, flat noses. Aderyn held her breath. Beside her, Suveer looked like he was reading the Codex, which reminded Aderyn that she was a Warmaster too and needed to stop being distracted by what might be happening with her friends.

[Improved Assess 4] told her these were both orc mashers. They stood in the doorway, not speaking, with their heads tilted back and their enormous nostrils twitching like they were scenting prey. A brief flash of fear struck Aderyn before she remembered tracking by scent wasn't something orcs could do.

One orc, the one whose tusks were almost long enough to reach his nose, turned to the other and grunted, "False alarm."

"Heard noise," the second orc replied. Strands of scraggly hair fell over its forehead to be brushed aside by one black-nailed hand.

Aderyn's astonishment at hearing human language on an orc's blubbery lips faded as Tusks slapped Scraggle across the ear. "Don't hear noise now, eh heh? Clean out ears."

"Clean out ears with your teeth," Scraggle spat.

Tusks slapped him again. Scraggle punched him. Then the orcs were fighting, bare-handed and barefooted, punching and kicking and kneeing each other. The fight took them away from the door so they blocked the exit from the zigzag hall. Aderyn's astonishment flowered into impatience. They didn't have time to wait for these orcs to work out their aggression on each other.

She put the <Wayfinder> away and dragged Suveer back down the hallway, out of sight of Ruan. "Use [Bonded Mind] to tell Ruan to attack on the count of three, all right?"

Suveer nodded. He looked alert, so Aderyn was confident this would work.

She returned to where she could see the orcs and held up three fingers to Suveer. Suveer nodded again. Aderyn folded down her fingers one at a time, three, two, one, and when she had a fist, she sprang from concealment, drawing her sword and attacking.

The timing hadn't been perfect, but Ruan was only two seconds behind her in attacking. Neither of them made any more noise than the sound of steel scraping across scabbards. The orcs were too preoccupied with each other to notice the new threat, and Ruan took advantage of their distraction to cut the head off Tusks' scrawny neck. Aderyn gutted Scraggle, who let out a pained but quiet groan before she slit his throat.

Congratulations! You have defeated [Orc Masher].
You have earned [7500 XP]

"Quick, shove them back inside," Ruan said. "Maybe we can keep our presence a secret a while longer."

Ruan and Suveer shoved the bloody corpses back through the door and maneuvered the door shut. As they did so, Owen's voice in her head demanded, *What just happened? Are you all right?*

Aderyn resisted the urge to snap at him. The team roster would reveal that she was uninjured, and *she* wasn't panicking over him. *I'm fine. Easy fight. Ruan is really good. Owen, we need to not use this skill except in an emergency, not while either of us could be distracted during a fight.*

There was a pause, and then Owen replied, *I still hate it that you're right. Okay. Emergencies only.*

Aderyn stepped back so Ruan and Suveer could avoid the dark charcoal-red smears of orc blood they'd made. She considered how they might clean up, then remembered that orcs killed each other for fun and this wouldn't be proof of humans running free in Charnel Keep. She turned her attention back to the **<Wayfinder>**. It still pointed toward the cross-hall.

The new hall was as wide and poorly-lit as the first one, the light dim and reddish without illuminating much. Aderyn turned left. Almost immediately, the **<Wayfinder>** led her to the left again, to a short hall which ended in stairs going up.

Another system defeat message flashed in front of Aderyn's eyes, revealing that her friends had killed another orc elite. She ground her teeth to keep from screaming in frustration.

Ruan didn't notice her moment of distraction. He headed for the stairs. "Stay behind me, in case this is where the prisoners' guards are."

Aderyn nodded. The **<Wayfinder's>** glow was deep red and the orb was warm to the touch. "We're close. I bet you're right."

They proceeded up the stairs, which were wide enough for Suveer and Aderyn to walk side by side behind Ruan. The distant sound of revelry or screaming had faded entirely, and except for the occasional scuff of Ruan's heavy boots on a stone tread, the stairwell was silent. They rounded a corner and kept going. There were no other exits off the stairs, and it felt to Aderyn like they were climbing past the second floor to the roof, though that might have been tension and the feeling they were going to stumble on orcs at any moment.

After the turn, the <Wayfinder> was again their only source of light. Just as Aderyn realized it might be a beacon to their enemies, Ruan stopped and held out a hand to bring them to a halt. "Top of the stairs. There's no light."

"Let me look." Aderyn brushed past him. Between [Darkvision] and the <Wayfinder>, she made out a single hallway leading left. She let the <Wayfinder> cool off and realized there was dim light coming from the end of the short hall, which turned right almost immediately. More torches. She hadn't seen any windows, and aside from the gaping hole above the atrium, she didn't think sunlight ever penetrated here. She clutched the orb in both hands. "There's only one way to go, but—"

"Then let's keep moving." Ruan headed for the hallway. Aderyn closed her mouth on a warning. They were so close, and the last thing they needed was to alert guards, either with sound or with light.

The narrow corridor snaked along for a short distance, making turns at random. There were no side passages and no doors—and then, when Aderyn had stopped hoping for one, it was there. The door was solid oak and looked sturdier than the ones they'd seen on the ground floor. When she neared it, the <Wayfinder> gave off a pulse of force and darkened. The rings stopped spinning, and the orb cooled off.

Ruan already had a hand on the latch. "Wait," Aderyn whispered. "We don't know if anyone's inside. Anyone evil, I mean."

"I don't hear anything. I think they're all downstairs at the party, or whatever that is." He forced the heavy latch open and pulled the door open.

The stench of blood and entrails assaulted Aderyn's nose immediately. The room beyond was pitch black, but the light grew rapidly, and Aderyn turned to see Suveer holding one of the wall torches. Surprise at his taking initiative faded as she returned her attention to the room. Torchlight flickered over the chair at the room's center and the motionless figure sitting in it. She couldn't see clearly because Ruan stood in front of the person, his head bowed.

"I thought," he said, then fell silent.

Aderyn joined him. The person in the chair was bound there, hand

and foot. The naked man was missing all the skin from his forearms, exposing raw muscle. Intestines draped over his lap like a grotesque skirt, dangling loose to the bloody floor. Blood caked his chest and pooled at his waist.

Aderyn's chest ached with helpless sorrow. "I didn't think," she whispered. "I forgot it doesn't know the difference between alive and dead."

CHAPTER THIRTY-TWO

"This can't be all," Ruan said. "I don't—I mean, the quest is still active. I can't rescue a dead man."

"Maybe Varoun and the others count." Aderyn turned her back on the corpse and met Suveer's eyes. He held the torch where it fully lit his face, and the horror there surprised Aderyn again, because she hadn't thought Suveer ever thought about anything beyond himself. She immediately hated herself for the spiteful thought, even though it hadn't been intended as spiteful. Suveer wasn't selfish, he was just inwardly turned. The difference mattered.

Ruan grabbed Aderyn's shoulder and turned her to face him. "Use the <**Wayfinder**> again. There has got to be someone left alive in here."

Aderyn nodded. "We have to be sure. If there's anyone not—" She swallowed and focused on the <**Wayfinder**> again.

Fortunately, the magic item stopped trying to lead her to the dead prisoner now that she'd found him. Around the corner from the door, the passage branched off in two directions. "It's showing me two results. One is closer than the other."

"Go on." Ruan gripped the hilt of the <**Galling Blade**> tightly enough to make his tendons stand out.

They didn't go far before they came to another door, as heavy as the other and with a latch that was even more encrusted with filth. Ruan shoved at it, then jerked his hand away. "I heard something."

Aderyn had heard it too—frightened exclamations from inside the room. "Hurry!"

Ruan muscled the latch open and wrenched at the door. Movement inside reminded Aderyn of sheep fleeing the wolf, huddling together for protection. "Suveer, the torch!" she whispered.

"Don't!" a faint voice from inside the room said.

Suveer, to Aderyn's surprise, entered the room first. Torchlight played over half a dozen filthy, terrified faces. Then one of the cowering prisoners stood upright and advanced on Aderyn, his outstretched hand pointing an accusing finger. "You!" he exclaimed in a raspy voice. "This is all *your* fault!"

"Me?" Aderyn exclaimed. She glanced around, but Ruan still stood at the doorway and Suveer was off to the side. The red-headed man, who wasn't a Southlander, was clearly pointing at her. "What are you talking about? Who are you?"

"That's right, pretend you don't remember your victim," the man said. For someone who was naked except for torn breeches, filthy, and trembling, he seemed remarkably focused. "If you had defended Shantos like you were supposed to, none of us would have been taken prisoner. Their deaths are on your hands, woman!"

Aderyn tried to shush him and gestured to Ruan to close the door, at least most of the way. The room was tiny and low-ceilinged and the idea of being trapped inside triggered all Aderyn's deepest fears. "Debran? And—are you all from Shantos?"

"Debran, it doesn't matter," a woman said.

"Of course it matters! Think how many of us died on the road here, or at the hands of these torturers!" Debran kept walking until his trembling finger poked Aderyn on the shoulder. "She is the architect of our downfall!"

"Oh, shut up," Aderyn said. "You were supposed to evacuate. I ordered you to evacuate. You chose to stay behind, like total idiots, and you want to blame *me* for what happened? If anyone's to blame, you are, for convincing these people to listen to you!"

"Aderyn, is this the time?" Ruan said. "We need to keep moving."

"Shut up," Aderyn repeated when Debran looked ready to verbally assault her again. "We're going to search for more survivors. You stay here until we come back."

"You can't leave us here!" the same woman exclaimed, bursting into tears. "They've been taking us, one at a time, and no one they take ever comes back! What if they return before you do?"

"We'll hurry." Aderyn felt uncomfortably like this was misleading. Not that they wouldn't hurry, but it was true she had no idea when the orcs would return.

"You're safer here than coming with us," Ruan said. "Aderyn's right, we'll hurry back." He gestured to Suveer to exit. Aderyn followed him. She exclaimed when he shoved the latch back into place. "Have to," he said. "Or do you think that delusional fellow *won't* follow us if he has the chance and thinks we've taken too long?"

Aderyn tried not to take pleasure in the thought of Debran stuck in that room. It didn't matter that he'd brought this on himself; no one deserved torture and death. He'd been through a lot and... he was obnoxious and selfish and while she didn't wish death and torture on him, she would indulge in a little petty smugness at having the upper hand.

The <**Wayfinder**> led them to two more dead humans before failing to react to Aderyn's heart's desire. The second one was down several narrow, twisting passages, some distance from where they'd left Debran and the others. Aderyn started to retreat, but stopped when Ruan didn't follow. "Ruan, that's all. Let's get those people out of here."

"I think we should explore some more," Ruan said. "We won't get another chance like this."

"Ruan!"

"No, really. The prisoners are safe in there for now, so why don't we look around? Maybe find some of that treasure the Assessment says is here?" He headed off in the opposite direction. "I see brighter light ahead. Come on!"

Suveer, still holding the torch, followed his brother. Aderyn cursed under her breath. They shouldn't be separated, and the prisoner escape was Ruan's quest, not hers. For half a second she considered leaving the brothers and finding Owen. Then common sense asserted itself, and she ran after the others.

For the first time since reaching the second floor, the corridor ran straight. They passed a darkened intersection, unlit by torches, but [Darkvision] continued to show her soot-blackened spots on the rough walls and blotches and smears of some dark substance on the floors. Just as Aderyn realized the light wasn't red-tinged anymore, they left the narrow corridors of the prison behind and came out on a series of windows through which silvery-blue moonlight flowed.

Relief flooded Aderyn at being free of the claustrophobic hallways. She took a few steps forward. The windows were more like floor to ceiling holes with no glass, about three feet wide. Above, the gaping glass-edged hole of the atrium ceiling showed a cloudless night sky; below, the gray tangled masses of the orc garden shifted in an ominous way that made Aderyn again think of plant monsters.

Ruan hadn't stopped to admire the view. He hurried around the atrium to where four hallways met. Aderyn, joining him a moment later, said, "This is really stupid. We don't know anything about where we are."

"So, use the magic item to find the treasure," Ruan said.

His relaxed cheerfulness was so inappropriate for their situation it put Aderyn on edge. "I don't want to find the treasure. The <Wayfinder> will know it's not my heart's desire."

"Oh, come on, Aderyn, who doesn't want treasure?" Ruan clapped her on the back. "If you won't, I'll have to search for it myself. Let's see..." He made a dramatic gesture of turning on his heel, just the way Aderyn always did when using the <Wayfinder>. "I see stairs over there. That might be a better way out."

"Or the treasure might be down there, on the ground floor, surrounded by orcs. Ruan, we can't—"

He shushed her, such a startling gesture Aderyn actually complied. "There's a door ahead, and one down the hall that way, across from the atrium. Let's try the nearest door." He waved at the hallway ahead. It was better lit than any of the others. Aderyn's sense of trouble, not [Sense Ambush] but good old fashioned paranoia, made the hairs on her arms stand up.

Ruan stopped at the door he'd mentioned and rattled the latch with no attempt at quiet. "Locked."

"Fine. It's locked. You tried it. Can we go now?"

"I'm not giving up. Hey, where did Suveer go?"

Aderyn spun around. Suveer was standing in one of the window holes, the toes of his boots jutting out over the edge, his hands gripping the walls to either side. Another warning tingle coursed through Aderyn. Slowly, she approached him until she was within grabbing distance. "Suveer?"

"It's a long way down," Suveer said, his voice again colorless and bland.

"Yes, it is." Aderyn calculated whether she could stop the young man before he flung himself off the edge. "Lots of plants down there, huh?"

"Monsters," Suveer said. "I Assessed them."

Aderyn blinked. Then she Assessed the ground below.

Name: Scimitar Tree [1]

Type: Plant

Power level: 14

Terrain: forest, marsh

Attack(s): weapon x6

Immune to: none

Resistant to: edged weapon damage, mind control magic and effects

Vulnerable to: elemental fire damage, elemental earth damage, toothed blade damage

You met these in their juvenile form once. Now, take a look at a grown-up one. Scimitar trees have the skills of a Swordsworn of their level and attack multiple times while you're still trying to find the arm they cut off. The best strategy against a scimitar tree is to deal damage to it from a distance beyond their sword range. Just a friendly hint.

You might find it interesting that scimitar trees live to be over a hundred years old. That's not long by tree standards, but when you consider that scimitar trees continue to advance in power level as they age, that makes them the kind of foe parents tell

their children horror stories about so they'll eat their vegetables and stop sucking their thumbs. If you want to live long enough to retire and have children to tell horror stories to, stay out of scimitar tree groves. (Bet you feel less guilty about killing those baby trees now, huh?)

NAME: Haematid [7]
   Type: Plant
   Power level: 15
   Terrain: any terrain of moderately high elevation
   Attack(s): special
   Immune to: mind control magic and effects, weapon damage
   Resistant to: none
   Vulnerable to: elemental fire damage, elemental water damage
   Special attacks: seed spray
   Haematids look like ordinary dandelions in their puffy state, ready for someone to blow and scatter the seeds. However, before a victim gets close enough to do this, the haematid sprays its seeds all over anyone in the vicinity. While at first this seems like an innocent, amusing trick, victims almost immediately discover that the haematid seed heads now buried in their flesh have begun to drink their blood. If left alone, the seeds will ingest blood for about thirty seconds before falling off.
   You thought that was the end of it, didn't you? Like mosquitoes, the haematid seed injects an anticoagulant into the victim's blood, but unlike mosquitoes, this doesn't make a person itch, it makes them bleed profusely from every tiny wound. Yes, it's as messy as it sounds, and it can also kill the victim by exsanguination. I hope your friends are quick with the healing! Come to think on it, where *are* your friends, Aderyn?

As if it was a signal, three system defeat notices flashed before Aderyn's eyes in quick succession, two elites and a masher. Aderyn gasped. "Ruan, we have to go now!"

"But I got the door open," Ruan said. "Let's just take a quick peek."

"You got—" Intrigued despite herself, Aderyn approached the door, which stood slightly ajar. Ruan wore a shit-eating grin that made Aderyn want to slap him, and he bounced on his toes like a little kid offered his pick out of the candy shop window. Behind her, footsteps told her Suveer had left the fatal drop and was following her.

Ruan entered the room before Aderyn reached it. She suspected he didn't want to give her any opening to drag him away. Bright light poured through the doorway, not reddish like torchlight, but sunny and warm and not at all what Aderyn expected from an orc stronghold. Tensing with anticipation, she pushed the door open wider, and stopped in the doorway, stunned.

The room was packed full of treasure. Ordinary objects like candlesticks and serving trays, but made of gold and silver, lay piled on shelves lining the room. Wooden chests big enough for her to bathe in were lined up in rows, fifteen of them, none of them padlocked. Smaller steel chests no bigger than a loaf of bread sat stacked on other shelves. One of them had its lid flung open, revealing heaps of cut jewels and a strand of pearls each the size of Aderyn's thumbnail.

Her eye was drawn to the back wall, where weapons racks full of swords, knives, polearms, and maces stood. Bows hung above them, and above that was a row of shields. Aderyn was sure if Livia were here, she'd be blinded by magical radiance.

Her earlier fear vanished. This was more treasure than she had ever dreamed of. It was—

No. What had the system Assessment said? *Greed is your enemy.* All of this was meant to entrap adventurers. How, she didn't know, but she took a quick step back so she could see the whole room and prepared to Assess it.

"There we go," Ruan said. His voice lacked the cheerful note from before, and now it sounded almost sultry, like he was coaxing a small animal out of its den. He drew a greatsword from the rack and made a few passes with it. "That's what I hoped for."

"What you hoped for?"

Ruan didn't look her way. All his attention was on the sword. It was beautiful in a showy way, with gems dotting the silver weave of the basket hilt and a brilliantly faceted ruby the size of a baby's fist clutched in wyvern's claws forming the pommel. Its silvery blade caught the light as if it was a gem itself.

Behind Aderyn, the door slammed shut. She spun around and grabbed the latch. It didn't budge. It felt sealed in place, like it was never meant to open.

The light dimmed like a cloud had passed across the sun. Something whispered in Aderyn's ear. It wasn't words, not even the almost-comprehensible words of spellslinging; it was the hiss of a snake and the breath of Darkshroud and the whisper of a smooth body gliding over silk. Aderyn put her back to the door and drew her sword. "Ruan, what did you do?"

Ruan held the silver sword at the ready. "Don't let it get to you," he said. His head turned slowly as if tracking invisible movement. "It wants us to be afraid, but all it has are taunts."

"'It'? What 'it'? Ruan, did you know about this?"

The gloom darkened and grew thicker until the room was filled with fog. A low, deep laugh echoed through the room, seeming to come from everywhere at once. "*Taunts?*" a voice said. "*I will tear your head off and drink the blood that fountains from your neck. Consider that a taunt, if you wish. I think of it as a promise. To myself.*"

The fog roiled, churning rapidly, and drew in on itself, collecting in a pool between two of the treasure chests. The room's brightness returned in a flash, and Aderyn blinked away pained tears. In her watery vision, the charcoal-gray pool surged upward and took the shape of something slim and curved. A serpentine body curled into a loose coil, thicker than the breadth of Aderyn's shoulders and scaled in shades of pearl and slate. Above the waist, a humanoid male torso balanced effort-lessly atop the snake half. The torso bulged as well-muscled arms burst from its shoulders and a head, not a man's head but a snake's, pushed its way up from the neck. A scaly hood unfurled around the snake's head, fully spread like a cobra about to strike.

The creature's narrow, forked tongue flickered in and out of its mouth. It didn't have lips to smile, but its lidless eyes with their elongated pupils fixed on Aderyn, and she was sure it found her amusing.

"*Three of you,*" it said, its sibilant voice threading its way through the air like the words had physical presence. *"I hope you are fond of each other. That makes it so much sweeter when I devour you, one by one."*

CHAPTER THIRTY-THREE

Aderyn took advantage of the time it wasted gloating to Assess it.

Name: Spectral Guardian

Type: Formless

Power level: 18

Terrain: any

Attack(s): special

Immune to: precision damage, all elemental damage except elemental air damage

Resistant to: weapons damage, mind control spells and skills

Vulnerable to: elemental air damage

Special attacks: ~~unknown~~ see below

A spectral guardian is a type of formless capable of taking the shape impressed upon it by its master. In its natural state, it is nothing more than a cloud of fog incapable of damaging anything but a pleasant sunny day. Unfortunately, almost no one ever encounters one in its natural state. More often, dungeon bosses summon them to guard (hence the name) anything they consider valuable. The creature who does the summoning gets to choose the form the spectral guardian takes, which in turn determines what attacks it has.

Be grateful you're a Warmaster with [Improved Assess 4], Aderyn, because anyone else wouldn't learn what I'm about to tell you. This spectral guardian was given the form of a serpentfolk magus, which is a kind of spellslinger. It knows only the spells *lightning bolt, vortex, spinning fire,* and *immobilize,* but those are more than enough to kill an incautious adventurer. In addition to those four spells, it has the serpentfolk ability to strangle anyone it catches in those coils, and its bite is a slow-acting venom that gradually weakens the victim until they can't make their lungs inflate, and they suffocate under the weight of their own flesh.

Unlike most formless, when the spectral guardian is given shape, it becomes vulnerable to [Outflank]. In all forms, it's made of fog, so wind attacks weaken it by dispersing its body. Yes, I realize you don't have any of those. Keep in mind what you do have, and wait until you've survived this fight to smack Ruan's secrets out of him.

Aderyn read all this in the time it took the spectral guardian to finish speaking and slither just like a real snake after Ruan. Ruan held the silver greatsword ready to attack. The two opponents faced off, the snake swaying slightly, Ruan balanced on the balls of his feet, both of them waiting for their moment.

It happened so fast Aderyn almost missed it. Ruan darted forward, aiming a blow at where the snake's human and reptilian halves merged. In the same moment, the spectral guardian lashed out, whipping its head, fangs extended, at Ruan's shoulder. Ruan converted his attack to a dodge and rolled out of the way. The spectral guardian hit a shelf instead and knocked three silver caskets over, strewing their jeweled contents across the floor.

"Aderyn, don't just stand there, we have to kill it!" Ruan shouted.

Aderyn drew her sword, but didn't budge from her place by the door. "You said it wasn't dangerous!"

"My information was wrong, are you happy? Stop arguing and come up with a plan!"

She had to come up with a plan? Aderyn indulged in frustrated fury for half a second and then Assessed the monster again, using **[Discern Weakness]**. No blue weak spots appeared—it was formless, that made sense—and it was covered by the red haze that meant resistance to weapons damage.

"Attack its torso, that's where it's weak/*It's a lie, it's not weak anywhere, but I'm misleading it*," she told Ruan with **[Secret Message]**.

The spectral guardian shook itself as if the impact with the shelf had dazed it, but Aderyn had been watching it closely and was sure it was pretending. It slithered around the room, heading for Aderyn. "*Lovers? Or just companions? Should I tear you apart first?*"

"Tear him apart, and spare me the trouble," Aderyn snarled. "Ruan, when we get out of this—"

She dodged the spectral guardian's attack and slashed at the back of its neck. It felt like hitting a brick wrapped in a feather pillow. Her sword sank half an inch into the monster's body before coming up against something solid. Immediately the spectral guardian jerked away, regrouped, and lunged for her again. It was fast, but **[See It Coming]** was faster. Aderyn thrust for the hollow of its throat. The sword penetrated deeper than before, but she still hit something solid, as if the creature was a stone statue beneath the surface.

The spectral guardian backed away, gliding gracefully. "*A Warmaster. How intriguing. It's been centuries since I saw one of your class capable of doing anything but cry in a corner about how useless she is. Is that one your partner, then?*"

Out of the corner of her eye, Aderyn saw movement. She didn't dare take her eyes off the spectral guardian, who was waiting for her to let her guard down, but she wasn't totally surprised when Suveer shoved her to the side. He was as unarmed as ever, and his body trembled, but he stood his ground. "Try to attack me," he said in a voice quivering with fear.

"Suveer, stay out of the way!" Aderyn shouted.

"**[Outflank]**!" Suveer shouted at the same time. The spectral guardian jerked forward as if it had been shoved as well and half-turned to face Ruan, letting out a furious hiss. Ruan pressed the attack from behind, the silver sword drawing traceries of light wherever it passed. Aderyn took advantage of the attack to slash the creature from her position. The spectral guardian hissed again and darted away. It put its back to the wall, knocking over some silver candlesticks, and raised both hands in a complicated gesture.

"Watch out, Ruan!" Aderyn shouted.

The spectral guardian's fists glowed white-blue, and a bolt of lightning speared through the air. Aderyn threw herself to the side, taking Suveer with her, though it was a futile gesture because there was no way **[See It Coming]** was faster than lightning. But she felt no pain. She hit the stone floor, landing partly on Suveer's shoulder, and Ruan screamed as the *lightning bolt* struck the sword and coursed down its length and through the Swordsworn.

"Ruan!" Suveer exclaimed. He pushed Aderyn away and crawled to where Ruan had fallen. Aderyn swept up her own sword and threw herself between the brothers and the spectral guardian. It continued to advance, but more slowly, and Aderyn Assessed it briefly and discovered the reddish haze of resistance was gone. Without pausing to dwell on this oddity, she leaped at the creature and slashed her sword diagonally across its torso.

This time, the blade bit deep, and the spectral guardian screamed in pain. No blood flowed from the wound, but the edges of the cut hung open, not sealing shut. Aderyn followed up her strike with another powerful blow, but the creature's tail flicked protectively across its injured body, blocking Aderyn's sword. Aderyn shouted in terror as the tail whipped around her lower body, coiling higher and higher and squeezing so all her bones ground against each other. She stopped trying to attack and raised her arms to keep them free. The spectral guardian's fathomless eyes met hers, and its tongue flicked out to caress her face.

"*Think you can defeat me, small one?*" it hissed. "*They've already abandoned you. I'll make you a deal—kill them, and I'll let you take whatever you want from this treasure room and leave. No hard feelings for any damage we might have inflicted on each other, yes?*"

Aderyn couldn't help it—she glanced over her shoulder. Ruan and

Suveer were at the door, trying to get it open. Ruan was using the <Galling Blade> to hack at the wood surrounding the lock, with no effect. It didn't matter that she disliked Ruan—his betrayal struck her to the heart.

Her breathing became labored as the spectral guardian's coils reached above her waist. "All right," she lied, lowering one hand to brush against the side of her knapsack. "Let me go."

The spectral guardian laughed. "*I just wanted to see how selfish you both were. I'm going to crush you out of existence, and then I'll do the same to your treacherous companions. I was never going to release you, you fool.*"

"That's all right," Aderyn gasped. "I can free myself." Her fingers found the <Rod of Unfettering> and snapped it free of where it hung on her knapsack. The carved chain flexed like a real one, and the spectral guardian spun away from Aderyn, shouting surprised obscenities and leaving her free of its coils. She drew in one glorious deep breath and ran to the door.

"Aderyn," Ruan said. "Look, it's not what you think—"

"Never mind that," Aderyn said. "Its protection against weapons drops for a few seconds after it casts a spell. We have to trick it into more spellslinging."

Ruan looked skeptical. His face and arms bore traces of burns from the *lightning bolt*, and Aderyn was sure if they'd been teammates, she'd have seen his low health bar. The Miracle Meal had probably saved his life. He nodded and dropped the <Galling Blade>. With the silver sword once more in hand, he stepped away from Aderyn and Suveer and pointed the weapon at the spectral guardian. If she hadn't been convinced the silver sword was magical, the fact that it hadn't melted from the *lightning bolt* would have proved it.

"You there," he said, his voice compelling attention. "You missed."

The spectral guardian, which had coiled in on itself as if regrouping, raised its head. "*I didn't miss, you fool. I don't know why you're not a charred heap of ashes, but it must be luck.*"

"This sword protected me." Ruan brandished it point first at the ceiling in a dramatic gesture. "I am its rightful wielder, and no spell you send against me will have power over me."

"*That's not true.*" The creature sounded bewildered. Aderyn took advantage of its confusion, and its focus on Ruan, to sidle along the wall. She couldn't use **[Outflank]** with anyone but her own partner, but the principle had merit regardless.

Ruan spread his arms wide, then held the sword crosswise over his chest like a shield. "You can prove it. Unless you're afraid I'm right, and you're the fool for letting me get my hands on it."

The spectral guardian shrieked in rage and thrust one fist at Ruan as if throwing a long-distance punch. Fire erupted from its fist and spun like a discus at Ruan, who dodged as if he had **[See It Coming]**. Aderyn leapt for the creature's unprotected back and drove her sword deep into its side. Again, she felt no resistance. She grabbed the edge of its hood for support and thrust again.

The hood jerked out of her grip. Sharp pain shot through her left forearm as needle-sharp fangs penetrated her flesh. Aderyn ripped free and staggered back, clutching her wounded arm. She didn't feel the effects of the poison, and for a moment she thought maybe she'd imagined the bite. But two deep holes edged with red-tinged blackness said otherwise.

The spectral guardian hissed with delight. "*You think you're so smart, figuring out my weakness. I plan to watch you die, choking on your own fluids.*"

Its tail whipped out again, lashing toward Ruan. Ruan stepped back, and suddenly Suveer was there, bracing himself against the strike. The tail wrapped around him more thoroughly than it had Aderyn, all the way up Suveer's body until only his head showed. Suveer struggled weakly against the coils.

"*Leave now, or I kill your partner,*" the spectral guardian hissed.

Ruan shrugged. "He knows the risks. It's his job." He raised the silver sword and took a measured step toward the creature, then another.

Suveer screamed, a faint, breathless sound, as the coils tightened. Aderyn reached for the <**Rod of Unfettering**> and couldn't find it—right, she'd dropped it after she'd used it on herself and the spectral guardian had knocked her off balance. She rushed to Suveer's side and battered at the spectral guardian's body, to no effect. "Ruan, he's dying!" she shouted.

Ruan ignored her. "It's called **[Draw Fire]**," he told the spectral guardian. "Warmasters take the hit so their partners can destroy their enemies. You're not invulnerable. You're just pathetic." With a single sweep of the silver blade, he aimed a head-chopping blow at the creature.

The silver sword didn't decapitate the spectral guardian. Instead, its tip tore through the creature's throat, knocking its head back so the blade bit deeper as it swung. The spectral guardian let out a choked, gurgling cry and grabbed its throat with both hands. Aderyn kept beating at the serpentine coils as Suveer gradually turned purple. "Ruan!"

Ruan thrust the blade at the center of the monster's chest, right at the tip of the wound Aderyn had previously inflicted. It drove deep, as if the weapon resistance didn't protect the earlier injury. The spectral guardian's fist began to glow bluish-white, and Ruan yanked the sword free and threw himself out of the creature's line of sight. But then the glow faded. The coils fell slack, and Suveer collapsed. Aderyn caught him. "Ruan, he's not breathing!"

Ruan joined them as Aderyn laid Suveer on the floor. He struck his brother on the chest, then struck him again. "He'll start breathing soon, I'm sure of it."

"Really? What makes you so sure? Ruan—oh, *damn* you, get out of my way!" Aderyn fell to her knees beside Suveer. A memory of Weston, lying still and unbreathing, triggered a second memory. She didn't know how Owen had done it, and she didn't have lifeguard training, whatever skill that was, but if she didn't try something, Suveer would die.

She covered Suveer's mouth with her own and breathed heavily into his mouth. A faint breath on her cheek excited her until she realized it was her own air exiting Suveer's mouth through his nostrils. She didn't know what to do about that. Finally, she pinched his nose shut and tried again. She did that for a few times—his heart was beating, didn't that mean he—

Suveer coughed into her face, spraying her with spittle. Aderyn reared back and wiped her eyes and mouth. She didn't think it was her efforts that had done it, but she didn't care.

Suveer lay blinking at the ceiling for a moment. "That was a lot of experience," he finally said.

"Yes, good work, everyone!" Ruan exclaimed.

Aderyn rose to her feet explosively. "What the *hell* are you talking about? 'Good work, everyone'? You knew about this place, didn't you?"

"Shh, Aderyn, we don't want to draw attention—"

"I think the lightning bolts and the screaming have done that!"

"All right, you're entitled to be angry, but let's get out of here first. You can shout at me later."

Ruan's placating tone made Aderyn want to scream again. But he was right. The fact that no one had come racing to see what was making all the noise was just their good luck.

Suveer was on his feet again, wobbly but able to stand without support. "We should take some of this," he said, staggering to the shelves bearing the caskets of jewels.

"Suveer, leave it," Aderyn commanded. She finally located the <**Rod of Unfettering**> and hooked it to her knapsack. "Ruan?"

"She's right. Besides, the sword is what matters." Ruan grabbed his brother's arm and towed him to the door. It was unlocked now, and Aderyn peeked out and saw and heard nothing. Breathing a sigh of relief, she slipped through the open doorway, followed by Ruan and Suveer.

No one waited silently outside to attack them. The four-way hall junction was still half lit by moonlight. Ruan gestured. "See? It's fine. Now, the stairs are this way."

"Stairs?" Aderyn frowned. "We have to go back for the prisoners."

"Oh. Right." Ruan cast a glance over his shoulder at the almost-visible staircase, around the corner from the treasure room. "I forgot."

"You *forgot?*" Aderyn clapped a hand over her own mouth as her outraged words came out too loudly. "It's your *quest*, Ruan. How could you forget?"

Ruan closed his hand over the silver sword's hilt. That one tiny motion brought everything into focus. Aderyn's mouth fell open. "You were never here for the prisoners," she whispered. "It was the sword. That's what you came for. You tricked us into helping you—"

"Watch it, Aderyn," Ruan said. He no longer had the cheerful, almost manic demeanor that had brought them through this dungeon. "I didn't trick you. It's true, my quest wasn't to save the prisoners, but does it matter why we save them so long as we do?"

"Who is 'we' in that sentence, Ruan?" Aderyn demanded. "You knew we wouldn't support you in a selfish quest—was that the Fated One quest all along, or did you lie about that, too?"

Ruan's hand on the hilt twitched. Aderyn's eyes fell on it. She didn't need to Skill Assess Ruan to know his ranks in [Superior Weapon Mastery] had gone up since the first time she'd Assessed him, weeks ago. And she didn't need to be a Warmaster to know those ranks were far higher than hers. He meant to kill her so she wouldn't tell the others, none of whom would be any more thrilled than she was at being used. She closed her hands into fists to stop their shaking.

A system message flashed across her vision, the defeat of an orc elite, and then another. In her moment of distraction, Ruan leaped. Aderyn darted out of the way and ran.

She didn't dare escape down the stairs, not when she had no idea what lay at the bottom. The abandoned atrium, with its monsters growing at the bottom, was no help. All she could do was race for the maze of the prison and hope to lose Ruan there.

Someone tackled her, an awkward grab that led to both of them lying on the floor, struggling to be free. Aderyn shoved Suveer away and got to her feet. "Thanks," she said sarcastically. "I guess you really were your brother's slave all along."

"I'm not a slave," Suveer said. His voice was quiet, not emotionless as it usually was, but he sounded as if he wasn't sure what he'd said was true.

"This doesn't have to end this way," Ruan said. He approached her slowly. The moonlight spilled through one of the empty window holes and painted the side of his body silver. "I don't want to kill you. It's not what you think, I swear."

"Then what is it?" Aderyn said, stalling. Her back and shoulders ached with tension. She couldn't use [Bonded Mind] without distracting herself and becoming unable to use [See It Coming]. And if she was destined to die at Ruan's hand, she wasn't going to make it easy on him.

"It's true my Fated One quest isn't to rescue the prisoners. I said it was because I knew you'd respond to that plea." Ruan's voice was low and persuasive. "The actual quest is to enter Charnel Keep and retrieve this sword. It was as hard to interpret as all those quests are, but Suveer and I stumbled across some prisoners who'd escaped this place, and they knew about the treasure. Specifically, this sword."

He raised its point slightly. "It's called <**Moonlight Dirge**>, and it has bonuses to damage you wouldn't believe. Plus the ability to cast *deeper darkness*, that's a spell of some kind, and if it's wielded in moonlight, it siphons damage from a victim to heal the wielder. They gave me the key to the treasury and some information about the guardian." He shrugged. "I wonder now how prisoners had this key. Maybe they were primed to mislead me. I guess it doesn't matter now."

The moonlight struck the blade and glittered darkly off the gems on the hilt. Impulsively, Aderyn said, "How injured are you, Ruan?"

Ruan's smile vanished. "You're smarter than you look," he said. "I'll make this quick, how does that sound? And I'll tell Owen you died fighting that spectral guardian. You'll be a hero."

"As if you know anything about heroism." Aderyn stood her ground.

Ruan shrugged. "It's not like you'll be alive to care. Suveer. [**Outflank**]."

Suveer stared at his brother. Then he took two steps away from Aderyn. "No."

Ruan lowered the sword. "What? Suveer, don't play games. [**Outflank**]. Now."

"You would have let me die," Suveer said. He didn't sound angry, or confused, just matter of fact. "She saved my life. Twice. I'm not going to help you kill her."

Ruan walked toward them. "Suveer, I've taken care of you for years. I'm the only one who believes in you. You're not going to take her side, not after all we've been to each other?"

Aderyn held still. In seconds, Ruan would decide he didn't need Suveer's help, and it would all be over. There was no point speaking to Owen. There was no point pleading with Ruan. He was her enemy now, which meant she had one chance.

As Ruan came level with the window hole, Aderyn focused on him. A dozen thin white lines sprang up on the floor, centered on Ruan. With a surge of mental effort, Aderyn shoved him along one of the lines of **[Reposition]**.

Ruan's surprised shout turned into a scream as he shot through the window hole and dropped into the darkness below.

CHAPTER THIRTY-FOUR

Aderyn didn't move. She heard the thud of a body striking the ground, and then terrified, agonized screams as dozens of blades struck their target, again and again. The blades kept slashing even after the screaming stopped, and then there was the sound of many feet running and shouting below.

**Congratulations! You have defeated [Ruan the Swordsworn].
You have earned [30,000 XP]**

Suveer stood motionless at the window hole, looking down. This time, Aderyn didn't fear he might try to jump. "We have to go," Suveer said.

Aderyn didn't ask him how he felt about his brother's death. Suveer's voice again had that dull, unemotional tone to it, and Aderyn had a feeling he was going to wake up to reality in a while and be less detached about her killing Ruan. "We have to get the prisoners to safety," she agreed. "Hurry."

Aderyn, you killed Ruan? What happened? Are you all right? Did he attack you? You're injured!

Aderyn slowed to a walk. **[Bonded Mind]** made it hard to do other things while carrying on a mental communication. Her legs ached with exertion and the aftereffects of the fight, and she wished she could stop moving entirely. *There's too much to explain now. Where are you?*

You have to explain something. *Did you find the prisoners?*

We did. Owen, I'm sorry, but more will have to wait until we get the prisoners to safety. She hadn't thought to look at the counter since being separated from Owen. It now read 15:24:44. *There's still time to complete our quest. Where are you?*

We've made our way through most of the lower floor. No Glasha visible. Must be upstairs, so be careful, okay? The last thing we need is for you to encounter him alone.

Aderyn shuddered. *The <**Wayfinder**> won't stop us running into orcs. Help me figure out where you are in relation to us.*

As she and Suveer worked their way through the halls to where they'd left Debran and the others, she determined her friends were in the northwestern corner of the ground floor, below the prison maze. *There are stairs south of you,* she told Owen. *We'll come down that way.*

Not a good idea, Owen replied. *The lower floor is teeming with orcs. Something happened near the atrium that has them all on edge.*

Aderyn suppressed feelings of inappropriate guilt. Ruan wouldn't have died if he hadn't tried to kill her. *We can't take the prisoners that way, but we need an exit.*

Hang on. We found stairs. Going up. Isold says, northwestern quadrant, but not the far west corner.

Aderyn came to a halt in front of the latched door. People were shouting inside the room, which annoyed her—what if it was an orc who came in response to the noise? *That will put you close to the prison maze.*

We're going up. Still don't hear anything nearby.

Aderyn put a hand on the latch, and jumped when Suveer put his hand on hers, stopping her from opening the door. "We won't get out if all those prisoners are with us while we search for an exit," he said. His voice was surprisingly clear and focused. "Especially that man who blames you. He will resist and maybe want to go his own way."

"That is a really good point, Suveer." Aderyn gave the door one final look, then pulled out the <**Wayfinder**>. "Let's join the others and make a plan. Two Warmasters together, right?"

"I don't have a partner anymore." Suveer, again, didn't sound angry or upset. "I'm back to being useless."

Aderyn grabbed his shoulder with her free hand. "Suveer, *listen to me*," she said. "I don't know why you think you're worthless, but you're not! Even without R—your partner, you still have all the skills you developed as you adventured. Some of them, like **[Keep Pace]** and **[Outflank]**, yes, those won't work until you find a new partner, but you still have them!"

"Ruan always told me my class wasn't useless," Suveer said. "He said it would be without him. I think he wanted me to believe that."

Aderyn blinked. "Um. I think you might be right. He wanted you to depend on him. But you can't anymore, and maybe now you can discover who you really are."

Suveer shrugged. For once, Aderyn didn't feel like slapping him. He pointed at the <**Wayfinder**>. "Are you going to use that?"

Aderyn gripped the orb more tightly. "Let's go."

To her surprise, the magic item glowed brightly the moment she focused on her heart's desire, and it led her around only two turns of the narrow prison hallway before she saw the glow of Livia's *orb of light*. She ran around the next corner and bumped into Owen, who grabbed her before she could trip and fall.

Owen converted his grab to a tight embrace. "You found us," he whispered in her ear. "Let's not do that again, okay?"

Aderyn nodded and hugged him in return, grateful for his support because she still ached all over. Being held by him felt so good it pushed the terror of the last few hours and the memory of Ruan's surprised, horrified face as he tumbled through the window to the back of her mind. She indulged in the feeling for a few seconds before releasing him. "We have to come up with a plan. This place is safe for now, because the orcs are occupied elsewhere, but that won't last forever."

"They were all at some kind of feast or party," Weston said. "It's why we encountered so few of them in the halls. But then something set off the monsters in the atrium, and that drew a lot of attention."

Aderyn felt Suveer's keen attention on her. Under his gaze, she suddenly didn't want to talk about how she'd killed his brother. "That's going to be a problem. The only safe exit we know about leads to the prison cavern, and that's as far from here as it's possible to be."

"Let's release the prisoners first," Weston suggested.

"They will be a liability," Suveer said. "They're naked and weak and not in a condition to be stealthy. We have to have a clear route to the exit before we let them out. Besides, one of them hates Aderyn and might ignore her instructions."

"Debran," Aderyn said to her friends. "From Shantos, remember? My bad luck he survived to make my life a thundering misery. Anyway, I agree with Suveer. The prisoners are safe for now—let's find them a way out, and then deal with Glasha."

"If the orcs are all downstairs, then the smart thing to do is search up here for stairs near where we entered," Suveer said. "Since the <Wayfinder> can't distinguish between stairs that are safe and stairs that aren't, right?"

"That's right." This new, confident Suveer unnerved Aderyn, even though it was what she'd wanted. "Let's get to the far side of the atrium before I use it. If there are stairs in that direction, being closer to them than the ones over here will help."

She led them through the now-familiar halls of the prison maze, rolling her eyes when they passed the room Debran and his friends were locked into. The prisoners were still shouting, and Aderyn could hear Debran's voice raised above the others. He was definitely a liability.

As they neared the corridor that opened on the hall around the atrium, Aderyn heard raised voices, guttural and growing gradually louder. Weston tapped her on the shoulder and, when she stopped, indicated that he should go first. He sidled along the wall and paused at the exit, then slipped around the corner and out of sight.

After a few seconds, Weston returned and gestured to everyone to back up a few steps. "There are orcs out there, clustered around the far wall. They're searching for something around the window hole. Livia can cast *mass invisibility*—"

"We wouldn't be maneuverable," Livia said. "Better to take our chances out in the open than risk one of us stepping outside the invisibility effect at the wrong time."

"All right. If we move fast, we can get out of sight in the other direction. There's an opening off to the southeast that could be a hallway leading the right way. Toward the prison cavern exit, that is."

"Aderyn? You're in charge now." Owen glanced at Suveer. "You and Suveer."

"Lead the way, Weston," Aderyn said.

She took one step, and her leg buckled. She collapsed to the floor. Owen gave her his hand. "Not a good start," he said with a smile.

Aderyn tried to rise, but her legs trembled beneath her and wouldn't move. She felt like she was wearing clothes made of iron with how heavy her body had become. Owen hauled on her arm, bringing her upright, but when he released her, she wobbled and grabbed his shoulder for support.

"Something's wrong," Owen said.

"Aderyn, your health bar is black," Livia exclaimed.

Aderyn closed her eyes in memory. "I forgot. The spectral guardian bit me. Poisoned me. It's slow acting, but it's been a while since that fight, so..." Her eyelids weighed so much she couldn't open her eyes. She leaned heavily on Owen and added, "It will be fine, thanks to the Miracle Meal. I need healing."

"There's no time," Weston said. "I hear voices from within the prison maze. Orc voices. There's a lot of them."

Someone scooped Aderyn up in his arms. "Follow me, and use the atrium walls as cover," Weston said. Aderyn sagged, unable to react even as Weston's movement jogged her up and down. At least it didn't hurt.

With her eyes closed, sounds were louder: Weston's light breathing, the slap of boot soles on stone, and, more distantly, the shouts of orcs. Aderyn didn't give much for Debran's chances if he and the others didn't have the sense to shut up.

Weston ran, paused for three seconds that felt like forever, ran again. The orc voices faded into the distance. Soon Weston set Aderyn on the ground, where she slumped. She felt so heavy, no longer as if her clothes were iron but like she was made of liquid metal that sloshed when she tried to move. Breathing was as difficult as if she'd been the one running. "Isold," she whispered.

The others were talking quietly a short distance away. "Isold," she said again, more loudly.

"It will have to be the **<Potion of Life>**," Isold said from close beside her. "I've never seen a poison turn a health bar black. It—" He stopped speaking. "They're coming!"

"Back, down the hall," Owen said. "Find a door. We have to get out of sight."

Weston picked Aderyn up again. He ran faster this time, holding Aderyn close against his chest to steady her. Aderyn tried to lift her arms to hold onto him, but they were too heavy. Even her fingers weighed too much for her to do anything but twitch.

Suddenly, Weston skidded to a halt. "Take her," he said, and shoved her into Owen's familiar arms. Owen crushed her close, his hand cradling the back of her head. He was breathing more heavily than Weston, and his heart beat rapidly as hers did not—no, when had her heart rate slowed? Each beat felt like it was fighting against an iron fist.

"Door's unlocked," Weston said. A door creaked open, and Owen hurried on a few steps before setting Aderyn gently on the ground. Aderyn couldn't move her lips to reassure him. She wished someone would reassure *her*.

Owen lifted her to recline against him. "Can you swallow?"

The possibility that her muscles might be too weak for swallowing was the final straw. Tears leaked from Aderyn's eyes. Why hadn't she remembered the poison sooner? That blistering idiot Ruan and his stupid, self-centered desires.

Someone's hand gripped her throat. "Hold the potion ready, and pour when I say 'go,'" Livia said. Another hand forced her lips into a curved, funnel-like shape. Aderyn, confused, could only weep harder. She was stupid, and she would pay for it with her life.

"Go!" Livia said. The cool glass of a potion vial touched Aderyn's lips. A thick, burning liquid that tasted of raspberries filled her mouth. She lacked the strength to fight, but the involuntary reaction to a foreign object pressing on her throat started her choking. She was going to die from suffocation before the poison could kill her.

Then she swallowed. It was involuntary—no, *telekinesis* had moved her muscles, stopping her from choking and pushing the liquid down her throat to her stomach. She convulsed, her entire body drawing in on itself, and then a freezing rush like icy water flooded her, chilling her to the bone. She felt impossibly aware of her body's workings, of how the potion was scrubbing her muscles and bones and organs clean of the spectral guardian's poison, fully absorbed in the sensation and simultaneously detached from the healing.

Gradually, the weakness disappeared, just as if the iron weight she'd imagined had slowly peeled away from her body. Aderyn opened her eyes to see Owen's face bent over her, upside down from her perspective. He looked so worried Aderyn caressed his cheek. "Just in time," she said.

"That was too close," Livia said.

A door opened across the room. Aderyn lifted her head from Owen's lap as he tensed. Beside them, Weston let a knife fall into his hand, and Livia took a step forward, clenching her stone fist.

The orc who stood in the doorway was as muscular as an elite, armored with a hardened leather cuirass, and between that and the short-cropped hair it took Aderyn a moment to realize she was female. She gazed at their little group indifferently, as if she didn't find them interesting. "I'm surprised you made it this far," she said, her voice guttural and as deep as a man's. "I'm going to have to kill a lot of my people for that. I never miss a chance to drive home a point."

Owen gently helped Aderyn sit unassisted and rose to his feet. "We're glad you came to us, Glasha. Saves us a lot of trouble."

"I'm sure you believe that. They always do." Glasha thumped the half-open door with one meaty fist. Before the echoes of the blow died away, three more doors opened, and more than a dozen orcs as big as Glasha surged into the room. The doors slammed shut with a thunderous clap. Aderyn didn't dare take her eyes off the orc commander general to examine the newcomers.

Glasha, for her part, never took her eyes off Owen. "Was the dead fellow one of yours?"

"No." Owen stepped forward, making the other orcs reach for their weapons. "But he was a good distraction."

Glasha's laugh sounded like gravel rolling around in a tin bucket. "Is this where you tell me how you're going to bring my reign of tyranny to an end?"

"No," Owen repeated. "This is where you die."

He activated the <**Sunsword**> and lunged for Glasha.

CHAPTER THIRTY-FIVE

Three of the orcs converged on Owen, blocking his way to Glasha. Aderyn scrambled to her feet and Assessed the room, reading as fast as she dared without missing facts.

Name: Orc Ravager [13]

Type: Monstrosity

Power level: 16

Terrain: any

Attack(s): multiple weapons, special

Immune to: none

Resistant to: bladed weapons, bludgeoning weapons, missile weapons

Vulnerable to: *daylight, sunburst*

Special attacks: fear

It's been a while since you encountered an orc ravager—Ornok, remember? They are the most powerful of the orc fighters and serve as Glasha's hands, controlling the orc army at her command. Beware their fear attack, because ravagers are the only orcs who know anything about teamwork, and in battle some will use their fear auras while the others take advantage of its effect on their prey. That's all. You don't have time for me to go into more detail, and it won't help you, anyway.

NAME: Glasha
>   Type: Monstrosity (orc ravager)
>   Power level: 18
>   Terrain: any
>   Attack(s): multiple weapons, bite, special
>   Immune to: none
>   Resistant to: bladed weapons, bludgeoning weapons, missile weapons
>   Vulnerable to: *daylight, sunburst*
>   Special attacks: fear, *raging fury*

No, I didn't mention Glasha is female, because it's irrelevant. Glasha climbed to the top of the heap in what passes for orc society through cunning, treachery, violence, and wicked self-interest. She is a ravager's ravager, a powerful swordfighter, and a brilliant tactician. In addition to her ravager's abilities, in combat she can become gripped with *raging fury*, which increases the damage she does on a successful hit and makes her likely to attack with her teeth instead of a weapon. It also decreases her chance of landing a successful hit, but not by as much as I'm sure you'd like.

If Glasha wins this war, she will murder or enslave every human in the Southlands. Then she'll turn her sights on the north. You received this quest for a reason, Aderyn. Now you know what it is.

Aderyn scrambled to her feet and drew her sword. "Watch out for their fear effect!" she shouted. The room was huge, but not so huge that [Amplify Voice] was necessary. Owen fought with the cold precision she knew so well, holding off all three ravagers at once. A flash of crackling blue light sent a gust of freezing air past Aderyn's face, and one of the ravagers cried out as ice speared through his body.

Weston's [Fire Dancer's Knife] shot past Aderyn, striking one of Owen's opponents, and then the other orcs converged on their group. Aderyn couldn't find a way past them for [Outflank]. She came face to face with one of the female ravagers, who snarled and raised her notched, heavy sword for a skull-cleaving blow.

As the blade descended, and Aderyn prepared to block, the ravager's expression became bewildered, and she shot five feet to the right of Aderyn. The sword whiffed through the air, nearly taking Aderyn's scalp with it. Aderyn knew [Reposition] too well to mistake it for any other maneuver. "Suveer!"

"I can move them around!" Suveer replied. He sounded surprised rather than pleased.

"Yes, but—all right, keep an eye on—" She decided not to give him instructions and further decided to save yelling at him for nearly getting her killed until after the battle. "We can control how they stand, so let's work together!"

Suveer was already gone, running to the far side of the room after an orc who flailed his arms as [Reposition] slid him out of reach of Isold. Aderyn gave up. Suveer would do his own thing, and hopefully it wouldn't get him or her friends killed.

She caught sight of Glasha again. The orc commander general stood some distance from the fight, her massive, muscular arms crossed over her chest. Her lip curled in disdain. Then she turned and left the room, slamming the door shut behind her. Aderyn almost cried a warning. Glasha was their target, not these stupid orc ravagers. But they didn't have any choice but to fight their way through.

Heavy tentacles of dark, rich earth sprang from the floor and *immobilized* three of the ravagers. Livia ran past them, ignoring them in favor of attacking a ravager menacing Weston. Isold had control of one and had compelled him to fight another ravager. Even Suveer was moving orcs around, five feet at a time, apparently growing more confident the more success he had in disorienting them.

Aderyn leaped to intercept an orc who attacked Suveer, using [Compel] to keep the orc's attention on her. She dodged the female's unexpectedly swift blows, infuriating the orc into roaring. The edge of the ravager's fear effect struck Aderyn, but she shrugged it off and went on the attack, aiming for the weak spots of throat and armpits and groin. The memory of the spectral guardian's poison made her feel lighter than usual by contrast.

**Congratulations! You have defeated [Orc Ravager].
You have earned [19,500 XP]**

The unexpected system defeat notice when her opponent hadn't fallen startled Aderyn into dropping her guard. The ravager seized her momentary distraction to stab Aderyn in the side. It felt like being punched rather than stabbed, and now it was the ravager's turn to be startled at how her attack had failed. Aderyn had never been so grateful for her <Gossamer Mail>. The ravager's grip on her sword loosened, just for a moment, but in that moment, Aderyn struck, and with a lucky blow wrenched the sword from her opponent's hand.

The ravager stepped back. Aderyn raised her mystery sword and with [Reposition] dragged the orc in one swift motion forward onto the blade. The ravager choked and involuntarily grabbed the length of steel embedded deep within her stomach. Aderyn drove it home harder.

**Congratulations! You have defeated [Orc Ravager].
You have earned [19,500 XP]**

It took some tugging to pull her sword free of the dead ravager, and another system defeat notice flashed as she did so. She heard Owen shout her name and discovered he'd made it to the far side of the orcs he was fighting. She shoved another orc aside and got into position for [Outflank].

"Glasha's gone!" Owen shouted. "What now?"

"We should go after her/*Pretend to turn your back, Owen*," she replied. [Secret Message] was still clumsy even now that she could speak to multiple people at once.

Owen half turned away. The ravager he'd been fighting laughed and aimed a blow at Owen's back. Aderyn dragged the fuzzy yellow ball that was its focus on Owen to herself. The orc let out a surprised yell as it spun around to face Aderyn. Before it could recover, Owen drove the <Sunsword> through its body so deeply the glowing tip emerged from below its breastbone. Aderyn slashed its throat and darted back to avoid the spray of blood. Another system defeat message appeared. Four down. No, five—the victim of Isold's **[Compulsion]** drove a knife through the eye of his fellow ravager.

"Aderyn, watch out!" Owen shouted.

Aderyn spun around in time to meet a pair of daggers aimed at her face. She dodged one, but the other scored a deep line along her cheek, cutting to the bone. She shrieked in mingled pain and surprise and threw herself at the orc, not thinking how stupid it was to try to body check something nearly twice her size. With the sword, she aimed a powerful blow at the ravager's neck. The tip of the blade struck the hollow of his throat and was deflected upward by the orc's tough skin, tearing through the corner of his mouth with its blubbery lips and cutting a line across his face to match her wound.

They faced each other, not moving, both breathing heavily. Then the orc roared in Aderyn's face, his hot, stinking breath on the raw wound making her wince. Aderyn let the fear effect wash over her, like a fog, and ignored it. She shoved him away with **[Reposition]**, moving him a good fifteen feet back to give herself time to recover her equilibrium.

Cold air riffled her ponytail as Owen's **[Weapon Mastery]** skill activated its elemental damage, and another system defeat message appeared. The chill was welcome in the overwarm, dim room that stank of orc, and it boosted Aderyn's morale. With a scream of defiance, she launched herself at the orc, who barely got his crossed daggers in place to block her attack. Aderyn disengaged and drove her sword into the orc's belly. It didn't penetrate deeply, so she tried again. Sharp pain, barely noticed in the heat of battle, shot through her below her shoulder. The orc backed away, stumbled, and collapsed. Aderyn pounced, wounding it a third time, and in seconds, the fight was over.

Congratulations! You have defeated [Orc Ravager].
You have earned [19,500 XP]

The system defeat message was blurry, and blinking did nothing to clear Aderyn's vision. She felt along the place where her chainmail arm opening was, and her hand came away bloody. Then Isold was at her side, pressing the **<Healing Stone>** to the deep wound. "Are we winning?" Aderyn asked, then felt stupid. She knew how many orcs they'd killed.

But Isold answered the question she'd intended. "Livia got hit hard, but I reached her in time. Everyone but Suveer has taken some damage. And I'm only guessing about Suveer, since I can't see his health bar. He's simply stayed out of the way of every attack."

"It's [Reposition], and I'm glad he's doing something." Aderyn wiped her bloody hand on her trousers and gripped her sword more tightly. "We'll survive. And we'll kill Glasha."

"We have to find her first," Isold said grimly.

Aderyn took the opportunity to examine the situation. Livia and Weston were fighting back to back, Weston with his rapier that flicked in and out almost faster than even Aderyn could follow, Livia with both fists wreathed in the magical glitter of *stone fist*. Suveer was, as Isold had said, darting around the room, moving orcs at random. And Owen fought two ravagers at once, using the <Sunsword's> brilliance to throw them off balance. Seven down. Six to go.

"Isold," she said, "work your way around to the left and neutralize the two pressing Weston and Livia. *Immobilize* looks like it's about to collapse, so we have to defeat those two before the three Livia trapped reenter the fight. I'll help Owen. Suveer—just stay out of Suveer's way, all right? I'm not sure how much strategy is going into his [Reposition]."

She hurried to [Outflank] with Owen just as one of Owen's two foes struck him a terrible blow to the side, making him stagger. Peripherally, she saw Owen's health bar drop, enough that she again thanked the Miracle Meal for keeping the hit from doing more damage. With [Compel], she wrenched the ravager's attention to herself. "Help me/*Focus on the one facing you*," she called out to Owen.

Just as she'd hoped, the ravager attacking her grinned and pressed forward, forcing Aderyn back. Aderyn moved just far enough to be certain he couldn't go on threatening Owen before using [Reposition] to slide him ten feet to the left, into one of the few open spaces. It was interesting fighting creatures who spoke her language! Interesting, and unsettling, but Aderyn wasn't going to let herself be thrown by the situation, or imagine herself into the head of an orc.

She followed the ravager, attacking before he recovered his balance from being magically moved. The ravager got his blade up to block her first swing, but only barely, and Aderyn shoved it aside and pressed the attack. Stumbling back, the orc roared in her face, and Aderyn winced at how the heat of its breath stung her wounded face. If her opponent had intended to frighten her, he'd failed, because Aderyn didn't feel even a hint of unnatural fear.

She blinked away a couple of overlapping system defeat notices and struck again, this time darting to the side to slash the ravager's legs. Sweat ran down her face and gathered in the long cut, stinging. The ravager took a step back, unhurt by Aderyn's attack. For a moment, the two stood facing each other, poised and waiting. Aderyn Assessed the monster again, hoping for new weaknesses. This time, in addition to blue points of light in the usual vulnerable places, the ravager's right knee was marked in blue. Aderyn kept her attention on the ravager's face. If the monster knew his knee was vulnerable, and saw that Aderyn had noticed it, he would protect it and she would lose her chance.

The ravager leaped forward, left leg extended. Aderyn dodged and struck his right knee, putting all her strength behind the blow. The orc screamed in pain, wobbled on his one good leg, and hit the ground. Aderyn was already within his guard and thrusting for the gap in his armor beneath his arm. The orc screamed again, dropped his sword, and grabbed Aderyn around the throat with both enormous, black-nailed hands.

Aderyn's gasp of surprise cut off along with her air supply. She overrode her instinct to claw at the ravager's hands and instead drove the sword blade deeper, twisting it. The edges of her vision fogged over, tunneling so sharply her air-starved brain told her she was falling backward into an endless, black well. Her grip on her sword hilt loosened and then fell away. With one hand, she tried to pry the meaty fingers away from her throat; with the other, she groped for the <**Rod of Unfettering**>. Her hands were too numb to grip anything. She closed her eyes. The last thing she saw before she slipped into unconsciousness were feathery lines of silver light.

Blackness faded from her vision, and she rose upward through a dark shaft whose walls rolled away from her the higher she got. She blinked. She was looking at a ceiling of dingy white plaster crisscrossed by thick oak beams, and something heavy lay atop her. In another blink, she remembered being throttled by the orc ravager, and she shoved and kicked with trembling arms and legs until its body rolled off her and she could stand. Her throat ached too badly for speech, but she breathed freely.

After a few blissful breaths, Aderyn Assessed the room once more. Only three orc ravagers remained, and as she dismissed the Assessment, another couple of system defeat messages popped up. They were followed swiftly by a flash of icy air and a third defeat message. Aderyn rubbed her throat, which only hurt worse. The room was still and silent.

Then Owen said, "Aderyn?"

"I'm fine," she tried to say, but her throat couldn't manage speech. She came to his side and hugged him instead.

"Aderyn and I are the only ones injured enough to matter," Isold said. He ran the **<Wand of Healing>** up his arm, making the deep slash seal up, then pressed the **<Healing Stone>** to the hollow of Aderyn's throat. She wished she could see the effect, to know what her throat looked like when it was translucent and glowed green. It was an idle wish, given that she cared much more about being able to speak.

When her throat felt less raw and her face no longer stung, and Isold had put away the **<Healing Stone>**, she said, "We don't have much time. Glasha clearly believed her ravagers could kill us, but she's not stupid. She'll know to the minute how long it should take them to do that, and if they haven't reported back by that time, she'll know we're coming for her."

"Then let's use the **<Wayfinder>** and get there first," Owen said.

"No," Aderyn and Suveer said simultaneously. Aderyn waved to Suveer to continue. "We need to take her by surprise by attacking from a direction she doesn't expect," Suveer said. "It's possible she has other of her minions positioned along that hall—" He pointed at the door Glasha had entered by— "and we'll have to waste resources fighting them. In fact, she's probably counting on it."

"What we need to do," Aderyn said, "is use *scry* to locate Glasha and then *transport* to move us directly to her location. How are your resources, Livia?"

"I'm doing all right, though I don't have enough reserves to use my highest-level spells. *Scry* and *transport* are no problem, now that I've seen Glasha to be able to *scry* her. Give me a second."

"One thing first," Owen said. "Suveer, I want you to join our team. It's safer for you, and you deserve to gain experience from these battles."

Suveer's eye widened. "Me? But after what Ruan did—"

"I don't know what Ruan did. You can tell us later." Owen extended a hand to Suveer. "Hurry up. We're losing time."

Aderyn's team roster flickered, and Suveer's name, class, and health bar filled the empty final slot. He didn't appear to be wounded at all, for which Aderyn was grateful.

Livia already had her scrying mirror out and murmured a few nonsense words. The mirror flashed once as if struck by a stray sunbeam, and then they were looking at Glasha's ugly, sneering face. The view expanded rapidly, dizzying Aderyn. It showed a room lit not by dim torches or sunlight but by lanterns that reflected off metal shapes that turned out to be armor. Not orc armor, which Aderyn knew was usually rusty and dirty and not at all reflective, but chain-mail and studded leather and steel plate. Human armor. Human trophies.

Three other orcs faced Glasha, two of them heavily built, one almost skinny the way Ahda the chanter had been. A door behind the skinny one opened, and another orc entered. Aderyn scanned the scene frantically, looking for anything that would give her a tactical advantage, but it was like trying to plan an attack by looking at a battlefield through a hole in a piece of cloth.

"Got it," Livia said, stowing the mirror in her knapsack. "Everybody huddle up. We get one chance at this."

"Go for Glasha. Ignore the others," Aderyn said.

They huddled together as Livia chanted the long, long syllables of *transport* under her breath. With a rumble of thunder, they were elsewhere. The light became somewhat brighter, and the room smelled not just of orc but of paper and grease and burning oil.

They broke their huddle, and Aderyn Assessed the room, looking at numbers instead of the long script of [**Improved Assess 4**]. Five ravagers. Three elites. A chanter. One grunt, the one who'd entered the room just before *transport* had taken effect. And Glasha. Aderyn rejoiced at how bewildered the orc commander general looked.

Owen didn't say a word. He leaped at Glasha, the <**Sunsword**> blazing. Glasha recoiled. She recovered immediately and drew her sword. Unlike most orcs' weapons, it shone almost as brightly as Owen's blade and had honed, unnotched edges. She brought it up to block Owen's attack.

The <**Sunsword**> struck Glasha's sword with a chime that sounded like ice cracking. A blast of arctic wind swept through the room.

Glasha's sword shattered.

Chapter Thirty-Six

Glasha, stunned, dropped the hilt of her broken blade. Everyone else froze in astonishment—everyone except Owen. He followed that first spectacular blow with a slash across Glasha's midsection. Glasha grunted and stepped back. Then she grabbed the nearest ravager and dragged him toward her. When Owen attacked again, she used the ravager's body as a shield. The ravager screamed as Owen's <**Sunsword**> impaled him through the chest. Aderyn's shock made the system defeat notice almost imperceptible.

Glasha snatched the sword from the ravager's dead hand and shoved the corpse at Owen, who converted his next attack into a dodge. "I'll kill you painfully for that," she snarled.

"Don't just stand there!" Owen shouted.

It had all happened in seconds. Aderyn rushed to Owen's side, but was blocked by the chanter, who held up a hand the way Isold always did. "You want to kill that one," he said, his voice breathy and not at all like an orc's. He pointed at Owen. "Strike from behind."

Aderyn lowered her sword and took two steps past the chanter, her movement dreamy. Then she spun around and stabbed the chanter through the chest. "Never again," she spat.

The chanter's lips moved, and he raised his hand again. Bloody froth stained his mouth. Aderyn pressed harder, forcing him back several paces, until he sagged and slid off her blade.

Congratulations! You have defeated [Orc Chanter]. You have earned [12,075 XP]

Aderyn put her back to the wall. The room was smaller than the one they'd fought the ravagers in, and the chaotic movement of the combatants made a tactical assessment impossible. Briefly Aderyn wished for a skill that would freeze a fight in place so she had all the time in the world to figure out tactics. Then she dove back into the melee.

She used [Reposition] to move an orc elite out of her way as she maneuvered to get behind Glasha for [Outflank]. Weston was again fighting to defend Livia, who looked like she was trying to find a position that would let her attack Glasha without hurting Owen. Aderyn didn't see Isold or Suveer anywhere. A ravager loomed up in her face; she switched its target to Weston and slipped around behind it.

Owen and Glasha fought as if they were the only two people in the room. Owen and Ruan had battled like equals; Owen and Glasha fought like equals who had waited their whole lives for the chance to kill one another. The <Sunsword> drew trails of light through the air, it moved so swiftly, but Glasha's stolen sword countered every strike, and when Owen forced Glasha back a step, she was quick to respond, pushing him backward in return.

The other orcs were defending their leader, Aderyn finally realized when yet another ravager got up in her face, screaming with incoherent fury. Frustrated, she used [Reposition] to shove him halfway across the room and ran for it, putting herself behind Glasha before the ravager could stop her.

The weird tug of [Outflank] affected her immediately. From where she stood, with Glasha's back to her, Aderyn clearly saw Owen's face, as intent and focused as it always was in a fight. He struck again, and this time Glasha took two steps backward, forcing Aderyn to move as well. Aderyn aimed a blow at Glasha's lower back, which was unprotected by her hard leather armor. Glasha shifted at that moment, and Aderyn's strike hit without penetrating deeply.

With a snarl, Glasha turned on Aderyn. "Sneaky little bitch," she said, and slammed her sword against Aderyn's shoulder. It struck like a hammer rather than a blade, knocking Aderyn back. She felt something crack, and her left arm went numb. Dizzily Aderyn took hold of the fuzzy yellow ball of light connecting her to Glasha and tossed it at Owen.

Glasha spun around—right into Owen's fist. The blow snapped Glasha's head back, stunning her so she didn't deflect Owen's next strike with the <Sunsword>. Charcoal-red blood spurted. Glasha howled in agony.

The remaining orcs howled in discordant unison with their leader. As one, they disengaged with whoever they'd been fighting and converged on Owen. One orc slid away sideways, and Suveer shouted with excitement. Weston tripped the orc elite he'd been fighting and slit the creature's throat as it fell. Then the orcs reached Owen, and what had been chaos turned into madness. Aderyn ignored the terrible stabs of pain from her left arm as she used only her right arm to wield her sword, but there was no way to apply any discipline to her blows. She thrashed about, hoping to do enough random damage to matter.

Someone grabbed her left arm, and agony spangled her vision with the bright sparks of near unconsciousness. "Sorry," Isold said. He steadied Aderyn and roughly pressed the <Healing Stone> to her broken shoulder. Aderyn shoved her fist into her mouth to keep from screaming at the pain, but in moments, it was gone.

"The stone is nearly out of charges," Isold said. "We have to win this soon."

Glasha howled again. Despite herself, Aderyn shuddered with fear. It was the howl of an animal that had reached its breaking point, a howl of fury and despair and the bone-deep desire to rend its prey. It brought all the other orcs to a halt briefly, and in that moment, Glasha threw her sword away and lunged for Owen.

Owen raised the <Sunsword>, but Glasha batted it away, ignoring the deep cut it gave her arm. She bore Owen to the ground, snarling and biting and hammering his chest and face with powerful blows of her fists.

Aderyn screamed and rushed at Glasha, raising her sword to attack the orc general's undefended back. This time, her stab drove deep. Glasha ignored it. She punched Owen in the face, apparently breaking his nose. Aderyn screamed again as the <Sunsword> deactivated. Owen's head sagged to one side. Blood streamed down his face.

Glasha sat back where she'd pinned Owen to the floor and howled in triumph. An orc ravager bowled Aderyn over when she aimed another strike at Glasha. The ravager bore her to the ground, laughing as he drew his dagger and pressed its edge to her throat.

Aderyn brought her knee up hard between his legs.

The orc let out a shrill, pained scream and dropped the dagger. Clutching himself, he fell to the side. Aderyn rolled to her feet and grabbed her sword. Three feet away, Glasha raised her heavy blade, preparing to cleave Owen's head in two.

Owen came to with a start. He grabbed the <Sunsword> hilt and pressed it against Glasha's chest. A chime rang out, and the blade of light extended—into Glasha. The orc commander general jerked as the sword cut through her armor and her chest and emerged out the back of her cuirass. Owen, his face set and tense, dragged the <Sunsword> through Glasha's body, cutting a gash from her chest to her navel.

Glasha let go of her sword, which hit the floor and bounced. Then she collapsed atop Owen, lifeless.

Congratulations! You have defeated [Glasha the Orc Commander General].
You have earned [40,000 XP]

In the shocked stillness that followed, another system defeat notice appeared as Weston slit the throat of an orc ravager. As the monster's body hit the ground, the other orcs scrambled out the doors.

Aderyn helped Owen out from under Glasha's body and hugged him, not caring about the mingled orc and human blood covering his armor. "I thought you were dead," she murmured.

"I almost was. Good thing the <Sunsword> works the way I expected." Owen made as if to kiss her, then swiped blood off his face and reconsidered.

"We defeated Glasha," Isold said. "Where is the system notice?"

"Yes, didn't we succeed at the **[Crush the Horde]** quest?" Livia said. "Or do we have to convince the orc army to retreat? I was hoping killing Glasha would be enough."

"It's not the Fated One quest I meant," Isold said. "The victory condition for defeating Charnel Keep was killing Glasha. And yet, nothing."

A powerful tremor shook the room. Suveer lost his footing and fell. Weston grabbed Isold's arm to keep them both upright, and Owen held Aderyn closer. Only Livia was unmoved. "Earthquake," she said. "I have a bad feeling I know what caused it."

WARNING! The death of [Glasha the Orc Commander General] begins the destruction of Charnel Keep. This event triggers a five-minute timer until the total eradication of this dungeon. Exit the dungeon before this time to complete the quest.

"Well, shit," Owen said. "I guess Glasha was a load-bearing boss."

Her heart sinking in anticipatory dread, Aderyn checked the Codex display. The twenty-four hour timer, which had displayed 14:10:51 in white, had been replaced by a nearly identical timer. This one's numbers were bright red, and the counter read 04:43.

"We can do this," she said. "Let's get the prisoners and get out of here."

THE PASSAGE LEADING TO THE PRISONERS' cell was eerily silent. Aderyn's fears propelled her faster until she stumbled to a halt in front of the door. She tried to work the latch, but the corrosion and warping were too much for her strength. "Weston!"

As Weston grabbed the latch, someone inside the room shouted, "Who's there?"

Relieved beyond words, Aderyn held back just long enough for Weston to fully open the door, then rushed into the room. "The keep is collapsing. We need all of you to run, now. Stay with us, and we'll get out alive."

Gasps, and a few muffled sobs, were the only response. Debran pushed through the crowd and got up into Aderyn's face. "We are not following the likes of you! You made up this preposterous story to cover your many crimes against—"

Owen appeared at Aderyn's side. With one hand, he shoved Debran backward, propelling him until the man ran up against the disgustingly filthy wall. "That's enough," he said, his voice dangerously calm. "If I hear one more word out of you, I'll lock you in one of these cells and you can find out firsthand if we're lying. Understand that I don't give a damn about your life one way or the other, and if you keep this shit up, I won't feel at all bad about abandoning you to your death."

Debran swallowed. His mouth opened. Owen leaned in closer. "One chance. Do I look like I'm joking?"

The man closed his mouth. He shook his head. Owen released him. "Everyone out. Aderyn, find us a path."

Aderyn stepped into the hallway and focused on the <**Wayfinder**>. She noticed in passing that the red number counter now read 3:05, and then she ignored it. Knowing how much time was left didn't help.

A huge tremor shook the keep. Aderyn braced herself against the wall until it passed. She knew the way back to the stairs they'd come up by, but both those and the ones Owen and her friends had found put them as far from the exit as they could be. With luck, the <**Wayfinder**> could shorten that path.

As she'd hoped, the magic item pointed her back toward the atrium. "This way," she commanded, and ran. The clamor of a dozen people following faded in her awareness. It was just her, and the glow of the <**Wayfinder**>, and the tremors that came more frequently now.

She emerged from the prison maze at a dead run and turned left, circling the atrium. The screams and shouts of orcs filled her ears, but they all came from the level below. Where she and her friends were, no orcs remained.

As she rounded the atrium, she remembered what Ruan had said about stairs—and sure enough, the <**Wayfinder**> pointed her toward a dimly-lit hole in the wall at the end of a hallway. The door to the treasury still hung ajar, but she ignored it, following the deep red glow.

When she reached the top of an unlit staircase going down, it pulsed once and cooled off.

"Hurry, down the stairs!" she exclaimed.

Another tremor shook the stones beneath her feet, and a terrible ominous creaking sound echoed from above. Weston ran past her, ignoring the shifting stones, with Livia right behind him. The prisoners stumbled behind, some of them barely moving faster than a walk. "Hurry!" Aderyn repeated, turning to hustle them along.

"The way's blocked," Weston said from beside her, startling her into a shriek. "The stairs are collapsed. We could get through, but not in less than three minutes."

"I can't move the stones fast enough," Livia said. "Maybe I can make a door through the outer wall, but I'm running through my reserves. That door would be thirty or forty feet in the air, and I don't have enough in me to cast *move earth* and make a safe passage."

Despairing, Aderyn cupped the <**Wayfinder**> in both hands again. "I refuse to believe this is impossible."

To her surprise, the orb began glowing again, the deep red that said she was close to an exit. "No—" she began. It was confused. It still thought the stairs were the way out. She turned her back on the stairs, and the glow deepened. Curious, she hurried back the way they'd come, following its guidance.

The orb took her around a corner and then fell dark and still again. Aderyn, blinking eyes that were dry from staring at the red glow, exclaimed, "The treasury? But that's—"

"Treasury?" Weston exclaimed.

"Weston, now is not the time for looting," Owen warned.

"I'm not that thundering stupid," Weston said. "But a treasury is something there might be a secret door out of. Come on!"

The room was still as disrupted as the fight had made it, gold and silver objects toppled to the floor, caskets of jewels upended and spilling their glittering contents across the shelves. Weston ignored them. He ran straight to the back wall and splayed one large hand over the stones. "It's here somewhere. Aderyn, do you see it?"

Aderyn turned [Spot Weakness] on the wall and shrieked again, this time in delight. "Right where you're standing!"

You have discovered a secret door! Your reward is [200 XP].

"I can move the stones," Livia said.

"No need." Weston felt along the lines where the stones met. The masonry was so exact the joins were nearly imperceptible. Against her better judgment, Aderyn peeked at the counter. 1:43. She resisted the urge to tell him to hurry.

With a click, one of the huge stones depressed half an inch, and a jagged line appeared, dark against the lighter gray. Weston got his fingertips around the exposed stones and pulled. Slowly, the secret door opened. "Go!" he exclaimed.

Aderyn got behind the prisoners and urged and pushed them onward. Two of them appeared near to fainting. She took their hands and dragged them with her.

The secret door opened on a dark hallway Livia immediately illuminated with *orbs of light*. Black, dry stones whose edges crumbled showed how old this part of the keep was. They also showed clearly the outline of another secret door, obvious from this side. Aderyn felt no pang of regret at leaving it unexplored.

The hallway extended a short distance before turning right. Aderyn, now near the back of the group, heard Weston shout, "Stairs! They're steep, so watch yourselves."

Owen grabbed Aderyn's elbow. "We need to move faster."

"They can't go faster!" But she pushed the prisoners harder, catching one woman who tripped and nearly fell. The woman was weeping soundlessly, as if Owen's threat to Debran had scared her into silence as well. Aderyn was too tense for compassion. Time enough to deal with fear when they were all free.

The stairs, when she finally reached them, were more than steep; they were practically a stone ladder. Aderyn urged the woman to turn around and descend that way. As the woman made her slow way down, Aderyn jigged in impatience. She refused to look at the red counter. There wasn't anything she could do about it now.

Finally, it was her turn to descend the steps, carefully—breaking a leg would be fatal. Owen followed her, blocking the light from above, but Aderyn found [**Darkvision**] still worked. At the bottom of the steps, she discovered why: a passage led to a rectangular opening through which the pale light of the moon was visible. Gasping with relief, Aderyn ran, overtaking the weeping woman and hauling her bodily along.

The two of them stumbled through the exit, and Aderyn slowed only to have Owen, running behind her, shout, "Don't stop! Get as far as you can from the keep! We don't know how far the destruction will spread!" He hooked his arm around the woman's free arm and said, "Aderyn, lift her, and *run!*"

They ran, **[Keep Pace]** accelerating Aderyn to match Owen's longer stride. Three seconds. Four. Five.

At six seconds after leaving Charnel Keep, the ground shook with a titanic rumble, throwing Aderyn and Owen to the ground with the woman between them. A roar of collapsing stone and timber filled the air, and a great wind rushed past, carrying dust and sand and the stench of unwashed orc bodies. Aderyn ducked her head to keep from breathing in dust and listened to the woman coughing as she wasn't so lucky.

When the tremors subsided, Aderyn pushed herself to her knees and looked behind her. Charnel Keep was gone. Not destroyed, not a pile of rubble, but vanished. All that was left in the spot it had been was an enormous, shallow pit that looked uncomfortably like the lair of a deep delver. Wind blew across its top, kicking up more dust, but nothing more dramatic happened.

Congratulations! You have completed the quest [Destroy Charnel Keep].
You have earned [51,000 XP]

Owen lay on his back nearby with his hand over his nose and mouth, breathing heavily. "That is closer than I ever want to come to failure," he said.

"We're not done," Aderyn said. "We still have to get back to civilization."

Owen closed his eyes. "Is it bad that that sounds trivial by comparison?"

CHAPTER THIRTY-SEVEN

They walked only as far as the first grove of sheltering trees. Debran was the least injured and weakened of the former prisoners, which struck Aderyn as either typical or unfair, but even he was struggling when just after dawn they finally found a safe place to rest. "Safer," Weston said. "Nothing here is truly safe."

"This would be a great time for *stone prison*," Livia groused. "Nothing gets through that, and I can cast it to be big enough to protect us all. Tight quarters, but... anyway, I don't have the reserves, so it's irrelevant."

"It's fine," Owen said. "We'll set watches, and eat, and get some sleep."

Aderyn settled next to Owen with her handful of beef jerky and green seedless grapes. "It feels like we were in there forever," she murmured. "Tell me what happened with you while we were separated."

"Aderyn, shouldn't you tell me—"

She shushed him. "I need something less intense to think about. And then I'll tell you about Ruan. Please?"

Owen put his arm around her and hugged her. "I understand. Well, without the <**Wayfinder**>, we did a lot of backtracking. I think Charnel Keep is—was—designed to confuse intruders, for all it's a straightforward design. We had to avoid the center, where their great hall was, because they were all having a feast or something and Weston said, when he peeked inside, there were easily a hundred and fifty orcs present. And we saw a lot more of those portcullis traps. Except they're not really traps, not in the sense of being something intruders set off. Not with the triggers being in the wall like that. Weston thought they were meant for crowd control by the orcs."

He shifted his weight, bringing Aderyn closer. "Anyway, we wandered for a long time, avoiding orcs and killing them when we couldn't. Every fight felt like it was the one that would alert the entire keep. There were some mazes like the cell block, though not as big. Then we discovered a shortcut. Remember this?"

He dug in his belt pouch and brought out a fat steel ring, covered in black wire mesh on one end and a faceted lump of quartz on the other. "Drorg's ring turned out to be a key, sort of. More accurately, it provides access permission to the user, like how in the Enchanterium the keys were badges or something. Once we discovered that, moving through the keep was easy. Then Ruan died, and we found the stairs up, and met you—that's all."

Aderyn tensed at the mention of Ruan's death, but Owen didn't say anything. She loved that he didn't push, and that lack of pushing made it possible for her to speak. "Ruan lied," she said in a low voice, though it didn't matter who heard. "His Fated One quest was actually to steal a sword from the Charnel Keep treasury. He told us his quest was to rescue the prisoners because he knew that would get us to come with him and provide support."

"That bastard."

"Yes."

"And you fought when you found out the truth?"

"More or less." The memory of Ruan's stunned face as he plummeted to his death shook Aderyn as it had not at the time. "I was lucky. Suveer refused to help Ruan kill me, and while Ruan was distracted, I used [Reposition] to shove him through that opening above the atrium. The scimitar tree did the rest."

"Scimitar tree? I didn't know that was there. You can get experience when you don't deal the final blow?"

"If you're fighting something, and you maneuver it over a cliff edge or into a trap or another monster, it counts as you doing the damage. Father says it's complicated and he thinks the system decides on a case-by-case basis whether to award experience, but I don't know anymore." She hugged Owen. "I'm glad Ruan is dead. His greed might have gotten us all killed."

"And now I feel guilty about my greed," Owen said. He dragged his knapsack toward him and unlaced the top. "I had the chance to grab some of that treasure while Weston was opening the door. I didn't go for anything in particular, there wasn't time, but I grabbed one of those little caskets."

He removed a silver box from his knapsack and opened the lid, which had a latch but no lock. Aderyn gasped at the sight of a pile of jewels, some rings half buried in the pile, and a tangle of golden chains. "Owen, it's a fortune!"

"Even divided among the six of us, it's a lot," Owen agreed.

"Divide what?" Livia said.

"Owen picked up some of Glasha's treasure." Aderyn ran her fingers through the mix of jewelry and gems. "I was going to be upset about him taking time away from our escape, especially since the system message told me greed is the enemy, but it doesn't matter. This could set us up for life."

"Oh, well, if you put it that way." Livia withdrew a matching silver box from her knapsack. "I figured, even Weston needed a few seconds to get the door open, and I didn't have anything else to do—"

"*Livia!*" Aderyn couldn't hold back a laugh.

"Then I feel less awkward about having taken something as well," Isold said. He removed a smoothly curved mace from his waistband. "I was about to take one of the coffers when I saw this. It is called <**Peacemaker's Burden**>, and it is specifically intended to be wielded by non-martial classes. Appropriate, since it's essentially a ball of steel welded to a stick and requires very little finesse. It has no bonuses to damage and it doesn't have an increased chance of hitting, but what it does have is the possibility of discharging *deep slumber* on a victim, knocking him or her unconscious." He smiled ruefully. "I've become tired of using the <Skeleton Ladder> for a purpose it was decidedly not meant for."

Aderyn rested her head on Owen's shoulder. Her heart felt lighter than it had since... she couldn't remember how long it had been since she last laughed. "I feel like we're close to success. I don't know what it will take to make the orc army retreat, but it can't—"

"You're going to jinx us," Livia warned. "Don't say anything about how it can't be that hard."

"All right, I won't." Aderyn ate more grapes. Around them, the citizens of Shantos, the former prisoners, lay huddled on the ground. Most of them appeared to have fallen asleep. "I hope—oh, I forgot to see if Glasha had Varoun's <Farspeaker>, since Zothemza didn't. Though I couldn't communicate with him if I had it instead. I hope they all made it out. Those caverns collapsed, too."

"They had plenty of time, even if Varoun used the <Wand of World Door> to get every one of them back to Ikharatia. *I'm* glad we didn't suggest they wait around down there for us. What a disaster that would have been." Owen twined his fingers with Aderyn's. "Let's talk plans. Once everyone's fed, I think we need to give the people from Shantos time to rest someplace that they're not at risk of torture or death."

"The Blighted Range is hardly that," Weston joked, "but I know what you mean."

"I think a few hours will be enough," Isold said. "None of them are injured in a way healing can fix, just exhausted and traumatized. Better we get out of the high-risk zone as fast as possible, and finish recuperating after that."

"I agree," Owen said. "But we should set watches as if it's nighttime. Aderyn and me, Weston and Livia, Isold and Suveer. An hour and a half each—what time will that put us at, Livia?"

Livia checked her pocket watch. "It's a little after seven a.m. now, so call it about one in the afternoon."

"We reached Charnel Keep a little more than twenty-four hours after entering the high-risk zone. By my math, that means travel took fourteen hours." Owen stared into space like he was doing more mental calculations. "With the civilians along, we won't go as quickly, but I'm sure they're motivated to get back to civilization, so I'm guessing we won't add more than a couple of hours to that number going back."

"And the sun rises and sets around six or six-thirty every day," Aderyn added.

"Right. Traveling at night is far too dangerous, so we'll cover ground today for five hours and, if we push hard, we could camp outside the high-risk zone tomorrow night. Livia, is there any way we can shorten that with magic?"

"There's one possibility I wasn't sure we should consider," Livia said. "When my reserves are full, I can cast *world door* seven times without exhausting myself. Tomorrow morning I could send the citizens back to Ikharatia and I'd still have some reserves left. It would take them to safety and keep *us* safer because we wouldn't have to worry about keeping them alive. But I wouldn't be in a position to defend us if we ran into something really dangerous, and 'really dangerous' is practically the definition of what we encounter here."

"It's still a smart idea," Owen said. "I love the thought of getting them to safety and especially putting Debran where he can't bitch at Aderyn anymore. But you're right we should consider other options. Anything else?"

"I can *transport* us about ten miles at a time, but we'd have to split into two groups, and I'm superstitious about separating the party. And ten miles might not be worth the power expenditure." Livia looked thoughtful. "A final option is for someone to go to Ikharatia via *world door* and borrow Varoun's wand, but we don't know where he is and, again, we'd be splitting the party."

"I don't know," Aderyn said. "That first plan is more appealing the more I think about it. We'll have to be extra careful, but we would do that anyway."

"I agree," Weston said.

"Does that mean sending me, too?" Suveer asked.

An awkward silence fell. Owen said, "Do you want to leave?"

Suveer shrugged. "Either I'm a useless Warmaster or I'm not. There are six former prisoners, and you said, seven *world door* castings. But that would leave you mostly defenseless. I don't know if you want me along."

Owen glanced at Aderyn. Aderyn, who was used to leaping to Suveer's support when he said things like that, found herself at a loss for words. Finally, she managed, "You're an adventurer. You have abilities these non-classed people don't. If you think you can fight beside us if something happens, we want you to stay."

Suveer tilted his head, fixing his one eye on Aderyn. "There's nothing for me in Ikharatia. Maybe I can be useful here."

The thought of Suveer as a permanent member of their team gave Aderyn an uncomfortable uneasiness that ran all through her body. She was sure he hadn't meant it that way, since they would be leaving the Southlands when the Fated One quest was complete, and Suveer might not want to leave his home. But where the thought of Jessemia joining them had pleased her, having Suveer there in her team roster forever just filled Aderyn with dread. It made no sense. She seemed to have gotten what she wanted, for Suveer to see his value, and it hadn't satisfied her.

"You can stay with us until we reach the city," Owen said as if he could read Aderyn's thoughts. "See how much experience you gain."

Suveer nodded. "I'm sure I'm close to seventeen now."

Owen rose. "Then that's settled. Aderyn, you and I will watch first, and I think everyone should nap if they can."

Aderyn followed Owen a short distance from their impromptu camp. "Thanks," she said. "I don't—Owen, this is awful, but I don't want him with us forever."

"How is that awful? He's really not a fit for our team."

"Because I wanted him to see his self worth, and now that he has, I don't like him any more than I did before!"

Owen sighed. "Come here." He drew her into his arms and held her for a few moments. "That is a problem only you could have."

"Owen!"

"That was meant as a compliment, sweetheart. Didn't it occur to you that you don't have to like everyone? Suveer has changed in large part because you believed he could. But he's still Suveer. He is still damaged from all those years under Ruan's thumb. You can't turn him into another person. And you shouldn't feel bad that you didn't."

"But—" Aderyn shook her head. "You're right. I guess I feel responsible for him, and I feel guilty that I sort of resent him still being here. I didn't ever think beyond getting him to realize his potential."

"It's all right. He can stay with us until we return to Ikharatia, and then we'll say goodbye. Maybe he'll team up with another partner, or maybe he'll retire. Level sixteen is respectable for any class, and for a Warmaster it's downright miraculous. But you—" He kissed her lightly. "You aren't responsible for him no matter how you feel about it. Let that worry go."

"I will. Thank you. I feel you've lifted a burden. I love you."

"I love you, too. Now, let's stay alert. Now that the immediate crisis is past, I'm feeling weary."

Aderyn's weariness grew as they walked the perimeter, and after an hour and a half she was ready to let Isold and Suveer take a turn. Sleep, even a short sleep, refreshed her, and when Weston and Livia got up to take their turn at watch, the movement roused her and she discovered she was slept out. She sat with her back to one of the dry, desiccated trees and closed her eyes, listening to the wind's voice rustling what few leaves were left and the sound of Livia and Weston's boots pacing around their camp.

Someone settled beside her. Suveer said, "I still don't know why you were nice to me. I didn't like you from the start."

Aderyn resisted the urge to respond sarcastically. By now she realized Suveer had no idea what small talk was. "I told you. You and I are the highest level Warmasters in the world, as far as I know. I liked the idea of being able to talk to someone like me, and you were it. And I don't like seeing potential wasted."

To her surprise, Suveer smiled. It was a thin, crooked smile, but she'd never seen him so much as twitch his lips in amusement no matter how good the joke. "Ruan said you wanted to be better than me. That you only cared about being the most powerful Warmaster. He said a lot of things to keep me away from you."

"He told you a lot of lies over the years, I think." Aderyn felt no shame at speaking badly of a dead man. "He knew if you ever met a Warmaster who knew the truth about our class, you'd figure out he was controlling you for his benefit."

"I know." Suveer lightly touched his ruined eye. "He meant well at the beginning, I think. Sticking with me even though I had a useless class—you know how people think. But all through our childhood, I was the one who tagged along after him. He had all the ideas and I followed where he led. So I had chances to break away that I never took, which makes some of this my responsibility."

Aderyn had never imagined having this focused a conversation with Suveer on any topic. "That sounds right."

"And it was easier to let him take the burden of leadership, even when I didn't like what he decided. Like it wasn't my fault if I did something bad because it was Ruan's idea." He drew his knees up and hugged them. "I should have stood up to him long ago."

Again, Aderyn didn't feel an urge to contradict him. "What matters is you stood up to him at the right time. You saved my life. I wouldn't have had time for [**Reposition**] if you hadn't distracted him."

"I'm glad. You saved my life, too." Suveer rested his chin on his knees. "I wish we had played Wall face to face."

"Yes, you have to be better at it than Ruan. Did you teach him?"

Suveer smiled again. "That was me playing. We used [**Bonded Mind**] for me to tell Ruan what moves to make."

"You—" Aderyn decided calling him a cheater was pointless. "You're right. I bet if we played each other, without someone else as an intermediary, it would be a fantastic game."

"It would." Suveer yawned. "I just wanted to thank you again. Even though I wish I'd retired years ago."

"What? Why?"

Suveer searched for words. "Because," he finally said, "I'm not sure being a level sixteen Warmaster with a terrible partner is better than being a level one Warmaster with no partner at all."

He rose and walked away while Aderyn gaped, stunned out of a good response. He'd said the words matter-of-factly, not denigrating himself, and yet the sentiment was so deeply depressing Aderyn almost felt like sliding into the black hole after him. And she'd had such hopes that he'd changed! Well, he *had* changed, just not as much as she'd thought. And she had the whole journey back to Ikharatia to get him to see things differently.

CHAPTER THIRTY-EIGHT

With a snap, the final *world door* oval collapsed, making Debran disappear. Livia stretched. "I actually feel better than I thought I would," she told Weston, who looked concerned. "I think my reserves may be greater than I realized."

"That's good, because I was thinking we could repeat that trick tomorrow morning," Owen said. "Especially since we'll be arriving in Ikharatia, where no monsters lurk to eat our faces and it doesn't matter how low your reserves are."

"I love this plan," Weston exclaimed. "I'm sick of the Blighted Range. This place makes me itch. I want a bath."

"Oh, don't say that. Now I can't think of anything else," Aderyn complained.

"No daydreaming," Owen said with a laugh. "Let's get walking. Unless it's safer to set up camp and wait the day out? Aderyn?"

Aderyn shook her head. "We're likely to make ourselves a target if we stay put. I don't know what kind of territory the monsters in this place have established, or if they patrol—you see the problem. If we keep moving, we might still disturb something, but the odds are in our favor."

"Then we walk." Owen stretched the way Livia had. "I shouldn't be complacent, but despite this being the Blighted Range and a real pit of a place, I feel like we're—"

"*Jinx*," Livia and Weston said at the same time.

Owen rolled his eyes. "Never mind. Let's walk faster then, how does that sound?"

Aderyn sympathized with Owen. The sun still blazed in the sky, which was yellow with haze and dust and heat, the air still tried to suck the moisture from her eyeballs and nostrils, but she felt good. The last of the prisoners had been rescued, and from here it was just a matter of surviving whatever monsters the high-risk zone threw at them. But, given how powerful those monsters could theoretically be, she wasn't about to be caught off guard.

She walked beside Owen, occasionally Assessing the landscape. The bright green lines never failed to amaze her. Maybe after a few weeks they'd stop seeming so miraculous. Her team had left the trees behind, and the orcs' "road" now passed through a barren landscape of rises too low to be called hills. Cracked soil covered with scatterings of loose gravel and sand looked as parched as the air felt. Aderyn's boots kicked up light puffs of dust wherever she trod.

"Stop," Livia said.

Aderyn turned. Livia stood motionless, stiff with tension like she was listening to distant noise with her whole body. "I feel movement beneath us," she said. "Like the deep delver. That kind of vibration."

"Crap," Owen said. "Is it after us?"

Livia shook her head. "I can't tell. But we have to assume it is. Everybody stay perfectly still. No movement. Maybe we can convince it we aren't here."

This made Aderyn uncomfortably aware that she wasn't balanced very well. The need to move nearly overpowered her. "When will you know?"

"If it's hungry, it will be more alert. We could be here for a while." Livia frowned. "Actually, let me try something."

She closed her eyes and clasped her hands in front of her at chest height. A tremor struck, not a powerful one, more of a jiggle of earth. It seemed the opposite of what they needed, and Aderyn was about to say so when she heard a deeper rumble, much farther away. In the distance, maybe a quarter mile to the north, the parched earth heaved, breaking the dry crust and sending more tremors through the ground. As the noise and shaking of the earthquake continued, Livia said, "Let's run. That should draw its attention."

"I thought you didn't want to use up your reserves," Owen said.

"That was a skill, not a spell. [Earthquake]. Different source of power." Livia jogged rapidly beside Weston, faster than her usual quick gait. [Keep Pace] kept Aderyn level with Owen, and Suveer turned out to be as fast a runner as Isold.

The tremors were subsiding when Livia finally said, "I think that's far enough."

"I hope so," Weston said. "I have no desire to fight another deep delver."

"Take a breath," Owen said. "Five minutes."

The words were barely out of his mouth before the earth shuddered beneath their feet, a stronger tremor than before. Aderyn grabbed Owen's shoulder to stay upright. "What was—"

The ground ahead of them exploded, sending chunks of earth and fist-sized rocks flying everywhere. A twenty-foot-wide wall of mottled-tan ribbed flesh shot up in front of them, rising higher and higher until it was as tall as the five-story mansions in Finion's Gate. The creature's body swayed and arched, its enormous round mouth ringed with circular rows of stained ivory teeth like a grotesque flower on a stem bending in the wind. It roared, and the wind of its stinking breath buffeted Aderyn so she again nearly fell. With another roar, it lashed its body once and then dove.

Everyone scattered as the monstrous worm thing hit the ground with a titanic thump, its gnashing jaw throwing up more chunks of earth and stone. Aderyn scrambled out of the monster's way and Assessed it.

Name: Terrorquake
Type: Abomination
Power level: 24
Terrain: subterranean; prefers flatlands and deserts
Attack(s): bite, special
Immune to: magic and skill effects with visual components

Resistant to: weapons damage, elemental earth damage
Vulnerable to: none
Special attacks: pulverize, grind, swallow whole

Remember the chaos worms? The deep delver? This is the granddaddy of them all. Terrorquake swims through earth and sand, usually at depths you can't imagine, coming to the surface to feed. It hunts by vibration as the deep delver did, but unlike that monster, it needs flesh to sustain itself—not a lot, despite its mass, but if you're the flesh it happens upon, that's small comfort.

Terrorquake is blind, so illusions and spells like *daylight* will have no effect on it. Its bite is powerful, but its other attacks are worse. *Pulverize* happens when it slams a creature into the ground or stone with its head; *grind* is when it bites a victim and keeps biting. I don't need to explain *swallow whole*, do I?

I rarely give you advice on how to fight a monster, but as with Darkshroud, I'll just say—get away from it as fast as you can, Aderyn. It's too much for you and your friends to kill.

"We need to get away!" she shouted with [**Amplify Voice**]. "It's a power level twenty-four monster, bigger and more dangerous than a deep delver but with most of the same attacks, and it's resistant to weapons and elemental earth damage. The system says not to try to fight it!"

"It's faster than we are, and it can track us wherever we go!" Livia shouted back. "How are we supposed to get away?" She and Weston were crouched together about ten feet from Aderyn. Weston held his rapier ready to attack. It looked fragile as a toothpick next to Terrorquake's bulk.

Terrorquake reared back and loomed over them, but didn't strike. If it had been a dog, Aderyn would have thought it was scenting the air for prey. "We stay still—"

Swifter than thought, Terrorquake dove again. Aderyn shrieked and dodged as Weston and Livia ran. "It tracks by vibration," Livia called out, "and I think that means sound vibrations in the air, too."

"Shit," Aderyn said, then clapped a hand over her mouth. They couldn't run without disturbing the ground, they couldn't talk without disturbing the air. She couldn't think of a single way to get out of this.

Terrorquake suddenly retracted into the hole it had made. "Nobody move," Aderyn said. "It's a creature of earth, so I'm guessing it only senses air vibrations when it's actually in the open."

Everyone remained still. They all looked like statues, lifelike ones painted to look human. Aderyn wished she could find the image funny. She turned **[Improved Assess 4]** on the landscape, but the green lines didn't inspire any plans.

"What do we do?" Owen asked.

She almost snapped at him that she shouldn't have to have all the ideas, but she *was* the one who came up with the ideas in tactical situations. "It will eventually come back. We need to not be here when it does. We could start running and hope it gives up, but that's a desperate, defensive strategy that's likely to get someone killed. If we were still in the mountains, we could lure it off a cliff. Damn it, everything I can think of depends on not being in its—"

With a roar, Terrorquake burst out of the ground scant feet from where Aderyn stood. She nearly fell into the pit its body made and scrambled backward just in time. Owen had drawn his **<Sunsword>** and watched Aderyn closely, waiting for her signal. Well, the monster knew they were there, and they couldn't survive if they didn't communicate. She ran for it as Terrorquake slammed its head into the ground right where she'd been standing. Even with **[See It Coming]**, it came close enough for the force of its blow to knock her off her feet.

Suveer called out, "What if we climbed on the boulders? Wouldn't that block our motions from being transmitted through the ground?"

"Yes! That was in a mov—a famous story from my childhood," Owen shouted. He threw himself to the side to avoid a blow.

"It might work, but as big as this thing is, I bet it feels the vibrations even through the rock," Livia said. "And it still leaves us stranded."

Terrorquake retreated again, leaving another enormous hole. Aderyn imagined she could still feel the movement of its body through the earth. "Let's try it anyway."

They all found boulders to climb on. None of the rocks were big enough to hold more than one of them, and the one Owen stood on was barely large enough for him to fit. They sat and waited. No Terrorquake appeared. The sun beat down on Aderyn's head until sweat dripped into her eyes. She wiped it away carefully. It might be paranoia, but she imagined a drop of sweat falling on the ground and drawing the giant worm's attention.

She didn't know how much time had passed before Owen said, "I think it's gone."

"Or it could be a trick," Livia said.

"It could, but we can't stay here forever. At the very least, we can make some progress before it tracks us down again." Owen slid down from his boulder. "Come on. Let's move quickly."

They ran, even Livia, walked for a while, ran again. The heat and arid climate combined to make Aderyn, for the first time ever, wish she'd thought becoming an adventurer through. This wasn't anything she'd imagined back in Far Haven.

Then she felt the tremors.

"It's coming back!" she and Livia shouted at the same time.

They all scrambled atop boulders just as Terrorquake erupted from the ground. One of the stones its body flung hit Weston in the head. He grunted and sagged in unconsciousness. Livia shouted something, and the earth where he lay rose and tilted to deposit him atop a large stone, but Terrorquake was already rearing up to pulverize Weston's inert form.

"That's it," Owen said. "We have to fight it. Come on, Aderyn!"

Isold's song filled the air, giving Aderyn a boost of confidence and strength. She and Owen attacked the worm together. It was round and eyeless and didn't appear to have a front or backside, but they came at it from the side opposite where it loomed over Weston. Livia shouted again, and magical energy wreathed her fists, but she looked tiny next to the gaping mouth.

Owen plunged the <Sunsword> into Terrorquake's side, and Aderyn attacked with her sword only a second later. It felt like trying to cut through old leather that had baked in the sun for years. The tip of her mystery sword penetrated only a few inches, and pulling it out took all her strength. Owen didn't seem to have more luck than she had, though ichor flowed from the wound he inflicted. Aderyn was sure if monsters had health bars, this one's would barely have dropped.

Weston stirred, holding a hand to his head. He moved so slowly it terrified Aderyn into racing to drag him to safety. Livia's punches seemed to do no more damage than the swords. When Terrorquake pounced again, Livia barely escaped the blow, though it didn't knock her over. She stood her ground and punched again, but it ignored her.

Aderyn Assessed the creature again, using [**Discern Weakness**] and finding, as expected, no blue points of weakness and a red haze covering its entire body except the open mouth. For a moment, she considered it—but no, this monster had a lot more teeth than the deep delver, and it moved too fast. She doubted limited paralysis would even slow it down.

Owen was still hacking away at Terrorquake's body opposite Livia, who continued to punch. Her lips moved constantly, but Aderyn thought she was swearing rather than spellslinging.

Someone else dropped to the ground beside the still-groggy Weston. "What if we trick it?" Suveer said.

Startled, Aderyn could only say, "What?"

"Trick it. Get it to go somewhere it can't get out of, or where it can't follow us." Suveer's cheek was bloody, like a stone had struck him, too, but his eye was clear and focused.

"How?"

Suveer shrugged. "You have the terrain Assessment thing. I hoped you would see something. Watch out!"

The two of them hauled Weston to his feet and ran, just steps ahead of the monster's attack. Weston was struggling when they came to a stop.

"I'm fine now," he said. "Let's kill this thing." He ran to join Livia, who was backing away from the hole Terrorquake left as it retreated again.

"We can't," Aderyn began.

"There's no other option," Suveer said as if she'd addressed him and not Weston.

"But, I mean—look at that! We're barely chipping away at it, and it's got all the time in the world to pick us off." Aderyn immediately felt stupid. Wasn't she the one who always said there was no point bitching about things you couldn't help? No, that was her father. He would have said the same, too—that they didn't have a choice now. Of course, he would also say "Better to die trying than die huddling in a corner," and she didn't want to die in any way.

But Suveer was right. She had skills she could turn against Terrorquake. She just needed to figure out which ones mattered.

She surveyed the scene. Owen's arm was bloody, though she didn't remember him getting hit. Weston didn't look fully aware yet, and Livia was supporting him. Isold watched in all directions, tensely waiting for the monster to reappear. And Suveer watched her expectantly. Time to use tactics to her advantage.

She put on the <**Lenses of Farsight**> and scanned the horizon rapidly, looking all around and down the road toward the south. Still no trees anywhere nearby. The road looked as rutted and destroyed as ever —more so, now that Terrorquake's eruptions had taken out a chunk of it. Beyond that—

She sucked in a breath. She hadn't paid attention to where they were in all the running, and she'd nearly forgotten the encounter days ago, probably because they'd avoided combat. "Those are black oozes," she said, pointing. "They engulf their prey."

"Engulf," Suveer said. "Are they big enough to swallow Terrorquake?"

"I don't know. But there are a lot of them, and maybe that's enough. Everyone, I have a plan."

Owen headed toward her. "What is—"

Terrorquake erupted from the ground beneath him, carrying him into the air.

Aderyn screamed. Owen grabbed hold of the edge of Terrorquake's mouth, dropping the <**Sunsword**> and hanging on with both hands as the worm rose higher and higher. Terrorquake jerked its head, tossing Owen into the air. Owen sailed upward, flailing as he reached the peak of his arc and then falling back toward the toothy, gaping maw.

An invisible force grabbed Owen and sent him shooting like an arrow in a different direction, in a smooth arc that ended with him landing easily on both feet. Another force swept up the <**Sunsword**> hilt and sent it sailing more slowly to where he could pluck it from the air. Livia gasped, "*Launch*. More control and faster than *telekinesis*. That took it out of me, though. What's your idea?"

"Hold off Terrorquake until it retreats again," Aderyn said. "Then prepare to run."

They were all getting tired from having to dodge the pulverizing attack, Aderyn saw. Terrorquake, by contrast, seemed to have unlimited energy, and the wounds they dealt it looked like scratches against its mottled tan hide. If this didn't work, they really were out of luck.

With a final roar of fury, Terrorquake slid back into its hole. "Follow me!" Aderyn shouted, and took off running. She'd already discovered that for once she had an Assessment skill that worked while she was moving. The [Terrain Analysis] feature of [Improved Assess 4] wasn't affected by her running, and the green lines stayed steady no matter how fast she moved. Now she looked for possibilities, and considered what she knew of Terrorquake. It was intelligent enough not to be fooled by basic ruses. It moved rapidly underground, but despite its fast strike, it wasn't as maneuverable on the surface. And it was able to guess where a creature would be next based on its movements.

"You have to stay close to me. Step where I step," Aderyn called over her shoulder. "Don't get ahead of me. We don't need to fight two battles at once."

"Where are we going?" Owen asked.

"We're going to see how clever Terrorquake is," Aderyn replied. "And hope it's just clever enough to trap itself."

The black ooze field spread before them, to Aderyn's eyes shimmering in the sunlight. She imagined she could feel the tremors of Terrorquake's passing, beneath and then in front of her. She hoped it wasn't her imagination. She would likely only get one shot at this.

"Everybody stop!" she shouted as she stumbled to a halt on the edge of the field.

Terrorquake burst from the ground in front of them, directly in the middle of the oozes. It roared in fury and reared back to strike.

The strike never came. Terrorquake jerked its head as if shaking off a fly. Then its entire body shook in uncontrolled convulsions. It sank back into the ground, not rapidly as before, but with a slow, ponderous motion like something dragged at its bulk. A black, tarry substance clung to its body and crept rapidly toward its mouth, then poured over the hundreds of sharp teeth. Terrorquake let out a roar that was more like the squawk of a terrified chicken.

Aderyn and the others stood motionless, watching the slow-acting drama play out. "This is disturbing," Isold murmured. "And strangely satisfying."

Terrorquake lurched. It emerged from the hole, covered in black tar, and just kept coming, yard after yard of giant worm body. They all backed away. "Maybe we should run now," Owen suggested.

The rumble of earth beneath their feet was all the warning they had. The ground broke open, and Aderyn screamed once before tumbling into the deep fissure Terrorquake's body had made. The sky disappeared. The ground heaved once more, dropping a load of stones and earth on her. She flung up her one free arm to protect her face, and something struck the top of her head, sending her unconscious.

CHAPTER THIRTY-NINE

She came to slowly, weighed down by the pressure of the heavy featherbed covering her whole body, all the way to her chin. Blinking, she stretched, or tried to. The featherbed pressed one of her arms to her side and pinned her legs to the strangely lumpy bed. Her other arm was caught on something that held it firmly in place, arched over her head. She tried to writhe free, and dust showered her face, making her sneeze. Her chest didn't inflate properly.

She opened her eyes on total blackness. She couldn't move, could barely turn her head. When she exhaled, her breath came back to her immediately as if there was a wall near her face. Dust filled the air, powdery and light. Everything smelled of dirt. Wherever this was, it was underground.

Underground.

She remembered finally, with a jolt, falling into Terrorquake's crevasse, of earth and stones falling on her. A cry of terror filled her chest.

She was buried alive.

A last scrap of sanity suppressed the scream that tried to burst from her, the awareness that she might not have much air and she shouldn't waste it. Then she was screaming mentally in wordless terror.

In her madness, she heard the voice in her head without understanding the words until whoever it was screamed her name so loudly it broke through her fear. *Aderyn! Aderyn, sweetheart, calm down. I'm here. You'll be fine. We'll get you and Suveer out, but you have to calm down, okay? Listen to me, no LISTEN, you can't panic or I'll lose you.*

Aderyn closed her eyes. There wasn't anything to see, anyway, and maybe she could fool herself into believing she wasn't buried. *Don't leave me.*

I can't leave you, remember? I think we'd both go crazy without **[Bonded Mind]**. *Livia's figuring out how to reach you right now. It won't take long. I promise.*

She hadn't spent so much time developing her ranks in **[Bonded Mind]** without learning every nuance of her husband's mental speech. *Something's wrong.*

Nothing's wrong. Livia's reserves are low, that's all, and she—no, DON'T PANIC, love, it's not like that. Her remaining spells aren't the sort that make this an easy retrieval. So she has to be careful. I wouldn't lie to you.

Aderyn wasn't sure that was true. She knew if Owen was in her position, and there was no way to reach him, she'd lie like thunder to keep him from panicking until all hope was lost. But she clung to his assurances anyway. *There must be a bigger pocket of space in here. I'm still breathing easily. The air is just full of dust, is all.*

That's right. Livia says you and Suveer are caught in a space between larger masses of earth. Do you see him?

I can't see anything. Nothing could persuade Aderyn to open her eyes again. But she said, "Suveer?"

Immediately, she coughed on the dust in the air. Her tongue felt furry with dirt, her mouth was dry, and she wished she hadn't said anything. But she heard, faintly, her own name spoken from somewhere beneath her. Whether it came from far away or the speaker was just quiet, she didn't know. Then, more loudly, Suveer said, "Aderyn. Are we trapped?"

His voice was the most beautiful thing she'd ever heard, reassuring her that she wasn't alone in this nightmare. "Owen says they are working on getting us out. Are you hurt at all?"

She didn't hear anything for a moment. Then Suveer said, "My arm feels broken, but that's all. You can tell me if we're going to die, you know."

"We're not going to die," Aderyn lied. Maybe it wasn't a lie, maybe it was true, but in her marrow she knew otherwise.

"I see." Suveer fell silent again for a few moments. Finally, he said, "Do you think the system looks like a person?"

"What? I don't know, Suveer. I never thought about it." In all the times the system had spoken to her, all the times she'd reflected on how its messages reminded her of a wryly sympathetic older sister, she'd never actually thought about whether that could be true on some level. Not the sister part, but the person with a physical body part.

"I'm not sure I'm ready to meet it," Suveer continued. "I don't think it likes me much."

That pushed Aderyn's fears aside in sheer astonishment. "Then it does talk to you! Why would you think that? It's always been... well, it can't be kind, it's not a person, but it seems interested in what I do. It's even answered my questions a few times."

"It tells me when I do things wrong," Suveer said, "and it's always critical. You know, how your parents rub it in when you make mistakes so you won't repeat them? It's like that."

Aderyn's chest ached from more than pressure. "My parents don't do that. They never wanted their children to feel humiliated by correction, they always said."

A rattle of pebbles suggested Suveer had moved slightly. Aderyn could picture his characteristic shrug. "I guess that's another difference between us. Anyway, the system wants me to be stronger, to endure pain so my skills will improve, and I feel like I disappoint it all the time, like I disappointed Ruan. Except, if Ruan didn't want me to succeed after all, maybe I shouldn't care what the system thinks either."

"Suveer—" Aderyn coughed again. The pressure on her chest was becoming painful. "Suveer, that can't be true. You aren't a bad Warmaster—"

"I don't know about that." He sounded perfectly matter-of-fact, not at all as if he was criticizing himself or reaching for compliments.

"I've watched you. You are good at [Reposition] even though you hadn't ever used it before, and you understand strategy. I don't know why the system would be hard on you, but maybe it really does care about you becoming better."

"Maybe." Another shower of gravel. "It doesn't matter anymore, does it?"

Confidence surged through Aderyn, borne up by a deep desire to see justice done. "Livia will get us out. And I'll help you find a partner, a real partner who will appreciate your skills. I promise."

"You're way too nice. The system said that too."

And just like that, Aderyn's confidence vanished. "The system talked to you about me?"

"Just once. It said you had ulterior motives. But I don't see how you could. It's not like I can benefit you at all."

A sick chill settled over Aderyn despite how warm her body was. She felt like she'd just learned Owen had been telling people how stupid she was behind her back. "No," she said, not sure who she was talking to.

The earth above Aderyn rumbled, and the pressure increased significantly. *Owen, it hurts!*

Sorry. Sorry! Livia's trying something else. Talk to me. I need to know you're okay.

Suveer is nearby. He says his arm is broken, but he's otherwise all right.

That's good. Your health, both your health, is still high. It's going to be fine, I swear.

Distantly, Aderyn heard Suveer speak over Owen's mental voice. "What was that, Suveer?"

"I said I feel lightheaded. Are we running out of air?"

Aderyn didn't feel dizzy despite how difficult it was for her to inflate her chest. "I don't think so. It is warm, though, and maybe that's why. Tell me what you're going to do with your share of the treasure."

"My what?"

"The treasure Owen and Livia brought out of Glasha's treasury. What are you going to do with yours?"

"I didn't think any of it was for me. I'm not really part of your team."

"That's ridiculous. You took part in the escape and you helped defeat Glasha. One-sixth of the treasure is yours. I'm going to save mine so I can build a house in Far Haven. That's the town I come from. My parents and my brother live there, and I hope my other brother and my sister will come back eventually too."

Suveer shifted his weight. "I can't imagine wanting to live near family. My parents will blame me for Ruan's death even though he was the thundering idiot who got himself killed."

Aderyn was uncomfortable with that line of discussion. "So, I'm building a house. Isn't there anything you want to do?"

Suveer didn't speak for a moment. "There was this girl," he said, almost dreamily. "I really liked her. Someone at court. She was always kind to me. I think I'd like to go back to Ikharatia and talk to her."

"That's a beautiful idea, Suveer. You could share a meal. Owen says where he comes from, men and women do activities like eating together or seeing plays together when they're courting. Not just community dances or galas, but the two of them alone together."

"That's very different. Where does Owen come from?"

Aderyn didn't know why she said what she said next. "Suveer, Owen is from another world. Another human world, not the demon world. He's not a demon."

"Another world." Suveer still sounded dreamy. "I know he's not a demon. A demon wouldn't marry a human woman. Did the system bring him here to be the Fated One?"

"I think so, yes. You're taking this awfully well."

"Everything feels so distant and unimportant," Suveer said. "And so what if Owen is from another world? He's still human, and maybe the Fated One couldn't be someone from our world. Maybe we had our chance to break the level cap, and we failed..." His voice faded.

Sudden panic gripped Aderyn, and she looked at the team roster. Everyone was wounded to some degree, with herself and Suveer the lowest—but Suveer's health bar was visibly dropping. "Suveer! Suveer, wake up and talk to me!"

"I'm awake," Suveer said, sounding more alert. "Are you afraid?"

Aderyn drew a shallow, cautious breath. "Yes. I'm more afraid than I've ever been in my life. Being deep underground terrifies me, and the tighter and closer the space, the more I'm afraid. If I didn't have you and Owen to talk to, I would probably be insane right now."

"Oh." Suveer sounded as if this revelation wasn't any more startling than Aderyn announcing she would have eggs for breakfast. "You know, those were the best times, when Ruan and I were separated enough for **[Bonded Mind]** to work. Ruan was always more of an equal when I was out of his sight. I don't think he liked seeing the reminder of his failure."

"I don't understand." If Suveer was about to fall into despair again, Aderyn really would go crazy.

"My eye. I lost it thanks to **[Draw Fire]**. He was quick to blame me —said if I'd been faster, it wouldn't have happened—but I knew him well enough to recognize his guilt. Ruan hated feeling guilty. He would do anything to make a disaster someone else's fault."

"I can believe that." Aderyn drew another shallow breath. "Are you trying to cheer me up?"

"I'm not very good at it, I know. I thought I could give you something to think about that isn't being crushed underground." He paused. "I shouldn't have said that last bit, should I?"

Aderyn tried to laugh, but it came out as a choked gurgle. "It's all right. Being actually crushed underground is worse than mentioning it."

Aderyn. Livia is trying something else. Let me know immediately if things get worse, all right? I love you. We'll get you out.

Aderyn blinked away tears. *I love you, too.*

The rumbling began again. This time, the pressure on Aderyn's chest eased noticeably. *It's working!*

That's just the first step. Hang in there.

"Owen says they're figuring it out, Suveer," Aderyn said.

Suveer didn't respond. Aderyn frantically brought up the team roster again. Suveer was still there, but his health bar was dangerously low. So, she realized, was hers. Maybe Suveer was right, and they were running out of air.

"Suveer!" she cried out.

"Still here," Suveer said. "Will you promise me something?"

"Sure, I guess. What?"

Suveer coughed. "When you're out, don't blame yourself. I haven't had much of a life, and there's no one left who will mourn me except you and maybe your friends. I want you to know I appreciate what you tried to do for me, even though I wasn't all that grateful at first."

"Suveer!" Aderyn calmed herself. "Suveer, don't talk like that. We're getting out of this."

"If we do, you can forget what I said," Suveer said. "But I'd rather not take the chance of not saying it and wishing I had." He let out a cough that sounded close to a laugh. "Though if the system absorbs us when we die, there won't be a 'me' left to wish for anything."

"Suveer—" Aderyn wished she had a hand free to wipe away tears. "I understand. It's not going to be necessary, but I understand."

"Thanks."

The rumbling started again, and the pressure increased. Aderyn screamed mentally, *Owen, no! It hurts!*

I know. Owen's mental voice lacked most of the emotional affect of his actual voice, but this time, Aderyn could swear he was crying. *It's the only way. Trust me, sweetheart. Trust me.*

Don't let go.

I won't. I swear it.

The pressure increased until Aderyn couldn't take another breath. Her vision tunneled, and black stars flashed in front of her eyes. Dimly, she heard Suveer say something.

Then the pressure was gone as if it had never been, and Aderyn felt like she was floating. Death felt surprisingly like being made of fog, drifting on the heavier air. She inhaled, and dragged a cloud of dust into her lungs. She coughed, and coughed, until her lungs were raw and her eyes and nose were streaming. Arms encircled her, and Owen clutched her to him and buried his face in her hair. He was muttering something she couldn't make out. "Owen," she said, and memory struck. "Where's Suveer?"

"Livia is pulling him out now," Owen said. "He was deeper than you. It's okay, love, everything is fine."

Aderyn was staring at the team roster. Suveer's health was almost gone. She disentangled herself from Owen's embrace. Beyond him, a long, deep trench extended for forty feet in both directions, tapering to nothing at the ends so it looked like a disembodied smile carved on the landscape. Livia stood beside it in her usual solid stance, her shoulders heaving with exertion. Aderyn walked to her side. The trench fell away into darkness. There was no sign of Suveer.

Livia's eyes were wide open, staring at nothing, and tension filled every line of her body. Aderyn was afraid to touch her for fear of disrupting her concentration. The ground rumbled, sending the barest tremors through Aderyn's feet. Still, Suveer didn't appear.

Livia let out a sigh that sounded like defeat, and Aderyn, suddenly furious at she didn't know what, shouted, "You can't—"

Without another sound, Livia folded at the knees.

Aderyn caught her before she could fall into the trench, and Weston grabbed them both and steadied them. "She was too close to her limit," Weston growled, but even though he held Livia close, his attention was on the crevasse.

"*No!*" Aderyn shouted. "We can't leave him there to die!"

Arms encircled her from behind. "It's too late, Aderyn," Owen whispered. "I think there never was any chance. He's gone."

Through tear-filled eyes, Aderyn examined the team roster. She was just in time to see Suveer's name blink three times and vanish.

CHAPTER FORTY

Aderyn kept staring at the team roster, not seeing anything but that empty space. Her body felt numb, as if her mind was floating free somewhere far from anything physical. "I told him we'd make it," she whispered.

Owen's arms around her tightened. "His health was dropping too fast, and he was deeper in the trench than you were. Livia exerted herself to exhaustion and it still wasn't enough. I was terrified we wouldn't get you out either."

"He knew I was lying. He knew he was going to die." Aderyn swiped a filthy sleeve across her wet eyes, not caring that it left a muddy streak on her arm. "Owen, he came so far only to die in this stupid, awful hole. It's not fair."

"I know. Fair isn't—"

"*It's not fair!*" Aderyn shouted. "If Livia hadn't wasted spells on that monster—"

"Don't blame Livia," Weston growled. "She saved your life."

"And she could not have saved Suveer at the cost of losing you," Isold said. "You were close enough to reach. Suveer was not." He cleared his throat. "Suveer jumped in front of you when you fell. He tried to stop you going in. That's why he fell deeper—he was closer to the center line of the trench than you."

Aderyn's throat closed up. "That makes everything so much worse," she said, and her final words dissolved into chest-aching sobs.

Owen turned her around so he could hold her close to his heart as she wept. The terror of being trapped under a ton of earth, of the darkness of the crevasse, struck her in flashes of memory interspersed with Suveer's voice coming to her in fragments of speech: *Are you afraid?... thought I could give you something to think about... I disappoint it all the time... she was always kind to me... what you tried to do for me...* It didn't matter anymore whether he remained with their team or not. But she pictured what she'd begun to imagine for his life, returning to Ikharatia, finding a real partner, maybe courting that girl, and her anger and heartsick grief made her wish she could fling herself on the ground and beat the earth with her clenched fists the way she had done as a child when she didn't get her way. Unfair. That was such a stupid, mild word for what had happened to Suveer.

She ran out of tears before she ran out of anger, but she didn't want to take it out on her husband or her friends. Instead, she hugged Owen and let the feel of his arms around her calm her enough that she could say, "We should move on."

"Are you all right?" Owen asked.

"I'm all right enough to know we need to leave this place." Aderyn looked around, wiping her eyes. "What happened to Terrorquake?"

"It was sucked into the middle of those black oozes," Weston said. "They pulled it out of the tunnel its body drove through the earth, and at the place where we were standing, the tunnel was just below the surface, and—" His voice cut off.

"I understand." She quickly ran back through the system messages and found the system defeat notice for Terrorquake. Over sixty-seven thousand experience. And—

"We leveled to nineteen," she said. It felt like something she should care about.

She disentangled herself from Owen and added, "We need to walk. Get as far as we can. Livia will be all right in the morning, and we can use *world door* to get back to the city."

"Wait," Owen said. "Shouldn't we do something? About Suveer?"

"Like a memorial?" Weston said.

"Well, yeah. I don't know what your customs are, but this feels wrong, just walking away from his body. Even though it's already buried." Owen winced. "That came out wrong."

"It's fine." Aderyn avoided looking at the trench. "Adventurers remember their dead in song and story, not in words said over their bodies. That's mainly because adventurers so often die in situations where their bodies are lost, like... like now."

"And I think it's safe to assume Suveer would not be happy if we delayed our journey over him, and ended up in greater danger or losing another of us thanks to that delay," Isold said.

"Oh. Well, all right then. I guess we walk. Weston, are you okay carrying Livia for a while?"

"I can carry her as long as we need. The sooner we're out of this place, the happier I'll be." Weston shifted the unconscious Livia in his arms.

They stayed with the road as best they could, recalling how few encounters they'd had along it during both journeys. As if the system knew not to push, they didn't meet any monsters that afternoon. Weston saw a handful of whisperweeds some distance from the road, but they didn't approach. "Guess word's gotten around," he joked. Nobody laughed.

They camped at sunset and let the little magical fire burn long enough to prepare a hot meal and some tea. Aderyn ate without tasting her food. The hot tea warmed her, but it tasted like water rather than herbs. She hadn't said much of anything from the time they left Suveer's body behind, and responded to questions with short answers she didn't elaborate on. After the meal, she waited as Weston and Owen kicked dirt over the fire, which dimmed it without dousing it, then prepared to take her turn at watch.

They'd discussed this, and Owen had said, "After what happened to me with Ahda the chanter, I don't think it's safe for anyone to watch alone. Aderyn and I will take first watch, and Weston and Isold can go second." No one had disagreed.

Now Aderyn searched the darkness for monsters and saw nothing but the tree line, close enough they would reach it in another hour of walking if they didn't intend to use *world door* in the morning. [**Dark-vision**] made the distant trees look like they were sketched in gray chalk, tiny and perfect and motionless in the still air. The illusion that she had stepped into a drawing persisted for a few moments until she shook herself out of it. She couldn't afford even so innocuous a daydream as that.

"Aderyn," Owen said. He'd been walking the small perimeter on the far side of the camp and now stood still.

She startled. "What's wrong? Do you see something?"

"No. Nothing's wrong. No monsters, anyway. I'm worried about you."

His words made her feel like drawing in on herself to protect a still-healing wound. "Don't. I'm fine."

"Don't blow me off, Aderyn. I know you better than anyone. I think you need to talk about what happened."

She cringed again, remembering that small, dark space and the dust choking her lungs. "It was terrifying, but it's over. I don't want to dwell on it."

"I meant, talk about Suveer." Owen's voice was low and invited confidences. "What did you talk about, before... you know."

"He died, Owen. You can say it." Immediately Aderyn regretted the harshness of her words. "I'm sorry. I know you're trying to help, but I don't think I'm ready. He—" She fought back more stupid tears. "I'm sorry."

"Don't be sorry. I can barely imagine how you must feel." Owen crossed the campsite and took her hand in his. "It's just—normally, I wouldn't push. You always talk to me eventually. But this time, I feel like leaving you alone is a mistake. You're going to dwell on what happened, and it's going to fester inside you until every memory you have of Suveer is tainted and foul. That seems like the worst possible betrayal of him."

His words touched her heart, easing her pain. They were the truest thing she'd ever heard. "Yes. Yes, you're right. My instinct is to wait for the memories to hurt less, but I think I'll be waiting a long time for that." She squeezed his hand. "Thank you."

"So, tell me. What did you talk about?"

Aderyn let herself remember those final, terrible moments underground. "About the system, and what happens when we die. And about what we would do when we were free. That's what hurts, Owen. He finally had things he wanted to do with his life, and now that's over. I think I'm grieving that more than anything."

"You gave him that. It sounds like he died free of whatever Ruan did to manipulate him."

"That's true. Oh, Owen, what little I know of Suveer's life makes me sad and angry, like how his parents were cruel to him in the name of correcting him, and Ruan constantly putting undeserved blame on him. And yet there was something inside him that survived that. Did he really try to save me from falling?"

"He did. And I'm trying not to feel inappropriately grateful that it was him and not me who leaped after you. He reacted so fast, Aderyn." Owen's hand briefly crushed hers. "When I thought you weren't getting out of there, I don't know what was worse—my fears, or hearing your terror. I thought, if she dies this way... anyway. If Suveer did something to help you with that terror, then I can't be grateful enough."

"He did. He wasn't at all afraid, did you know? Not of being buried and not of dying. And that made it easier for me." Aderyn let out a long, deep breath. "If I dwell on the sheer unfairness of it all, bitterness and anger breed inside me, and it's like I'm trapped in the crevasse again. But that means dying a different way. And if Suveer tried to save me, I owe it to his memory to not destroy my life through anger."

"You're still the wisest person I know."

"I don't feel wise. More like in this case, Suveer's death, and his life, gave me perspective. And I want to celebrate that."

Owen drew her close and kissed her briefly. "You sound much calmer. Not as if there's an eruption of pain brewing beneath the surface."

"I feel calmer. Thank you for pushing." She withdrew from Owen and turned her gaze on the distant horizon. Still, nothing moved. "I hope we make it through the night. I still feel hollow inside, not from grief but from everything we've done in the last forty-eight hours."

"I agree. I'm practically counting the seconds until sunrise." Owen returned to pacing the perimeter. "But I feel like it's going to be all right. Maybe that's wishful thinking."

"I'll take it," Aderyn said.

She understood what Owen meant. The sky was clear for once, not hazy, and the nearly-full moon sailed high overhead, brightening the trees and the tents and making the gritty, stony plains look like snow-fields. In the north, it was winter, and the snowfields were real. Aderyn let herself daydream for a moment about where the [Fated One's Destiny] quest might lead them next. She would welcome a northern winter after the unrelenting sun and heat and humidity.

The end of her watch came with no attacks or interruptions, and she crawled into her bedroll next to Owen and let him put his arms around her. [Read Body Language] told her how relieved he was to have her safe in a way he would never say out loud, for fear she would think he thought his pain mattered more than her suffering. She'd never loved him more.

The next thing she knew, the tent walls glowed with the first light of the sun, and Livia shouted, "Everybody up! It's time we left this thundering wasteland behind. Breakfast in Ikharatia!"

Aderyn scrambled out of her tent and hurried to hug Livia, who returned her embrace tightly. "Thank you for saving me," she whispered.

"I'm sorry it wasn't enough," Livia responded. "I don't—I didn't like Suveer much, but I tried, Aderyn, I swear I tried to save him. If I'd held back when fighting Terrorquake ''

"Don't," Aderyn said. "If you'd held back, maybe something worse would have happened. We can't play that game. And Suveer didn't resent it, I know."

"It still hurts." Livia wiped her eyes. "But it's time we moved on. I'm sending you back first. Don't argue. Call it inappropriate guilt if you want, but I'm superstitious that you evading death from your worst nightmare means something terrible lurks in this blasted wilderness to take you out a different way."

Aderyn laughed. "I'm not going to argue. Let's do this."

She stepped into the rough wooden oval of *world door* with more than usual eagerness. Livia's skill had grown, because the walls weren't as indistinct and the floor barely wobbled, but it still felt like forever before she stepped through the exit and the humidity of Ikharatia slapped her in the face, miserable even at this early hour.

Livia deposited her outside the city gate, where a couple of guards stared at her in disbelief. She had to look strange, disheveled and filthy with her hair in disarray, and a northerner at that. Beside her, the oval of *world door* formed again, and Isold's figure appeared. Aderyn waited impatiently for two seconds before remembering her <**Farspeaker**>. Varoun wouldn't have his, but someone might know where he and the escaped soldiers had ended up.

It didn't take long for Chandar's face to appear in the mirrored oval of the <**Farspeaker**>. "General Aderyn! Are you all right? Where are you?"

"I'm in Ikharatia," Aderyn replied. "Have you had word from Varoun?"

"He's here—wait a moment." The view swayed wildly, and then it was Varoun looking out at her. Aderyn's relief buoyed her up more than she'd expected at seeing the old Moonlighter well and alive.

"Aderyn. You survived. I'm so relieved," Varoun said. "We all made it safely back to the war camp outside Shantos. I wanted to follow your progress, but I didn't think I should contact you for fear of alerting enemies to your presence."

"Thank you, sir, that was wise." A million questions bubbled up inside her, but the one that won out was, "Is the orc army still a threat?"

"We have pushed them back from Shantos and Tielana, but they continue to attack." Varoun scowled. "Did you fulfil your Fated One quest?"

She heard the unspoken criticism in his words—you must have failed, or the orcs would be gone—but before she could respond, Isold said from over her shoulder, "The orc commander general and all her important leaders are dead, and Charnel Keep is no more. With so much of their leadership gone, I imagine word of all that will be slow in reaching the armies."

"I'm sorry, I shouldn't have implied a criticism," Varoun immediately said. "I am grateful beyond words that you and your friends succeeded. Was anyone lost?"

Aderyn swallowed. "Ruan and Suveer are dead, but that's a long story I don't think we have time for now. The rest of us made it out alive, and we rescued a handful of citizens of Shantos."

"One of whom probably doesn't deserve it," Weston rumbled.

Aderyn looked around. Owen was caught frozen in the middle of *world door*, which would have relieved her mind if she didn't have so many terrible imaginings about what crisis might affect Livia when she was alone in the Blighted Range. "Do you want us to return to the front, sir?"

"I do. I need someone to direct the defense of Tielana. I realize it's asking a lot of you, if you've only just returned from the high-risk zone, but this war isn't over."

The thought of going back into battle after the terrors of the last few days sickened Aderyn, but she said, "I'll do it."

"Thank you. I'll join you in the capital shortly so I can send you to Tielana," Varoun said. He turned to speak to someone not in range of the <Farspeaker>. "Wait a moment, Aderyn. This messenger is from Tielana. You'll want this intelligence before you plan the defense."

Someone put a hand on her shoulder. "Aderyn, what did Varoun say?" Owen asked.

"He wants me at the front near Tielana." Aderyn tried not to cringe saying those words, but Owen wasn't fooled.

"Aderyn, you've been traumatized," he said bluntly. "You aren't in any condition to lead troops."

"Yes, but—"

"Aderyn," Varoun said, "the scouts at Tielana report movement in the orc army positioned there."

Aderyn's heart sank. "If they're attacking, I need to go there as soon as possible."

"They're not attacking," Varoun said.

A system message flashed its silver letters in front of Aderyn's face.

Congratulations! You have achieved all the victory conditions of [Fated One's Destiny: Crush the Horde].

ACHIEVED Death of Glasha, orc commander general

ACHIEVED Death of Ornok, second in command
ACHIEVED Death of Zothemza, orc elementalist
ACHIEVED Death of Drorg, orc cavalry commander
ACHIEVED Death of Ahda, orc chanter
ACHIEVED Destruction of Charnel Keep
ACHIEVED Orc army retreats

You have earned [75,000 XP]

"It's over," Aderyn said. "The war is over."

CHAPTER FORTY-ONE

The throne room, glowing gold from the gilding decorating the walls and ceiling, felt smaller than before, which might have been the many people thronging it, but might also be that it no longer intimidated Aderyn. The cool breeze from above, not generated by anything Aderyn could see, kept the close-packed space from being unbearably hot. She wandered through the crowd, nodding politely at those who acknowledged her but not pausing to talk to anyone. By now, three days after the orc army's retreat, word had gotten around about what she and her friends had done, but to her surprise the story hadn't led to people pestering her for details. Southlander politeness appealed to her.

She saw Owen approaching through the crowd and waited for him to join her. "I'll be sad to leave the bathroom facilities behind," he murmured. "Maybe I need to talk to Marrius, someday when this is all over, and see if a Spellcrafter can replicate what I know from, um, where I come from."

"That was cautious of you for once!"

"Yeah, well, I *can* be taught, Aderyn." He clasped her hand and raised it to his lips.

Trumpets sounded, and Aderyn turned to watch the queen's attendants enter the throne room. This time, they carried nothing but unlit candles in brass holders. The crowd divided in half, pushing Aderyn and Owen back. Disappointed at not having a better view, Aderyn shifted to find a place to look past the heads and shoulders of those in front of her.

A woman standing beside her noticed. With a smile, she put her hand on the small of Aderyn's back and pushed her gently forward. The tall man ahead of Aderyn half-turned, registered who she was, and made a path for her to stand at the front of the crowd. Aderyn decided not to protest. She'd had an important role in the war, and maybe that meant she was entitled to be there at the end.

She was in time to see the four attendants range themselves along the foot of the dais, to either side of the gilded white thrones. Behind them, two armed guards dressed in gray and gold surcoats flanked the thrones. As still as they were, they looked more like statues than living people.

A rustle of movement as everyone around Aderyn bowed heralded the entrance of the king and queen. Aderyn bowed as well. She didn't owe Devendra allegiance, but she respected the queen, and bowing felt appropriate. Owen must have felt the same, because he bowed, too.

Devendra glided past, as expressionless as the guards, and didn't meet Aderyn's eye. That felt strange, and Aderyn didn't know why. It wasn't as if she and Devendra were friends, and obviously the queen didn't owe Aderyn anything. Well. That wasn't true; she owed Aderyn gratitude for her service, and for saving her life and protecting Colan, but those weren't anything Aderyn was going to demand respect for. But this felt as if Devendra was deliberately avoiding making contact, and that was unusual enough to rouse Aderyn's curiosity.

Colan walked beside his mother, not holding her hand this time. He did meet Aderyn's eyes, staring in astonishment as he had the first time they'd met. Aderyn didn't wave or smile. She didn't want to make the boy uncomfortable. Behind the royal pair, a guard strode, unarmed and bearing only a golden cushion on which rested a crown. It was clearly sized for an adult, so it didn't surprise Aderyn that Colan wasn't wearing it. The slim golden band, unadorned by precious stones, was topped by a series of filigree points and looked exactly as Aderyn had always imagined a crown should look.

Devendra helped Colan onto his throne and gracefully took a seat beside him. The guard with the crown stood between the thrones, looking as impassive as the others. Aderyn turned her attention to the doors in time to see them swing shut. No one spoke, and the room was silent except for the barest rustling of fabric.

The *boom, boom, boom* of someone knocking on the door startled Aderyn, it filled the silence so completely. Still, none of the courtiers reacted. Aderyn expected Devendra to tell someone to open the doors, but it was Colan who responded. In his high child's voice, he said, "Who knocks at the door?"

"One who has served this kingdom well." The voice was muffled, but Aderyn recognized it as Varoun's.

"What does my servant request?" Colan said. He spoke stiffly in the way of someone reciting a memorized text.

"To lay down my burden," Varoun replied.

"Open the door and bid my servant enter," Colan said.

The door swung open, and Varoun, dressed in his armor and with his sword hanging by his side, walked at a measured pace down the aisle formed by the watching courtiers. He came to a halt in front of the thrones and bowed deeply, first to Colan and then to Devendra.

Colan glanced at his mother, who widened her eyes and made a little gesture with one hand. The boy swallowed and said, "General Varoun, your report."

"I accepted command of the army of the Southlands with the express purpose of defeating the orcs that threatened to destroy us," Varoun said in his clear, decisive voice. "That threat has been eliminated. With your majesty's permission, I return command of the army to you and request relief from my duties." He drew the <**Wand of World Door**> from its sheath at his hip and extended it to Colan.

Colan took the wand in both hands and looked briefly uncertain. Devendra motioned to him to give the magic item to her. Colan handed it over quickly and wiped his palms on his trousers. Aderyn controlled a smile. That was a nervous gesture they had in common.

"I relieve you of your command, General Varoun," Colan said. "Please kneel."

A rush of noise suddenly filled the room, men and women

exclaiming or asking their neighbors what Colan had said. Puzzled, Aderyn watched Varoun, who knelt stiffly but not as if Colan's request was a surprise, as it seemed to be to everyone else.

Colan swallowed again and closed his eyes briefly. His lips moved in silent speech for a couple of seconds. Then he climbed off the throne and approached Varoun. "Varoun, you have spent your life in the service of this kingdom. Now I require a greater service. As of this moment, I abdicate my claim to the throne and proclaim you, Varoun, king of the Southlander kingdom."

The room erupted in shouting and exclamations. Aderyn, stunned, remained silent. She looked at Owen, who was as astonished as she, then at Varoun, whose back was to her. Despite not being able to see his expression, Aderyn was certain he'd known what was coming.

Devendra rose from her throne and walked forward to join Colan, who was biting his lip as if he'd come to the end of what he'd memorized. "Be silent," she said, pitching her voice to be heard over the noise. "Your king demands your respect." She put a hand on Colan's shoulder and squeezed gently.

Colan startled, then turned and nearly ran into the guard holding the crown as the man stepped forward. With his small hands, he gripped the crown tightly. Moving slowly as if he was afraid of dropping it, he walked down the steps of the dais and put the crown on Varoun's head.

The shouting and demands for explanations faded and died. Varoun continued to kneel for a few moments, his head bowed as if the crown weighed more than it did. Then he got to his feet and extended a hand to Colan, who clasped it tightly. "Thank you," he said. "I know that was hard. Thank you for your faith in me."

He lifted his head and turned to face the room. "I swear to execute the duties of a king to my utmost abilities," he said, his voice ringing out as Devendra's had. "I will serve this kingdom as I have done before. This was not something I sought, but the needs of the kingdom—" He glanced briefly at Colan, who was looking at the floor— "must take precedence. Do you bear witness?"

There was a tense, silent moment that felt like it went on forever, long enough for Aderyn to imagine a dozen scenarios in which the Southlander kingdom went up in flames as a dozen nobles challenged

Varoun. Then someone pushed to the front of the crowd. Janesh. He faced Varoun fearlessly. Then he went to one knee and bowed his head. "You have my allegiance, your majesty," he said. "As I am certain you have that of everyone in this room."

It was a clear warning, and it worked. Raggedly, everyone except Aderyn and her friends knelt, murmuring variations on what Janesh had said. She concealed a smile. Varoun didn't look like he thought it was funny, but tension left his body, and he inclined his head to Janesh.

Out of the corner of her eye, Aderyn caught furtive movement. When she looked up, Devendra gestured again, indicating that Aderyn should join her. People were rising and surrounding Varoun, so Aderyn and Owen made their way through the crowd and were joined by Isold, Weston, and Livia. Devendra held Colan's hand and guided him through one of the doors flanking the dais, not the one leading to the command center.

This door led immediately to a short flight of stairs rising to a long hallway lined with doors. Devendra opened the first door on the left and spoke quietly to whoever was inside. "Colan, Anagha will help you choose what you will take with you. I am going to speak to these people, and I will return soon." She hugged the boy, and for once she looked like nothing more than a mother who loved her son. "Remember, only the most important things."

She shut the door on Colan and said, "Join me in my sitting room. I'm sure you have many questions."

The sitting room was furnished in tropical hardwoods and colorful linens, with gauzy drapes that moved in a breeze with no source. They gave the impression of window curtains, though the room was windowless. Devendra sat heavily on one of the sofas and waved her guests to do the same. "Surprised?"

"I'll say," Owen said. "You had to keep it quiet, didn't you? A king's abdication is immediate and final, and you needed to set things up so no one could interfere."

"You're clever," Devendra said. "That's right. There are many who would fight over the right to the crown if they knew I intended Colan to abdicate. This way, if they choose to fight, they will be in rebellion against their rightful ruler."

"All right," Livia said skeptically, "but let's be blunt. Varoun is old. How does making him king do anything but push the instability problem back a few years?"

"Varoun is a good choice for more than one reason," Devendra said. "Have you met his son, Mansur? Mansur has been involved in governance for twenty years, as a magistrate and arbiter of law. He is well known and popular throughout the Southlands, someone trusted by all to choose the well-being of the country in every instance. And he is married with seven children. When I chose Varoun, I chose a dynasty. I have no qualms about turning the kingdom over to him and his family."

"I suppose," Aderyn said.

Devendra eyed her narrowly. "You question my choice? Or do you question my authority to make that choice?"

"Neither. I was just thinking, Varoun could justifiably have expected to retire after this." Aderyn smiled. "It's just me and my inappropriate sympathy again. He's an excellent choice."

"He would not have accepted if it hadn't meant freedom for Colan and Rila. And now I will take my children north and make a new life for them." Devendra rose. "And you. We owe you a tremendous debt."

"We didn't do it to incur debt," Owen said. "But you know that."

"Nevertheless. Varoun and I are agreed that you can call on this kingdom at any time for whatever you need. Though I imagine you're headed north again."

Aderyn and Owen exchanged glances. "We definitely are," Owen said.

THAT NIGHT AFTER DINNER, they gathered in Owen and Aderyn's room. "We could ask Varoun to use the **<Wand of World Door>**," Weston said. "Conserve Livia's resources."

"I'd prefer to continue expanding my ability with the spell," Livia said. "Are we sure we want to go to Finion's Gate first? Now that I've traded *acid ray* for *greater scry*, I can take us anywhere in the world."

Aderyn lay back on the bed and called up the Codex to review again the new quest that had appeared after the completion of **[Fated One's**

Destiny: Crush the Horde]. She couldn't help remembering what Ruan had claimed about how difficult the Fated One quests were to interpret. This was the complete opposite of difficult.

She focused on the gold dot in her Codex display and watched it enlarge.

[Fated One's Destiny: Eye of the Storm]
Bring peace to the Northlands.

Reward: [100,000 XP] plus any experience gained in the course of completing the quest.

That was all. No details. No quest victory conditions. Just that one line. Aderyn dismissed the Codex and closed her eyes. She wasn't even sure what "the Northlands" meant. There were lands north of Finion's Gate, and even though most of them weren't in the high-risk zone, nobody went there. So, how could a place where no one lived be in conflict?

She sat up and pulled off her boots, then her stockings, and wiggled her toes. "We don't have any idea where to go in the Northlands, so we'd end up traveling all over the place and wasting our efforts. Someone in Finion's Gate will know more about the Northlands. Until then, I'm going to relax." She tossed her stockings in the direction of where her sword stood propped against the wardrobe in the corner, then one boot after the other. The second boot struck the mystery sword's hilt and knocked the weapon over.

Isold, who was leaning against the wall, bent to pick the sword up, and froze. "That was unexpected," he said, straightening with the sword in his hand. "I thought we were going to find someone to cast *heritage* on this weapon."

"We were! I forgot. We can do that in the morning, before we leave." Aderyn held out her hand for the sword.

Isold shook his head. "That is unnecessary. Apparently my ranks in **[Knowledge: History]** have increased enough that what used to be a tickling sensation of almost recalling facts has become actual knowledge. I know whose sword this was."

"*Whose* sword?" Aderyn said. "Not what magic it does?"

"I said before it has only minimal magics. That remains true. The sword's importance lies not in what it is capable of, but in who previously wielded it."

"Stop drawing out the suspense, Isold. Was it someone famous?" Owen asked.

Isold shook his head. "Yes, and no. This sword belonged to Aurelon."

"Who is—oh, I remember! The one we learned about in the Repository. The man who destroyed a city at level fifty." Aderyn gasped. "And his sword was lying around in the Enchanterium for the kobolds to pick up? What are the odds of that?"

"That's only strange because we know who Aurelon was, sort of." Owen took the sword from Isold and half-drew it from its scabbard. "But his name has been forgotten except by us. That makes it damn weird that we should be the ones who got his sword."

"But why would someone who was level fifty have such an ordinary, barely-magical sword?" Aderyn held out a hand to Owen for the sword. "It's beautiful, granted, but shouldn't Aurelon have wielded something that shot lightning bolts out the tip or could cut through superdense metal?"

"Let me tell you everything my skill knows about the sword." Isold leaned against the wall again and raised his hand, ticking off points on his fingers. "Aurelon wielded the sword at two different times in his adventuring career. I don't know the specifics of what level he was at each time, but I know he set the weapon aside for several levels before taking it up again as a high-level adventurer. Or, rather, what we would consider high level, since this was before the level cap and reaching level forty or above was not abnormal. During that second period, the sword became famous through association with him. Its lack of powerful magic was a point of pride—Aurelon claimed he didn't need help to defeat his enemies."

"Jerk," Owen muttered.

Weston eyed Owen. "Does that mean someone proud and arrogant? Or should we take it literally?"

"The first thing. I didn't like Aurelon when we heard about him in the Repository and I like him less now. Somebody who brags about his skills is exactly the kind of person I could see destroying a city and not caring." Owen gave the sword to Aderyn. It didn't feel any different, but in her imagination it radiated more mystery than before.

"At any rate, Aurelon traded on the mystique of the blade for several levels. I don't know why he brought it to the Enchanterium, just that it was meant to be temporary. I imagine it needed mending or reimbuing with magic. The rest, I also don't know, but my guess is he did this shortly before he disappeared." Isold's eyes narrowed as he regarded the sword. "And before whatever occurred to create the level cap happened. Otherwise, he would have returned to claim his sword."

"That is a thundering weird coincidence," Livia said.

"It's exciting, though, don't you think?" Weston said. "Aderyn's carrying around a piece of history."

"We don't know what kind of history," Livia said. "If this Aurelon was evil—"

"You don't believe that, do you?" Aderyn exclaimed.

"I'm just saying, don't rule it out. And if he *was* evil, maybe that sword has done some evil things." Livia's gaze fixed on the sword. "Maybe it's not a heritage to be proud of."

Aderyn shuddered. "Now I'm scared to wield it. What if it corrupts me?"

"That's unlikely." Owen put an arm around her waist. "Either Isold would have known about its history, or Livia would see that in its magic. Besides, you've had plenty of chances to be corrupted over the weeks you've used the sword. I think you're safe."

"I can't answer that question, and Livia has a point," Isold said. "But if an item can pick up impressions from its user, good or bad, there's nothing to say it can't change over the years. You are the last person in the world I would expect to be negatively affected by someone's dark experiences."

Aderyn blushed. "Thanks, Isold." She sheathed the sword and leaned it against the wall. "I'm going to go with how amazing it is to have a connection with someone that powerful. The witness at the Repository didn't think Aurelon was completely evil, right? And maybe someone who's level fifty sees the world differently. At any rate, I'm not going to worry."

"Good decision," Weston said, his words ending in a yawn. "So, we're leaving tomorrow?"

"If we're all done," Owen said, "we'll go to Finion's Gate in the morning. Good night, everyone."

Aderyn stayed seated on the bed while the others left. Owen shut the door and returned to her side. "Are you doing better?"

Aderyn snuggled into his embrace. "Are you asking if I'm ready for sex?"

"I am not. You're still traumatized, and I have no intention of even implying I think we should share that intimacy until you're ready. I just don't know what I can do for you. The nightmares—"

"I think, if I wait for those to stop entirely, we'll never have sex again," Aderyn said with a smile. "It helps if you hold me, you know. As long as you're near, I know I'm not buried in that trench."

"Holding you." Owen made an exaggerated "I'm thinking" face. "Hmm. I guess I could put up with that. It's a real sacrifice."

Aderyn kissed him, and for the first time in days felt the faintest stirrings of desire. "Let's sleep, then. I'm excited to see how Finion's Gate looks in the winter."

They cuddled close despite the warmth of the room. Owen fell asleep almost immediately. Aderyn's body ached with weariness, but the nightmares that had plagued her since returning to Ikharatia filled her mind and fought her body's sleepiness. If she wasn't dreaming about being trapped in a pocket of air with stones and dirt pouring down on her, burying her more deeply, she dreamed of Suveer, who in the dream floated free of the rockfall and spoke nonsense words her dreaming self knew were spells that failed to save them. Then she would wake, drenched in sweat with her heart pounding, and cry herself to sleep again in Owen's arms.

To distract herself, she opened the Codex and whispered, "Advancement."

Name: Aderyn
∞ Jacob Owen Lindberg
Level: 19

Class: Warmaster

<u>Skills</u>: Bluff (18), Climb (15), Conversation (17), Intimidate (13), Sense Truth (20), Survival (11), Swim (3), Knowledge: Monsters (20), Knowledge: World Lore (12), Knowledge: Demons (2), Unite

<u>Class Skills</u>: Improved Assess 4 (33), Awareness (22), Knowledge: Geography (19), Spot (19), Discern Weakness (32), Dodge (20), Improvised Distraction (19), Outflank (27), Draw Fire (15), Keep Pace (25), Amplify Voice (22), See It Coming (29), Basic Weapon Proficiency (Swords) (17), Read Body Language (19), Basic Map Access (9), Compel (13), Spot Weakness (11), Secret Message (7), Bonded Mind (15), Sense Ambush (8), Reposition (8), Truesight (5), Darkvision (5), Interchange (0)

[Interchange] had some good possibilities. It let her switch places with any ally using teleportation. Aderyn wasn't sure she understood the phrasing "any ally." If the skill meant it could only be used with members of her team, wouldn't the system have said so? Probably the wording was to distinguish between creatures who were enemies and creatures or people who were not. But instinctively Aderyn felt "ally" could be a useful distinction in the future.

Her eyelids were so heavy she couldn't keep them open, and her mind was foggy, signs that her distraction wasn't working. The terror of being entombed jolted her awake briefly, but it wouldn't work forever. Desperately, she reached for any other memory. Suveer. He'd done his best to keep her from being afraid, even though he was dying. Even though he thought she was too nice. No, that was wrong, it was someone else who'd told him that.

Another jolt struck her, this one of a memory she'd forgotten in her fear and grief. Before she could stop herself, she whispered, "Why did you tell Suveer I had ulterior motives?"

There was no response. Aderyn immediately felt stupid. It was the system; it didn't have to tell her anything, and even if it did, it had reasons for its actions that were incomprehensible to humans. But the feeling of having been betrayed by someone she trusted prompted her to repeat herself. "Why did you tell Suveer I had ulterior motives? You know I didn't."

Silver lines formed in front of Aderyn's face, bright against the room's darkness.

I never spoke to Suveer.

As a child, Aderyn had walked into what she thought was an empty room, felt the brush of something soft against her forehead, and then screamed when the spider whose web she'd disturbed skittered across her face. She'd never forgotten the thrill of terror that had flooded her body. The system's five words brought that feeling back, the sense of wrongness and fear. "I don't understand. Suveer said you talked to him."

I never spoke to Suveer.

"Then..." Aderyn swallowed. "He didn't make it up. I know he didn't. Who talked to him, if it wasn't you?"

She strained to see anything in the darkness. No more words appeared. She lay there, not moving, until her breathing and heart rate slowed. The system hadn't said anything to Suveer, but Suveer didn't have the personality to make up a story to confuse Aderyn. Something else had communicated with him. Something... or someone.

Fear and tension wearied her beyond her capacity to fight. She fell asleep, not drifting peacefully but in a sequence of exhausted images, none of them familiar. Her last coherent thought was of those silver letters proclaiming an impossible truth. There was someone else out there who communicated like the system. Someone who knew who Aderyn was. Someone who had lied about her to Suveer. For the first time in days, the thought of nightmares about being buried alive didn't frighten her.

She had an unknown enemy. And that enemy might be impossible to fight.

Appendix: Character Sheets

NOTE: These character sheets represent the status of the companions at the end of the book, which means it reveals everything the companions learn about their skills throughout the story. If you haven't finished the book, don't read this unless you don't mind spoilers!

Name: Aderyn
∞ **Jacob Owen Lindberg**
Level: 19
Class: Warmaster
Skills: Bluff (18), Climb (15), Conversation (17), Intimidate (13), Sense Truth (20), Survival (11), Swim (3), Knowledge: Monsters (20), Knowledge: World Lore (12), Knowledge: Demons (2), Unite

Class Skills: Improved Assess 4 (33), Awareness (22), Knowledge: Geography (19), Spot (19), *Discern Weakness (32)*, Dodge (20), Improvised Distraction (19), *Outflank (27)*, Draw Fire (15), *Keep Pace (25)*, Amplify Voice (22), See It Coming (29), Basic Weapon Proficiency (Swords) (17), *Read Body Language (19)*, Basic Map Access (9), Compel (13), Spot Weakness (11), Secret Message (7), *Bonded Mind (15)*, Sense Ambush (8), Reposition (8), Truesight (5), Darkvision (5), Interchange (0)

Italics are paired skills with partner

Name: Jacob Owen Lindberg
∞ Aderyn
Class: Swordsworn
Level: 19
Skills: Assess (15), Awareness (19), Climb (14), Conversation (17), Sense Truth (16), Spot (16), Survival (11), Swim (13), Knowledge: Demons (2), Unite
Class Skills: Superior Weapon Proficiency (33), Advanced Armor Proficiency (27), Knowledge: Monsters (17), *Exploit Weakness* (32), Dodge (22), Parry (22), Improved Bluff (19), *Outflank* (27), Trip (10), *Keep Pace* (25), Disarm (12), Intimidate (19), Charge (13), Two-Weapon Fighting (17), *Read Body Language* (19), Basic Map Access (9), Overrun (11), Shatter Confidence (7), *Bonded Mind* (15), Weapon Mastery (longsword), Anatomist (11), Combat Momentum (6), Crippling Strike (3), Whirlwind Attack (0)
Italics are paired skills with Warmaster

Name: Weston
∞ Livia
Class: Moonlighter
Level: 19
Skills: Assess (17), Climb (18), Conversation (15), Intimidate (14), Survival (11), Swim (6), Knowledge: Social (16), Knowledge: Demons (2), Unite
Class Skills: Pick Locks (21), Advanced Sneak Attack (21), Superior Weapons Proficiency (17), Advanced Armor Proficiency (17), Improved Detect Traps (22), Disable Traps (20), Improved Spot (25), Awareness (19), Dodge (20), Stealth (25), Improved Bluff (19), Dirty Fighting (14), To the Heart (23), Hide (13), Improved Thrown Weapons Proficiency (18), Disguise (5), Hide in Plain Sight (9), Improved Evasion (11), Basic Map Access (9), Escape Artist (7), Unarmed Combat (4), Improvised Weapon (5),

Glibness (4), Improved Sense Truth (18), Coup de Grace (3), Slippery (0)

Name: Isold
   Class: Herald
   Level: 19
   Skills: Assess (15), Awareness (19), Bluff (14), Climb (9), Conversation (12), Intimidate (8), Sense Truth (21), Spot (19), Survival (11), Swim (5), Knowledge: Demons (3)
   Class Skills: Perform (singing) (26); Knowledge: Magic (17); Knowledge: Monsters (19); Knowledge: History (18); Knowledge: Social (14); Knowledge: World Lore (17); Identify Magic Items (20); Charm (21); Distraction (15); Improved Map Access (19); Inspire Courage (19); Fascination (15); Persuasion (14); Perform (drum) (16); Suggestion (15); Resist Magic (12); Shout (8); Hypnotize (14); Find Object (9); Coercion (8); Break Enchantment (9); Perform (flute) (6); Cause Fear (7); Sleep, Mass (6); Mimic (2); Compulsion (3); Greater Shout (0)

Name: Livia
   ∞ Weston
   Class: Earthbreaker
   Level: 19
   Skills: Assess (10), Awareness (12), Bluff (10), Climb (6), Conversation (13), Intimidate (18), Sense Truth (14), Spot (15), Survival (11), Swim (6), Knowledge: Demons (2), Unite
   Elemental Powers: Earth, stone, acid
   Class Skills: Knowledge: Magic (22), Matchless Elemental Blast (earth spray, shower of small stones, rain of large stones, stone sphere shrapnel, burning rocks) (19), Earth to Mud/Mud to Earth (12), Mage Armor (shifting stone slabs) (16), Excavate (13), Summon Elemental Hammer (9), Basic Map Access (9), Tremorsense (11), Sculpt Earth/Stone (10), Speak with Stone (5), Pass Through Stone (6), Counterspell (3), Earthquake (2)

Spell List

0-level spells: Daze; Drench; Light; Telekinesis, Minor; Mending; Freezing Ray, Minor; Root; Spark

1st Level spells

Air Bubble; Break; Force Shield; Grease; Heat Metal (slow); Loose Bonds; Mudball; Sunder Weapon; Thunder Punch

2nd Level spells

Create Pit; Dust Cloud; Earth's Endurance; Thunderstomp; Mirror Image; Mud Minion; Improved Mending; Protection from Fire, Mass (big earth dome); Skip

3rd Level spells

Iron Spike Attack; Thunderstomp, Greater (directed); Clairvoyance; Dispel Magic; Immobilize; Telekinesis, Greater; Daylight

4th Level spells

Stone Ladder; Stone Sphere; Transport, Minor; Invisibility (self); Earth Glide; Stone Fist; Daze, Mass

5th Level spells

Hungry Pit; Dismissal of Demons; Scry; Lighten Object; Darkvision; Passwall; Burrow

6th Level spells

Move Earth, Major; Stoneskin, Mass; Invisibility, Mass; Dispel Magic, Greater; Truthspeak

7th Level spells

Immobilize, Greater; Sunburst; Reverse Gravity, Localized; Summon Large Earth Elemental; Greater Scry

8th Level Spells

World Door; Greater Polymorph; Launch; Iron Body

9th Level Spells

Stone Prison; Dispel Magic, Superior

AND NOW A SPECIAL MESSAGE...

Did you enjoy this book? Want more LitRPG adventure goodness? Then the LitRPG Books Facebook group is for you! Find new recommendations, connect with fellow readers, and more!

About the Author

In addition to the Warmaster series, Melissa McShane is the author of many fantasy novels, including the novels of Tremontane, the first of which is *Servant of the Crown;* The Extraordinaries series, beginning with *Burning Bright;* and *The Book of Secrets,* first book in The Last Oracle series.

While her home remains in the mountains out West, she currently lives in Kerala, India, with her husband and two rambunctious Persian cats who believe they own the house. She wrote reviews and critical essays for many years before turning to fiction, which is much more fun than anyone ought to be allowed to have.

You can visit her at her website
www.melissamcshanewrites.com
for more information on other books and upcoming releases.

To subscribe to her newsletter, which is published monthly, visit **www.melissamcshanewrites.com/contact-me-2/join-my-mailing-list**

Also by Melissa McShane

The Book of Harmony
The Book of War
The Book of Destiny

THE LIVING ORACLE
Hidden Realm
Hidden Enemy
Hidden Pursuit

THE EXTRAORDINARIES
Burning Bright
Wondering Sight
Abounding Might
Whispering Twilight
Liberating Fight
Beguiling Birthright
Soaring Flight
Discerning Insight

THE NOVELS OF TREMONTANE
Pretender to the Crown
Guardian of the Crown
Champion of the Crown
Ally of the Crown
Stranger to the Crown
Scholar of the Crown
Servant of the Crown
Exile of the Crown
Rider of the Crown
Agent of the Crown
Voyager of the Crown

Tales of the Crown

COMPANY OF STRANGERS

Company of Strangers

Stone of Inheritance

Mortal Rites

Shifting Loyalties

Sands of Memory

Call of Wizardry

THE DRAGONS OF MOTHER STONE

Spark the Fire

Faith in Flames

Ember in Shadow

Skies Will Burn

THE CONVERGENCE TRILOGY

The Summoned Mage

The Wandering Mage

The Unconquered Mage

THE BOOKS OF DALANINE

The Smoke-Scented Girl

The God-Touched Man

Emissary

Warts and All: The Deluxe Expanded Edition

The View from Castle Always

Winter Across Worlds: A Holiday Collection

www.ingramcontent.com/pod-product-compliance
Lightning Source LLC
Chambersburg PA
CBHW051443260626
47162CB00001B/221

* 9 7 8 1 9 6 4 5 4 5 1 9 6 *